# I am a Cat

## Louise Hudson

Best Wishes
Louise Hudson

# Copyright Page

For Frankie and Rocky

# CHAPTER 1

When he shouted the command, "Jump!" my throat closed up and I stopped breathing. My feet inched obediently forwards, tentatively, towards the edge of the ledge. Don't look down. Do *not* look down!

As the sweat streamed down my neck, tickling my collarbone, the man called to me. "Take your time!" He meant it kindly but I knew he was having second thoughts about including me in the squad. Did he guess how petrified I was?

Had anyone suspected the attack of nerves that had hit me as I cowered in the roadway waiting for the bridge to be cleared? Traffic had already been diverted but interested spectators milled about everywhere. When I sat down on the kerb the icy stone gripped at my thighs, making me shudder. Taking some deep breaths I prayed that no one my mother knew would be there, but this was unlikely as her generation rarely showed interest in anything adventurous or exciting. There was one newspaper reporter, complete with camera, so I kept my hand by my face, just in case.

There were six of us doing the jump, two friends, me and three guys. Needless to say, one of these was the real reason for my ostensive bravery. Mel was tall, kind, humorous, clever, and he had a car. What more could a girl ask? I just wished he noticed me a bit more. But once he'd seen me jump – everything would change.

Then I was being called. I stood up trying to look nonchalant. Trying to look as if I did this sort of thing every weekend. But my armpits were already moist and my face and head were burning. Minutes later I was out on the parapet with the solid comforting wall of the bridge behind me. Swaying slightly I felt as if I was hovering above our house, listening to myself having that last conversation.

"I absolutely forbid it!" my mother had screamed, in the way that mothers do. "We've had this conversation before and I've not changed my mind." So I tried another tack – stressing the huge sponsorship donation that would be made to charity. Still, she didn't see it my way.

"But, why Mum?" Trying to sound reasonable, and not whining.

"Because it's dangerous! Because there's no need to put yourself through that sort of thing. You could kill yourself!"

"People get run over by buses."

"Yes, just going about their business, but no right minded person would dangle herself from a bridge, goodness knows how high up, and expect to live to tell the tale."

It didn't even cross my mind that she might actually be right. I patiently explained that people do it all the time and that bungee jumping is one of the safest sporting activities around. "It is all so well regulated, nothing can go wrong." I even believed it myself.

But she just would not budge so I had two choices. Cancel my place on the team, which had taken a lot of training and wheedling to get into, or go and do it anyway. No contest! It was a college event and as I had not proved myself adept at anything else it seemed a good opportunity to make my mark. No, I wasn't going to give up.

I stamped up to my room and slammed the door, causing the cat to stare up from where she lay curled on my bed. "It's all right for you," Yes, I remembered the words quite clearly now. "You don't have problems like this. I certainly wouldn't mind coming as a cat next time around!"


Someone was shouting from the side of the bridge. "Everything all right?" The man called to me again, sounding a little tense. "When you're ready!" I turned my head and tried to smile. Yes, of course I will make the jump. I wanted to reassure him.

Quite vividly my brain flashed snippets of my life into this nightmare. College, my bedroom, my new red handbag, childhood moments, aspirations, what I'd been planning to do next week. Mel! He was there just a few yards away. Watching, waiting. They were all waiting......for me.

Not daring to look down at my feet I tried to recall the instructions given at the training session but my mind crashed on crazily. Jumbling, jostling. Please let it settle; just let me stop this rollercoaster. I closed my eyes. But I didn't jump. Very slowly, I just stepped out into space.

During the restless, sleepless nights of the last few weeks I had wondered whether it would be like floating or flying, as in angels or birds, or if it might just be like dropping a stone.

Although this was my first time, I had read all about it, and had received meaningful advice from others who had actually done it and who considered themselves experts. I vaguely knew what to expect but the rush of feeling is impossible to put into words. Fantastic. Exhilarating. Terrifying! I shrieked briefly as my insides were jolted up above my head then thudded down through the soles of my feet.

"It's like taking off in an aircraft," they had told me. But it wasn't at all. This was just so unbelievable. The zing of bouncing every whichway is completely abandoned, absolutely uncontrollable, which must be why so many people enjoy the thrill it gives. Up and down, I twanged. Spinning a little, but I didn't mind. The worst (or best) was over now. I had really done it! I would become one of the college heroes. One who had risked her life to raise money for a good cause (although at that moment, not surprisingly, I couldn't remember what it was.)

The bouncing simmered a little. Disconcertingly, the spinning started to accelerate. Suddenly, everything began to lurch wildly. The harness was going berserk. Dipping, swinging. Swaying from side to side. Then, eerily, everything seemed to be moving in slow motion. Somewhere in the far distance people were shouting. For a split second I seemed to have dual vision. My mother's face swam before me, taut with concern, forbidding me to do the jump. (My father patting her arm and telling her, "Don't worry, she's got far more sense.")

Then as I fell, the rocks and bracken and the rushing, swooshing air of Death swirled up impatiently to meet me. I squirmed my face away, sure that if I didn't look down at her she would be cheated and I should be saved. Turning my head, searching for the bridge above, I tried to shout. Then I screamed. Then again, more loudly. My wailing and whimpering echoed mockingly as the rocks tore at my flesh.

*Goodbye!* I thought silently. A cool breeze pillowed my head. Nothing…

Suffocating heat, smelly stickiness, nausea. Yes, nausea was definitely my initial feeling. Warm lumps of wriggling movement everywhere, poking into me, climbing over me. Molten liquid jelly, stopping me from breathing. What sort of a joke is this? Retching emptily I attempted to roll away. No chance! Something like tacky flypaper glued itself to my face and shoved up into my nostrils making it impossible to inhale.

Hysteria took over. What has happened to me? So I didn't quite make the bungee jump, but, where have I ended up? Not Heaven. Definitely not Heaven – not with all these smells and stickiness and fluff stuff. The other place? Possibly. Or maybe, just maybe, it was all a bad dream.

But it definitely was not. A huge nobbly surface, sharp as a razor blade, slapped down on to me, attending to my immediate discomforts by sweeping itself over and over again across my body until gradually my unfamiliar form could wiggle itself unfettered. The congealing mess that had been all over me was licked away.

I yelled out in the pitch blackness. 'What am I doing here? Where is here?' But I couldn't hear my voice. There was just silence. 'Where's my Mum and Dad? Where's my tea?' No one answered but ridiculous squeals and other disturbing sounds surrounded me.

Ugh! So where am I? What am I?

'Tell me what is happening!' I demanded into the dark. 'Tell me! WHAT?' I tried to shout but it didn't work. I must still have a head, I realised, because I was able to think. I still had some sort of a brain, because something inside me was whispering gently. What was it whispering? I held my breath and tried to concentrate. The voice was repeating again and again, '*You are a cat!*'

No! No! NO! Why couldn't I hear my screams above the sniffling and whining going on around me - what were those noises? Surely they couldn't be...? They certainly were animal sounds. Oh no! I can't be, can I? Is it conceivable that I can possibly have been born again as something else – something cat-like? Am I a kitten then? I desperately tried to look at my body or move something. But nothing was operational. I smelled strange. Everything near me smelt strange. Ponged! Why was I here in this stinking place? Ha! Don't try and tell me I'm a cat, I snorted. This is just the worst sort of hallucination, I told myself firmly. But the scrambling and scratching went on all around me. This din must be other kittens - my litter, my existence. As my limbs struggled towards some movement I touched my own back. Strewth! There must be some dreadful mistake! But this was positive proof. I stopped screeching and squealed instead. Fur? It felt like fur. And my foot, the instigator of this fresh panic? Not foot – paw! Plus another three. And a tail! Shrieking again, I shuddered and juddered and inched about my allotted space (which wasn't much as each time I stretched anything, it connected with more, foreign, fur.) 'I hate it! Hate it!' I yelled, and then fell asleep.


Some cats deliver their offspring in unusual places. The boot of a car, suitcases, drawers filled with undies, a bathtub, garden sheds – all these are known to be quite usual venues in which to make one's appearance. My first glimpse of the world, through pussy eyes, was much more traditional and comfortable, although at the time I didn't appreciate this.

My cat mother, being an aged, experienced producer of multiple young families, had apparently indicated her preferred maternity bed some days before the birth. From the many and varied nurseries she had used previously she chose her favourite. She wanted warmth, comfort and privacy for what might well be her last contribution to cat-kind. Her old bones protested against most movement, let alone the rigours of further procreation. It was only the fact that she could no longer move fast or spring away speedily that had landed her in this latest pregnant state. Her human keepers, who had cared for her since kittenhood, were also elderly and well past welcoming new feline families. Realising this might be the last shared happy birth occasion, they gladly let her sleep on the bottom shelf of their airing cupboard until she was ready.

"Just three little darlings!" These were the first words my furry ears heard when I woke up. (How on earth had I been able to fall asleep? At a time like this!) "What little sweeties, aren't they Cuthbert?" The frightful female voice gushed, drooling a waterfall of spittle down on us. Who was this creature? What had I come to?

"Only three this time?" Old Cuthbert chuntered, prodding into the darkness of the stifling delivery room with podgy trembling fingers. So what did he expect from the poor old cat who, I gathered later, had probably produced more litters than was good for her? "We usually have more, Celia," he whined.

"But aren't they the darlingest, sweetest..," Celia spluttered and sprayed through ill fitting false teeth. She droned on and on. Even at that early stage I decided I did not like the sound of the two C's. Chuntering Cuthbert and Spluttering Celia were not my cup of tea. And that was before I was able to actually see them.

After days and nights of doing practically nothing except sleep and suck milk (difficult to acclimatise to, having spent years noshing fish and chips) my eyes finally decided to open and I looked carefully at my siblings. Truly, they were beautiful. One black and fluffy and one an unusual creamy white, and fluffy. Actually seeing them, touching them and hearing them brought home the sorry state of my situation. They both, after a few days, assumed an aristocratic air which I supposed came with the fluffiness. From the onset, in spite of their close proximity, they remained distant towards me, thank goodness. They cuddled and whimpered together but they ignored me completely. This, I learned later, was because our culture was very different. When one is born again in a different guise, no instructions or guidance are given as what to expect. One moment you are an ambitious girl, doing a bit of bungee jumping on a Saturday – young vivacious and quite attractive, even though I say it myself, and then the elastic gives way and you're laying in the dark on someone's mohair sweater, alongside an old cat with protruding nipples. Before you've had chance to come to terms with all this, two pulsating bundles of softness keep rolling into you.

I tried to lay quietly, searching my mind for that strange whispering inner voice. Obediently, it reminded me gently that it was my own wish for whiskers and a fur coat – the last words I ever spoke in my home before leaving for the bridge. Had my own cat done this to me? I loved my cat, I'd always treated her well. Why would she do this to me? How could she do this to me? What had happened? I clearly remembered then, someone leaning over railings of a very high bridge shouting, "She's going down!"

Watching Mother Cat wash herself, I wondered half-heartedly if I should try to do the same. After systematically exploring bits of my strange hairy clothing, the thought of licking them did not hold much appeal. The only good thing about this abominable state was that my mind still seemed to function logically; but this made it all so frustrating and completely beyond reason. In spite of the fact that I was apparently only able to squeak, I tried to comfort myself with the fact that I could understand every word that Cuthbert and Celia said - the only trouble was, there was no way to answer them. Conversely the strange grunts and squeals that poured from Mother Cat and her other offspring meant nothing to me. It was like being at some horrendous fancy dress party, wearing a bearskin and gag. Every time I tried to ask a reasonable question, all that came out is what sounded suspiciously like a weak, infantile meow.

Once again, this peculiar voice deep in my little head, put me right. (Mental help on this new way of life is obviously going to come in dribs and drabs.) Apparently cats are firmly divided into two camps, according to the information fed into my befuddled mind. The first group is made up of those who were cats or other animals in their previous lives, and the second – to which I belonged – are humans who had requested rebirth as an animal.

*But I've changed my mind,* I told this stupid annoying inner voice. *There is no way I want to be a cat, or pretend to be a cat, or whatever is happening to me. I want to be a person. I want to be myself again. Curses to this nightmare!*

There was, naturally, no response whatever to my mental outburst. Then my newly acquired mind-mentor floated the depressing news that the two groups of cats could never communicate with each other although they could with other members of their own 'group'. I searched this new dimension of my brain for information on other animals – cows, elephants, lions – would I be able to laugh and joke with them? And how would we communicate? My mind changed gear for one brief second and I saw my college lecturers as enormous venomous snakes - this gave me a fleeting feeling of pleasure. I waited hopefully but no more information on this was forthcoming. I supposed I would have to wait for the next instalment.

Mother Cat and her two pretty babies obviously belonged to the other animal group, this is why there was no rapport between us. Anyway, I discovered that pussies have a very limited verbal vocabulary apart from purring. (This, I grew to understand, is not necessarily a sign of contentment, more an involuntary noise made in order to feel they are participating in any conversation or argument that is going on). They only have a small repertoire of cries. These are used mainly for fighting, copulating and persuading people to open doors or cartons of cream. As every cat lover knows, cats talk mainly with their ears, both to each other and to their humans. This vital data was of little use to me in the early stages as, after exploration with shaking paws, I didn't think I had any ears. When I strained to squint at the other two, they appeared to have little holes where ears should be, so this was obviously the norm. Although we did not share the same background and there was apparently no way of us conversing, they weren't hostile and occasionally attempted to include me in their childish antics. There was always plenty of room for me on the piece of old blanket which replaced the original labour-room mohair jumper and they were warm little bodies to snuggle up against.

Some things I found especially difficult though. It was only after quite a long hesitation, when I got really famished on our first day together, that I was able to follow their lead and pummel the milky cushion of Mother Cat before selecting a nice pink entrée to the world of instant food. (I screwed my tiny face up and tried not to think of chicken balti and roast beef and Yorkshire pudding.)

All this licking and sucking and nibbling made me think, with nostalgia, of my own, recently departed, quite passable human body. Apart from being slightly overweight I had had good legs, a reasonable face and my boobs had been adequate. Tentatively, I explored with my forepaw to see whether I did, indeed, have little buttons on my new coat. Yes, there was something there that resembled a nipple – just. And another. Good Gracious! There was another lot further down!

I squeezed my eyes together tightly so as to stop the tears settling on my small whiskers. But there were no tears. Perhaps cats can't cry.

And now, I am a cat.

# CHAPTER 2

After what seemed like years to my poor befuddled brain, we had to endure the turmoil of our first move – out of our warm secure birth place and into the vast chilly regions of the kitchen floor tiles. Why couldn't they have a carpeted kitchen like civilised human beings? But maybe the old minders couldn't afford carpet. I tried to remember whether people who were affluent had carpets in kitchens, or whether they had tiles, or was it all laminate now? But it was irrelevant as there we were, sliding and skidding in and out of a basket, which wasn't really big enough for us all, in the corner by the sink. (I dreaded to think how poor Mother Cat had managed with her previous, multitudinous broods, but then she may have had a larger accommodation.)

Quite early in my new (unbelievably loathsome) life came my first experience of the litter tray, just across the floor opposite our bed. Shock number one! (Well, really about 101 after all the others I was experiencing.) Yes, of course I knew about litter trays before. They were things that cats used, to wee and splat in. But, actually having to perform in one! Never, never, never! Me? Not in a billion years!

But what was an alternative? None! (Oh, where is my comfortable Armitage Shanks with its padded plastic seat?) But, needs must. Whiskers aquiver and hissing menacingly I steadied my trembling frame (which always left these things until the last moment) to sway over the waiting box. This definitely demanded more skill and perseverance than I, at that stage, possessed. Mother Cat had carefully demonstrated, diligently disguising her samples without upsetting the tiny granules too much. Then her two fluffy clones had mimicked her moves triumphantly. I could hardly wait (literally) for my go. Nothing to it I felt, pushing aside the indignity. Believe me – no human (or ex human) could ever imagine the dexterity required to hold wobbling rear end steady over small rectangular plastic tray. Sufficient to record that my first belching attempt managed to distribute the entire contents of my bowel around the rim and, with some artistry, in quaint patterns across quite a few of the pristine white floor tiles. (Was my bottom being purposefully bolshie or what?)

Mother Cat watched with horror then rushed across to usher me back to the others and the comparative sanctuary of our basket, gathering us to her as if she feared the worst. Poof! I thought, two seconds with a floor cloth and I could dispel the disaster. Then I remembered who, or what, I was. No longer could I do these simple chores. 'I can't even pick up a damned cloth!' I shouted, but my whimper just caused Mother Cat to snuggle up against me. And with good reason, it transpired, for just as if someone had summoned her, Spluttering Celia waddled into the kitchen. Two lumpy tree trunks towered over us - this was the closest my nose had come to her legs. A worn corduroy slipper kicked the side of our bed causing us all to claw on for dear life.

"Cats!" she spat. "Who did this? Just you tell me, which of you?" Somewhat expectedly, there was no answer. "I'll wring your neck!" she promised as if this might prove an incentive for instant confession. "I'll kill you!" she spluttered (as if the neck wringing might not do the trick). Then she screamed "Cuthbert! Come here at once!" Cuthbert shuffled in, yet more scruffy corduroy slippers creeping towards us.

"Look!" she yelled to the poor man, who clutched at his Sporting News as if it were a lifebelt.

"Ah! A little accident." He nodded. His wrinkly's mind assessing the situation with alacrity.

"Little? Little? My new floor is ruined! I told you they should be in the garage like all the others she's had."

"Now, now." He lifted the journal in a pacifying gesture, which Celia mistook for an act of deep aggression.

"Don't you wave that thing at me! Full of rubbish it is, and ways to lose your money. You and your blasted horses! Get your nose out of that rag and get the cloth and wipe this mess up!" Orders issued, she stooped until her moon face was almost on our level. Petrifying I can tell you! I just wish I had met her when I was wearing my other skin. I would soon have....

"Give me that!" Her chubby hand snatched at the precious 'News'. "It will do to mop the tiles. Then, you can wipe it up."

"But.." he stuttered, clutching at his treasured newspaper. "It will leave print marks – black smears on the white…."

He was too late with his attempts to save the destruction of the day's racing form. Frothing at the mouth his spouse crumpled the pages and fell to her knees, embossing jigsaw-type bits of horse and jockey on to the wetness of the floor where my misdirected splodges had occurred. "Now, wipe it!" she shouted. "And do the sides of the tray as well!"

"You..You – WOMAN!" he wailed, almost tearfully. She glared at him. "No more cats!" she spat. "Ever!"

He coughed. "All right  Dear, don't upset yourself." If he had hoped by this, to salvage the remaining pages, he was out of luck. The furious woman stamped out of the kitchen, the offending crumpled mess held at arm's length with the unused sheets clamped stiffly beneath her other arm. "Dustbin!" she fumed, wrenching open the back door and clomping outside.

We watched, hardly daring to breathe. Mother Cat wiggled her ears and the others responded in similar fashion. They looked at me sadly. Well, I suppose I was hardly Top Cat that day.


Now that my eyes were completely open, I could make out the layout of the room. There was something silver and shining that immediately caught my attention over by the far wall. I tried to ask Mother what it was but even with frantic waggling of ears she couldn't manage to convey anything. The two fluff balls watched and wiggled their apprentice ears, then the three of them had a good laugh, no doubt at my expense. What a trial this new life was turning out to be already. Surely, if they have such a stupid dual system, mothers and offspring should all belong to the same clan. At this rate I will never speak to anyone (or thing) again. *Ah*, but my inner voice hinted, *there is the advantage of being able to think like a homo sapien – for the time being at least.*

This cheered me a little. Thank goodness for my human brain! Then I thought about my humans – my previous family people. I shuddered. What about my mother? How would she feel if she knew her daughter had become Cat Woman? But, I reasoned, to her I was simply 'gone' like my cousin.

"Whatever you do, do it with style," he had once said. And sure enough his going was even more stylish than mine. He bade goodbye to life whilst attempting to prove it was possible to take off from a shed roof and remain motionless in the air. He was well into model airplanes as a hobby and worked as a cleaner at the local RAF camp. Consequently he felt he knew all about the principles of flying aircraft and was convinced he could adapt these to a more personal scale, so long as the wings strapped to his middle were strong enough. (He wasn't terribly old, but, in thinking back, I realise he must have been a bit advanced in the senility stakes.)

After a precarious take off, Cousin, who was built rather on the same lines as an ox, touched down heavily in the centre of the vegetable patch. His face, I learned afterwards, became embedded in the moist earth and the seedling potatoes, resulting in lots of quick breathing in of rather more roughage than was good for him.

He choked to death. Commiserating friends and family were told he had suffered a fatal accident whilst flying. (The RAF connection had its uses).

I sighed. My poor mother must think that compulsive fatal jumping is in our genes.

Ah well, back to the nightmare scenario that is me. How can I even begin to accept what is now? Now. When is now? And what the hell is happening? How can I really believe I am a cat? Who did this to me? And why? Oh, why?

I yelled and hollered obscenities into the air but no one took any notice and it just made me feel worse. I steadied myself with difficulty. Perhaps if I could just try to accept it (just temporarily, oh yes, only very temporarily) perhaps someone or something would come along and take me away. Out of my purgatory. My heart was pounding and I was panting like a stupid dog. Where was that inner voice that comforted me before? Gone! Nothing. Not even my own mind could save me. Was I a mad human or a mad cat? Did it matter? I was just mad. I shut my mouth and was quiet for a few moments.

'Help!' I yelled. I must keep on trying. But nothing happened. No one came to rescue me. Then I clamped my jaws together again and slumped down. Where is my beautiful life? Where is my beautiful body? Am I still beautiful even as a – well, whatever I am now?

Stretching as much as I could in the confined space of the basket I stared at the occupants. I refuse to call them family. How can they be my family? My great, great grandfather had been a Lord (or so my mother had told me). What were these cats' ancestors? They wouldn't even have had proper grandfathers. Alley cats or wild beasts – that's where they came from I bet. As I looked at them, the little ones looked so innocent and Mother Cat was purring so contentedly at them and, yes, across at me. This charade wasn't their fault. I really will try to be nice to them I decided. They haven't done me any harm.

Although I had studied the kittens in detail, I had no idea about my own appearance. Hands and feet sprouted only whispy hair of indeterminate, doubtful colour and tail was not long enough to coax around for examination. I gazed across the kitchen at the silver shinning thing I had noticed earlier. I worked out that it must be some sort of pedal bin, and figured that if I could get to it, the reflection would show me what I looked like and put me out of my misery. (I had never been particularly vain, you understand, but this appearance thing was becoming quite an obsession – especially as old Celia seemed to be picking up and cuddling the others more than me. This suited me fine but did make me slightly anxious.) A mirror would have been better, as even from that distance it was obvious that the distant silver surface was rather scratchy. But mirrors were hung high, necessitating large leaps on to furniture, which was beyond my young capabilities. (Completely out of the question as I was having difficulty enough negotiating myself over the edge of our wicker home.)

Once out and on the floor I staggered away from my family. (There, 'my family' - I really am trying) who were taking no notice anyway. The hazardous journey took me past various familiar appliances – washing machine, dryer, dishwasher, ironing board. I remembered them well and wondered wistfully if I would ever again throw in dirty jumpers or stack messy plates. Even the previously dreaded ironing board held a kind of attraction. (Somehow I felt a vague feeling that it might be good to try to climb up it.) They all looked so different from this low angle as I slewed past them. They all looked so huge!

At last the shiny round bin was within scrambling distance. Then suddenly, right in front of me, stood a shaking, trembling, apparition. Was that mixture of carrots and rustiness really me? Why had I bothered to make the trek? My quivering image sneered back at me. Moving hesitantly sideways to the lesser scratched surface did not improve my appearance at all.

'I am a ginger cat,' I admitted to myself, noting, with no sense of relief, that there was the makings of a white chest and white bits splattered about elsewhere. No wonder nobody wanted to pick me up. Horrors upon horrors! A rotten ginger cat! Why, if I've got to be a creature like this for a while (please – only for a while. Please?) Why can't I be something special? A thoroughbred, a champion prize winner, a rare exclusive strain? But ginger with vague white bits... Could anything be worse? 'I wish I was dead!' I screamed. And screamed. And screamed. But it did no good.

My misgivings were compounded the next day at the Kitty Christening Ceremony. Celia's splutter gave way to gurgling as she clasped the little black bundle to her ample bosom. (The rage of the mis-targeted litter box seemingly forgotten in the joy of this occasion.)

"You, my little fluffy beauty will be called Blackie because you are so beautiful and black." Drips from the corners of her mouth swayed down on to my luckless sister. Cuthbert, adjusting his floral pinafore, grunted approval.

"And you," she gently lifted up the other little snorting creature. "We will call you Creamy because that's what you are, my little treasure." (Very predictable, I thought.) Cuthbert nodded dutifully at his wife who now held one baby in each arm. There was no room for me even if she had wanted to pick me up, which, thankfully, she obviously did not.

"And you, there," (No endearment here I noticed. Had she deduced that I was the filthy culprit-of-the-tray or did she merely dislike me?) "What shall we call you?"

No, please God, No!

"Yes!" she interrupted my unanswered prayer, "You will be Ginger!"

Oh no! Please! Why not - Tigress, Marmalade or even Jaffa? – but not just common Ginger....

She put the others down and patted my head firmly to cement the decision. Mother Cat stopped washing her bottom and looked at me with some sympathy – she had seen it all before.

"You are my little ginger Tom," the old woman said, withdrawing her hand hastily as I flayed my yet-to-grow claws in her direction.

'I am NOT a Tom – I am a girl!' I shouted lustily but no one heard me. 'A woman, A female!' My protests were not even noticed. 'I've got tits and other things!' I roared, shaking my angry body at them. I even rolled over to show my stomach lest someone should take the trouble to check. But no one did.

# CHAPTER 3

Those early days in Cheshire rolled into weeks and I and my sisters became adept at dashing about the kitchen, springing on to low furniture and tripping up our humans at every opportunity. Sometimes, in the evenings, we were taken into the living room to watch television. The others couldn't have cared less and filled the time hiding and springing out at nothing and generally being childish and making a nuisance of themselves, but for me it was heaven to see Coronation Street again. Although I had never been a TV addict, I missed watching the programmes I used to enjoy. Maybe, I thought, we might be allowed to stay up for the late news one night, so that I could catch up with the real world. But after dear Blackie and Creamy had successfully unravelled the fringe around the bottom of the settee, no one was allowed out of the kitchen prison again, except for Mother Cat as she was an established member of the household.

Then, one day, Lucifer paid us a visit. Lucifer was a small brown dog of doubtful parentage who belonged to the minders' daughter, Lynda. From various conversations, I had learned all about family members and knew that Lynda was coming that day, with Lucifer, presumably to gawp at us. The rest of my family apparently had no such forward information as they were extremely alarmed when a car stopped outside in the drive, by the kitchen door, and Lucifer sprang out barking his joyous greetings. Mother Cat and her offspring ran into their basket, each trying to crawl and hide beneath the others. As the old minders shuffled into the kitchen I stood by the door unnoticed.

"Put the lead on Lucifer before we open the door," shouted Cuthbert as his daughter tapped at the window. "Then bring him through into the house. The cats are out here!" He sounded unusually firm.

"OK. Just a minute!" Lynda slammed the car door and admonished the yapping dog, whose paws appeared, clawing at the frosted glass pane in the top of the door.

"How lovely to see you, Dear!" gushed Celia, sucking excitedly through her cavities. She threw open the back door, clearly ignoring the rules set out by the old man. A chocolate streak darted straight past us, towards the far corner where the pussy family cowered.

"He'll go for the cats!" Lynda screamed through the doorway, though her attention was primarily occupied by emptying the contents of her car.

"Where's his lead? You shouldn't have opened the door until he had his lead on," muttered her father crossly.

"Woof Woof!" Lucifer yapped, happily bounding towards the basket.

'Steady on,' I thought, glad I was out of the line of danger safely behind the open door. 'You'll frighten the living daylights out of them.'

The mass of brown hairiness stopped in mid track, turning slowly to stare fully at me.

"Look!" shrieked Celia (this time she wore the floral pinny.) "Lucifer's seen Ginger. He's going to chase Ginger Tom!"

Glaring at her I thought, 'Stupid woman!' then I looked in the dog's direction and thought, 'Hello, what have we here?' (Why don't I feel afraid? Aren't cats supposed to be scared of dogs?) My whirling brain tried to cope with the absurdity of the situation.

Lucifer waddled over and stood in front of me and put his head on one side. 'Hello,' he returned my greeting. 'You must be one of the new arrivals everyone keeps going on about.'

'I can speak to you!' My whiskers started to tremble with excitement. 'Well, not actually speak, but our thinking – we can talk to each other by our thinking.' I was sniffling and squeaking convulsively. What the devil was happening to me now?

He nodded wisely, which must have been difficult as his head was still hanging over to one side. I couldn't believe it – rapport at last! Even if it was only with a mogrelly dog.

'Steady on, yourself,' he retorted haughtily. 'I'm not a mongrelly dog, I am a cross breed. Remember, I can understand every little think you have.'

'Thought,' I corrected him automatically. (English, especially grammar, had always been my strong point.)

"I do believe he's frightened of Ginger," Celia lisped, yellowing fangs sucking over her lolling lips. "He's not growling or snarling and he seems to have forgotten about the others."

"Rubbish!" Cuthbert was again striving to prove himself head of the household (easier now that he was not wearing an apron or flourishing a floor cloth.) "You put the lead on him. He could eat that cat with one swallow."

'Beastly thought, silly old twat!' Lucifer snorted.

'Yes, they're both a bit senile.' I was desperate to keep him by me – to fire questions at him. 'But how can we understand each other? I can't exchange words or thoughts or ear wiggles with anyone else?'

As Lynda, fastened the lead to his collar I became frantic lest I should lose my new found ally.

"Come on!" The younger woman, also fat and dumpy like her mother, tried to drag Lucifer away but he wasn't having any of it.

"Woof!" and "Growl!" he told her, trying to dig his claws into the tiles but she didn't understand and he started to slither towards her.

"Why isn't he chasing Penelope? He always chases Penelope." The old man scratched his balding head. Penelope? So that was Mother Cat's official title. Spluttering Celia had always referred to her as Puss Puss or You Dratted Cat, according to the prevailing climate.

'We can talk,' Lucifer started, slumping down and stretching out his legs at angles so that no amount of lead pulling would dislodge him. Lynda looped the end of the lead over the door handle ."Sit down!" she told her dog, "I'll walk you in a minute." She beamed at her parents, anxious to start chatting. "He won't get far now."

'We can talk,' Lucifer continued patiently, knowing full well he could tug free if he needed to, "Because we are Zoons – we used to be people. Neither you nor I can converse with animals that were animals in a previous life, but we can both chat away – through thought – with any other Zoon.'

Ah, it all becomes as clear as mud. But at least it went some way towards explaining things – that is, if you're crazy enough to digest all this nonsense. Best humour him for a bit, find out what on earth he was going on about.

'Zoon?'

'ZOON. You and me, we're Zoons.' At first I thought he was having me on, some sort of shaggy dog story, but no his thoughts were doggedly serious. 'It was sweltering hot in that damned car.' His tongue flopped noisily, trying to stop the rivulets of saliva from escaping at the corners of his mouth.

'Aren't you a good traveller?' I didn't really care but felt I must keep him with me, keep him interested.

'No way!'

'Look, I don't mean to be rude but I've got loads of things to ask you. Do you mind? Just in case they take you away before we've had chance to talk'.

'Well, you would have, wouldn't you, not long having been here – fire away!'

'Do I understand it correctly, then, that you're telling me we're all split into two groups and that animal animals can only communicate with each other and those who used to be humans are, well, whatever..'

'Zoon is the general term. It covers all of us of the higher intellect – cats, dogs, horses, cows, elephants – the whole shooting match. It includes anyone who has stupidly told a particular animal that they would like to 'come back' as one of them. That's what does it, just that little momentary wish put into words.'

I shook myself from head to tail. This is clap-trap, I told myself firmly. 'What? You mean just because we've said something silly in the heat of the moment, it happens?'

The dog nodded his head. Pieces of unruly hair fell over his eyes. 'Yup!'

'So we might have come back as anything – if we'd said it?' I blinked. This was the barmiest thing I'd ever heard.

'Yup! You could've been a kangaroo,' he elaborated, shaking his hair back.

'How do you know all this? You're making it up.'

'I could be,' he said reasonably, 'But I ain't. Anyway, can you think of another way of explaining it?'

I shook my head in bewilderment. 'But how do you know about all this?' I persisted. He patiently explained that it is incumbent upon Zoons to tell any newcomers they meet, details of what they know. In this way the novice can adapt more smoothly to its new way of life. 'That's the theory, anyway,' he said. 'My dog mother told me about it when I was only a few hours old. You can imagine the shock. What would that news do to a poor pup?' I swallowed, still not even starting to believe what I was being told. 'She was cruel to tell me so soon. Before I'd even realised it was really happening to me. Spiteful! Now I know why they're called bitches.' He finished vehemently.

'Why Zoon? What does it mean – does it stand for something?' I hadn't time to waste on his self pity.

'Dunno.'

'I just can't believe any of it. It's so difficult to take in.'

'You'd better believe it. Only snag is one doesn't initially know which lot folk belong to. Dreadfully confusing at times, I can tell you. When you're dying for a good chat and everyone else sits around waggling their ears at each other.'

'Well, do you, er, we, have to do anything – to give out and receive these messages? You still haven't explained how we do it, how we, well, think-talk.'

'Not difficult to work out,' he sniffed, 'It's the eyes. You give and take with the eyes. If you're facing the other way I can't tell what you're thinking, that's when you can have your naughty thoughts,' he added wickedly. 'And,' he went on. 'Your feelings come through with your message. For instance you can do it softly, crossly, happily – just like tones of voice in speaking.'

25

I just sat and stared at him, dumbfounded. But, goodness only knows, it was something to latch on to, even if it made no sense at all. What else was there to think? Find out more, I willed myself urgently.

'It's all so strange but I suppose you're used to it by now. How long have you been – I mean – well, you know what I mean?' In spite of my desperate need for facts I couldn't help being curious about him, and I told myself, I must keep this dialogue going at all costs.

'Well, I've been in this itchy coat for about two years. I was a butcher before.'

As he became more conversational the adults gazed at us in astonishment. Now that their welcome endearments had petered out they stared toward Lucifer and me as if hypnotised.

'A butcher? What on earth made you want to be a dog?'

'Ah well, I didn't really. I mean, it was just a chance remark I made, which is usually the case of creatures in our predicament. There were so many damn dogs who used to sneak into the shop and help themselves when my back was turned, or empty the scrap bin all across the shop floor.' He paused as if trying to remember details. 'One day I said something like, "In my next life I'll be a dog – they have it made," and, well, here I am. I lost a fight with an unfriendly meat cleaver and the next thing I said was, "Woof".'

I laid down next to him digesting all this.

"Heavens above!" fat Lynda spouted from the other side of the room. "They're actually sitting together. Lucifer, have you taken leave of your senses? You always chase cats!" She sounded utterly bewildered. Lucifer ignored her, turning back to me.

"The car always exhausts him," she said, "But never like this. Let's take this off you, you're panting like mad." Lynda unsnapped the lead from his collar, slipping it from the door handle. She coiled the leash and viciously rammed it into one of her copious bags. Her voice sounded genuinely worried about her pet's uncharacteristic behaviour. "He always chases after cats," she whined to her parents. "Well, let's see the others. This one's certainly a bit strange." She threw me a nasty suspicious look.

"I still think that dog ought to be on the lead," Cuthbert protested but the two women ignored him and headed towards the other cats who were watching tentatively from their corner.

'Ah yes. I was going to have some sport there wasn't I?' Lucifer looked across to where Penelope was bravely peering over the edge of the basket. Two tiny heads behind her strained to see what was going on. 'Yes I enjoy a tussle with good old Lady Penelope.' Lucifer lumbered to his feet, trying to summon up enthusiasm for his expected demonstration of doggytude.

'Don't you dare!' I warned, jumping up. I was amazed that my back arched ominously and that my short fur was actually fluffed up and standing on end. God, I must have looked pathetic! I realised I was behaving like a regular cat; I made myself keep repeating 'I am Me! I am Me!' Determinedly I told myself to get a grip. This dog maybe could help me, advise me. I slackened back and tried to look more amiable. Lucifer grinned at my powerful puss pose and I fought to stop myself from shrieking with frustration.

'All right, all right. I don't feel up to it anyway.' he retorted. 'You know that car journey made me feel quite sick. She drives like a maniac.' To everyone's relief he slumped back down on to the floor again. Even Celia, who I am sure would have welcomed my elimination, could not have borne further attack on her new kitchen tiles.

"Well let's look at them." Fat Lynda peered into the cat basket. "Here Penelope, let's see your babies."

'Makes you sick to listen doesn't it?' my companion snorted.

'Well, they are rather sweet – well that's what I would have thought before, before…'

'Useless,' he interrupted, 'just like old Pen. Can't do anything. No sense at all, just whisker and ear twitching. Hyperbolic ears that's what that lot's got. Can't even hold a conversation. But you moggies from Cheshire are always the worst - the absolute pits.'

27

'What do you mean?' My tone was wary, especially as he seemed to be smirking.

'Cheshire cats are the looniest of all – they are always grinning.'

'Ha bloomin' ha!' I could feel my tail flick about a bit.

'It's only my little joke, I'm only kidding. You're OK,' he said soberly. 'I bet you were a clever girl.' My striped body relaxed and I felt my little white chest puff out. I lay back and stretched as much as I decently could without rolling over.

'Good looking woman, I shouldn't wonder,' he said licking his lips lasciviously. My whiskers twitched happily at him and from somewhere deep inside me came this almighty thumping and thudding - almost like a diesel engine - each time I breathed. Good Lord, I was purring for the very first time!

'Well,' I said when I had composed myself sufficiently. 'Thank you, kind sir, but how do you know I'm a female – everyone else thinks I'm a Tom just because I'm ginger.' I hated admitting to be ginger. I would have much sooner been a Persian or a Burmese or even a Siamese -though having to make all that noise all the time would be tiresome.

'You think like a girl,' he said immediately. 'Anyway,' he turned on to his side and started to close his eyes. 'I never had any trouble telling which was which. I never had a problem with that sort of thing.' He managed a lopsided leer, even with his shaggy eyes shut.

"The stupid dog's exhausted," Lynda was obviously taken aback by his undoglike attitude. "How can a car drive exhaust a healthy dog?" The question held a note of concern.

'The way you drive would exhaust anyone,' he said, his eyelids fluttering dangerously.

'Don't go to sleep, Lucifer!' I begged him. Me! Pleading with some dog! But I couldn't afford to lose eye contact otherwise our communication would finish. According to him, anyway..

'Can I just ask? Is there anything else important I should know?' There was loads more no doubt, but just how much

28

could I stomach? 'Anything that might help me?' Put pressure on him. Don't lose him yet.

His stubby ears inched forward. 'Possibly just something. Not the sort of thing usually passed on. Bit upsetting.'

'What?'

'Well..'

'Get on with it!'

Lucifer blinked and shook back his hair again. 'Memory,' his stare muttered slowly. 'Your memory will start to go. Each day you'll remember less and less of your life as a person. The people you knew, the things you did. Places, feelings. They will gradually go.'

'What do you mean – go?' My eyes opened wide

'What I say. Each day you will start to act and think more like a cat. Eventually, if you live to be a grand old age you will become complete cat and not know anything else. If you die young you may still remember some things about being a person but not if you live to be an old cat. Your human mind will go blank.'

'Impossible!' But I knew anything was possible in this horrific saga. 'This can't be true!' But I realised, even without looking at the brute, that this could be, and probably was, true. Or was he just making it all up to frighten me? Well, if he was he was certainly succeeding. My eyes pierced into his. No, he really believed it himself.

He looked at me with sympathy. 'I hated to tell you, but it might make it easier. I was told, not early on but soon enough. I don't think it helps much though. Sometimes I think it would be better not to know. But it does explain why you search about, trying to think of things. Trying to remember..' His gaze trailed away despondently. 'Can't recall much now,' he admitted. 'Except what I was and what made me come here – you never forget that,' he said bitterly, coughing to cover his embarrassment.

I gulped and gulped again. 'It's all mad!' I spat at him. 'You're mad!' He nodded slowly. 'I understand how you feel,' he said, settling himself more comfortably. 'I felt like that. Angry, puzzled, humiliated. No rhyme nor reason. But I promise you each day you'll feel it less. You'll be less angry. Every week you will feel more accustomed to it.' He shifted his legs so that his paws could curve around to his body, instead of sticking out awkwardly.

'Marvellous!' I hissed through clenched teeth. 'Every day my memory gets worse and every week I feel happier about it! Well, let me tell you, Mr. Stupid Rotten Dog, I will not get accustomed to it, as you so quaintly put it. I will not!'

'Yes you will,' he interrupted, completely unperturbed. We sat staring at each other.

"I just don't understand what is happening." A voice wailed from the other side of the kitchen. "They seem to be almost chummy."

I fired a deadly look towards the stupid fat Lynda. What might she and the old idiots come as next time? Well, whatever it was it would serve them jolly well right. As for Lucifer, or whatever his cursed name was....

'It is not exactly my fault,' he chipped in defensively. 'I'm just the messenger.'

'Don't give me that!' I snarled

'True,' he said after some consideration. 'Perhaps I shouldn't have given you that. But you did say you wanted to know as much as possible.'

I glared at him. 'Well, I feel as cross and as stupefied by the whole thing, as much today as I did yesterday, and last week,' I added for good measure. But in order to avoid further communication he shut his eyes firmly. I didn't know if he was asleep or not.

I crept back towards the door and crouched against the wall. So this is what madness is about. I have turned into a crackpot. My life, loves, hopes, dreams – gone! Meowing, purring, scratching, sleeping. Is this to be me from now on? Not even a proper cat. A raving lunatic cat that talks to dogs. But if I can talk and listen, I reasoned, some creature, somewhere, might know the way out. The way back. I would humour them all, go along with it. Collect as much information as I could, then when the time came I would be ready. Ready for what? My mind was drowning, submerged. I took some deep Yoga breaths, holding in as my instructor had taught me. No good. Little snorts shot out past my tongue. Jeeze! I couldn't even control my breathing. My mind reached out, searching for avenues of hope. Trembling, I tried to think about God. Could he help? I was sure he could, but would he? I would talk to him in a nice civilised way – not blaming, just asking - Why? But I hadn't spoken to God (apart from a couple of words on my way down on the flight to catland) since I was at junior school. I tried half-heartedly. He did not hear me. I shouted and spat and swore. I drummed forepaws against the door, clawing with my no claws against the wood. I stamped back-pads on the famous white tiles. I went bananas.

"Ginger Tom's having a fit," Cuthbert observed.

"Wicked destructive cat!" spluttered Celia looking up from displaying the treasurers of the cat basket. "Stop it at once!" She was not really distracted, though, as she knew I could do little damage.

"He's got no claws." Cuthbert confirmed my humiliation publicly.

'You just wait until I have,' I threatened him. 'I hate you all!' I was exploding again.    But it was really just a squeal, even to my own ears.

# CHAPTER 4

Shortly after Lucifer's visit I realised that the next momentous event was to be adoption day, or should I say, the passing-out parade. I should have anticipated this but when Chuntering Cuthbert casually mentioned it one evening, as the old folks stirred their cocoa at the kitchen table, it came as a bit of a shock. (I suppose it was worse for the others as they wouldn't understand what was going to happen unless Mother Cat gave them some sort of warning about the next and probably most important stage of their lives.)

"Three lots of visitors to see you lucky kittens the day after tomorrow," Celia giggled. "I only hope they don't all choose the same little girl – or boy," she added looking at me spitefully.

'You silly old bat!' I tried to yell at her but she just ignored my squeak. 'I'm a girl!' Just because I had crapped over her wretched tiles there was no need to turn me into a transvestite. For some reason this gender thing had started to worry me greatly and I desperately needed to drive the point home. Action was needed! Flinging my body at her foot, which was covered only in a glittery pink bed sock, I sunk what miniature teeth I had into her hot swollen toes. She squawked like a parrot and danced around the kitchen, slopping her drink down the front of the old man's pyjamas. He, in turn, yelled, as the hot liquid scalded his white crinkled chest and, as he grabbed at her arm, her cup tilted up and the cold white tiles turned into a sea of delicious warm brown stickiness. (My sisters and Mother Cat had no idea what all this was about but they set to with glee, lapping enthusiastically at the unexpected bounty.)

"You dreadful cat!" Celia's shaking jaw yelped. In fact, her whole body seemed to wobble in her rage. "You ungrateful moron!"

The others stopped lapping for a second and looked up questioningly. Ears twitched violently as they asked Mother to explain – which of course, she couldn't as she only understood a few words of Language. Suffice to say, tone was well comprehended and she marshalled the girls back to safety hoping that the storm would subside and the feast could continue later.

"You wretch!" the old lady spluttered lifting her injured foot off the floor. "After I've looked after you and given you every comfort."

'You wouldn't let us go in that nice warm room to watch TV' I hissed at her. The others were cowering somewhere in the depths of the wicker and I felt a bit vulnerable, paddling in the middle of the chocolaty pond, back arched like an idiot and tail lashing to and fro uncontrollably.

"Blasted cats! No more – ever!" the old man grunted, clutching his sodden pyjama jacket. "Come on up to bed, Dear. We'll clear all this in the morning."

But Celia wasn't through. Never, it emerged through seething teeth, had one of her 'little ones' turned on her. Not even a spit or claw, let alone actually biting her foot and attacking her poor bunion which she had nursed for so long.

"I hope no-one chooses you!" she shouted at me venomously. "Then I can have you put to sleep – though that is probably too good for you!"

"Oh come on, Love." He mopped his scalding, throbbing front with a 'Come to Bournemouth' tea towel. "It was probably only meant in fun."

"FUN!" roared his anguished spouse. "He's drawn blood. Look, I'm bleeding into the cocoa!" As she lifted a leg and aimed her silk covered bunion in my direction, her other foot squelched, hesitated, then slid out in a straight line behind her as she did the splits in the middle of the kitchen floor.

This was the time, I decided, to make myself scarce, so I moved quickly. Lifting my splattered brown paws from the puddle I hurried back to the basket, burrowing frantically until I was hidden underneath my cat family. Not a whisker or tail in evidence.

By the noise she was making I realised there was a strong likelihood that the grand parade of would-be owners, in two days' time, would be hosted by an elderly fat woman with her leg in plaster.


"Oh, Oh!" sang the first delighted visitor on the important day, as she stepped across the newly scrubbed, glistening kitchen floor. (I can still conjure up a sharp image of Cuthbert operating bucket and cloth.) Tiny stilettos stopped tap-tapping as she bent over our basket. Mother Cat had obviously recognised a few familiar human words and picked up the signs, as she had spent hours scratching and washing herself and us (yes, she gave me a good going over as well – she was very fair and showed not too much favouritism.) I quite enjoyed being groomed – rather like someone brushing your hair with a Mason Pearson and then combing it down smoothly afterwards. Anyway, we all looked a treat. Cuthbert had made our bed nicely (Old Bat couldn't bend down because of her bandaged leg. I wondered, in passing, how the red throbbing bunion was faring encased in its white sweaty tomb.)

"This is the little black treasure then?" the woman said eagerly, dropping her handbag and reaching towards my apprehensive sister. "May I?" The kitten was grabbed without waiting for the old people to reply. "What a sweetie pie! Are you going to be my Blackie then?" Whew! How glad I was that this female was ignoring me. "I shall have to change her name – I mean Blackie isn't very imaginative is it? No offence of course," she rushed on ignoring the pained look on Madam's face. "Yes, yes, she's adorable. I'll definitely have her. Can I take her now?" Tucking poor Blackie under her arm, she turned to retrieve her little patent leather handbag which stood by the basket, waiting.

"I'm glad you want her," Celia said carefully, "But as I explained on the 'phone, they are not quite ready to leave their mother. Could you possibly collect her next Saturday? I think they need a few more days together." Hopalong Cassidy was making sure everyone knew who was in charge.

34

"Yes. Yes, Saturday will be fine." The visitor reluctantly deposited Blackie back with Penelope. "About midday, would that be all right?"

"Afternoon would be better, after 2 o'clock," The big C remained in control. "My leg is troublesome sometimes in the mornings," she whined, eliciting sympathy.

"Yes. Yes," the lady tutted, "How did you have your – er – accident?"

'By trying to kick the poor hard-done-by cat!' I shouted, but my weak squeak was rewarded with a very nasty look from her with the gammy leg. "I slipped," she said in the sort of tone one might use after being hit by a tank.

"Ahhh. I see." The handbag was back in place under her arm and the stilettos tap-tapped on their way. "Two o'clock, Right!" Off she went.

Guest number two arrived almost immediately (or rather, guests, as this one had brought her man along, presumably to stand and nod because that's all he did.) Mother Cat sat back so that we took centre stage in the basket. Dear Penelope, I quite liked her – she had obviously been through this procedure many times before. I could almost feel that she was saying, "Smile, Purrr," to us, her offspring, wanting us to look our best.

"Hello pussies!" The floral tent bent over us, enormous pudding breasts tumbling towards the low neckline precariously. "Are they all available still?" Cuthbert opened his mouth to answer but was immediately relegated to standing by the door with nodding guest man.

"No, I'm sorry," our incapacitated chargehand said in a businesslike manner. "The little black one has already gone." I snuggled closer to Penelope. Bouncing hydrangeas of varying purples and pinks vibrated before my whiskers.

"There's no contest," she said at once. "The little white one is cute. Is it a Tom?"

Celia shook her head, her teeth rattling in a negative gesture. "The cream kitten," she said with emphasis on the 'cream', is a she. The ginger one's a Tom." She shot me a baleful glance which I returned, hoping she could read my murderous thoughts. 'Wrong!' I screamed but no one heard.

"I didn't really want a female – you know all that operation and things." The frantic flowers swung to and fro making me feel quite dizzy.

"The cream one's a nice looking cat," the nodding man tried hesitantly.

The undulating floral arrangement swung around. "Of course it is!" she snapped. "It's just, well more bother, you know that." The man nodded obediently.

"The operation's much easier these days, quite a simple matter, just a few minutes." Celia wheedled, and so it was settled. Two down, one to go.

"Saturday? Agreed!" The botanical woman swished her flowers about for the last time whilst her husband nodded.

So, this was it then. Like a cattle market or slaves being plucked out or left unwanted. Never in anyone's wildest dreams could there be such humiliation. Human to cat was grotesque enough. Cat of uncertain sex was bizarre. But cat being ignored on open owner-market was just beyond acceptance. Then I consoled myself, if the first two viewers were anything to go by surely my chances must get better. No one could be a worse surrogate Mum than Tappy Heels or Flora Bunda. Then my unpleasant little inner voice assured me that things can always get worse. OK, if that's the case I will be brave and put an end to it all. Self destruction. I would pass away peacefully before the third threat could arrive. Then I realised that a modern kitchen (where one cannot reach anything except the floor) provides scant opportunity for self demise. Also – cats have nine lives, don't they?

The third prospective cat owner arrived quite late in the evening. "It's a Miz Ballenger – and she said she would be here by six at the latest," Celia grumbled because she had cleared away the tea things early in readiness. What on earth would Miz Ballenger be like, I wondered vaguely, not that it would be any of my concern – she would no doubt enthuse over the others and ignore me, but I was getting used to this. Hells Bells! Might I then have to stay with the two C's for ever? No. I consoled myself that Celia would never allow this. She would find some method of being rid of me. I dared not even consider possible alternatives. Suicide and slaughter are very different, even if they do both meet the desired end.

Miz Ballenger eventually arrived at about nine o'clock with a trumpeting of car horn and battery of engine revs.

"It sounds like one of those sports cars," Celia spluttered, as if owning such a vehicle carried a serious stigma. "Yes," she lifted the curtain gently, "It's a great low red thing – all that noise at this time of the night!" she snarled. The other kittens were asleep but Mother Penelope stretched and had a little wash as the front doorbell rang.

"You're very late. We had almost given you up," old peg-leg remonstrated, leading her guest through the hall and into the kitchen.

"Sorry!" the woman said carelessly. "Had to work on." She ignored the aged people's frowns of disapproval and strode over to our basket. I looked up at her with some interest, mainly because I could immediately tell that she was wearing Opium. My uncle had given me a tiny bottle last Christmas which I truly treasured, and the fragrance reminded me of him, of my family, of my friends at college, of…

Having always believed that people who enjoy the same scents are naturally kindred spirits, I studied the newcomer. About 25, tall, with short copper-colour hair cut in a bob. Make-up was minimal but the face peering down wore a healthy, energetic look. Then I noticed the trousers. What a strange outfit to wear to work. Whatever did she do for a living? The snakeskin (or sharkskin or whatever skin) clung snugly to slim hips and the short black waistcoat was a garment I would have killed for. It was the sort of gear I would dream of wearing. That is, before…I fought back the threatening, now familiar, panic attack and forced myself to look at her more closely. There was something magnetic about her manner – something warm. Her long tapering fingers sported two diamond rings, and a discreet but expensive looking bracelet matched a similar neck chain. Miz Ballenger was obviously a woman of some substance I decided. She was also very different from the previous visitors. She didn't coo baby-talk and she didn't ask about availability.

"That's the cat for me," she decided at once, pointing a rather impressive pink fingernail in my direction. She didn't bend down patronizingly but squatted so that her eyes were on the same level as mine.

"Come here, Pusscat," she invited holding out the palm of her hand in front of the basket. She had a reassuring friendly voice and I found myself clambering over my sleeping companions towards her. "Very smart, very nice." she said approvingly. She sat back on her haunches and stroked me a couple of times without attempting the undignified task of grabbing hold of me. I nodded courteously. "You are very beautiful," she said softly and I could not stop myself from purring loudly. "And you obviously know exactly what I am saying, don't you?"

'Yes of course I do,' I remarked but, as usual, no one heard.

"Yes, Ginger is still available," Celia said quickly, relief sounding in her voice that everything had worked out so well and that the danger of me being left on her hands had been averted.

Miz Ballenger stood up and I jumped from the basket and trotted over to her. I sat down prettily at her feet (you know, front legs straight, toes slightly outwards and tail wrapped neatly around.) I prayed she would take me away in her sports car there and then. "Ginger?" Her eyebrows arched. "I think we can do better than that," she said smiling at me.

What a lovely person!

"Well, it's a Tom – so it was natural to call it Ginger." The old lady dragged her poorly foot over to the table so she could plonk her ample body down on one of the shiny pine chairs.

"You don't look like a Tom," my new owner said thoughtfully and before I had time to even shake my whiskers she had scooped me up and cast an experienced eye over my tummy and nether regions. "Definitely a little girl," she said gently lowering me back into my place in bed.

"Well!" the old man said in an embarrassed sort of way.

"Are you sure? I mean, I thought all ginger cats were Toms." His wife was obviously not pleased at being proved wrong.

"Quite sure," the visitor said emphatically. "Now will it be convenient for me to collect her next Friday?"

The old woman opened her mouth to object but then thought better of it. At least she was getting rid of me. "Yes, I suppose so." Celia obviously did not enjoy someone else taking the initiative. "But after two o'clock please." She would at least have the last word.

The scaly skins squatted down again beside me. "You see," the young woman said thoughtfully, "You and I have the same colour hair – well almost. When I was a girl at school they used to call me Ginger or Copper Nob and I hated it – they are no names for a lady."

I automatically rubbed against her arm hoping she could see that I was smiling at her. She twisted around to look up at the old man.

"What did you say her mother is called?"

"Penelope," Celia chipped in.

The woman straightened up again. "That's a lovely name," she told Mother Cat thoughtfully, causing her to preen and twitch her ears like mad. "So," she looked at me again intently. "What about Penny – daughter of Penelope? You are almost the same shade as a shiny new penny and it would keep the family name going. What say you?" She addressed me directly and I nodded, speechless with happiness. Again I tried to mould my face into a smile. (I know cats can smile as I've seen them do it often; I just hoped she noticed.)

"Good, that's settled." She stood up and stretched out her hand to Celia who I noted for the first time in my short life, was actually smiling. They shook hands formally as if to seal the matter. Then she turned and smiled at me.

"Penny it is." she said. "Until Friday Penny, and by the way, my name's Tina."

And with a throaty blast from her car's exhaust, Tina departed. For a few brief moments I actually felt happy. Then I shook myself. What was the matter with me? Nothing had changed. I was still a wretched animal instead of a proper person. But, I had to admit that, although everything was completely abhorrent and I was still sick inside, I no longer felt like doing away with myself. Not quite so despondent.

I gave myself a mental shake. Nonsense! Keep fighting it!

Then I wondered vaguely what it might be like, living with this woman, Tina.

# CHAPTER 5

My last week in the family basket passed uneventfully. The old minders ignored me completely and they really didn't take much notice of the other girls either. I suppose the end being nearly nigh meant we were no longer of much concern.

Spluttering Celia's foot seemed to bother her a lot because she was even more short tempered than usual; this was endorsed by the fact that Cuthbert spent most of the day in his shed at the bottom of the garden. Time seemed to pass very slowly. The others, of course, never knew what day it was but by counting the tins of Happy Kitten Food, which were visible when the cupboard door opened, I knew how long it was until Friday. (Tin replenishment took place on Saturdays.) I was glad that my departure was to be the first as I think it might have made me sad to be the last to leave Penelope Mother all on her own again. I would also have grave doubts about Celia's intentions towards me should there be no-one else to snuggle up to and hide under when she came towards the basket.

Friday at last! I did my stretching exercises and had a very thorough wash. I made sure my fur was fluffed up and that my feet were spotless. Two o'clock came and went, with no sign of the woman, Tina.

"What time did she say she was coming?" the old man kept asking after tea.

"I said, after two," the old lady replied. "But I meant soon after two, not after five." She was obviously not happy – maybe she dreaded a no- show, leaving me still on the wanted list.

"Well you should have said a definite time. You know how late she rolled up last week," he replied unnecessarily. The only acknowledgement he received was one of her frightening looks. Now I know the true meaning of 'if looks could kill' – hers most certainly could.

"Let's play cards for a change until she comes," he suggested helpfully.

She strode from the kitchen and turned on the telly, loudly, in the other room to let him know what she thought of his suggestion. The old man sighed. None of this was really his fault, he told himself.

Where was Tina? By six o'clock I was getting anxious which Penelope sensed as she kept giving me an encouraging lick. Maybe my saviour had changed her mind and didn't want me after all. Maybe she had found a more appealing feline companion. I closed my eyes and forced my attention back to the manicure I had started earlier, which had been abandoned due to something nasty and sticky having become wedged into the little pad on my rear near-side paw. (I suppose cats have a proper name for all this but to me it was rather like being a car, something positioned in each corner to keep you moving.) Then the telephone rang. I strained the points of my inadequate ears to hear what the old man was saying. There were lots of Yes's and No's and I Think So's but nothing that meant anything to me. Or to the old girl because she rushed into the kitchen to cross-examine him.

"I hope she's coming. What time does she call this?" she shrieked at him.

"She's had a bit of a set back," he said slowly, turning from the 'phone. "She was nearly here and something went wrong with her car."

"Poof!" spluttered the woman. "She should get a proper car instead of that boy-racer thing."

He nodded passively. "She's at a garage the other side of town. They can fix it in about an hour."

"That means she won't be here until very late," she snapped.

"Yes I know, that's why I said I would take the kitten down to her. It would save us waiting up and would shorten her journey – she's got a long way to go back."

"You, What?" Celia stammered, hobbling around the kitchen noisily. "Why should you put yourself out? If she had come at a civilised time this wouldn't have happened."

"I can't see what the time has got to do with it.."

"Oh, shut up. You make me so angry sometimes!" Her face went very red and she started to sweat profusely. What a grand cabaret for the pussy audience! We watched with great interest wondering if she might even hit him. But I felt so relieved. I really was on my way. Purring loudly, to my own disgust, I savoured my imminent escape.

"Oh all right, very well, go!" she frowned. "If you're silly enough to go out at this time of night.." (It must be at least seven o'clock, I thought. What cloistered lives some folks lead.) "Anyway," she threw me one of her glances. "At least we'll be rid of him."

"Her," corrected the old man, taking his life in his hands. She ignored him. "You'd better get the cat box in from the garage. I don't want that ginger animal wandering all over our nice car seats."

The cat box! How can three such little words strike fear into the very soul of an intelligent, normally good natured - what was the word – Zoon?  I remembered cat boxes. During my human lifetime I had squashed, stuffed, neigh forced, various poor animals into receptacles loosely referred to as 'cat boxes'. I prayed my transport would be different, comfortable, the latest thing in puss luxury. When he brought in the bright yellow coloured, plastic container I burrowed beneath the old woolly cardigan. Penelope cowered down flat, with legs stretched out trying to become invisible – she had obviously encountered the thing before. Blackie and Creamy watched uncertainly.

"Good riddance!" Celia winced as she bent to grab at me. No one was going to do her out of the delight of actually imprisoning me in that monstrosity. But it meant getting away from her and nearer to Tina, so I gave in gracefully, without even scratching her hand.

For anyone who has never had the pleasure of being ensconced in a small cat carrier I will explain just how it feels from the victim's point of view. Unless your owner has thoughtfully put in some bedding or covering (which, naturally, mine had not) the floor is freezing cold and dangerously slippery. They always put you in so that your bottom and tail are at the end where the wire mesh grill might have given you a view of what was happening. Then, the clasps are fastened with loud clicks, like a prison door closing I imagine. A finger is usually then poked through the grill into your hind quarters, or through the slits along the top so that jagged fingernails catch in your sensitive ears, and as the digit wiggles about on your fur annoyingly, the same someone asks in a silly voice, if you are all right. (This was the old fellow – she had gone back to her telly.) I looked across to the where the litter tray stood and wondered what would happen if I wanted to... But no, perish the thought! There was a long way to go apparently – a very long way in cat-cramped-in-box-with-no-food-or-drink-or-hygienic-means-of-relieving-one's-self terms. Penelope cried out quite loudly. Mainly, I felt, with relief that she was not going to be the traveller after all, but also, I liked to think, that she was saying goodbye to me. I struggled to turn around for a final look at the basket which had been my first home in this new strange world – not an easy feat as my paws kept sliding away from my body. It must be dreadful for a large fully grown animal in one of these things, I thought. Funny, I had never considered the drawbacks of such a situation in my previous life. Suddenly the carrier was hoisted up. Because I was so light, I suppose, it seemed to swing this way and that; it was rather like being on one of the best rides at Alton Towers.

"I'm off, then!" he shouted raising his voice about the decibels thudding out of the lounge. As he bent to collect his keys from a low shelf my cage zoomed up into the air and just as swiftly lost height to return again to arm-carrying height. Then, jiggle, thud, jolt and bump, as we made the crossing of the kitchen and out to the driveway. I was then unceremoniously dumped on the windy drive whilst he undid the car. My teeth (which were still mainly gums) clanked together and although my fur billowed out on its own accord to try and protect me, I was absolutely freezing even though, by the look of the trees and foliage, it still seemed to be only autumn. The back seat of the vehicle was piled with cushions, rugs and various stuffed animals and teddy bears. Cuthbert more or less threw me down somewhere in the middle, not bothering to check that my cage was level, consequently I slithered to one end where I crouched in near agony during the drive through the town to the garage. The journey was more frightening than my worst fears. Being huddled up in the corner of the box, all I could see through the side grill was a clump of some material – probably a cushion. I tentatively crawled along the side of the carrier to get a better look. Angrily I shouted out but the engine, which complained loudly about being left in second gear all the way, drowned my cries. What have I done to deserve this? I demanded to my inner voice, to God, to anyone who might be listening. But no one was. There was no reply.

With a flamboyant arm flourish, Cuthbert changed firmly into first gear and with excessive noise we grated to a standstill. (Next time, I will definitely be a camel or a squirrel – some creature that did not have to put up with this.)

"Hello! And thank you very much for bringing Penny." Tina was a woman of few words (to the old man anyway). She unclipped my chamber of torture and gently lifted me out. The old man nodded and loaded the yellow carrier back into his car which trundled off as soon as he had gratingly sorted out the gears. Holding me firmly but not squashingly, Tina opened the door of her lovely red car and (oh joy!) placed me on a curly white sheepskin pad on the passenger seat. It was only a two-seater vehicle but in the floor well she had positioned the latest cat loo, complete with privacy hood and little Perspex swing entry door. The lovely lady had thought of everything. But this wasn't all. From the glove compartment she took a small bottle from which she poured milk into a minute plastic bowl. "Thirsty?" was all she said as I gratefully took a few laps. Then I went to sleep as she smoothly slid the car forwards.

"You will be mainly an indoor pusscat," Tina told me during my tour of inspection of her home. She lived in a top floor apartment – quite spacious and light with very comfortable looking furniture. "But we do have a small roof garden." She opened French doors and I poked my head out hesitantly, ashamed about feeling so nervous. (But, I reminded myself, my reincarnate being was small and vulnerable, quite different from the substantial bungee-jumping girl that I used to be and whose mind I still seemed to partly share.) The flat roof (sorry, garden) seemed big but it was dark and the perimeters were indistinct even with the city lights blazing below.

"Yes, come!" she said shepherding me back into the cosiness. (What wouldn't I have given for a flat like this instead of my small bedroom at home which always seemed so untidy.). "You will be able to go out there in a few days. Better get used to the inside first. It's noisy outside but you will be safe – no one can get into our little garden, only," she added a bit darkly I thought, "Tabatha Cat, from over the roof. She is a remarkable wall jumper, though I fear that one day she might come to a sticky end, poor thing."

Then I went to bed - a lovely little fur house with a curved roof and a duvet type cover to wriggle into.

During the next day or two I explored every inch of the apartment whilst she was at work. Yes, I was allowed on the seats and no, she didn't rub butter into my paws to stop me roaming (there was nowhere to go to but I wouldn't have gone anyway.) The only down side was that on my second day I had discovered a sliver of wallpaper hanging away  above the skirting board in the kitchen – just at my eye height. Tantalising though it was, quivering in the draught, I fought with my conscience. So badly did I feel the need to tap it with my growing claws, so tempting was the sure knowledge that I could rip the thing clean off, possibly bringing down a long strip of the stuff. But my conscience won, reminding me how much I liked being with Tina and how unbearable it would be to be sent back to the Old Minders.

I avoided the wickedly inviting kitchen for the rest of that day but almost by telepathy Tina stooped to examine the torn paper that evening. She dabbed at it with something from a small bottle which helped to flatten it back against the wall. This was just as well because that was when she introduced me to knee-time. She made sure, in my first days, that she was always there to feed me at about six, then she would eat whilst

I washed myself and did my hair. Then we would watch TV together and I would sit on her lap, for knee-time, and get a lot of attention. I realised that this might not have continued had I attacked her kitchen wallpaper, so I didn't even consider the matter after this, even though I was fairly sure I could have worked the errant strip loose again.

She was good to me, though she did get a bit unreasonable about my attempts to jump on to the settee. 'Of course my nails dig in,' I tried to explain. 'It's the only way to cling on and pull myself up.' So we compromised. I would sit and gaze longingly up at the cushioning, looking what I hoped was appealing, and purring like mad, and she would lift me up. "Soon you'll be able to do it in one leap," she assured me.

We talked a lot – or rather she did – and I did a lot of meaningful looking and hoped she would understand my catribution to the conversation. She told me about her work and her mother and her car, but mainly about her work. I became quite an expert, in theory, on organising conferences, which is what she did for a living. Venues were selected by us both scrutinising glossy hotel brochures and convention centre leaflets. Guest speakers were arranged, transport was booked, accommodation reserved, flip charts, back projection, lights, power points and cloakroom facilities sorted out. Although I could not actually give an opinion, Tina shared her problems and concerns with me, constantly inviting my advice. How I wished I could speak to her! So many times could I have helped, particularly when she had to arrange events in London where I had lived most of my human life. Yes, I knew which good hotels were near to Marble Arch, I knew unusual places to entertain and feed delegates – such as Tower Bridge, The London Aquarium, H.M.S. Belfast. But, sadly, I wasn't able to tell her.

The best part, I thought, was choosing the menus and wine. I knew for certain that I would have no trouble in guzzling the banquets we were ordering but I wondered vaguely whether the taste of wine would still be appealing to me now. Were there, I mused, any alcoholic cats around? Tina seemed to drink quite a bit – every evening, in fact, when she got back after work. I watched and counted her points; although her excess made me feel quite uncomfortable it also made me envious. But I didn't say anything. Perhaps once I had got my paws under the table, so to speak, the time might be right to experiment. An opportunity may arise. Who knows – the future might be, a glass of Chablis for her and a saucer full for me.

# CHAPTER 6

The roof garden was rather special. Fresh air, some sunshine and more than a little wind – but it was wonderful to be able to go outside. I had never really been 'outside' as a cat although somewhere deep in my human mind were visions of trees and fields, streams and parks. These must have been well known in the past but my memory seemed to struggle when searched for more details. Could I really remember any specific place? Any park? Any forest or wood? No. But was it really important? No, I supposed not. Not now.

Tina's garden was a remarkable make-over of a large flat roof. There was wooden decking, a bench seat, a tiny square of grass (which she cut with shears) and several small areas of stones and pebbles of different colours and sizes. The top of the apartment block formed one wall of the garden, into which were set our French doors. The walls on either side were quite high too, one had a criss-cross wrought iron insert. This was great because if I stood up on my hind legs and stretched my forepaws up on to the metal I could just get my head through the lowest bars. The world far below was fascinating. Constant movement of snail-like traffic, lights and noise. At first I was a bit apprehensive although I instinctively knew that if my head went through, so could my body probably, but this was not an option. There was going to be no trying as the fall the other side would certainly be fatal so my back paws were kept firmly on the ground. I realised too that in a little while, when my face filled out, care would be needed lest I got stuck in my watching position. By then, though, my legs would be longer, so my eyes would reach high enough to be able to see through, without all the stretching and straining and poking my head through the bars. The wall at the far end of the garden was lower than the others, but still far too high for me to jump to, at my age, even if the will had been there. It had a long flat top which projected out from the wall over the edge of the stoned area. Tina could stand and lean her elbows on it comfortably – she used to relax there quietly sometimes, either deep in

49

thought or watching. I had no idea what was the other side of this wall but as no noise came up directly from that area it must have led on to other buildings.

Once she said to me, "If you're really good and brave, I'll lift you up so you can walk along the wall." She meant it kindly, as a treat and couldn't understand my flight indoors and consequent hiding behind the washing machine.

'Please don't ever suggest it again,' my eyes, nose, ears and tail implored, but how could she know that I had met my demise by jumping off something very similar? I would just have to make sure not to go anywhere near the far end of the garden when she was in one of her 'leaning' moods.

Tina had installed a cat flap in the bottom square pane of the French windows to allow me free passage. The room that led out on to the roof was a sort of utility place, housing washing machine, dryer and dishwasher. There was a small sink and a wide shelf over the machines. This was where my basket lived. As it was quite high Tina had put her step stool against the wall so that I could spring up its two steep steps to access the shelf. "In a few weeks," she told me knowingly, "You'll be able to leap straight up and we can dispense with your stepladder."

I scratched and purred to show my appreciation. It was so frustrating not to be able to say exactly the right words but she usually seemed to get the general gist. When she talked to me though, she asked so many questions that really needed answering. It was an extremely difficult situation to deal with. Even at that early age I was determined to try and converse by making sounds as near to the important human words as possible. For instance, when she said, "Thank you," to me (usually when I rubbed against her or licked her hand) she said it in a sing-song sort of voice. For ages I practised Meow making it MEE – ow and lowering the last part like she did. I was quite proud because to me it sounded just like 'Thank You' and I used it at every opportunity – when my dinner was served, when my milk was poured or when she helped me to get up or down anywhere. The other word I worked on was OUT. During the evening she would lock the flap (she was obviously afraid I might jump up on to the far well and fall off in the dark – silly lady, didn't she realise that that wall was my deepest nightmare?) When needing to go out after dusk I would take up position in the utility and gaze longingly at the glass doors. Eventually she would ask, "Do you want to go OUT?" emphasising the Out as if it were a very important word. I trained myself to Meow as I waited for her to turn the door key and tried to make it sound like Out – a sort of M'owww but I just couldn't finish with a t sound. So I dropped the M' and concentrated on the OWWW as loudly as possible. This was rewarded handsomely because after about a week of rehearsals she said, "Penny, I do think you're actually saying OUT to me when you want to go in the garden. You really are a clever girl, aren't you?" My fur puffed up with this praise and I rubbed against her legs and completely forgot that I had wanted to go out.

I did try to emulate other words but as we couldn't hold a real conversation there was little point in my working my whiskers off. I could get most of my necessary requirements with my limited vocabulary, purrs and little snuffles and grunts which Tina seemed quite partial to.

She obviously liked me rubbing against her legs and stroked me a lot when this happened but I was very careful not to brush against her when she had dark trousers on or long skirts. "Your beautiful copper hair just sticks to these dark materials," she groaned once after I had ruined the effect of a stylish black trouser and bolero suit just before she was going out somewhere. (Even her chastisement was not hurtful as she always took care to include some nice words as well.)

I sometimes thought about Lucifer dog wistfully and wondered if there would ever be any more real conversation in my feline years. Almost resigned to perpetual silence and never being able to communicate properly with anything or anyone again I was happily surprised when Tabatha came into my life. She did not just 'come in', she hurled herself in, over the flat parapet of my garden one Thursday morning. (I knew it was Thursday as Mr BBC 2 had said so at breakfast time.)

'I'm Tabatha,' she said unnecessarily. I knew she must be as she was the only cat Tina had mentioned.

'Yes I know.'

What? I can understand, was my first gleeful thought.

'Yes I am a Zoon too,' she said, daintily licking her front paws which had been the main landing gear. 'Did your minder tell you about me then?' She seemed pleased.

'Yes, she said you were the only one who comes in here – into my garden.' I purposely added the 'my garden' – start as you mean to go on had always been my motto. However grateful one was for conversation, territorial limits had to be observed, even if she had previously had unrestricted access.

'Your name's Penny. Your minder calls you quite loudly. You're an unusual colour for a girl. Very nice!' My whiskers wiggled as I thought 'Thank you.' I also tried my verbal 'Mee oww' on her.

'Oh, you're trying to humanize. Yes I tried it at first but it was a waste of time – no one understood me.'

'Are there many, er, Zoons around here? I mean do you talk with lots of – well – like us?'

She sat back, up straight, and curled her silky black tail around her. She wore the most beautiful fur coat, cleverly marked with unusual shaped black and white areas. (I was careful not to even think the word 'patches'. Somehow I had the feeling that this description might offend such a dignified and personable creature.)

'Yes, I'm lucky,' she read me immediately. 'My minder brushes me daily. Well, you have to with long hair like this, don't you? And of course,' she added hastily, 'I do a great deal of grooming and washing myself.'

I turned my head away slightly so that she could not intercept my thoughts (I remembered Lucifer telling me this wheeze. If they can't see your eyes, they can't read your thoughts.) Tabatha, it seemed, was a just a tiny bit vain.

'Yes,' she went on as I turned back to her, 'In answer to your question, I do have many friends. I live in a rather fine building over there. One of the better places, you understand?' She tilted her head towards the end wall over which she had made her entrance. 'None of my acquaintances are such good jumpers as I am, so I usually do the visiting. I live on the ground floor – we have a real garden, big you know.' I shut my eyes as the thought 'oneupmanship' (sorry, 'oneupcatship') slid into my mind.

'Oh?' I waited politely for her to go on, knowing that she would.

'Yes, I've lived there for – well two or three years, though I don't feel that old,' she added hastily. 'My minders are a young married couple. Quite well off.'

'You mean,' I tried to think of something that was not too offensive but that might bring her down a bit. 'You have to share your minder with someone else. Another person?' The way it came out sounded as if it were slightly improper.

'They share me,' she retorted firmly, closing the topic.

'Isn't it difficult getting up here when you live all that way down?' Changing the subject completely seemed a good idea.

'There are ways,' she replied mysteriously. 'I have perfected routes to all sorts of places. I can even get across to the park on my own.'

'Park?'

'Yes, it's not an enormous one but it's pleasant enough to go for a stroll there. Are you a good jumper? I mean, when you're a little bigger might you be able to leave this roof yard of yours once in a while?'

I shook my head so violently that my poor ears tingled. 'No chance!' I said vehemently, 'I don't like heights. Not at all,' I added loudly. 'I'm quite content in my roof garden.' (I stressed the word 'garden'.)

'You may grow out of it,' she said yawning. 'Well, in the meantime you're a little land-locked in this yard aren't you?' I looked up at the sky and wondered if we were really going to get along. But as she was my only companion at that time, I vowed to try not to alienate her even though my whole furry body objected most strongly to my lovely garden being called a yard.

'It's nice of you to visit me,' I said.

'Well, I felt it my place to welcome you to the neighbourhood as no one else can get up here. I'm rather late I know, apologies, but there's been a lot of entertaining going on.'

'Entertaining?'

'Well, you know how it is. Lotty has been unwell so I have been popping along to her place to cheer her up. And Timmy and Jules – they live in the next place to me – they had me in to share their dinner the last two evenings when their minder was away. And dear old Moggybones (that's not her real name – she is the Marquise of somewhere, really top drawer.) Well, Moggybones gives delicious milk-and-biscuit mornings. She lives in a little house at the end of the mews and her back door boasts an ever open puss-flap. And she has a wood burning stove in her kitchen which makes it ever so warm. So hospitable when everyone else's central heating switches off.' She paused for breath and stretched out a paw to inspect immaculately tapered claws. 'You would be surprised at the number of guests who frequent Moggybones's gatherings.'

I gazed down at my own paws and felt very glad that I and my door-flap were well out of general reach.

'Dear Moggybones,' she drawled on. 'Is quite old but she certainly knows how to party. Would you believe? She and Timmy and Jules managed to prise open her minder's fridge door and they took out a lovely lump of salmon. Timmy and Jules really have the knack of acquiring things and they do it so professionally. None of the minders ever knows something is missing.' She intimated that these notorious pilfering pussies were held in universal high esteem – or at least by the near neighbourhood.

Tabatha sniffed into the air, stretching her long neck gracefully. 'I don't suppose you have any delectable morsels of anything in your pad?' She looked intently across at my cat-flap as if half expecting a silver tray of goodies to appear.

'Sorry,' I mumbled. 'Tina only leaves me crunchy things in the morning and I've eaten them all.'

'You must keep an eye on your weight, you know.' She straightened her slender body and gave it a little shake so that her hair fell into place making natural waves from her neck down across her back. (Somehow it conjured up dim and distant memories of the back of a golden retriever dog I must have known, except that this fur was a different colour. The waves were very similar though.)

'Yes, it is true,' she went on before I could say anything, 'I do like my food, but only delicacies of course.' (Of course!) 'But then, I do look after my figure. I go climbing and jumping and I walk without fail every day. None of your laying about on walls in the sunshine. Anyway, the sun makes me feel hot and sticky – unfeminine somehow.' She gave another little yawn and I half expected her to cover her dainty mouth with a silken paw.

'I don't lay in the sun on the wall either.' My stammer was defensive and she gave herself another all over shake.

'No of course not,' she agreed, 'But then you don't like heights – you would be afraid of falling off.' She giggled and wrinkled her nose and I felt miserable. 'No,' she went on more kindly, 'No, you really will grow out of it. Then we shall go out together. Don't worry, I wouldn't let you get into any danger.'

I sighed trying not to think again of that bridge and all the cheering people spurring me on to jump.

'What is the other side of the end wall?' One must make an effort to show interest and, anyway, I was quite curious.

'Not much,' she sniffed. 'It drops down on to a slate roof. Bit of a hazardous climb in the wet. Or you can skirt around the edge in the drain pipe gutter but that's difficult – there's a sheer drop down to a lower roof. Over the slates is best – then the other side you can slither down to a flat ledge. Then you really need to jump down a long way to the next level. Coming the other way, up to you, is worse because one has to leap up. But it's all good fun – you'll see in time.'

'I will not!' I thought, not bothering to avert my eyes.

'Yes you will,' she answered, 'When you feel a bit more confident and sociable. There are others who will probably brave the journey to come and have a look at you but they are only cats. No cultural exchange there, just the usual whisker and ear movements. No, if you don't venture out you'll have to rely on me, I am afraid, but I'll come often, never fear. And I'm sure old Gull will put in an appearance.' I could see she was getting ready to take her leave.

'Gull?' I asked quickly as she positioned herself for her leap upwards on to the ledge, her coat glistening in the pale sunlight, whilst her back feet explored the ground for the best take-off point.

She looked over her shoulder at me. 'Yes, Gull – he hasn't really got a name, we just call him that because that's what he is, although I don't know why we have seagulls here, we are nowhere near the water.'

'Is he - Gull - one of us?'

'Oh, yes, he is a Zoon all right – one of the old stagers. It is not just cats you know. Zoons come in all shapes and forms.'

'Yes I know,' I said quickly to at least gain some credibility. 'I met a dog called Lucifer who..'

'What a horrible name!' she interrupted. 'Anyway I must be off. Lottie is giving me lunch and then I am going to try out her minder's new bed. Do you know – they have carpets and duvets and curtains and nightclothes and bathrobes all to match. All black!' she finished triumphantly as if trying to shock me with this decadence.

'Gosh!' was all I could manage as air traffic control cleared her for take off. Legs flexed, body bent crouched, then instantaneous thrust up from the ground, producing a dynamic spring, arms stretched forward, then all four paws landing firmly on the wall top.

"See you soon, Penny. Nice to have met you. 'Bye..!' Tail held high, she crouched again, her nose jutting out firmly in the direction of intended travel. With a slight jiggle of her neat hindquarters, she bounded away out of sight. I listened for some sound of safe landing on the slate roof but could hear nothing above the distant hum of midday traffic.

I sat for a moment, contemplating, then went for an extremely brisk trot around my lovely garden, about half a dozen times until my breath came in snorts and my paws smarted. After all, one must look after one's figure.

# CHAPTER 7

My next encounter with Tabatha was rather unfortunate. I was taking my late evening trot around the roof when suddenly, out of the dusk and gloom, a feline figure landed with a thud on the wall just above my head. Instinctively I catawalled, using language I wouldn't normally think of. Intruders were most certainly unwelcome on my premises. The figure shook and shuddered so I managed a few grown-up-cat type snarls and stood on my hind legs and did a lot of spitting. The visitor let out a strangled Meow as it backed away along the wall.

'What a nice way to greet me, I do not think!' Tabatha transmitted angrily across the gathering darkness. It was difficult to make out exactly what she meant as I could only just see her eyes.

'Tabatha, I'm truly sorry.' And I was. Backing away I made room for her to jump down on to the grass. 'I didn't know it was you.'

'I should hope not,' she muttered climbing gingerly from the wall. My welcome had obviously shaken her. 'I'm not used to such scenes,' she murmured.

'Well,' I replied levelly, 'I'm only protecting my domain. I'm not having just anyone think they can scale my wall.' My tone was firm yet reasonable so that she would get the message without taking offence.

'I'm not a prowler,' she said haughtily, 'I came as a friend.'

'You are,' I interrupted quickly.

'And', she went on undeterred. 'Such screeching! Real alley cat stuff. Quite feral.' Then she regained her composure. 'But I realise you must have been afraid – it is nearly dark, I'll admit. I must have startled you landing like that. I'm normally much more sure-footed but the tiles are so wet that my grip just wouldn't hold as I took off. I had my claws trimmed on Monday which doesn't help these rather strenuous activities,' she finished in her oneupcatship voice as she inspected a front paw.

After that Tabatha visited me two or three times a week but she never came again after dinner time. She usually appeared during the morning and I got into the habit of not eating all my breakfast crunchies and saving a little milk (which I didn't seem to enjoy as much as I used to) just in case she should be desperate for some refreshment. I nearly had a heart attack one morning when Tina scooped up my uneaten breakfast and poured the morsels back into the packet. After this I ate very slowly and kept going back to the saucer every few minutes so that she would understand I wanted them to be left. Although I couldn't compete with Moggybones's salmon or milk-and-biscuit parties, Tabatha seemed to appreciate the meagre snacks I provided and we gradually started to get on more amicably. She didn't mention my fear of heights and I tried to ignore her tendency towards snobbishness. In spite of her sometime haughtiness Tabatha was a worldly wise puss and a mine of information.

I asked her, 'Why are we called Zoons? What does it mean?' She always enjoyed answering my questions as it gave her an opportunity to air her knowledge. What she didn't know I think she made up but it was done so entertainingly that I never had the heart to challenge her, even when I suspected she was wrong.

'Zoon,' she said slowly and precisely. Her eyes moved in such a way that the word would have rolled about her tongue had she been actually speaking. 'Zoon,' she repeated. I waited patiently. 'It is an ancient word. A word used by the Greek philosopher Herodotus to describe the belief by ancient Egyptians that human souls could return in animal form. This is something you must not forget as it is your responsibility to pass this information on to another animal who does not already know it. Every one of us is charged with telling at least one other and certainly the younger ones. Sadly,' she added, 'some of us die without ever knowing about this duty.' For some reason she looked quite unhappy about this; maybe she was thinking of the loss of a friend or someone close.

'Surely,' I said, 'It's not all that important to know what we're called and why, is it? What terrible thing will happen to us if we don't ever know?'

She looked at me condescendingly. 'Nothing will happen,' she said, sniffing. 'Except that the fact that you know, and have passed it on to someone else, will stand you in good stead in your next reincarnation. It helps to determine whether you come again as another animal or as a human. It's a little bit like the laws of Karma. It's like collecting good points.'

'Sounds a bit far fetched to me,' I said boldly, risking her wrath. But she merely replied, 'It is all part of our culture and we should appreciate it.'

Although I still felt the whole thing was a load of rubbish – what alternative was there to believe? How else could I cope with this ridiculous situation which was daily becoming more plausible? Maybe Lucifer had been right after all. Every day I seemed to be less human. Each time I went to sleep I prayed I might wake up rid of this sentence that had been thrust upon me. This misery I had somehow been damned with, and find that it was all a bad dream and that I wasn't a cat at all.

Tina was working hard and often came home late in the evenings. Sometimes she didn't come home at all. On these nights she left me a serve-yourself feast. At the stroke of six, the plastic container's lid would flip open and there, lo and behold, a meaty meal for one pusscat; albeit sometimes a rather dried up meaty meal, and milk for afters in the other part of the tray. At first, in this new life, I wondered how a curry-loving human, with a liking for the occasional lager, would fare on Whiskers, Kit-e-Kat and Munchies washed down with frequent gulps of milk. This born-again business, though, is quite weird really – I hardly noticed the difference in my enforced diet change though I did still continually lust after a glass of something.

My opportunity to discover whether or not I was a potential wino-paws presented itself one Saturday when Tina spent the evening alone in front of the TV. (Very unusual – she generally went out at weekends.) A Chinese take-away appeared on the coffee table and my share was allocated to a dish thoughtfully placed on the (rather garish, I thought) multi-coloured rug in front of her living-flame gas fire.

She seemed to indulge in more than a few G & T's before opening the Chardonnay. (I wasn't actually counting as the Blind Date repeat was riveting that night.) Towards the end of the bottle she mumbled something like, "S'time for bed," and without even shutting me into my night quarters, the utility, she staggered off towards her room. (She left the lounge light on so she must have been sozzled. Still, she had been working hard lately…) She had carried her tray, and my dish, into the kitchen and the tempting remains of the wine stood glistening in its bottle on the draining board.

My whiskers quivered in anticipation. Worth a try, I decided as she disappeared into the bedroom. If I knocked the thing over the precious contents would dribble down the furrows in the drainer before I could even lap a little. And, dreadful thought, I might even break the bottle. (Would Tina ever forgive me and, just as importantly, would I cut myself?) The clean shallow dish, which the rice bowl had stood on, gleamed up at me. The convenient dip in its middle was where a puddle of something nice might easily form. If I could negotiate it towards the inviting bottle and then, carefully, tap the Chardonnay over on to its side the liquid would drip out into the dish and then - hey ho!

The dish was heavier to move than I anticipated. Finally, after a lot of shoving with my back, it was just about the right distance from the wine bottle. With my front claws I dragged the crumple of her used napkin and positioned it so that a make-shift cushion was formed below the lip of the dish, stretching towards the bottle. For good measure I also enlisted the aid of the sopping dishcloth to form a more substantial pillow for the bottle when, and if, it tipped over. Then, slowly, keeping one foreleg near the base of the bottle, I twisted slightly, gently tapping my back legs against the glass, near to the bottom, and wriggled about until the bottle wobbled. Another paw-touch, in just the right place, tilted the wine towards the napkin and the brightly painted plastic dish. It fell more heavily that I had expected, quite hurting the paw which was trapped underneath but the scrunched cloths softened the impact and the dish remained safely in its place. Very carefully, I withdrew the smarting under-leg which was helping to support the bottle and the wine started to trickle out into the dish. I watched hypnotised, as best Australian liquor made its way into my treat receptacle. Then came the point when no more could dribble out unless the bottle was tilted yet further. But I decided I was not into this type of technical manoeuvre. There was ample sensuous amber liquid swirling around beneath my nose to satisfy my curiosity. Hesitating for just a second I approached the dish. The smell (sorry bouquet) of the shimmering wine made my claws retract and stretch out again. Mmm! Delicious! Slowly I lowered my neck until my head was parallel with the crazy gaudy flower motifs. I extended my tongue gently, letting it drop gradually until it touched the drink.

Taking a deep breath and carefully folding my whiskers back to prevent damage I slurped and then slurped again. Purrrrrrfectly gorgeous! Gulp, gulp! Thankfully tongue was working quick and well. At first I was afraid that Tina would come back into the room and catch me but after the first half dozen quaffs this seemed a matter of indifference; the problem at hand was how to tip the bottle so that the remains of the drink became available. Well, to cut a long story short, the bottle somehow fell off the dish and, still firmly caught in the serviette and cloth, its neck hung out over the floor at a curious angle, allowing the nectar to flow freely all over the laminated surface below. Knowing that this was Tina's pride and joy I jumped down ready to adopt a protective role. (Yes, actually jumped – my first real leap, and, amazingly, I didn't feel a thing.) I lay by the quite large pool and by just letting my head loll over to the side was able to start the mop-up operation without physically having to stand, although my left ear got quite wet and soggy. (It was probably fortunate that I was rendered immobile because, in the prevailing condition, I might easily have drowned in the stuff.)

Then, night time came quite suddenly, just after the flashing lights and nasty noises started. I was certain someone was trying to flatten my head with a very robust hammer in time to the music which seemed to beat through my head. Then, I slept. Or, more accurately, I passed out.

Tina was not amused the next morning. She was also nursing a hangover.

## CHAPTER 8

At the beginning of my second month with Tina, I met Gull. I was prowling about the garden (I no longer trotted or strolled), when this bedraggled moth-eaten looking thing swooped on to the wooden bench.

'Who are you?' I spat, although I knew very well who it was because Tabatha had mentioned the creature several times. 'And what are you doing in my garden?'

'Well, your Pussyship,' he looked at me rudely, straight in the eye, with his watery pale yellow beady slits. 'I've been coming here for the past hundreds of years and I don't intend to stop now just because you've moved in.'

'Hardly hundreds of years,' I stared right back at him. He'd better watch out. In a few weeks time I could see him off. Pounce on him, grab him, trap him, drag him into the utility, chase him behind the freezer.... My fuzzy mind took off – I completely lost control of myself.

'Well it seems like hundreds of years,' he thought back wearily, ignoring my train of malicious ambitions.

'Well, how old are you?' I demanded, arching my back in order to look more vicious. I jumped up on to the bench so as to be prepared, should war break out. (How frustrating it was to know what I should be doing to this intruding character but unable to carry any of it out because I was still too little.) I stared as boldly as I could but, for all his years, he was a big bird. Wondering vaguely if I was supposed to attack big birds like him now, or, more comfortingly, when I was grown up, I stepped back.

His long curved beak pointed straight at me. 'My name is Gull. And, what business is it of yours anyway, what my age is?' Before I could think of a reasonable thought he went on, 'I'm not as ancient as you think. Just had a hard and eventful life. Was old in human form, but there's still a bit of life left in me now,' he chuckled and lowered his beak. 'Got a poorly wing. Can I rest here a while? It's safe here, nothing can get me. Except you and there's nothing of you yet.' He laughed unexpectedly.

Before I could manage an answer another, much smaller gull landed on the arm of the bench. This garden was certainly getting crowded, I decided. But here was one that could be easily despatched. Not too big and a bit stupid looking.

Gull interrupted my thoughts. 'This is my friend Cedric,' he said, not even looking at the other bird.

'Well, this isn't a dickies' gathering,' my glance said ferociously (or so I hoped.)

'Cedric is different,' Gull remarked turning to gaze affectionately at the newcomer.

'I'll say, a bit loopy. I might even chase him off.' Then I reminded myself that Gull was quite a size, even with an injured wing.

The older bird nodded, reading my thought train. 'Cedric is a very, very special friend,' he said meaningly, emphasising the word 'special'. 'And no, you won't worry him. I'm quite a reasonable fighter.' He spread his feathers and I marvelled at his magnificent wing span.

'OK,' I met his eyes. 'You can both rest here for a while.'

'Thank you,' he replied gravely, nodding his grey head, which I felt should have been covered with thicker feathers. Searching my reduced brain I frantically tried to recall, way back in my earlier life, if I had ever come across a balding seagull, a cat fighting a seagull, or a gay seagull.

'Don't worry about any of it,' he advised as they both hopped simultaneously down on to the seat next to me. This was a bit too close for comfort. An energetic growing cat (albeit it with alcoholic tendencies) sitting on a bench with two birds of the feathered variety. Thankfully no one could see this astounding spectacle.

'Well,' Gull said in a businesslike manner. 'What's this we hear about you being afraid of being high up?'

'How on earth did you know that?' the thought spluttered its way over to him.

'Tabatha, of course,' he said. (Of course! I should have known.)

'I used to be scared of being up too high,' Cedric offered, sheepishly fluttering his eyelashes.

Staring at him coldly I replied, 'Well, fancy that. A seagull who doesn't like flying too high.'

'That's unkind,' Gull interrupted as Cedric hid his head under his wing. 'We, Cedric and I, have come here to give you our help. We got him over his difficulties so I am sure we can get you over yours. We'll soon have you airborne, no sweat."

This took a while to sink in. Was I getting this right? Two gulls were predicting confidently that they were going to get a half grown cat to fly?

'No, no!' Gull cut in. 'Not fly. Just get you used to jumping up and leaping down again. Get you used to heights. Get your confidence back so that whilst you're here you will be able to jump down or across to somewhere else.'

'Not across the roof tops!' my whiskers twitched and my tail trembled.

'Yes, exactly! Across the roof tops! How can you live up here and not be able to jump and climb for goodness sakes? It's madness. We'll show you how, don't worry,' he repeated.

I was speechless (sorry, thoughtless.)

Cedric had recovered his head to its rightful position and was now looking at me with interest. 'It's right,' he twittered, 'Gull did it for me'.

I'm sure he did, I thought to myself looking away, not wanting inappropriate thoughts to intervene in this surprising exchange. 'How are you proposing to do this, even if I agreed? Which I very much doubt.' Curiosity was getting the better of me again.

'Ah, that's more like it,' Gull hopped about a bit and wiggled the wing which hung down lower than the other. 'Just relax and I'll tell you what we thought we would do. You see, after I had helped Cedric we came across a cat who had similar problems to yours.'

I laid down tentatively and listened to the most ridiculous monologue about days of planning and discussions with Tabatha and some other cat who used to have trouble jumping about. I was almost falling asleep with boredom when the big old bird brought me up with a jolt. 'The scarf will go under your belly and will be tied in knots on the top of you – on your back. The ends will be left flowing.'

Was he going mad?

'I can tie knots,' Cedric wriggled proudly. 'I was on a ship for a time. I know how to do it like the seamen do. It was easy to pick up and I have a good strong beak. A very strong beak.' My ears were really hearing things now. Here we have a seagull who was a sailor!

Gull interrupted my thoughts with a shrill squeak. 'We came to help you,' he reminded me, rather savagely I thought. Then he described his outrageous plan.

I, the star of the production, would be positioned on my low wall, which, on the other side, overlooked the slate roof that Tabatha had told me about. 'You would have to practise jumping up and down from the wall into your own garden until you get the hang of it,' Gull instructed. (Ha! Would I ever?) Then, he went on, next would come a short trial jump down to the top level of the slated roof. He assured me it was only a marginally bigger jump than it was from my garden to the wall top. They, Gull and Cedric, would both be escorting me (that is jumping without flying, just to show how easy it is – except that they had wings to use in an emergency.)

After this first mythical leap, the frightening story got worse as Gull became more excited. Next, with this scarf still tied securely to my body (most securely fastened by Cedric, who, I was assured once again, was good at tying knots) I would be encouraged to jump from one ledge to another, slightly further each time. (The reason for the decorative scarf was not at all apparent at this point.) Then, it appeared, the next and final stage of this horror (I was now sitting bolt upright on the bench, shaking, either with abject fear or hysteria at the ridiculousness of the idea – I don't know which) would be even more of a leap, again with an escort each side. At about this juncture I couldn't help wondering about the contraption which was supposed to adorn my middle person. Surely it wasn't to keep out the cold or make me look elegant as I flew off into pussycat heaven? No, nothing quite so sensible. Gull explained with gusto that if, for any obscure reason I took off badly, leapt badly or landed badly, then he would swoop down and catch the scarf end in his beak. Cedric chimed in to say he would gather up the other end of the material (in his very strong beak.) and together we would all make a safe landing.

'In your dreams. Count me out. No way!'

Gull was mortified. 'Don't make rash judgement, just think about it for a while. Tabatha, the other kitty, and I – and of course, Cedric, have planned this meticulously, even down to the precise ledges and roof tops. There is nothing to fear. Every detail will be gone over many times. We will make you a jumping, leaping cat, never fear.'

'You will make me a dead cat, either from a death-wish falling accident or a heart attack!' I retorted, swishing my tail.

'A bit uncharitable, I would say, Cedric.' Gull was offended. He gathered up his wings and steadied himself, ready for flight. Cedric copied his every move.

'Think about it,' Gull advised. 'Probably a bit of a shock, knowing that we all want to help you. I can understand that.' He hopped up on to the seat back. Cedric put his head on one side. 'You should be grateful,' he shot at me snidely.

Gull cut in, 'We'll be back. Talk about it then!' He sailed away, up towards the sky, closely followed by Cedric.

I jumped down and quickly washed my shoulders. Then I headed hastily for my pussy flap. In the safely of the space beside the sink unit I concentrated on washing my whiskers – not that they were scruffy or anything – I just needed to do something useful, something to blot out the encounter with the mad gulls. Maybe his stupid wing would fall off and I would never see them again.

# CHAPTER 9

As Tabatha steadily demolished my breakfast the next day I took her to task on Gull's preposterous suggestion.

'He means well,' she informed me. 'And it very nearly worked with Joey.'

'Joey?' I spluttered. 'Who on earth is Joey and what do you mean – it very nearly worked?'

Tabatha cleaned her whiskers meticulously, rather enjoying, I fancied, keeping me guessing for a while. 'Just imagine how difficult life must be for a fully grown Tom cat that cannot climb or jump because he is afraid – much more serious than it is for you,' she added, as we strolled out on to the grass. 'Yes, I'll tell you about Joey.'

I waited while she stretched and gave her coat a little shake. Although I was consumed with a need to know all about it, I fought to hide my impatience.

Joey, it seemed, had in real life been an athletic, healthy man. Climbing mountains, cycling rallies and running marathons had presented welcome challenges. Although married, he had had little time or energy left for his wife (this much he had admitted to Tabatha when recounting the misadventure that had forced him to lead a cat's life.) His woman had patiently accompanied him in his pursuits, driving him around the country, dragging their caravan behind. During every spare hour away from his work as a sports instructor, she encouraged and applauded his triumphant wins. It was on one of these trips that he met his downfall - literally.

On arrival at a camping park, Joey had sited their caravan at the highest point overlooking a forest. Then, he realised that there was an even better pitch nearby which would offer an uninterrupted view of the adjacent artificial ski slope, where he would be competing the following day. He insisted on immediately repositioning the van, in spite of the fact that it was getting dark. He and his long suffering spouse pushed and shoved to reconnect the caravan to the car and it was duly shunted about until he was satisfied with the new spot. After hastily unhitching the outfit he instructed his wife to park the car at the side of the 'van. Following these exertions, and because they were so far from the main camp site facilities, a sudden heaviness of the bladder necessitated his quick dash into the 'van toilet compartment. Slamming the washroom door behind him and dancing from foot to foot in his anxiety for relief, he freely acknowledges he must have rocked the caravan about somewhat.

'To cut a long story short,' Tabatha was obviously enjoying relating the events as she paused for maximum effort. 'The wife moved the car away, he jiggled the caravan and as neither had remembered to pull on the trailer handbrake, the 'van slid slowly forwards. It had gathered momentum as it trundled down the hill and although Joey tried to free the jammed door he was securely imprisoned. His wife ran after the rattling, rolling vehicle, screaming to attract attention. This she certainly did, as the entire camping fraternity rushed out to watch the spectacle. Lurching dangerously, the clattering wheels only slowed when they reached the depths of the duck pond outside the glass fronted restaurant. This was always crowded with guzzling gourmets in shorts, at that time in the evening, and they streamed out on to the wooden decking to see what was going on. Even the nearby ski lift ground to a halt in order to observe the proceedings.'

Tabatha paused again, wrinkling her nose at what was obviously her favourite part of the incident. 'Ducks scattered, the door flew open and Joey stood just inside for all to see, with his trousers around his ankles.' She gave a little chortle. 'Then the van toppled, door side down and Joey drowned, trapped in two feet of muddy water.'

'Well!' was all I could manage before Tabatha resumed her story.

'So now he's a cat, he won't even go up a slight incline, let alone a hill, or roof or tree. Very sad.' she finished, sniffing delicately into the air. 'He should have been such an active cat too. Now, not only can he not tolerate heights, he is now not active at all. Not at all, since Gull....'

70

A feeling of apprehension made my neck fur stand on end. 'What do you mean?' I asked suspiciously, 'Why isn't he an active cat. What actually did happen when Gull tried to help, with one of his ideas?'

'Well, Gull only has one idea – the one he told you about – this was what they tried on Joey.'

I blinked, 'And?' Did I really want to know this?

Tabatha swished the tip of her tail. 'Well Joey went along with it – I mean he was so desperate to become really macho.'

'And?' I prompted again.

'Well, they all took off from the ledge, Joey panicked and flayed about in the air, Gull and Cedric couldn't catch the ends of the scarf material and Joey broke both front legs when he fell. He doesn't go out much now at all.'

'How dreadful!' I gasped. Half of me felt sympathy towards the unfortunately incapacitated Joey and half of me wanted to burst out laughing at the absurdity of the escapade (yes, cats do laugh, but quietly.) Every tingling part of me was thankful that I hadn't agreed to the barmy birdy plan.

Having related the tale with gusto, Tabatha didn't seem at all surprised that I was adamant about not wanting to try Gull's rehabilitation scheme. She did make a half hearted attempt to sway me by saying that a scarf of stiffer material was his current recipe for solving what he called the 'teething troubles' of his plan. Not a chance!

Tabatha was really quite a nice puss, when you got to know her and when she relaxed her haughtiness. During our chats I learned a great deal, much of which helped me through my later cat time. I asked her once what happened to us when our lives ended. 'Ah, well,' she told me. 'It only needs someone to say that you could be almost human, or next time you'll come as a human, or something that registers with whoever above makes the decisions on these matters, and, well, you're a born again person next time.'

'You mean – we revert back to being a human being again, just like that?'

Tabatha nodded. 'Not quite, just like that. Someone has to make the wish for you,' she repeated, sounding a bit sorrowful.

Possibly miserable, I thought, that no one had ever mapped out her future in this way.

It occurred to me that if one's cat-life was unsatisfactory and the magic words had been said by a human, one could commit hari kari and hey presto, start afresh again. This, I discovered later, was not quite as easy as it sounds. Cats do have nine lives – or at least they are clutched from obscurity several times, which makes ending it all rather difficult (look at poor Joey). The other snag is that being a born-again-human does not necessarily guarantee the nice cosy lifestyle one may have enjoyed in a previous existence. The next time around as a human, might happen in a starving, under-developed country. Or, as a feline, in a darker continent where cat meat is part of the usual daily menu. It all seemed very much the luck of the draw. I nearly asked Tabatha again about the Zoon business and how the fact of passing the word on to another creature would help in a future life. But I didn't because I couldn't take yet another lecture on culture and standards, subjects dear to her heart, on which she might pontificate indefinitely. She was right though when she said that you might be better off remaining a contented creature on four legs, rather than hastening to a new existence on two, which might turn out to be very disappointing and uncomfortable.

My almost tolerable life, that had come to revolve pretty much around Tina, Tabatha, Gull and Cedric, was all too soon halted. And halted by the very person I had grown to love – Tina, herself.

It had never occurred to me that my being with Tina would not continue indefinitely. She had her work, of course, and she brought colleagues home from time to time. Friends too, visited the flat and I put up with them all. They were too inconsequential to either like or dislike. I just tried to ignore the brief intrusions into my comfortable little world. The only one I really hated was a loud voiced woman called Greta who referred to me as Catbag. 'Hello Catbag!' she would shout and then wondered why I disappeared behind the settee.

It was my modus operandi to make myself scarce whenever Tina had company. She didn't seem to have a steady boyfriend. Various men came for the evening and on some occasions stayed the night (an occurrence I frowned upon as I strongly felt such goings on usurped my standing in her affections) but there wasn't a regular suitor.

Then one day my life crumbled. Clark strode into the apartment brandishing champagne and flowers and laughing a silly raucous American laugh.

'This is Clark,' Tina said almost shyly. 'He is a colleague from our associate company in the States.' If the massive towering guy felt it odd to be introduced to a diminutive red-haired cat he was at least courteous enough not to show it.

'Hi!' he acknowledged genially. (As he was wearing some sort of cowboy type hat I had half expected him to say, 'Howdy!') This time I did not flee behind the sofa. I sat on the mat and watched carefully.

After the bouquet was arranged in a vase and the champers had been drained Tina asked plaintively, "But what about Penny?" She gazed at me intently for a few seconds but then switched the look to adoring, and to him.

"Yep," he said, obviously pretending to consider the question, "That sure needs thinking about."

Thinking about? What on earth were they talking about? I pointed my ears towards them and disregarded the requirement for urgent de-gritting of my back paws. Slowly I got the picture. Clark - what a daft name - was over here to lure my Tina to the New York office. (And this was not all the lure was, I felt).

'It's a wonderful opportunity,' he gushed. (Never trust a man who gushes, I tried to warn Tina).

"I know, but all this?" She waved an arm vaguely around the room, finishing in my direction. "You can rent the flat out." He was ready with all the answers.

"What if it's not a success – if I don't make it?" She was sounding positively female and hesitant – not at all like my Tina.

"Make it? You'll wow em!" he bellowed and laughed his great roar. He took her hand and I knew he had won her over as he said quietly, 'Please come Tina. Your career would really take off and I'll be there all the time with you. I will guide and help you. No strings. But I'd like to have you there." Ye Gods – no strings! I could feel the noose tightening around her lovely neck even as he spoke.

'What about me?' a little voice fluttered deep inside my furry chest, which was pounding with worry.

"Penny could go to my sister," Tina said suddenly as if reading my thoughts. I didn't even know she had a sister. Anyway, there was no way I was going anywhere. "Claire would love to have her." I'd never heard of Claire. "She has a farm and two little girls. Penny would like it there I'm sure," She didn't sound at all sure and, as I tried to hold her gaze, she lowered her eyes.

'What is all this, Tina? I won't go anywhere. I want to stay here!' I would have some sort of attack, I decided immediately, faint, do whatever cats do in a crisis. 'Tina!' I yelled, but she did not even glance at me. I looked sadly at the two of them but their eyes were locked. Slowly I crept towards my pussy flap and my beautiful roof garden.

'I'm to go to a farm and two children,' I reported to Tabatha sadly the following day.

'Children?' she screamed as I nodded wretchedly. 'You poor, poor little mite!'

Gull and Cedric and Tabatha came to my farewell. The birds brought gifts in their beaks.

'A large lump of cheese from Timmy and Jules,' Tabatha told me, 'And a two whole sardines from Moggybones as she feels badly that you could never attend one of her do's.'

Gull had transported the chunk of Edam (which Tabatha immediately set upon) and Cedric (in his ever-so-strong-beak) had conveyed the sardines wrapped in a damp tissue.

'I love sardines,' I lied. I hated the things – all gritty and bitty and oily. Wondering how not to cause offence to my well-wishers I said, 'Look, let's all share this lovely feast.'

Tabatha, having already gulped down most of the cheese, looked at the silver fish which had fallen into several pieces, and said, 'Good idea! If you've got any Munchies left we could have them too.'

Gull and Cedric, it transpired, liked the odd sardine so I ate a couple of my cereals whilst Tabatha demolished the remainder of the cheese and a handful of Munchies. Some sort of speech was expected from me as, when the food was gone, they sat back and waited. I thanked them all for coming and for bringing such a glorious meal.

'Please thank Moggybones and Timmy and Jules as I am sure they acquired the cheese course from someone's frig,' I transmitted with lots of emotional blinks of my eyes. 'And thank you bird-men for carrying all this so perfectly.' I wiggled my whiskers at them.

Gull nodded gravely in recognition of such praise. 'Cedric has a very strong beak,' he said magnanimously.

After extended sorrowful goodbyes the seagulls flew off and Tabatha positioned herself on the wall.

'Goodbye my little friend,' she held my eyes warmly, 'Remember all that we have talked about. Gull will try to locate you through his flying acquaintances (he mixes with some very well connected racing pigeons, you know) but he may not be able to. Have you no idea where you are going? No? Goodbye then, Penny Pusscat!' Tabatha jumped out of my life.

'Bye bye,' squeaked Gull from somewhere above. 'Bye bye, your Pussyship, you really turned out to be a nice one!'

'Goodbyeee!' shrilled Cedric in the distance.

I was alone in my garden. In the apartment I could hear Tina packing up her things. Much later, she gave me a special dinner of freshly cooked liver and kidney. Then we were together in the lounge, quietly because the television and music centre were packed away. The settee and easy chair were surrounded by boxes and cases and the room looked discarded and unloved, its ornaments and personal touches stripped away.

"I love you so much and I will miss you such a lot, my lovely Penny," Tina said stroking my back gently as I sat on her knee.

'If you love me how can you leave me?' I tried to shout out but my mouth just opened and quivered. My heart knew that the same question had been asked the world over and would continue to be asked for ever.

Clark, the laughing hunk, had jetted back to his New York office leaving Tina to tie up her loose ends (including me) and to follow in a few days. I tried not to think of him and the way he was taking her away from me, ruining our lives.

Tina watched me as if hoping to see some sign of understanding, of condoning. She sighed deeply. "I will be back, it's not for ever and then we can be together again."

But I was not convinced and from the falter in her voice, neither was she. I tilted my head on one side and gave her my undivided attention. Then she said something that was to stay with me and bolster me in the following weeks. "Penny, my precious puss." She stopped stroking and looked deep into my eyes. "You understand every word I say to you, I'm sure. You could almost be human." The moment passed and she carried on tickling the underneath of my chin – something which she knew I particularly liked. If I were to believe what I'd been told, with those few words Tina had given me the promise of being a person again in my next life. I was momentarily overjoyed. I now need not be a cat-person for ever and ever. And then, if my new role didn't suit me I could revert back again to cathood by saying, 'Next time I'll come as a cat.' The power of choice was so immense that I carefully washed my back to hide  my feelings. So exuberant was my toilet that I rolled over and fell off her knee on to the rug.

Quickly she knelt down to console me. "Poor darling!" she whispered. 'You're going to be all right." Tina cried a little, soft silent sobs which dripped down on to my neck fur. There was so much sadness inside me but I just did not know how to cry so I washed behind my ears with such gusto that she sat back and laughed, although her eyelashes still glistened. "You always do that when you're embarrassed, "she giggled. "Everything will be fine, Penny, you'll see. You will have a wonderful life on a farm – you're growing big now and you need more space to roam. And Claire will love you."

But it turned out that Claire did not love me.

# CHAPTER 10

As a human I had never been at ease as a car passenger, but as a feline it was a thousand times worse. Not only did I feel nauseous but the fact that I could not fix vision on horizon made my head spin. That last journey in Tina's lovely car was a nightmare even though I roamed freely as I had done on previous trips (mainly to the dreaded vet for necessary jabs). Tina was preoccupied and drove fast, braking and accelerating suddenly, jolting me around the foot well. I jumped on to the passenger seat but my paraphernalia loaded there constantly reminded me of the reason for the journey and I felt desperately sad as well as sick, so I jumped down again and hid under the seat.

"Nearly there!" she announced briskly as we finally turned off the main road into a wide gateway which led to a narrow smooth lane. Her tone reminded me of my grandmother's many years ago, when I was nine and she had deposited me at boarding school for the very first time. The timbre was almost severe but with an underlying catch deep in the throat.

The tarmac gave way to a dirt track which further on splayed out into a short wide shingle drive leading to the farmhouse. Perching precariously on top of my bedding I could see that the track continued through an open five bar gate to the side of the house then on towards the farm out-buildings. I gazed at the rusting agricultural machinery buried deep in a giant patch of nettles at the side of the broken gate. The farm track was heavily rutted and weeds grew prolifically. Some bedraggled birds perched on upturned bottomless buckets, watching our arrival. Tina turned off her engine and we sat in silence staring out through the windscreen. Abruptly she got out, slamming the car door hard.

The front door to the house was huge. The wood was traditionally beaded and studded although some of the old metal decoration had fallen out, leaving uneven pits of faded colour. Probably oak, I decided, which must have been handsome in its day. Now, a nondescript grey paint hung from the sagging timber in curls, discoloured bare wood showing through in patches. Tina reached up for the iron bell pull, whose chain disappeared into a hole higher up the wall. The jangle of metal chimes echoed from somewhere deep in the house, which was to be my new home.

My first impression of Claire was that she was plump, rosy and untidy. (She was also impatient, bossy, lazy, greedy, loud, complaining and had no discipline over her two horrible children, I discovered later.) She was everything Tina was not and on appearance alone they made unlikely sisters. (Perhaps she had been adopted?) Tina scooped me up from the car seat in a rather businesslike fashion and was swinging me into the hallway. I realised from the brief sibling conversation, that there was little love lost between them.

"I'll look after her as best I can," Claire puffed, dumping my bed in a tiled passageway that led from the kitchen to a scullery. This was cluttered with Wellington boots, old clothes on a row of hooks, an old fashioned deep white sink and lots of jars and giant bottles. "But she'll have to take her chances. I have my hands full as it is."

"You won't forget to feed her – I've brought a good supply of her favourite food?" Tina was trying to hide her anxiety. "And she does like her morning cereals."

Claire shot me a contemptuous look. "I'll do the best I can," she repeated nodding. "She'll sleep out here, but in the day she can get down by the Aga, that should suit her well. The other poor things have to live in the barns. About a dozen of them at the last count."

I cowered down by Tina's leg. 'Oh, please don't leave me!' I begged. But she did.

Amanda was Claire's 'little scallywag'. In reality she was a six year old monster who wore a constant frown and screamed a lot. She shouted and stamped her feet and kicked out at everything in sight which she took a dislike to – particularly me. Fortunately the great crumbling house boasted copious full length cupboards, shelves built against walls, windows that did not quite close, rooms that no-one ever went into or cleaned and numerous places where one could hide and sleep undisturbed. The constantly banging, unclasped, windows offered speedy entrance and exit which was useful for someone in my tenuous position. The door from my passageway into the scullery was seldom closed and the old window in there had two panes of glass missing, so escape was possible from various points, thus avoiding Amanda easily when necessary.

More difficult to evade was Sally, the pigtailed tormentor of anything that moved and was smaller than she was. (A wide category considering that at 10 she mirrored her mother's bulbous physique.) Whilst Amanda kicked and spat at me and pulled my ears at every opportunity, Sally practised tactical warfare. She would tie things to my tail if she found me sleeping soundly or put a box over me so that I awoke in a pitch black stifling cave. She would tip my milk on to the tiled floor which meant my licking up the dirty drink before Claire could chastise me for making a mess. Sally would creep after me trying to discover my hideaways so she could shut me in. She was once so successful that I was imprisoned in solitude for 24 hours in the upstairs cleaning cupboard. Quite peaceful and not so serious, apart from the problem of being hungry. But during my confinement, alas, nature took its course and, although I crossed all my legs and wound my tail over my rear end, I was forced to emit a rather squiggy mess on the feathers of a gaily coloured dusting broom. Fortunately it was the farmer himself, Fred, Claire's husband, who eventually heard my cries and released me. He appeared not to notice my indiscretion – or pretended maybe, in case he had to clear it up.

"Poor cat," he sympathised, patting me as I rushed by his legs, "What a stupid thing to get yourself shut in there." I made haste to my passageway, hoping some food had been left for me but the tiles beside my bed were cold and barren.

"Who's a naughty pussycat?" shrieked Sally leaping out at me. "Where've you been then? Missed your dinner last night, didn't you? Bet you're hungry. I threw it away this morning 'cause it'd gone all hard and lumpy. Threw it out to the yard cats. Loved it they did!" How I hated that brat! Even more so when she taunted me. I trotted through the kitchen, with as much dignity as I could muster. "What a naughty, nasty cat!" she screamed with delight, as the family was gathering around the long pine table for lunch. "Who made a poohy mess then? A smelly, poohy mess!" she sang out. How on earth did she know? I looked sideways at Fred as he pulled out his chair. No, he had not given me away I was sure, and I knew no one else would go to that cupboard for days, weeks probably and by that time my mistake would have disintegrated.

"Yucky poohy cat!" Sally continued to chant. It was then I realised that in my haste to depart the cupboard and my misdemeanour, the usual body checks had been forgotten. From my rear end, next to my tail joint, three or four stout little feathers of bright colours stood up proudly, fanlike, making me resemble, I supposed glumly, a sort of circus miniature peacock (or peacat). Yes, when I turned my head from side to side the picture became obvious as did the sticky heaviness around my hindquarters. Claire shrieked at me and I was collectively chased from the warm cosy room through the open scullery door and out into the back yard. I belted across the driveway and scurried into one of the barns.

During my second day at the farm I had made a brief tour of the outbuildings but the roofs were high and the dark beams and rough floors made me wary. There hadn't seemed much point in going too far from the house in the cold so I had decided to delay exploration proper until it got warmer. After my escape from the house that evening, however, I settled gratefully on a bed of hay and started the laborious job of cleaning myself up. Pausing for breath about half way through I thought, 'What I would give for a long soak in a warm luxurious foam bath. (Yes, the memories of such ecstasy came flooding back.)

'A bath? Sounds like heaven.' This reply seemed to come from the hay-strewn floor. I stopped my ablutions and sniffed around.

'I'm here!'

'Where? Who?' I asked warily. Good Lord! A mouse! The tiny creature sat almost between my forelegs.

'You cannot harm me.' It blinked it's diminutive eyes. 'Because I am one of you ..us, you know.'

'Yes, yes, I see that,' Life had gone mad. I was talking to a mouse. But, a mouse Zoon, no less, so, grateful that Fate has at last dealt me some luck, I made a supreme effort to be friendly. Yes, even to a mouse! We chatted for a while and he seemed a decent enough sort of mouse. (I had little to go on through, as I had never met a mouse before.) I told him of my plight and he listened intently. He said he would try to be extremely supportive and he valiantly tried to make helpful suggestions. One of these I found astounding.

'If you're hungry, and you must be famished,' he winked knowingly. 'You should catch yourself a meal.' I stared at him. 'A bird or a, .ahem…, a mouse', he went on conversationally.

I shook my ears disbelievingly. 'No, not me,' he giggled hastily. 'But I have a lot of enemies I wouldn't mind out of the way - mices that have not been nice to me. Even my own, very large family will not have much to do with me because they know I'm different, but some mices have been really nasty, cruel – you wouldn't believe it if I told you.' Thankfully he did not tell me. I suppose it's a hazard that because the majority of animals belong to one group, when the other few meet, some feel compelled to hold long, mostly boring conversations which usually terminate in a monologue. What transpired next was surprising to say the least.

Monty Mouse (he adopted this name, he told me, as his human life grandfather fought under Montgomery in the desert in the Second World War) set out to lecture me on how to stalk and catch one of his brethren. 'You just cannot rely on them for your keep,' he pointed out, jerking his head towards the farmhouse.

When I explained that my cat mother, Penelope, had neglected to instruct her brood in the art of hunt, kill, eat (there having been plenty of quick pouched sustenance) Monty, without any preamble, declared himself Tutor Extraordinaire.

'I have been hunted, unsuccessfully of course, by more cats than I could count and have witnessed more mouse casualties than that, so I am in the rare position of knowing it from both sides. You could have no better teacher!' he boasted, reminding me a little of Jerry of 'Tom and Jerry' fame, when he stuck out his little chest.

'May I suggest that every morning you will meet me here for your lesson.' He really was enjoying this. 'The examination test at the end of your training will be your extermination of my worst enemy – The Black Mouse. Then', he continued swishing his tail importantly. 'Then you can kill whom you chose.' He glanced away briefly, 'Except present company of course. You do understand that?'

I nodded to dispel any anxiety. 'Don't worry', I told him. 'I will be in your debt and so grateful for the tuition, that I'm sure we'll be friends.' I made an effort to sound humble but my whiskers quivered with amusement at the whole ludicrous idea.

'Friends?' he pondered, 'Does that mean you will protect me?' He looked so earnest that I nodded.

'Yes, from your enemies, once I know how.'

He paused for a moment. 'Even the yard cats?' he asked incredulously opening his eyes wide.

'Yes, I suppose so.' I felt ashamed of my hesitation but I didn't much like the sound of the yard cats; the reverent way everyone spoke of them suggested they were not a very alluring bunch. Coming up against them could be a bit different from dealing with an occasional mouse. Suddenly it dawned upon me that I needed to be able to stand up for myself and indeed, to be able to feed myself if needs be. 'Are the yard cats very vicious then?' I was trying to sound casual although I was shaking inside at the very thought of such confrontation.

'Nah, they just think they are. But, problem is, there's so many of them.'

'None like us, you know, Zoons…?' I asked hopefully.

'Nah. Don't know of any, but naturally I don't go too near to find out. They're all ear twitchers. Nut cases, most of them.

Dash about pouncing on things you can't even see. But good hunters. Lost a lot of good mices through them,' he finished soulfully.

When I crept back into the house through the scullery window, the tiled floor beside my bed was still bare of food. Fred was in the kitchen doing some paperwork whilst the others sat in the living room watching TV. I fixed him with a determined look and meowed loudly. Nothing. Again I tried. Nothing. After he disappeared to join his miserable family I slid into the larder and jumped up on to the big white bread bin. On the lower marble shelf was some jelly leftovers and pieces of cake. I have never gone much on jelly but after a few mouthfuls I felt better. The cake was good – at least big Claire was a reasonable cook. Then I came across the board of assorted cheese. Taking care to only select a little of each (to avoid detection) I then finished my meal with a mouthful of cold stew from a dish that was hiding at the far end of the shelf. As I sat on the larder floor and washed my mouth and whiskers I vowed to attend my future hunting lessons with a definite, positive attitude. I just might well need independence from this family.

# CHAPTER 11

The next day a letter arrived for Claire. "It's from Tina," she announced sourly at breakfast time, sniffing at the prettily decorated envelope. "Doing all right for herself it seems. But then she always did, that one."

No-one paid any attention to her or the contents of her letter. After a few seconds she screwed the crisp notepaper into a crumpled ball and aimed it vaguely at the overflowing waste basket in the corner. I sidled across to where it had fallen and patted the ball towards my corridor. This was my first real frustration at not being able to read. Tina's neat handwriting curled across the wrinkled paper, and I swear I could smell her perfume. My eyes misted over as my paw caressed the words – how I wished I knew what she had written.

"Daft cat!" spat Sally. "Trying to read the letter from your Mummy! What it says," she said spitefully, grabbing the paper and tearing it into shreds. "Is - Don't feed the stupid cat – she's getting too fat!" She showered the pieces all over me and I wept inside.

Claire put her slippered foot under my backside to facilitate my speedy, if undignified, flight from the room. "Take all that rubbish outside with you!" she shouted after me whilst Sally slid back into the kitchen.

But there must have been something in Tina's letter about looking after me, as a good dinner was provided in my bowl that evening. Or maybe it had a little to do with the cheque that accompanied the letter, which I had watched Claire stow away safely in her worn handbag. Unpalatable though it was, it seemed my very existence might just be dependent upon periodic payments between the sisters. Perhaps I would only be fed on the few days around receipt of that important envelope.

Taking no chances I plunged attentively into Monty Mouse's training sessions which were conducted privately and discretely in the lower barn. The dreaded yard cats inhabited the larger far barn and most of them were out hunting when I crossed the yard for my morning lessons. My ultimate test of prowess – The Black Mouse, had, as yet, remained unseen, although smaller rodents had scurried across my path from time to time. As the days went by and my stalking, springing and pouncing became more professional, fewer miniature livestock risked making an appearance. My skills, which were becoming finely honed, had not escaped notice.

'Is he really black and very big?' I asked during a 'stalk and make yourself invisible' session.

'Very black and very big,' Monty assured me, tentatively licking at a graze I had inflicted during the previous 'pounce and kill' practice.

'I've never seen a black mouse,' I said, ignoring the 'very big' information.

Then, after a few more days, Monty made his announcement. 'You are ready,' he said gravely, 'to make your first attack. Probably,' he added thoughtfully, 'There won't be a kill this time – that would be too much to expect, proficient though you are becoming. Just treat it as a trial run. But if you do your pinpointing accurately and make a good precise jump on your prey, that would be an encouraging starting mark.'

Pompous little prig, I thought turning away hurriedly lest he caught my drift. Looking back at him again I retorted, with as much seriousness as I could manage, 'I will do my best,' almost adding, 'Sir' but checked the thought hurriedly, remembering the time and patience the small mouse had contributed to this part of my development, which should rightly have been executed maternally.

We both agreed that this preliminary important stepping-stone of my first catch should be negotiated whilst Monty was not present. (He thought I might feel too inhibited if he were watching over me.) He gave me the strictest instructions to avoid 'friendly mices'. 'Do not use for practice the brown and white patchy one, the one with beige spots on his head, the one with only half a tail, or the little fellow with a striped coat.' (A mouse with stripes? But nothing would surprise me now.)

It was decided that sometime during that week I would carry out the elementary test and the result should be reported back at the next training session. (Although I had no doubt Monty would probably stalk me to do his own private check before that.) 'Then I can tell you where you went wrong,' He was obviously really enjoying this, I could see. 'Then, then we aim for The Black Mouse.' I wondered why he hated this silly black mouse so much.

It all happened sooner than we expected. The next morning I was up and out early, determined to have a private rehearsal of hunting and generally moving quickly and quietly. I laid low in the long grass and weeds by the old buckets and rusty tractors, until the yard cat gang had departed for their morning activities. Vigilance had accustomed me to their ways and routine. The majority would leave after whatever they had foraged for breakfast, stopping briefly to drink discarded milk from the milking shed gutters. Behind them in the far barn, the nursing and expectant mothers would remain with their seemingly hordes of baby kittens and young cats. None of these strayed far from their camp so it was safe for my lessons and training in the near barn until mid afternoon when the marauders returned, swaggering and pontificating about their day's exploits. Then they all seemed to go to sleep in the undergrowth or under the rambling hedges until evening.

I mentally assessed my skills in a factual way before making my way to the barn. There was nothing wrong with my jumping up. I could leap quite efficiently from a semi-crouch to several feet and from a standing or moving position could reach even higher with little effort. My balance was good. Parading along narrow walls or ledges (which would have terrified me a few short weeks ago) caused me no concern as long as I didn't look to either side. But I still could not make myself jump down from any respectable height, even to land softly on piles of hay. Low surfaces to floor had been mastered but from anywhere above a few feet, my descent needed to be staggered. My fluffy brain just would not allow me to step off and leap through the air as I would have wanted to. Monty had worked hard with me on this but the mental block still remained. I just had to go down in easy stages.

On this morning though, I felt that I could conquer the world (so long as it did not necessitate jumping from too high up.) I climbed the bales of hay and sprang up on to the roof rafters, secure in the knowledge that the stages for my easiest way down were in place. I would rest, laying on the knurled beam just under the roof slates, and watch for movement. A young bird or inexperienced mouse might just chance that way. The oak was wide and comfortably cool even though the morning was already quite warm. I was beginning to relax and starting to close my eyes (in order to concentrate my efforts, you understand) when I heard a sound. It was the specific sort of sound that my training had enabled me to identify - a creature moving somewhere near. Very slowly I opened my eyes wide. Very quietly I turned my head to one way and then the other. There was nothing below in the hay at either side of me. It must be on one of the ledges I had climbed to reach the top of the old building. Silence, then the sound came again. Nothing on the level below me or the piles of bales to my right. Then I checked the left side of approach, hardly daring to breathe in case it advertised my presence. And then I saw it. Way, way down below, almost as low as the crop-covered floor, on a bank of bales, a long pink tail rhythmically lashed to and fro making the swoosh, plop sound that had alerted me. Nothing else moved. The owner of the demon tail was certainly fast asleep. I inched forward slightly on my beam and moved my head fractionally to get a better view. The rump of the animal was a light brown colour and I noted with relief that it did not appear on Monty's list of 'good mices'. No stripes or spots and the tail was indeed very full length. I shifted forward slightly, holding my breath, then swung my head from side to side in order to determine the exact location of my intended prize. Narrowing my eyes to slits I calculated the precise take-off position required to bring my leap to the accurate attack mark. Standing up cautiously, my tail assumed its automatic balance strategy. I breathed deeply for a few seconds then did not need to breathe at all. The lump in the hay beneath me rose and relaxed in slumber, oblivious of its imminent danger. Quietly I tested all four sets of claws on the worn beam. The wood splintered obediently. I ran my tongue carefully across my teeth as they would be required to administer the ultimate death blow. Like razor blades and syringe needles, I acknowledged with satisfaction.

The long tail below continued to lash left and right, left and right until the sound became unbearable. Swaying my body minutely, my back legs pushed and my front paws stretched forwards. The hot polluted air swam up to choke me. I spluttered and quickly steadied in mid stream. As I landed, dead on target, my right paw beat out at the half hidden mound, the blows administered directly between its ears. (Monty Mouse had insisted – always thump to stun before going for the kill.) Surprise was on my side. Before my captive target had awoken properly I had given its head a good battering with both paws (thankfully they had grown to be quite heavy and well formed.) As the creature squirmed its pointed nose around to investigate what was happening, my bared incisors sunk into the brown fur at the pressure point behind the neck. There was a strangled shriek and a token writhing and then this silent warm carcass lolled in my jaws. My teeth clamped frozenly together as I jerked my head from side to side to dislodge the limp body from the hay. As the animal swung free I was amazed at how enormous it seemed. I unhinged my mouth and bit my victim quite aggressively to make sure it really was dead. Maybe it was just my imagination but as I dragged it out on to the wooden planks that fronted the near barn, the thing seemed almost as big as me. Depositing it gratefully after the few yards of stumbling and pulling, I was able to get a good look at it for the first time. It certainly wasn't the Black Mouse  - it was a great deal larger. Enormous, in fact. Gazing dispassionately at the blood oozing from the shrew's lethal wounds I might have expected to feel some revulsion at what I had done. Elation on my achievement swept over me instead; indeed a form of job satisfaction on a task performed efficiently. When I studied the wound for which I had been responsible, it occurred to me that perhaps there would be expectation of my having to tear it apart and feast upon the bloody flesh. Yes, I was certainly proud of myself but not to that extent. I twitched my whiskers and shuddered, for a moment feeling quite sick. Suddenly I was not in the least hungry. My feeling of success was gradually tempered by the need to creep away before anyone could attribute the corpse to me.

'Penny, Penny Cat!' shrieked Monty Mouse who appeared from nowhere. 'What HAVE you got there?' My bossy little tutor cowered away at first as if to make sure the body was completely safe and incapable of inflicting reciprocal harm.

'I've caught a mouse,' I replied with renewed pride, sitting back and waving my front paw expansively. (I might as well get the deserved credit, after all). 'Quite a large one,' I looked at the creature uncertainly, glad that it was immobile.

Monty gaped at me. 'Oh, Lordie, Lordie!' he spluttered, his eyes wide and staring. For a second I was taken aback. I had expected pleasure at such speedy first stage accomplishment.

'It's not The Black Mouse is it?' I asked, fearful that I had overstepped my grade too soon.

'Mouse?' he echoed, creeping forwards slightly. 'My dear girl – that's not a mouse, it's a bloody rat – and a bloody big rat!'

My mouth muscles sagged and I scuttled back quickly from my dumped trophy. Blood dribbled from its wounds but, reassuringly, its long tail had stopped lashing. 'I had no idea,' I spluttered, 'I was up on the beam and I jumped on it.'

'You jumped?' shrilled Monty unbelievingly. 'From the top beam?'

'Yes.'

Suddenly I was a champion! It did not seem relevant to mention that the enemy had been asleep at the time and that no actual battle had ensued.

'My, my,' chanted a grey silky face through the adjoining stinging nettles. 'A young cat like you, not even a wild one, catching a rat! And it looks ever so much like one of the Leader Rats,' the yellow eyes added, staring straight at me.

'You're a Yard Cat,' retorted Monty Mouse taking a few shuffles backwards. 'I didn't know any of you could, well, talk.'

'Well you don't know everything, clever dick mouse!' the yellow eyes turned to him. 'There are one or two of us who aren't so stupid.'

'Sorry,' Monty said hurriedly, painfully aware of his vulnerability in this new situation, standing between two cats.

'S'alright,' the head said passively. 'I'm Minnie, by the way,'

Minnie-by-the-way trampled out of the nettle bed to reveal a beautiful light grey silken body, well kept and groomed but unmistakably swollen with pregnancy. 'What a marvellous rat!' she gazed at me with unabashed wonder. 'And it is definitely one of the Leader Rats. Did he put up much of a fight? I'll bet he did!'

My tail was flicking and my whiskers twitched. 'Well...' I said modestly gazing down at my improbable conquest.

'What a marvellous catch!' she sighed.

Monty straightened to his full height, which wasn't very high. 'I have been teaching Penny to hunt,' he put in hastily as if anxious for his share of the honours. (The glory, he obviously felt, should not all me mine.) If Minnie might have been surprised by this revelation she appeared not to show it. She continued to gaze from the dead bleeding rat to me and I felt embarrassed.

'Look,' I said uncomfortably. 'Now that we have met, maybe we could get together sometime and have a chat?' It would be good to talk with someone other than the mouse and I thought perhaps this suggestion may terminate the present rather awkward situation.

'Wonderful!' she breathed, heaving her heavy underbody around. 'But I am a yard cat,' she admitted sheepishly, looking sideways at Monty. He knew all about yard cats and I did not.

'I know that,' I said quickly. 'So what? You can probably teach me to really hunt.' Monty immediately looked hurt but Minnie smiled.

'No, no,' she protested. 'I could never catch a rat. Not a Leader Rat like you did. Wait 'till I tell the others. Not many of them have got rats and lived to tell the tale.' Then she was gone. The weeds and wild flowers closed over her silky back and Monty and I stood looking at the unappetizing corpse.

If I had lived with a nicer family I would have dragged it to the farmhouse, through the scullery into the kitchen and made a formal presentation. But there was little doubt that Claire would scream and that Sally and Amanda would chase me out again. So Monty and I left the rat where it was, hot and sticky, its drying matted blood issuing quite a smell. Tabatha and Lucifer had been right; as the weeks had turned to months, cat feelings were overtaking human thoughts and only a tiny part of me felt ashamed that I had killed this creature in cold blood.

The next morning when I made my way to the near barn for lessons, the rat confronted me, spreadeagled over a pile of stones outside the barn door. I was gaping at it (or rather the remains – most of the middle bits appeared to be missing.) when Minnie-by-the-way appeared at my side.

'It is so beautiful,' she enthused. 'We brought it out here last night to show it off properly. It's too magnificent to eat it, all of it,' she finished looking away with some ill ease. 'I expect they'll finish it off tonight,' she said lamely. 'Everyone has seen it. The yard cats say you can join them, you know, hunt and things, if you like.' Although the invitation was almost casual this was probably the equivalent of a royal command. Monty had explained something of their hierarchy; their organisation seemed a very closed shop. This was a gesture of the highest order and I summoned up as much discretion as I could remember.

'Minnie, this is most kind,' I said carefully. 'But I am not a strong cat yet so I may let them down in their hunts and fighting. I haven't been used to fending for myself. There is still much for me to learn about living in the wild. Also, like you, I was human in my last life, and it may be difficult to fit in. You said there were only a few of the gang who are like us. How do you manage to talk with the others? I thought they just twitched whiskers and you could never understand each other...'

'Ah, she interrupted me, 'When a cat gets older, really old, just before you lose your human side finally, often you find you can talk to both sides. Then it all goes and you're permanently a cat, down to the twitching only. Your mind stops thinking any human thoughts and apparently you don't remember anything that went before.' She paused briefly then hurried on, 'Most of us die before we get to this stage. I've only known two cats that could talk, both sorts of talk – they were really, really ever so ancient. We've got one old girl now. She's been going for years and years – no one knows just how long. This is how we talk with all the others – she's a sort of interpreter. Don't know what will happen when her human side disappears – she can't have much longer to live anyway. Her eyes and claws have gone and she can hardly move about. She's had so many litters of kittens, poor thing. Everyone is related to her.' She stopped short and rearranged her tummy which must have been cumbersome for her now that the weather was getting warmer.

I seized the advantage of the break in her story. 'Minnie, please thank your friends and say I am honoured that they asked me to join them. Perhaps sometime in the future when I have really proved myself..' (I hoped she would pass this on verbatim. Humble was what I certainly wanted to appear when I thought about some of the thuggy types that frequented the far barn.) 'And,' I added with inspiration, perhaps they would like to take the Leader Rat back with them as a gift?' (They would have it anyway but it seemed a good idea to score a bonus point.)

'Oh!' Minnie smiled and purred a little. 'Will you give us the next one or two rats you catch?' She still wore the expression of admiration which made my ears sweat a little.

'Well...' just a slight modest hesitation. The last thing in the world I needed was to catch another monster like the mess congealing on its altar. 'Maybe, but then I might just play with the next one and then let it go. Who knows?'

This seemed to satisfy her well. Tormenting a large rodent and letting it escape to provide more sport later seemed even more cavalier and foolhardy than just going on being Greatest Rat Catcher. I started to amble inside my wooden schoolroom.

'Will we talk after, your lesson with Mouse?' she asked shyly.

'Monty is his name,' I told her. If we were going to become buddies we would need to sort a few things out. 'No more references to catching mice – or rats either,' I stipulated firmly.

'Right!' she said. 'I'll wait outside here for you. Better you don't come up to our barn. You know, some of them are a bit territorial and, if you're not actually joining us...'

'That's fine,' I cut in. There was no way I wanted to be anywhere near the yard cats HQ, even if I did appear to be the flavour of the month for an hour or so.

# CHAPTER 12

The warm summer had turned to autumn. One of the yard cats had slaughtered the mouse with only half a tail and another yardie had pounced on 'the little fellow with the striped coat' and frightened it to death. Consequently Monty Mouse became understandably depressed and entrenched in deep mouse mourning. He withdrew from circulation, perhaps fearing for his own wellbeing now that the hunting seemed to be moving closer to home.

'It always happens when the weather gets colder,' he said. 'The pack doesn't like to go too far from the warm buildings. They catch what they can nearer rather than venture further away.'

My tuition ceased. 'Only for a while, you understand?' he had spluttered, looking anxiously over his shoulder.

But I was relieved. Sessions in the barn had become boring. I was, by this time, well versed in most aspects of what was needed – starving or being the loser of fights was no longer a probability. What Monty had omitted to teach me, Minnie-by-the-way had added. There cannot be many cats so well educated by peer and prey. My farmhouse dinners appeared most evenings. When they did not (either because Claire had forgotten or couldn't be bothered or because Sally had got to my dish first) I simply trapped something outside. These days I was becoming quite partial to eating al fresco. My initial revulsion at eating flesh and other bits that had not been cooked seemed to be disappearing. I could not work out whether this rather convenient development pleased me or depressed me, as it must mean I was becoming more of a real cat. As the days got chillier I spent more time sleeping by the kitchen Aga. My bed was rarely shaken or freshened and my draughty corridor got cold at night, so I appreciated my blissful time by the warmth of the cooking range. For some days I had lain listening to the excited chatter of the terrible daughters as they appeared to be getting more animated than usual about something.

'We'll have the biggest Guy in the world,' Sally told Amanda, who shouted, 'Yes!' Amanda might scream and shout at everyone else but she knew Sally had the upper hand so there was generally superficial agreement between the two.

'I will make him,' Amanda offered in her usual grating high-pitched screech.

'No,' Sally corrected. 'You will help me.' Amanda opened her mouth to shout then closed it and nodded as her sister continued. 'He will be an old scarecrow – but he'll have a smart fur collar.' After some whispering they both sniggered and looked pointedly in my direction.

I lay considering this with more than a little concern when Fred the farmer said, 'I hope you girls don't mean what I think you mean. That is not a matter for joking.' His eyes too rested on my tail which wouldn't quite fit with me in the slot between Aga and wall.

'Dad!' shrilled Sally, 'Whatever are you on about?' They ran off, still giggling, leaving me with a nasty uneasy feeling deep down inside.

From the innermost part of my mind I probed for remembrance of guys and scarecrows. The days had grown short and dismal and everyone wore gloves. It was definitely getting colder. I gazed at the kitchen wall calendar for a clue. It was the same sort as the one where, in my previous existence, dental appointments or visits to the hairdresser had been recorded. The neat squares with their bold black numbers did not mean a thing to me now. Once again I felt the frustration of not being able to read. Then I saw the box of fireworks on the sideboard and I knew. November the fifth! But when was it, how many days were there before I would need to hide? I knew without doubt that I would need to hide. Not simply because animals are notoriously afraid of the sound of fireworks; my trepidation stemmed from hardly daring to think what involvement for me the terrible duo might be planning. The heap of rubbish and surplus limbs of trees in the field by the yard grew daily into a monster bonfire. Even the yard cats seemed to disperse and I did not see Minnie-by-the-way for several days.

I bumped into Monty Mouse in the tractor shed and he told me, 'Just keep out of the way, right out of the way,' adding darkly that the animal mortality rate always rose in early November. He did not know which day the fire would be lit but I didn't have to wait long for a firm indication of the timing of the festivities.

'They can have a couple of sparklers – then nothing else until tomorrow,' Fred told Claire, much to the girls' delight when they arrived home from school one afternoon. Each armed with a sizeable packet of sparklers they demanded matches.

'No!' Fred said firmly as he strode outside. 'Your mother will light them for you.'

Claire lit the first pair, which were waved decorously around the room, then she left the matches on the kitchen table (either carelessly or to avoid being pestered every few minutes to relight.) Gazing at the fairylike stars and pretty patterns the little metal sticks made as they were swished around, helped me to remember Guy Fawkes night more clearly. The warm spluttering and the burning sparks reminded me of former happier times. Chestnuts and hot sausage rolls and frozen fingers clutching cans of Coke.

Claire stomped out of the kitchen, armed with the TV times and a plate of rock cakes. Sally winked at Amanda who sidled to the door and closed it carefully. Then Sally lifted the big square chopping board from the table and barricaded it neatly across the small alcove into the larder. There was no way of escape from the room. I watched mesmerised as Sally very steadily struck a match and lit two fresh sparklers. My heavy heart relaxed slightly as she dropped the lighted match into the sink. Not much harm can be done with a sparkler, I remembered. Not much, that is, unless it is held against one's fur.

The next few moments were a blur.

Sally's voice saying softly, 'Let's make stupid cat into Queen of the Fairies!'

Then as she ran towards me I cowered against the door, praying that someone would come in. 'With my wand I dub you, Queen!' she cried, dipping the silver star encrusted metal towards my head.

Ducking I tried to run sideways but Amanda cut me off, bringing her own lethal weapon down on to my back. I tried to inch alongside the familiar safety of the Aga and then both sticks of fire touched me simultaneously and the hot pain seared through my body. But it was the crackle and stench of smouldering hair that made me throw up all over Sally's shining white designer trainers, which had been bought specially for the following night's celebrations. As Sally shouted a string of her favourite swear words and tried to kick my nose in, Fred swung open the door just in time to prevent my complete extermination.

'Nothing too serious,' the vet said after his ministrations an hour later. 'Just keep puss warm and comfortable and away somewhere in the quiet. More shock than harm, I'm glad to say. But just keep her away from any more fireworks.' He smiled at Claire as she lowered me with exaggerated care into the pet carrier.

She scowled at him and said, by way of mitigation, 'Well, you know how it is, the little one dropped a sparkler and it just caught the cat.' (I wondered if she really believed this or, more likely, was just covering up for them as she usually did.)

'Yes, I know how it is,' he said kindly, looking from Claire to the two girls who had switched on angelic smiles. They managed to look amazingly innocent as they both nodded toward me with a show of sympathy.

My bed and some food were ceremoniously carted up to the upstairs cleaning room. 'She likes it so much there, that's a good place for her – out of our way,' Claire said after grumbling about all the upheaval I was causing.

There I spent the next two days. A tray of moist earth was placed near the door for my convenience which I found uncomfortable and distasteful but I supposed they had never heard of proper cat litter. This tray, thankfully, propped open the door just a few inches so although I was not actually shut in, there was wonderful peace and quiet. Being out of sight from everyone, not a soul came near me except Fred who exchanged the remains of my dinner for fresh food and milk the following day. (He had no doubt warned the persecution pair that I was off limits, for the time being.) Perhaps I was sleeping extra soundly to obliterate my anguish but I didn't hear even one bang of a firework. After some lengthy slumbering I started to feel better. I ate all my food though the milk had soured miserably (you'd think that on a farm it would be fresh enough to last a day but it was probably stale when they put it down.) The dirt tray became offensively smelly in spite of my constant attempts to make it presentable. But I stayed where I was for a few more hours until the next morning when I felt the time had come for me to leave my sick quarters. Choosing the middle of the day I crept down the big stairway and into the kitchen. Thankfully it was all quiet. My torturers would be at school, I knew, and it seemed that Claire was out as her dilapidated old van was not parked haphazardly outside the window as it usually was. Fred would be working of course. His plate of cold meat and slices of bread were laid on the table ready for his lunch. I jumped up on a chair (which movement pulled agonizingly at my poorly back) and scrutinised the food but it did not appeal to me. My appetite had diminished, even for freshly cut meat. I needed to breathe in clean air, some exercise and I needed to be out of that house.

Suddenly I felt desperate for a drink of milk so I wandered into the dairy. No luck there so on into the main milking shed which I thought would be empty at this time of the day. It was not empty as the cow boy, who helped out generally, was hosing down at the far end.

'Hello cat!' he called in a friendly way. I had encountered him before and thought him the nicest person on that wretched farm, except for Fred perhaps. As he laid the hose down on the concrete floor I trotted towards him. He automatically reached up and poured milk from the slop-can into a rather scruffy and not too clean metal tin, as I had hoped he would. I rubbed against his dung-covered boot in thanks and acknowledgement but he at once returned to his hosepipe and the swilling out of the far milking stalls. He was a kindly lad who always had a word for all the animals. He was known for his slop-can of discarded milk, kept ready for any thirsty creature, when by rights, this should have been thrown away. I was so appreciative of my drink that I did not notice Monty Mouse who, as always, had materialised from nowhere.

'Hi!' he trilled, scampering along the still damp floor gully.

'Hello!' I lifted my head from the now empty dish and licked my whiskers.

'Lordy, Lordy!' he squeaked, 'What have you done to yourself?' He studied the gaping bald patch on my back and the sore skin beneath. 'Let me guess. Not firework night?'

'More or less,' I said, telling him briefly what had happened.

'Dreadful, dreadful,' he shook his tiny head sorrowfully. 'Though I like the bit about her shoes being ruined with your vomit. Great, that!' Then he became his usual serious self again. 'You can't stay there, in that place. Not after this you can't.'

I sighed and said I thought he was probably right but what choice did I have?

'Come, live in the barn with us mices,' he offered, then quickly considering the improbability of this, shook his head again. 'Or the yard cats. Join them, you have had an invite and you can hunt as well as any of them, thanks to me,' he added importantly.

Before he had even finished I shook my head. 'I do not want to become a yard cat,' I replied, then, jokingly. 'Anyway, if I did I would have to hunt you!'

Mine was a miserable situation so we sat and talked of other more general topics. I learned that Minnie-by-the-way had safely delivered her kittens – four beautiful little bundles, Monty said. Then he added soberly, 'What a shame they have to grow into horrible cats.'

'Not all cats are horrible,' I retorted angrily.

'You know what I mean.' He squirmed, then lightened the subject speedily. 'One of Minnie's sisters had some too last week. She had five. Not as sweet as Minnie's. The sister has had loads before, but these are Minnie's first. She's only very young. About like you,' he added thoughtfully. 'Anyway,' he assumed his schoolteacher authority once more. 'Come to our barn tomorrow morning. We will have a serious talk about everything. Something has to be done.'

He tore off, squashing himself down to squeeze through a very small hole in the wall. He was like a wizard, I decided, always disappearing suddenly and appearing again, usually when he was needed. I lay in the weed patch for a while then forced myself to go back to the farmhouse. Someone had dragged my bed back to the scullery and the same someone had left me a dish of rather dubious food – obviously not Tina's pay cheque time-of-the-month. (My heart fluttered but I forced myself not to think about her. There were more urgent things to concentrate on at that moment.)

As I washed thoroughly I thought about what Monty had said. How long could I stay in this environment? A question that was reinforced by Sally shouting, "Hello, baldy cat! Who's a baldy cat then?" when she ran past on her way in from school. Worse was Amanda who, as she passed my basket, prodded my wound with her sticky thumb. 'Ugh!' she screamed, wrinkling her nose.

I flattened myself down on the blanket and wished my quarters could permanently be upstairs in the store room, out of the children's easy range. Monty had told me that in my escapade I had probably used up one of my lives. Even though I had cheated death-by-burning, I could just as easily have died of shock, he said. But neither of us really believed I had nine chances. Anyway, on reflection, it may be infinitely preferable to just slip away from life rather than have to endure and escape from so many future virtually fatal situations. Especially as I remembered the remarks Tina had made about me almost being human, which would automatically ensure I was going be a human again, next time around. (Oh, I really did hope so!)

On this cheering thought I dropped off to sleep without having touched my unappealing meal.

Monty was already seated on one of the hay bales when I passed the barn entrance the following morning.

'Hello!' I greeted him brightly, then saw his thunderous expression. 'Is anything the matter?'

He gulped and jumped up. 'Dreadful! It's dreadful! Lordy, this hasn't happened for ages!'

'Calm down' I said but he was so overwrought that he danced from one front leg to the other.

'Oh Lordy! If you knew what they're going to do!'

I thought at once of the girl enemies but they were at their lessons. The yard cats then? 'Who?'

'The bloody farmer, that's who!' he snarled. (I wouldn't have expected a mouse to snarl but he did.)

'Fred? What is he going to do then?'

Monty took a deep breath. 'Minnie's kittens, her babies. He's going to drown them.'

'What?' What did he mean? I must have heard wrongly.

'And her sister's and some other little ones. They're all going to be drowned.'

I shook my head until my ears smarted. Trying to stop my back from automatically arching (because the stretching hurt) I stammered 'Why? What on earth for?' but I knew the answer.

Claire was constantly going on about how the place was overrun with yard cats and saying things like 'we only need enough to keep the mice and rats down. The rest are just scavengers and make a mess everywhere.' Only last week Fred had nodded and said he would have to think about doing something. This, then, was what he had decided to do.

'It's barbaric,' I whispered, 'Poor Minnie. Poor babies.' That lump in my throat was there again although as an apprentice complete cat I realised things like this happened. The laws of killing and survival were becoming second nature to me as each day passed. 'But this is barbaric,' I repeated lamely.

'It happened before, when I was very young,' Monty said sadly. 'There were even more of them then. Food was scarce and because cats catch rabbits that humans could eat, fully grown cats perished too, I can tell you.' His words hung on the still crisp morning air.

'How? How do they do it?' I asked softly, although I did not really wish to be told.

'A bucket. A dirty great bucket,' he mumbled. 'He puts water in it, drops the little ones in and then puts another pail over the top to hold their poor heads under the water.' Monty almost sobbed the last words, his whiskers moving with emotion and his tail quivering.

I stared down at my paws. 'Can't we do something?' But I knew the answer to that too.

'What?' he said simply. 'What could we do? Even if we pooled our resources – all we have is a pack of mices and some hard-headed yardies – and they don't much care. They've seen it all before and as long as it's not them they aren't bothered.'

'How do you know about this? Maybe you've got it all wrong?' Putting my prayers into words did not help at all.

'He and his old cowman have already got the things out waiting by the water trough in the yard, and anyway, I heard them talking about it.'

Mention of the old cowman made me start. He was, to me, a distant figure who always seemed to be brandishing a long stick with which to hit the cows. He was always shouting and swearing.

'What about the farm boy? He would never do a thing like this. He's a kind lad.' I was clutching at straws.

Monty looked at me, his eyes brimming. ''Phoned in sick. Said he couldn't come to work until this afternoon. Couldn't stomach it I suppose. I'm not surprised, he's a good sort as you say. He's never tried to stamp on me if I get in the way. Farmer wasn't too pleased. Heard him tell the cow man that the lad will have to watch it otherwise he'll be out of a job. Although,' he went on thoughtfully. 'Young help is not easy to find out here. They all go into the town to work. Better pay,' he finished morosely.

We stood looking at each other. Somewhere outside there was a series of clanking sounds and men's voices were shouting. Crouching down I tried to bury my ears in the hay by shovelling it about with my paws. My contortions pulled at my injured back again but this was minor discomfort compared with what Minnie-by-the-way must be suffering. Monty burrowed beneath the tied bale. But we both could hear the real or imagined cries of the infants as they were being slaughtered so near to us. After a while the clanking of metal stopped and the men's shouts trailed away. There was silence when we lifted our heads.

I must get away from here, I vowed silently, selfishly. To Monty I said, 'This is a terrible day. I will go now, to try to find Minnie,' I added, shaking off the wisps of hay that clung obstinately to my uneven coat.

'The yardies will be gone out,' Monty said matter-of-factly. 'Only the others, well, some of the others, will be there,' he muttered. 'You will be perfectly safe going to their barn. Give her my best,' he said vaguely, looking away. He was recovering already. In the animal kingdom, others' misfortunes are seldom of any consequence for more than a minute or so.

As I marched purposefully towards the far barn, strategically avoiding the yard area, the older female cats went about their routines as if unaware of the morning's tragic happening. There was no sign of little Minnie. However much of a cat I become, in all the senses, please God, I implored, do not ever let me lose my feelings. As I searched the bushes and along by the wall, my whole being reached out to try to find my silky grey friend, who had been deprived of motherhood so cruelly. And, I shuddered, by those of a supposedly superior intellect. It made me quite abashed to have had any connection with their species. As she was about my own age Minnie's thoughts and emotions would be similar to mine. Basically still half human, her hurt would be very real. What words could I say to comfort her and would she want my offer of friendship and support?

I found her at last, alone, curled up in the weeds by the nettle bed. As I crept in beside her she turned her anguished yellow eyes towards me.

'Minnie, my lovely girl,' I stammered inadequately. She closed her eyes tightly so that further communication was impossible. Quietly I curled myself close to her back and gently licked the spot between her ears. She moved slightly and gave a little grunt of assent. Her limp, sagging belly spread uselessly over the dandelion leaves, the proud little nipples redundant. How much simpler it would be, I thought sadly, if we were both just ordinary cats. By the next day we should have forgotten all about it. But we were not ordinary cats and because Minnie would not be able to dismiss her hurt, and my sore back constantly reminded me of my misfortunes, I thought it seemed sensible that we should team up together. We lay closely entwined until the afternoon became chilly. Life must go on, I decided practically, but not in this same way. With my left paw I gently touched her nose and she opened her eyes gradually as if sensing I had something to say.

'Let's go see if the farm lad is in yet.' I started gently. 'The milking is over and I feel like a drink.'

Minnie roused herself carefully, giving her front paws a perfunctory lick. 'Good idea,' the grateful amber eyes said, 'I'm ever so thirsty,' and we walked together slowly through descending dusk towards the milking sheds.

# CHAPTER 13

Minnie-by-the-way and I agreed to run away together. Although she had always been a yard cat she was keen to learn about better living standards and it seemed that if we joined forces the two of us might improve our lots. The Yardies were tough, selfish and often cruel, she said. How she envied cats born into a real domestic life with families, warm beds, central heating and regular food. She confided too that what she could remember of her previous existence, life had even then not been entirely happy. Abuse in her childhood had led to lack of proper schooling which in turn meant she had had no qualifications for work. She had been obliged to take up cleaning and washing dishes in a 'rather nasty' (as she put it) hotel in central London. It was strange that as humans, living within a few miles of each other, our paths had never crossed. Predictable, I supposed, given our very different lifestyles. Her years had been hard and depressing whilst mine had been encouraging and promising. There was no way I would have had to work as a cleaner when I left school. Although Minnie's human life had been longer than mine our endings could not have been more different. I had suffered a self-inflicted demise whilst engaged in something useless and indulgent; she had died after falling down a flight of stairs whilst trying to escape the unwanted attentions of an hotel client. Now, in this life, we were equal and we made a pact to always stay together whatever fate had in store for us. I realised this was probably not tenable but it seemed to cheer her up. Who was I to dampen her optimism right at the very time when I too needed to believe in something or someone again?

'Where shall we go?' I asked at our first planning meeting a couple of days after the destruction of her young family. It was all right getting away from it all if we had somewhere to get away to.

The weather was becoming colder and the attraction of living rough and eating off the land receded with every gust of wind and each shower that held more than a hint of snow. The horrible children and their slovenly mother continued to be horrible and slovenly but, since my burning ordeal, Fred the farmer made sure I had food each day although the quantity and quality varied greatly, sometimes it was just fatty scraps in congealed gravy scraped from the family dinner plates. But it was food I did not have to go out in the freezing weather at night to catch for myself and, during the day when the house was quiet, the warmth of the Aga almost made the nastiness of the family bearable. As the days crawled by my resolve to run away weakened but whilst we sat cosily in the near barn Minnie became even more enthusiastic.

Monty Mouse had received the news of our possible departure with mixed feelings but he said he would attempt to attend as many of our planning meetings as he could. (In order to give advice.)

'It will be hard for you Penny cat,' he observed. 'But things will not improve and be any better here for you than they are now.'

'What if Tina comes back and I'm not here?' This recurring desperate thought was unbearable.

'She might never come back,' Minnie retorted. 'After all, she left you and you said she had sold her home and not let it as she originally was going to. No, she's there for good.' I did wonder if a little of this was a case of sour grapes as Minnie had never known a good home, either as a human or cat.

'You have to think about now. You life can't go on like this.' Monty brought us back to the agenda in his best lecturer's manner. 'What will those monsters do next to you?'

He was right, of course. My tail was constantly being trodden on (purposely) and Amanda had tried to cut my whiskers with some nail scissors the previous afternoon when I was sleeping. Fortunately this was averted when I heard her gum-chewing molars churning close to my ear, and sprang up to defend myself. Aware that the shining instrument was virtually on my cheek, my protracted claws had connected rather successfully with her grubby little hand. She screamed hysterically waving her arms about as the blood trickled all over her white cotton school blouse.

106

Sally had immediately come to the rescue, kicking out at me with a heavy black school boot. 'Clear out, you rotten cat. Don't come into this house again! Mummy! Mummy! Look what this rotten cat has done to poor Amanda!'

'But 'poor Amanda' tried to cut my whiskers and stab me!' I yelled out, dashing between the chair legs to avoid further punishment from the boots.

Sally ignored her screeching sister and picked up a book which she aimed, accurately, in my direction. The sharp blow to my head slowed the progress of my departure somewhat but I managed to slip into the corridor and out through the scullery.

'Don't you ever come back!' shouted Claire somewhere behind me as I limped as quickly as I could to the sanctuary of the near barn. But I did go back.

About mid-evening I crept in to see if by chance there was any food as I certainly did not feel up to hunting. There were no dishes in sight so in desperation I helped myself to some cold pork from the bottom larder shelf, thankfully not stowed away yet in the fridge. I didn't bother to disguise my theft. Whatever happened now there was no way for me to remain at the farmhouse. So I just didn't care any more. A good helping of baked beans from a little dish at the end complemented the meat well and made me feel much better. My bed was still in the passageway but I felt it prudent not to avail myself of its relative comfort until later when everyone had gone to bed.

'Yes,' I replied to Monty, rubbing the lump on the back of my head hesitantly with my right forepaw. 'Yes – what will they do to me next? That is, if I am allowed to go back into the house. I slept in my bed last night for a while but not easily. I wouldn't put it past those sadists to creep down at night to do me in.'

Suddenly the warmth of the cooking range evaporated into insignificance. It was no good being warm and dead.

'But,' I repeated. 'Where will we go? It's not really conducive to just wandering about.'

'Join the yard cats, just for the winter, then you two can slip away when the warmer weather comes.' Monty offered.

'No!' Minnie stated resolutely, 'I don't want to stay here. They are jeering at my poor belly and making nasty cracks about who is going to have a go at me next. They say that the Tom who can father the most kittens before next summer is chief of the barn. It's all ever so horrible. And I'm frightened,' she finished quietly. Monty and I nodded understandingly and my mind blocked out nasty thoughts of the time when yard Toms might forcefully turn their attentions to me. I shuddered as Minnie went on. 'Anyway if we stayed, you, Penny, might become like them. The females are crude and coarse and dirty and slatternly, most of them.' She looked down at her immaculately clean coat and purred a little.

'I would never become like them,' I assured her. 'But that doesn't matter. We're not stopping.'

'Well, stay here in this barn.' Monty tried. 'Though it would be difficult with all the mices that live here. You would both just have to promise not to catch any of my friends. Not to catch any mices at all, because I know them all.'

'That's kind but it's not practicable,' I replied. 'For one thing, how would you tell them we are friendly? Unless you have a very old mouse that speaks to both groups, only you and those like you would know. The others would be scared stiff and would take off, I don't doubt. Also,' I added truthfully. 'We are cats and we will be hungry. It's against very nature to expect us to sit and watch you scurry about whilst we are starving. Come on, Monty, a thoughtful idea but it just wouldn't work.'

'No, 'Minnie chimed in. 'I couldn't promise not to touch anyone. I am a trained hunter,' she looked at me sideways. 'With lots of experience.'

'Penny caught a rat,' Monty reminded her. Then we reverted to meaningful silence.

'We will all think where you might go,' Monty announced. 'And we will meet here tomorrow and pool our ideas. Now I must be off, there are things to do.' I was just about to ask exactly what things he was always rushing off suddenly to do, but he had already effected his usual disappearing act.

'Let's go and get some milk,' Minnie suggested.

# CHAPTER 14

The next day was fine, sunny and unusually warm.

'I've decided where we will go,' Minnie announced to Monty and me as we sat in the barn doorway. We waited. 'We shall go to my brother's – he would love to have us. And he's a Zoon, of course.'

'Your brother?' I knew she must have many brothers but hadn't realised one might have a house.

'Not his house,' she mocked, reading me immediately. 'His owners' house.'

'Your brother might love to have us but would his owners?' was my immediate response.

'I'm sure,' she nodded her silky head. 'My brother says they are very kind people, always feeding strays and animals that pass by.'

'Where does this brother's benevolent family live then?' Monty, ever the realist.

'In the town,' Minnie said. 'But', she added thoughtfully. 'I don't know the address exactly. It's precisely due west of here so all we need do is follow the sunset.' This sounded pathetically simple.

'And just keep going until you get there?' Monty put in sarcastically.

'Well, yes,' she bridled, adding helpfully, 'I know it's by the main road, the one that our lane leads out on to. So if we just go west along it...'

I swished my tail impatiently. 'Have you been there before?' Minnie shook her head apologetically. 'Then how do you know where it is? Due west and by the main road? It sounds too haphazard to me. Hardly acceptable directions, do you think?'

'I know all this because Robson told me,' she said haughtily.

'And who on earth is Robson?' Monty and I chorused.

'Robson is a very wealthy cat. A very good pedigree,' she added as if this may be pertinent. 'My brother, Sooty – because he is black,' she explained unnecessarily. 'My brother met Robson when they were on their holidays at the boarding kennels.' She made it sound like a five star hotel somewhere quite exotic, instead of the usual row of smelly wooden huts which I supposed it to be. 'Robson,' she savoured the name. 'Was in one of the pavilions – you know, a split level chalet accommodation with its own garden exercise run.'

Monty and I nodded patiently.

'Well Sooty's chalet – that was a nice one too, I think, but not really posh like Robson's,'

We waited again as there had to be a point to all this.

'Sooty's chalet faced Robson's and, both being Zoons, they got chatting and became quite pally.'

'Yes?' I prompted encouragingly.

'Well Sooty told him he had been born and raised on a farm (he just said farm, I don't think he said he was a yard cat).'

'Naturally,' Monty interjected.

Minnie narrowed her eyes to slits. 'We are not ashamed of being yard cats,' she told him haughtily.

'Just don't want it advertised,' Monty finished smugly.

'Just get on with it,' I interrupted. Now was not a good time for confrontation.

'Well, Robson said he knew our farm as his house is not all that far away. He said he lives in an enormous place on the edge of the village with big lawns and a lily pond.'

'Yes, Yes,' prompted Monty who I could sense was tiring of the whole thing.

'Well, Robson, as he lives so close by,' another linger over the name. 'Volunteered to come to see me and tell me how Sooty was getting on in his new home and all his news.'

She launched into further enlargement of how wonderful Robson's life was and how the two caged animals swore undying friendship (at least for the length of their holidays in the kennels.)

Minnie then related how her brother had always looked after her in the yard and protected her when they were young. They had been very close and she recalled the mixed feelings she felt when she heard that Sooty might be going to a real home. Gladness and joy that he was escaping to a more comfortable life and sadness and tears when she realised he had gone from the yard. In those days, it seemed, Fred usually took unwanted cats to the cat-care home to, hopefully, be re-housed with people who wanted pets – he must have had more compassion then and it was probably less trouble than drowning them. But, Minnie confided, these days there were too many unwanted animals for the home to accommodate so she supposed that's why Fred had reverted back to the pail and water.

'I was asleep in the hedge when they took him and the others away on that day to the recycling place. I s'pose I'd have gone too if they'd found me.' She shuddered and let out a nervous purr. No, cats do not only purr when they are pleased and happy. Sometimes they purr in times of anxiety or stress and frequently when they feel unwell. They also purr very loudly when they want something, such as cream or fish or attention. But knowing owners soon learn the different meanings. (Tabatha told me all this.) 'When I woke up,' Minnie finished, 'Sooty was gone, along with other family and friends. Only a few, that weren't about at the time, were left here.)

Remembering this obviously made her feel sad as she wiggled her whiskers and glanced away from us. Monty and I took care not to make any comment. 'Well, I had no idea where he had gone.' She pulled herself together. 'Until one afternoon when Robson appeared at the farm yard gate,' She moved her shoulders backwards and forwards at the memory and lowered her head shyly. 'Well,' she went on, 'When he explained who he was and confirmed that I was the sister of his friend in the kennels, there didn't seem much point in inviting him into the yard – it's always so filthy – so we went for a walk.'

'Yes?' Monty thrust into her reverie unkindly.

'Well,' she continued, shifting to a more comfortable position. 'He told me all my brother's news. Where he lived, all about his owners, and we got on very well together,'

She rolled over on to her back, then, remembering her manners, sat up straight and shook herself. 'We met a few times and went walking in the meadows.'

'Did he take you to his house?' I asked, keen to know if this might be a landmark for our impending travels.

Minnie shook her head. 'I really liked him but he was, well, ever so intellectual. He must've been a very important human man before, and now he is a very well respected local cat. Even the yard cats had heard of him because they called me Lady Muck because I tried so hard to keep myself clean, which is very difficult here. They said I was dolling myself up to meet with the snob nobs.'

She paused briefly then raced on again, 'He is a champion British Blue – that's why he liked me, I think, because my grey colour fitted in with his so well, even though I'm not actually a pedigree,' she obviously thought this all needed to be explained. 'Well, because we got on so well, this is how I came to have my little family.' Her tone faded as she paused, realising that she now had no family. I wondered, sorrowfully, if their kittens had all been a lovely soft silky grey colour.

'And then? After all this walking etceteras?' Monty cut in, keen to finish the session.

'Well, as I say, he is well known and has a lot of appointments – I wanted to see him again but he was always having to go off to shows and, well, we drifted apart..' Her thoughts trailed away.

I smiled ruefully at her misplaced trust, feeling that Mr Aristo-British-Blue-Robson would probably have jumped on any soft pussykins who crossed his path. But I might have been doing him an injustice. Then I suddenly had the most disturbing thought. What would happen if someone like him, with or without an enormous pedigree and startling good cat looks, jumped on me one day with evil intentions?

I stood up and shook myself violently. No thanks! I told myself adamantly. I'll stick to catching the occasional meal, that's as much of a cat as I want to be for a long, long time.

'Can't you get in touch with this Robson?' It was evident from Monty's tone that his impression of Cat Casanova was similar to mine. 'So as to find the exact location of your brother.'

'No!' Minnie twitched her tail slightly, a movement which gave way to energetic lashing from side to side. 'Don't know exactly where he lives. He explained where Sooty is very clearly, in case I ever wanted to visit but he never told me how to get to his own house.'

'The Yardies would know,' Monty persisted.

'No,' Minnie was firm as the energetic lashing subsided. 'I doubt it. They only know fields and meadows and gardens and kitchens of workers' cottages. Anyway, I don't want to see him again. Not after all that has happened. We can find our way to Sooty's. We just go towards the sunset along the main road. The house has a big wood woven green gate and is right by the bus stop after the 30 mile sign in town. It is just after the canal bridge Oh, yes! I remember he told me the house has lace curtains.' She finished triumphantly.

'We should find that easily I suppose,' I said tartly, 'What if they have a new gate or have painted it? Anyway I'm not good on colours – are you?''

'Now, now,' Monty realised his departure might be speeded by reconciliation. 'It seems straightforward. You can always come back if it gets too difficult.'

Minnie-by-the-way looked at me, the question brightly in her yellow eyes. I flicked my tail impatiently.

'If it is fine,' I announced airily, 'We will go in the morning.' Then almost immediately, I regretted such a hasty management decision.

'What about the sunset?' she whispered. 'It doesn't set in the morning – not 'till late afternoon. We won't know which way.'

'You will go in the opposite direction to where the sun is, if there is any, which I doubt.' Monty pointed out usefully. The meeting was ended.

Fred left me out some food that evening. Quite a big dish of leftover stew and potatoes and a full saucer of milk. I avoided the vegetables but polished off the meat, gravy and milk, feeling that it was quite a substantial meal as befitted my

Last Supper. Both Sally and Amanda had continually kicked me as I tried to get some sleep under the kitchen table but they were soon ensconced in front of the TV in the lounge and forgot about me. Claire clearly did not want me in her house and had shifted my basket right to the coldest, dampest part of the scullery by the broken window. She ignored me completely and never fed me. But at least I did have some shelter and the food Fred put down for me.

What was I letting myself in for if I left? I asked myself this as I had a good wash on the doormat. The coward in me would have backed out then and there and chanced my luck staying where I was (at least until the spring) but for Minnie. I couldn't let her down at this last minute. Still, I consoled myself, we could always come back, as Monty had said, though it is doubtful if the farmer's family would be overjoyed to see me again. Presumably the despicable Claire would continue to enjoy her sister's financial generosity whilst not mentioning my absconding

Before I curled up amongst the damp rags in my draughty basket, thoughts of Tina, her apartment and our lovely roof garden flooded back. I blinked quickly and drew some comfort from Monty Mouse's promise that he would get word to me at Minnie's brother's house if Tina ever did come back. Monty had good friends in useful places. He had mentioned he was on chatting terms with several of the cows, though I could not imagine them ambling into town with a message for someone who lived by the bus stop. More promising, I felt, was the acquaintance of a family of crows. Monty had, apparently, saved two newly hatched chicks when they had fallen from their nest high up above the barn roof. The parent birds (both Zoons) had promised a favour in return if ever it was needed. Monty had told me he had, only a couple of days before, reminded the family of this and mother crow had agreed loudly. 'Of caw caw caw cawse!'. It would take – well, only a few minutes to cover the distance to Sooty's home, because they always fly in a straight line, taking the least possible time. Hence the saying…'as the crow flies'. I sniffed and sniggered at my humorous thoughts and promptly fell asleep.

# CHAPTER 15

It was fine and the winter sun was already trying to break through the drabness of the scullery when I roused myself earlier than usual. My customary mid-night walkabout had been abandoned in favour of getting as much rest and warmth as possible before our imminent adventure but my bed was damp and uncomfortable and lumpy so I stole into the kitchen as soon as Fred unlocked the door. The welcome heat of the Aga against my side fur made me question again the wisdom of forsaking what few comforts I had.

When noises on the stairs indicated the arrival of the rest of the family my departure from the kitchen was swift. It was even quite warm in the cowshed where I waited patiently for my dish of milk from the farm boy. The cows were tethered in pens and their offerings of fresh warm milk slurped into the greedy rubber-tipped fingers of the waiting metal machinery. Their sweating bodies combined with the steaming cow feed grain made the temperature almost comfortable – if you could stand the smell.

'You're early today, you are,' the boy remarked, salvaging a tin that had obviously been used several times before. But the milk was delicious and still frothing and I tried to ignore the hard congealed crust around the edge. I wished he would wash his dishes out occasionally, especially when they started to become smelly. Minnie arrived just as I had finished.

'You'll want some too?' the boy asked already refilling the tin.

Minnie-by-the-way had made a special effort with her appearance. Her coat was glistening in the sunlight that crept in through the grimy windows and there was no dirt between her claws. Her whiskers seemed more springy than usual and her tail fur was spotless (not easy when everything one's tail touches in the yard is squelchy and messy.)

'I am ready for the journey,' she announced after meowing her thanks to the boy.

'I'll be just a few minutes,' I told her, 'I will come out to the near barn. Monty will want to say Goodbye.'

For some reason I suddenly had the urge to go back into the farmhouse and have a last look around. There might also be the chance of seeing an envelope from Tina laying on the front mat under the letterbox. (I could tell her letters by the way her company logo was stamped across the envelope and by the tiny flower motifs on the back. I remembered with a pang that very first note that had been torn up and thrown over me.) Hurrying through the scullery I noticed that my basket had been turned upside down and someone had dumped a pile of old newspapers on top of it. If I needed one last prompt to support my departure this was it. Past the reassuring cooking range and quickly under the kitchen table where the horror-girls were having breakfast.

'There's that spiteful cat again!' squealed Sally whilst Amanda leaned down from her chair and tried to grab at my legs as I fled past.

As I raced by Claire at the bottom of the staircase she shouted, 'I thought I told you not to come in the house!' but as she was carrying a basketful of dirty washing she could not lunge at me or do anything potentially harmful.

I gazed at the letters laying on the scrap of carpet at the bottom of the big front door. Just letters. No pretty flowery envelope. No last reminder of the happier part of my cat childhood. No last faint hope that the dreadful Claire would open a letter and read aloud that Tina was coming home. No. Miserably I turned back to run the gauntlet of getting to the scullery again so as to make my escape. Past lumbering fat Claire with her overflowing plastic basket, past Fred as he came from the kitchen to collect his bills from the mat, and then a smooth dive beneath the kitchen table to comparative temporary safety. If no one saw me, I might warm myself en route for a last few minutes by the blissful Aga. But someone did see me.

Screaming, I bolted towards the door on my final exit, Amanda's scalding hot coffee running all down my back. Rushing out into the garden I could hear her shouting,

'Mummy! Look what that stupid cat has done! It's knocked my drink over!'

Monty Mouse and Minnie-by-the-way were waiting for me by the barn door and whilst Monty spouted instructions, Minnie attempted to clean my smarting back.

'The time is certainly right,' Monty admitted shaking his little head solemnly. He pointed his nose upwards and sniffed, as he so often did when he was changing mood or subject. 'I will walk with you to the end of the gravel driveway,' he told us, adopting his usual disciplined manner. 'Then you will have to go along the dirt track until you reach the tarmac bit. Do you remember how to get to the road?' he asked me with some concern.

'Only when I came here,' I said. 'I saw it from the car.'

Tina's car! I blinked furiously.

'Oh, I know it like the back of my paw,' Minnie said brightly. 'I've been hunting all along the track and quite a bit of the tarmac road, but I've never been out on to the main road,' she amended. 'I usually go across the fields – don't like roads.'

Fine, I thought. Here we are about to set off, walking goodness knows how many miles along one of the busiest roads I had even seen, and now she tells me she doesn't like roads.

'It is straight through,' Monty confirmed although he did add that he had never been further than the end of the shingle drive. 'My legs are too small and too old to tear about doing such long distances,' he said.

We went the grassy way out of the yard and past the farmhouse, pausing by the rusting old farm machinery to watch Claire marshal her little beasts into the van for their trip to school. We waited until they had driven off then I strode forward out into the middle of the drive, Minnie sashayed along at my side and Monty trotted, gamely attempting to keep up with us.

'I should walk to the side,' he advised breathlessly. 'Less chance of being seen under cover of grass and undergrowth. Don't want to cause attention to yourselves.'

'Thanks,' we both said together, veering our course up on to the slightly raised verge at the trackside.

'Good luck!' Monty said cheerily as we reached the end of the shingle. 'Although you will not need it if you are sensible. Remember all I have taught you, Penny Cat and you, Minnie-by-the-way, keep away from good looking macho moggies.'

He was being brisk and positive but I knew he was worried for us and unhappy about loosing his friends. We would all miss our conversations and I felt a surge of gratitude for his help and teachings, even if they were a little over the top at times. We said our farewells by the old gate and Minnie and I started off again; she slinking easily, gleaming in the sun, me with a damply matted coat, smelling sickly of sweet coffee, and limping slightly. We made our way along the track towards our first goal, the tarmac, turning only for a last backward glance. Monty was already scurrying away, hurrying, no doubt with relief, towards his familiar territory.

By the time we had reached the main road the sun had disappeared. We stood together in the weedy pathway, shuddering visibly as each huge lorry thundered past. Even more frightening were the cars that seemed to tear by in a continuous stream with a loud whoosh.

'It's the rush hour,' Minnie stated. 'When everyone is going to work and school.'

'I know what the rush hour is,' I said irritably. I should do, having been part of it for so many years in my previous existence.

'Anyway,' she snapped back, 'Where is the sun? How do we know which way to go along the road? I knew this would happen.'

Her previous optimism seemed to be evaporating by the second.

'That's not a problem,' I assured her, wondering myself how on earth we could be sure of the right direction. Where had the sun been in the sky when we were strolling along the tarmac lane chatting? I couldn't remember for the life of me. 'Let's rest a while,' I suggested, playing for time.

'Rest?' she was contemptuous. 'We've only just started. There's a long way to go yet.'

As we cowered back against the prickly hedge my self esteem was saved. Saved, by all people, by the fat, nasty Claire who at that moment turned her old van from the main road into the lane towards the farm. Knowing that she was returning from the school run and that the school was in the town, our direction towards the town was crystal clear. Then I saw that the devil daughters were still in the van. They must have forgotten something and had had to turn back. A slight niggle gnawed inside me. Supposing, just supposing they had gone to a shop or somewhere not in the direction of school? But no, I calmed myself. If they had gone shopping they would have carried on after they had made their purchase. No, they had definitely come back for something.

'OK,' I said nonchalantly, assiduously hiding my bright coat behind the tall weeds so as to avoid recognition if anyone looked in our direction. 'We go this way.'

I pointed my nose purposefully toward the rear of the turning van.

'How do you know?' Minnie was instantly suspicious.

'Trust me,' I said. Then she beamed. 'Oh, yes, the old van. Must have come from the town, she must.' Minnie was quite bright when she wanted to be. We kept well under the hedge as we trotted along but even then the slipstream from passing traffic continually ruffled our furs.

'This is not very pleasant,' Minnie complained as the flying dust settled on her eye whiskers. (I'm sure they're not called eye lashes – they are far too long and wavy.) So we decided it made more sense to follow the road on the other side of the hedging which was certainly an improvement. Once in the field our progress enjoyed a renewed lease of life. We alternately trotted, strolled and ran, only stopping to drink from a muddy pond after scaring away a few tattered ducks.

'Pity there's no ducklings around,' Minnie said washing her face and carefully dislodging some mud from a back paw.

'Surely you are not hungry already?' I questioned almost sternly. Killing mice and even the odd small rat had become a part of my life but I still did not relish the thought of trapping a large bird, either for sport or food. The only one I had ever eaten was an injured chick found lying in the farmyard. But that was when I was extremely hungry one night and, anyway, I was doing it a favour really. Apart from feeling that my jumping through the air once (to land on the Leader Rat) had given me some empathy with birds, albeit very briefly, the feathers and fluff were quite unpalatable and had a way of sticking to one's face and whiskers. And in my limited experience, dead, bedraggled feathers did not smell very nice either.

We continued our journey for what seemed like hours, carefully crossing side roads and turnings leading to houses and farms. We used the inside of the hedgerows wherever possible but sometimes had to walk along the path at the roadside which made us both feel uneasy. There was one very nasty area when there was a sheer drop to a quarry immediately inside the barbed wire fencing, with no pavement at the edge of the road. After debating whether we should attempt to cross the main road to the safety of the opposite verge or whether to try to walk along the edge of the pit keeping directly beneath the wire fence, we agreed on the latter. If we crossed the road it would mean re-crossing to get back again at some juncture and the edge of the quarry only ran a short way alongside the road before it widened again into a meadow. In order to come to this, quite major decision, Minnie had climbed a small tree from where she could report the lie of the land ahead. Fortunately the lowest strand of barbed wire was reasonably high so the only thing we had to watch out for was the safety of our tails (which, as you know, cats always hold rigid and vertically when engaged in serious walking.) Negotiating the periodic metal posts was complicated but nothing we couldn't handle. We were glad, though, when we were able to crawl under the fence, back on to more secure ground.

Shortly afterwards our efforts were unexpectedly rewarded when we passed a short driveway leading to a cottage. We could hardly believe our eyes when there, on the spotlessly clean white stone step, stood a large plate containing food. We crossed the space that separated us from our lunch, quickly and quietly as there was no camouflage, and to our delighted surprise saw that our repast consisted of chunks of meat and some thin biscuit pieces. Had we been able to read the word DOG embossed on the lip of the dish, we might have shown more prudence, but as it was we leaned our necks over and began to hastily choose the pieces we would eat first. Hungrily we ate from opposite sides. It was the first time Minnie and I had taken food together (apart from mice) and I was astounded at the amount of noise she managed to make, crunching, gulping, slurping. Then I realised that she probably had never eaten from a dish before, yard cat table manners would be entirely different. Using her method also meant that she consumed far more than I did which signalled a lesson for me if we were to share future meals. When the dish was licked clean and whiskers and faces had been attended to a sudden tiredness engulfed me.

'I would like to rest,' I said, yawning and stretching.

'Mm,' she glanced over her shoulder. 'Have we time? I wonder how far we still have to go.'

'Well, at least we're not hungry now. That will do me for today.' I replied looking about for somewhere comfortable where there might be no disturbance.

Although the traffic still roared past distantly at the end of the front garden I knew sleep would come easily.

'I shall be starving later,' she informed me, also yawning.

'But you ate most of it.' I protested, wondering how she kept so slim.

'Sshh,' she whispered turning her head, 'Look, there's a place over there.'

I turned towards where she was looking and saw the sweet little wooden house by the wall that had caught her attention.

'Yes?' she asked, starting to move towards it.

I looked around us cautiously. There was no-one in sight, no movement anywhere nearby, save the road vehicles.

'Ideal,' I agreed stepping after her.

As we neared the small wood building, some familiarity with the deeply pitched roof and the small curved entrance doorway nagged at my brain. It reminded me of something I had known some time in my past. But what? I just couldn't remember. A coil of thick silver chain lay abandoned on the flagstones outside the small hut as if it had been dropped carelessly. At the front was a round metal dish, the clouds flying by above reflected in its watery contents. Minnie was almost there, ready to climb through the archway and flop down inside to sleep when I noticed the red rubber ball lying by the dish. And there was a sort of doll made of foam, or something soft, which looked pitted and chewed, its clothes painted on and one of its arms bitten off. Then we both saw the giant brown paw that flopped languorously out through the doorway as its owner inside must have stirred. My neck hairs shot upwards as memory returned.

'It's a dog kennel!' I shouted with my eyes but Minnie could not understand as she had her gaze firmly away from me, glued on the huge paw ahead. 'And it's occupied! Flee! Run!' Even though I had spurted forward to be level with her she still didn't look at me. She stopped by the chain and turned, almost casually, to me. Thank God!

'Dog kennel!' my eyes spat toward her as I surreptitiously started to walk backwards as silently as I could.

She had obviously never seen or heard of a kennel before but she knew Dog, for she suddenly let out a piercing yowl and for one dreadful moment I was certain she was going in for the attack. Still trying to reverse, I stumbled over the chain. Enough was enough! No cat can successfully run backwards so I spun around and started to sprint away from the enemy. Self preservation took control - Minnie would have to fend for herself. Three ear splitting 'WOOF's' and noises of large animal scrambling about on small wooden floor preparatory to climbing out of his lair, unfroze Minnie who miraculously appeared at my side. Racing back past the front door and streaking under the hedge we were in close range only just long enough to hear a human voice shout,

"Down Butch! Down! How dare you chase after little pussy cats. Come here, boy, come here!"

Sounds of a chain being dragged over stonework gave way to canine complaints of howling and barking as the animal was presumably re-tethered. As we ran non-stop towards the middle of the adjoining field, the human shouts were subsiding.

"Bad, Bad, Boy! Fancy doing such a naughty thing after eating all your lovely dinner. Shame on you!"

Minnie and I smiled at each other with relief as we flopped down in the long grass to rest.

# CHAPTER 16

Curled up together cosily in the middle of the field of tall grasses we slept longer than we intended and it was nearly dark when we woke.

'It's still a long way,' Minnie complained sleepily, rubbing her eyes with a front paw that looked decidedly scruffy.

'It can't be that much further, we've come miles already, I'm sure,' I said giving myself a thorough shake.

'Not miles,' she smirked. 'You've got no sense of distance, have you? I don't expect you've ever been a whole mile before.'

She was quite right, of course. My exercise around the roof garden had hardly been energetic and my weeks at the farm had been roughly divided between dozing by the Aga, sleeping in the near barn and relaxing in my basket. As a feline I had probably never travelled, by paw, a mile in one go. Ostensibly I chose to ignore her unkind remark.

'We can make our way just as well in darkness,' I said bravely but we both knew my night experience was severely limited. (And, no, cats cannot see completely in the dark but they do have far better night sight than humans.) 'Or we could rest a bit more.'

'You are a right one,' she chided. 'All you want to do is sleep.'

'And all you want to do,' I retorted. 'Is to eat and eat.'

She nodded her smooth grey head. 'Yes, we make a good pair,' she said happily, refreshed by the rest.

I too felt much better – she was right though, I did seem to need quite a lot of sleep. All this hunting and practice-fighting and rushing about might well suit a yard cat but it was not for me.

'Do you know?' I told her gaily, 'I feel a bit like the Dick Whittington story, going on a long journey like this.'

Minnie had obviously never heard of Dick Whittington as she made no comment. She was pretty and had a nice personality, I decided privately, but she wasn't very intelligent. Bright yes, I remembered past assessments, but not that intelligent. Still, it only needed one of us to be the brains of the outfit.

'Great Hell!' she turned at me, stopping abruptly and crouching down almost flat against the ground, 'What on earth is that?'

As a low flying jet 'plane appeared over the distant hills, the thunderous roar of its engines engulfed us.

'You must have seen a 'plane before?' I was astonished at her, cowering against the earth. Surely she remembered from her earlier days even if one had never come over the farmyard.

'No, never!' she whimpered, laying quite still.

'But when you were, you know, before?'

'No, I always lived in the town,' she said defensively, then she paused. 'Yes,' she said quietly. 'Yes, I do know about 'planes. I think I can remember now.'

There was something sad, I thought to myself, about our memories fading. I dreaded this happening to me but knew it was likely to, eventually. Maybe because I was slightly younger and had had a more active and varied human life, maybe it would not affect me. It made me wonder if she might have known about dog kennels too and just forgot. I shook myself again, determined not to dwell on it.

We walked briskly through the dusk, and the traffic built up to a crescendo again – evening rush hour. The passing scenery changed very little, with fields and more fields seemingly never ending in front of us. I tried to shake off the nagging feeling that perhaps, just perhaps, we were walking in the wrong direction. It seemed so long before there was any sign of our progress. Minnie did her spasmodic scouting bit, climbing trees and scaling walls to report on what was ahead of us. I began to despair that signs of an approaching town might never appear and before long I started to become weary again.

'Night time may not be good for arriving at your brother's,' I suggested, desperately needing to rest.

'Better than in broad daylight,' she retorted. 'When everyone for miles can see us coming.' She had a point but I persisted. 'If we get there when it's pitch black, Sooty might be asleep behind locked doors in the house.'

'He would never sleep at night,' she scoffed. 'Remember, he's a yard cat by nature.'

I sat down abruptly, sighing. 'Was a yard cat,' I corrected. 'You said yourself it's been a long time since he went. He may be very changed and his ways might have altered. If he goes for holidays to the kennels he sounds very domesticated now.'

She thought about this, slumping down beside me. 'S'pose you could be right. But I can't see him sleeping in a box or a basket like you did.' The suggestion seemed like an insult to her. For a few silent seconds I thought longingly about my bed at Tina's apartment, warm and soft and inviting. The cat family basket before, at the old Minders' home, even seemed attractive now, and my poor unkempt bed at the farm would have been an improvement on the icy cold wet grass on which we were squatting.

'If you're that exhausted,' she said condescendingly, 'What about, if we slept for a bit now and got up very early and hurried there first thing – before people were about?' She was at least trying to compromise.

'But we still don't know how much further we have to cover,' I mumbled yawning, the prospect of slumber starting to become a reality.

'Let's have a look then,' she said, jumping up on to a fallen tree branch. 'Look over there!' she instructed shrilly. 'I can see a row of houses, it's a way off but it looks more built-up than it is here. In fact there are buildings on both sides of the road down at the bottom of the hill.' She paused. 'When you come to think of it, it doesn't take the farmer's wife long to get those girls to school and come back and they go right into the town – I've heard the farmer complaining about them spending money in the shops during their dinner hour.'

'But they go by van,' I said morosely, cheered slightly but not convinced.

Then, as I turned, over to the side of the wall I could see a stone outbuilding, a small barn or tumbled down workshop. It beckoned like an oasis in the desert. 'Look - could that be our bed for the night?' I asked hopefully.

Minnie slid further along the branch and strained her neck forwards. Now that the town was in sight I thought she might argue about not continuing our trek but at that moment the drizzle started.

'Looks OK to me. Roof's gone a bit but I can see some straw or something inside. Probably a pig sty or place where the sheep go,' she said knowledgeably, jumping down beside me. 'I'm ever so hungry,' she announced unsurprisingly as we hurried towards our shelter through the light rain. 'Do you want something? I'll get it for you,' she offered as we got closer. When we reached the building we realised just how decrepit it was. But there was bedding, as Minnie had seen from her branch, and there was still some part of the roof intact. Shaking my head in answer to her question (I was perfectly able to hunt for my own food if I needed to) I slouched down on some hay in the dry corner of the shed. Even as my eyes closed I heard a slight rustle, some scurrying, then almost immediately, crunching and the smacking of lips. Minnie then gave herself a good wash, managing, as she did everything else, to do it noisily. So, perhaps now that she had eaten (whatever it was) we might get some peace and be able to rest. I had barely settled, it seemed, when she prodded me with her back.

'Wake up,' she said softly, although there was no one about, 'It's time to get going again.'

Yawning and stretching I stared at her disbelievingly. 'What are you talking about?' I stuttered preparing to turn around and resettle.

'Time to go.' She lent against me roughly, prodding me with her spine as she dug her feet against the floor.

'You have no idea of the time,' I murmured, shutting one eye.

'Yes I have. The traffic is starting and there are people on bikes.'

What on earth was she rabbiting on about? She read my one open eye. 'I've been up on the roof – you can see ever such a long way from there. Folk are starting to go to work. We really must get moving. Go up on the roof and see for yourself,' she goaded me, knowing full well I would decline with vigour. 'It's not so bad, even though there are a few slates and bits of wall missing.'

I gave up and got up. 'I presume you have already had breakfast,' I said sarcastically and she nodded agreeably.

'Too right! But nothing too heavy,' she added glancing over at a bundle of feathers by the doorway.

I drank water from a puddle outside, had a quick wash and we started on what I hoped was the last leg of our trip. Traffic was about and apart from the lights of moving vehicles I could make out street lighting through the far hedges. We kept up a good regular speed, only deviating to circumnavigate a group of young ponies who, on spotting us trailing through their meadow, decided to investigate. Their silly neighing and stamping of hooves as they cantered towards us caused the detour as neither of us felt in the mood for unnecessary conflict. We were soon under the hedge and when we ducked out on the other side we found ourselves in a sort of park or playing field. Wooden benches were scattered about alongside a narrow paved path, and a sports pavilion of some sort loomed out of the semi-darkness. The high wooden boundary fencing was a nuisance as we had to work our way around it – Minnie could have managed to climb up easily and balance along the top but although I could jump, it was probably out of my range and there was no way the walking-a-tightrope bit would appeal. I was grateful that my little grey companion did not even hint at it. We squeezed through the iron railings of the high gate and warily crossed the lane beyond the end of the park.

'This looks like a bridge,' I observed, seeing the low walls either side of the main road, which was, thankfully, still relatively quiet. 'The canal bridge,' I emphasised, for, as I turned my head, I could see the ribbon of still, murky water, wandering into the distance between buildings and, further away, yet more open countryside. 'Look, the canal!' I almost shouted with joy.

'What's a canal?' she asked quietly trying to follow where I was looking.

'A canal? Well you know, like a river but not flowing. Man made, still. It has locks,' I added hoping this might jog her memory.

I didn't know whether Minnie really had never seen a canal before or whether, once again, the recollection had become vague. There was no point in labouring it so I just said, as kindly as possible. 'It's no big deal. Just a stretch of water used mainly for holiday boats, though sometimes they still do transport goods along it in narrow barges. There's nothing to worry about – there's no way it will bother us. We just cross the bridge on the pavement and we're on the other side. We won't even see the water,' I reassured her, suddenly realising how she must feel about being near to water. But she didn't say anything – merely kept quite close to me. We crossed the bridge in single file, with Minnie keeping up close to my tail. Fortunately there was no one about and the passing drivers were concentrating on the road in the half light. We scrambled back into the hedge as soon as we could but had to keep bobbing in and out when the greenery gave way to boarded fencing. We were now passing gardens instead of fields and meadows.

' That looks like the speed sign,' I told her, glancing up at what looked like a giant lollipop. The circle on top of the pole seemed a very long way up above us.

'Yes,' she said absently.

The speed limitation could have read 100 for all I was able to tell but no, I checked myself, only two figures. Once again I cursed not being able to decipher anything.

'Is it the right sign?' she asked watching my consternation, but before I could reply she fixed me with a jubilant stare. 'Look! There's a bus stop, and there just by it is a big gate.'

'Is it green?' I said automatically, realising then that for me colours were now extremely difficult to determine. I could just about manage blacks and whites and greys.

'I don't know,' she said mournfully. 'But', she perked up. 'It's a woven sort of gate.'

'That must be it,' I said with an authority I did not feel.

Discreetly I looked across the main road to the houses opposite, just in case we were on the wrong side after all. There were gates of varying shades of light and dark but I was relieved to see nothing with a woven or interlaced appearance.

'And it's got lace curtains!' she cried with glee.

I hesitated to tell her that the houses each side sported lace curtains also. 'Well, we're here,' I flopped down by a weeping willow tree that had somehow got entangled with the privet hedge.

'You're not tired again?' she asked anxiously lest I should demand rest before making inroads into what could be our future home.

'Of course not!' I snapped. 'But we should have a plan of action. A plan of entering. We can't just walk up to the front door and say we've arrived.'

Minnie was so happy and had started purring furiously. I felt cautious and very aware that we might be shown the boot and be chased away even if her brother did live there and was pleased to see his sister. His minders would not know who we were; to them we were just another two vagrants.

'There's Sooty!' she screamed, bounding off towards the garage, which was set back along a paved driveway at the side of the house.

A tall statuesque black cat stood motionless in front of the closed garage doors. His yellow eyes glinted in the half light and even from that distance his fur gleamed and shone in the street lights.

'Sooty! Soo-ooty!' Minnie turned briefly to me before shooting across the garden to the paved area.

'Good gracious! Mercy! It's Minnie! What on earth are you doing so far from home? From the farm?' His purring engine was thudding at full speed and I felt like an interloper as they rubbed against each other, no doubt whispering private endearments.

I settled quietly on the grass at the edge of the perfectly manicured lawn. Then they sat down together, oblivious of me, the interested onlooker, and talked and talked with their eyes. I was not close enough to know what they said and began to wonder if I should creep away for a while but the cars and lorries were pounding past the gates and as there was no field to escape to; moving more than a few feet filled me with terror.

'Penny, come here! Meet Sooty, my long lost relative.' Her tone was warm and happy and even as I got up she turned back to her handsome black brother. Familiar glinting yellow pools turned in my direction and I shook myself carefully, wishing I had filled those minutes on my own by having a good wash and groom, only I hadn't thought of it.

'Hello,' he said amiably, then, 'Hel – lo!' as if catching me in the light for the first time.

'This is my friend, Penny,' Minnie said with affection. 'She was living at the farm as I told you and..'

'Well,' he drawled, licking his lips, 'I AM pleased to know you.'

I nodded uncomfortably and said, 'I am pleased to see you too,' but I felt uneasy, not really that pleased at all.

His gaze turned back to Minnie as he gave her his approval of me and then I was treated to the full volume of his feline charm.

'What a wonderful coat you have, Penny, and such unusual markings.'

His eyes held mine almost hypnotically as I twitched my tail and murmured, 'Thank you.'

I sat down again, carefully drawing my feet into my body and curling my tail around, razor wire fence style. He was Minnie's brother and I wanted no unpleasantness for her so I looked away. Had I continued to return his stare he would have received my message of 'not in the slightest bit interested', but he was probably not the sort to be put off easily. I had met his type of bloke in my human life - they usually regarded a rebuff as a challenge and continued even more forcefully with their pursuit. Minnie, thankfully, seemed blissfully unaware of the signals being put out by her brother or the way in which they were being rejected by me. As long as this dark-haired monster continued to lick his lips at me I would remain firmly keeping my distance.

'A right little darlin',' he tried again, dropping the I-am-a-semi-detatched-house-with-a-garage-cat pose and reverted back to type.

'I am very tired,' I managed to convey, hoping for at least a stay of sentence until I had decided how to handle such a delicate situation.

'She's always tired,' Minnie laughed. 'And she says I'm always hungry.'

Whether this was a direct hint that she had not eaten for about two hours I couldn't tell but fortunately salivating Sooty remembered that his role as a perfect host might add to his chances.

'Yes, I'm sorry,' he flashed his white teeth briefly, glancing in my direction to see if it might be worth one last try. 'You must be hungry, of course.'

Minnie nodded immediately.

'Come into the garage,' he said, leading the way through a small purpose-cut hole in the door. 'I usually eat in the kitchen, naturally, but well, for the last two nights it's been the garage for me. Sorry it's in such a mess and full of rubbish.'

He led the way and Minnie licked her lips expectantly. 'Is it breakfast?' she asked hopefully.

''Fraid not. Just my last night's leftovers. You see,' he added sheepishly, 'You have come at rather an awkward time.'

He looked despairingly around the building which was, indeed, crammed with junk.

'What do you mean?' his sister demanded, tucking into the dish of the remains of slightly congealed Felix. Than she added feelingly. 'I can see why you left this. It's not very fresh is it?'

'It's last night's,' Sooty answered cuttingly. 'It doesn't usually keep very well for more than a few hours.'

'It would be horrendous in the heat. Good job it's winter time otherwise it would be inedible,' she said munching into another mouthful. Why, I thought are they spending all this time on discussing the way cat food keeps or does not keep?

'Why have we arrived at a bad time?' I interrupted impatiently.

If it were relevant we should know about whatever it was as soon as possible. Sooty studied me for a few seconds then turned his gaze to Minnie (who was still tucking in, of course).

'Well,' he started. 'I don't quite know how to tell you this, but, well, we are moving. Mr and Mrs and me. We are going to another house. If only I'd known you were thinking of coming I could have warned you not to. I could have asked Robson – have you seen much of him lately, by the way – I could have asked him to let you know. We still keep in touch through a mutual friend who lives about half way between us.'

Minnie ignored the bit about Robson and was not really listening at all to what was being said, as she continued to eat ravenously. (Obviously Sooty had no inkling that he had been made an uncle, even though it had only been for such a short time.)

'Where are you moving to?' she asked automatically then, as the implications hit her, she stopped eating abruptly. 'Moving?' she repeated incredulously, 'What do you mean, moving? How can you move? We have only just got here!'

Sooty looked at me as if for support. 'It was decided months ago,' he said apologetically.

Just as he said the words there was a roar of a large diesel engine outside.

'Sounds like the van now.' He sounded almost relieved.

Minnie stared at him as if in a trance. 'You can't move!' she said stupidly. 'You just can't! We have come to live with you.'

The big cat seemed to crumple for a moment, sagging down into his coat and dropping his head so it almost brushed against the floor. 'Yes... Well, I know, I'm sorry,' he mumbled quietly, 'But there's nothing I can do about it.'

'What about us?' Minnie screamed at him. 'You can't just go off and leave us!'

# CHAPTER 17

If Minnie could have wept I know that she would have. Feeding forgotten, she gazed helplessly from me to Sooty, who was looking distinctly uncomfortable.

'Where are you going to?' I asked, not because there was any point in knowing but someone, somehow had to keep things going.

'Not far,' he said gratefully. 'Not far at all. About ten miles, in fact – I know because Mr and Mrs have talked of nothing else for weeks.'

'It may as well be a million miles,' Minnie said mournfully, her eyes glistening. 'It took us ages to get here from the farm and that was hardly any distance. You can't possibly be moving.'

Sooty edged around a pile of boxes and sat down on the side of an old mat. 'Look girls,' he cajoled, 'Come and join me and we'll talk about it. Penny?' he looked at me almost pleadingly. 'Let's try and decide what's the best thing to do.'

Minnie stood her ground and arched her back up as high as she could.

'I hate you and your Mr and Mrs!' and, surprisingly, she spat at him.

I shuffled over to the old piece of carpet to squat beside Sooty. It seemed the least I could do. We were surrounded by stacks of boxes crammed with other boxes, tools, electrical things, books and various bric a brac. Pieces of wire and electric cable seemed to stick out of each receptacle and things like walking sticks, umbrellas and garden tools leant drunkenly against every vertical surface. Decades of oil and paint spills decorated our mat, which was punctured with holes and torn in places. It was definitely not the sort of sitting place I would have chosen.

'Come?' he invited, sensing my hesitation and moving to make adequate space for the three of us.

I felt a bit sorry for him and scowled towards Minnie. 'All this isn't his fault,' I pointed out but my whiskers trembled as I selected a few square inches that were not covered with cobwebs, dust and rusty nails. For the next 15 minutes we thrashed about our problem, Minnie at last deigning to join us.

'There are three choices then.' I was obviously the most practical one and the siblings seemed to expect me to take charge. 'One is that we, Minnie and I, try to secret ourselves away in the van somewhere – hide, that is,' I amended, catching Sooty's quizzical look. 'With the furniture. And then hope that your 'Mr and Mrs' will take us in when we're discovered. The second option is that Minnie and I go back the way we came, to the farm.' As I paused, Minnie rolled her eyes and flicked her tail.

'The third possibility,' I lumbered on. 'Is that we try somehow, to cover the distance to the new house after you have gone. All 10 miles of it.' I added, feeling weary and exhausted at the mere thought of it.

'What a choice to have to make!' Sooty said with some feeling.

'S'all right for you,' Minnie snarled, 'You don't have to worry. Nice cosy cat box in the car, to a nice warm home. You've got it on a plate.'

She turned venomously to me. 'If it wasn't for you, I could go with him. If there was only one of us...'

More than a little taken aback, my claws gripped at the rug beneath us and my tail twitched ominously. 'I can easily go back to the farm.' I said testily. 'At least, Monty would be pleased to see me,'

Sooty frowned darkly. 'And who is Monty?' he asked suspiciously.

'A mouse,' I replied sweetly.

The big cat was naturally surprised but he didn't dwell on it. He shook his head decisively. 'No way. Penny's not going anywhere alone. She brought you all the way here, my lass.'

Minnie drew herself up and moved away from the crouching Sooty. 'I brought Penny here, don't you mean?' she spluttered. 'It was me who found us somewhere to sleep – I went up on the roof, and caught breakfast, and didn't get tired every few minutes. I am the hunter and the climber.' She finished holtly, as if aware, for the first time, of her brother's growing interest in me.

'Yes,' I sang out cattily. 'I can only hunt and kill Leader Rats!'

There was a short silence. Sooty looked at me with awe. Although he had been away from the farm yard a long time, he obviously remembered the Leader Rats.

'I'm impressed,' he signalled. 'Aren't you?' he stared directly at his sister.

There was a silence before Minnie nodded her head and said softly. 'Sorry. Didn't mean all that. It's just that I'm ever so upset and shocked. What on earth are we going to do?'

'Look,' Sooty stretched out more comfortably. 'Let me tell you about the new place. I know all about it 'cos I've been there, just for a weekend when they went measuring up. Then you can decide.'

'But the van is outside, we heard it.' I said urgently.

'Shush!' he whispered, almost sensuously, 'There's plenty of time. It will be there all day. Listen first, talk later.'

We listened. The new house, was, apparently, a much older building. It had more rooms than the modern brick built dwelling which we were sitting by and, the black cat told us with pride, several stone outbuildings.

'I could sleep there,' Minnie beamed, her mood brightening. 'I don't much fancy being in a proper house and sleeping in a poofy basket.' We did not remind her that she probably wouldn't be invited to anyway. 'I mean, WE could sleep there,' she amended, looking sideways at me.

Although I was tempted to mention my preference for a warm, comfortable bed, rather than roughing it on some dirty floor, I looked away quickly so the others would not catch my drift. Our future sleeping arrangements were the least of our worries.

At that moment the internal door into the house opened and a head covered in curlers appeared. This was Mrs, draped in a tent of quilted dark coloured dressing gown. She stared down at us.

138

"Heavens!" she exclaimed in quite a reasonable tone, I thought, seeing that she was suddenly confronted with what must look like a rug full of strange cats. "Having a farewell party then, Soots?" she asked genially, then. "Well, if you are, you'll need more foodies than that." Her eyes rested on Minnie and me for a moment as if she half expected us to scamper away. The fact that we stayed exactly where we were prompted her to dash back into the kitchen.

Sooty grinned. 'Told you,' he boasted. 'Really nice, my Mr and Mrs are.'

Billowing back into the cluttered garage, his hospitable owner scooped up the dirty food dish and put down a larger plate of a freshly opened sachet of meaty pieces in jelly. "Milk coming up!" she trilled, trotting off again.

Licking my lips I advanced towards the feast, suddenly remembering I had taken nothing since my last drink of milk in the cowshed back at the farm. Minnie was in like a flash and our host watched with unconcealed masculine amusement as I strove to forget manners and upbringing and compete efficiently with the little grey gannet who was attacking the offering with such gusto. After a few gobbling moments, whilst I transferred my attentions to the newly brought milk saucer, Minnie licked the food platter clean. 'What a hungry girl!' Sooty observed wryly. 'Did you get enough Penny? I can always ask for more. A quick yowl in the right tone should do it.'

'I'm fine,' I said hastily.

At least I had had some milk. Although thankful for his concern I was still fairly certain that his consideration was not strictly of the platonically friendly kind. Mrs had shut the communicating door very firmly behind her when she withdrew again to her kitchen, maybe fearing that our social gathering might permeate into the house. I washed myself laboriously, wishing there was some pleasure to be derived from the chore but I still found it slightly repulsive to have to do all that licking. Minnie, as usual, finished her after-meal ablutions and coiffure in double-quick time, shaking and preening her coat, whose condition belied the fact that she had recently crossed rough terrain, climbed trees and roofs and slept in a pig sty. In contrast, my fur seemed to be sticking out in unruly clumps, a fact that did little to deter Sooty's amorous advances.

'I'd love to have you with us,' he purred softly, rubbing against my front paws. I shifted my legs hastily.

'Well?' I looked at them both. 'What do we do?'

'Of your three choices, you mean?' he asked, allowing his thoughts to be led back to the business in hand.

Minnie sighed. 'I'm not going back,' she vowed, taking a last speedy lick around the empty dish.

'Well, you can't stay here. The family coming in has got two dogs. Ginormous they are! Came once to look over the garden – see if it's big enough for them. Frightened the daylights out of me.'

'Dogs!' Minnie shrilled. 'No, I certainly can't stay with two dogs. No way! I vote we hide in the van.'

Sooty nodded and finished off the few drops of milk which for some reason Minnie had left. 'Good choice. What say you Penny?'

Penny did not feel like saying anything that would bring her into permanent easy contact with the imposing black cat so I just purred a little (as one does in circumstances like these.)

Then we traipsed after Sooty to look at the evil mechanical monster that was manoeuvring in the front garden and which had dashed all our hopes. Vaguely, I remembered car transporters and draw-bar lorries; somewhere in my past there must have been removal vans and insatiable giant trucks ready to swallow up whole households of furniture. Nothing prepared me, though, for the real size of the 'Gladstones Great Removers' vehicle. Perhaps it was just that now I was obliged to spend my life so near to the ground, everything looked massive. We crept outside to watch the belching diesel monster reverse into the driveway. Even backed up right to the open garage door the nose of the cab overhung the pavement in front of the house. The men had to move it even further into the road so they could lower the wide slatted ramp, up which tables, chairs, beds and the collected junk of years of hoarding would travel.

'There will be plenty of places to get into to hide out of sight,' Sooty told us, thoroughly enjoying the excitement. 'I wish I was coming with you.'

I wish, I thought to myself, that we could change places and that I could sneak into the cat travel box. I could endure a few miles in the thing. Yes, I was sure I could.

"Do you want the piano first?" Mr cried, flinging open the front door as the men discussed their plan of action.

There must be something about the mention of the word Piano that freezes removal staff in their tracks. The three men stood rooted to the crazy pavement path.

"Piano?" one squeaked. "Piano?" As if he could not believe his ears.

"Didn't we tell you?" Mr bounded down the short flight of steps which led from the front door. "It's only a baby grand. Upstairs in the front bedroom. Got to go up in the attic in the house we're going to." He was a round, bald, jolly-looking man. From the look on the removal crew's faces at that moment I feared for his life.

The head of the gang thrust his hands purposefully into his overalls pocket. "Nothing was said about a, a GRAND PIANO, going from upstairs to upstairs." He was obviously trying to control his voice but it shook nevertheless.

"Only a baby grand," Mr answered him happily.

The three men stood in a picket line between their van and Mr. This was definitely going to be a battle, and for a few moments Minnie, Sooty and I sat quietly, unnoticed, at the side of the garage.

"Are the men here?" shouted Mrs, diving down the steps, tugging at her foam hair rollers. "Oh, what a big van!" The giant quilt swirled around her as she clenched up her toes to prevent the fluffy slippers from slipping. "What a big van," she repeated gazing up at it.

Her husband let out a deep belly laugh. "Nearly big enough for the Grand Piano!" he roared.

The three warriors before him stood firm, solid in their resolve to invoke the small print in their agreement, which clearly states that two weeks' notice must be given and special terms agreed before any transportation of pianos can be considered.

"But, we don't have a piano," the bewildered wife said, thrusting her curlers into her dressing gown pocket. "Of any sort. Grand or otherwise. A record player – yes," she added helpfully.

"Ho, Ho, Ho!" spluttered Mr, face screwed up with glee. "No piano? Silly me! Ha ha ha!".

Three men and three cats stared dumbfounded as he doubled himself over with raucous laughter. One billowing lady floated towards the immobile removal van, flouncing like an unruly eiderdown.

"Now Charles," she remonstrated. "What a wicked thing to do. Fancy upsetting these good, helpful people before they've even started. Shame!" She might have been scolding an errant child by her tone.

The head man looked sourly at his companions. "Let's get started boys," he said ignoring the convulsed figure at the bottom of the steps. "Carpet's all up, Love?" the chief addressed Mrs's dressing gown.

"They are staying," she said haughtily. "We are buying all new ones where we're going." She clearly felt she needed to emphasise this very important fact to the three impassive faces.

"Sooner we get started, sooner we'll finish," number one man said in his monotone.

"Well said, old son," Mr straightened himself. "Please excuse my little joke." He grinned at them.

"Always has to have his little joke," Mrs explained, patting the frizz of her now curler-less head. "Would you like me to tell you where to start?"

"Not necessary," one of the others spoke for the first time. "But we would like to take a look around the house."

"Good thinking," agreed Mr, standing back and waving them towards the front door with arms outstretched expansively.

"Will it all go in?" Mrs fluttered.

"Everyone asks that, M'am," the head man nodded reassuringly, "But it always, well almost always, does fit. Unless, of course, you have a surprise grand piano you forgot to mention when you booked the job." Mrs looked at her husband and roared with laughter. "Touche!" she guffawed. "I'll go and put some clothes on."

"Might be a good idea," agreed the third man as they trooped towards the house.

'Best keep out of sight,' Sooty said, leading us back down the side of the garage through into the rear garden. 'We can relax for a while,' he said knowingly. 'They will take a break at lunchtime and that will be the best time to hide away.'

'How d'you know all this?' Minnie asked, admiration in her look.

'Mr told Mrs. They load up in the morning, have a break then drive on to the new place, then unload. There's no one in where we're going so we can get there at any time but we've got to be out of here by 2 o'clock at the latest.'

'Why?' she probed.

Sooty shook his head. 'Dunno,' he said honestly.

'When do the people come with the dogs?' Minnie asked anxiously.

'Sometime after two I guess,' he replied with authority. 'When the completion's done, whatever that is.'

I smiled to myself. For all his macho egotism, our black friend was not exactly worldly wise.

The back garden was an average size – mainly lawn and flower boarders. A low hedged wall ran along the end boundary. We settled under a small tree which leaned heavily towards the wall. 'We bought this last year,' Sooty told us. It was still firmly tied up to a tall stake and looked as if it could do with a good dousing of water. Still, I supposed no- one really cared much about it now.

'What the 'ell is that?' Minnie jumped up wide eyed as a long yellow and black roof appeared to skim the top of the wall and hedge. Sooty tapped his teeth together in amusement.

'That, my child,' he informed her. 'Is a canal boat. 'Big boats' they call them.'

'Narrow boats,' I said automatically.

After narrowing his yellow eyes in my direction he went on, 'These boats go up and down the canal – it's just a bit further over on the other side of the wall - they're mainly holiday rental boats but some, I think, are still carrying stuff, you know, goods and things, like they used to in the old days.' He paused as if sensing I might interrupt with an amendment, then continued. 'Not so many this time of the year. Mainly summer things. But some people do have their own and use them all year round – mostly at weekends.'

I curled up and prepared for a nap. It must be all this fresh air, I told myself. Anyway the other two had a lot of catching up to do. My eyes closed gently as Minnie said with vigour. 'I'm glad we're not staying here. There's no way I'd live by this, er, canal.'

'Why?' Sooty stretched out, curling dangerously close to my back.

'She doesn't like water,' I said sleepily. 'Now if you will excuse me...'

'Not again! You've not been awake for more than an hour or so,' Minnie snapped impatiently.

'Leave her,' her brother said casting what I felt was a rather protective stare at me. 'Anyway,' he said crisply. 'Our new place is by the canal too. Has to be so that Mr can get on with his fishing all the time. It's good though,' he hurried on, seeing Minnie's uncertain frown and shivering of whiskers. 'Cos he often gives me the small fish he catches. Makes a nice change.'

As I dozed restlessly, continually aware of the thud and thump of the furniture being carried or dragged up the distant wooden ramp, my fluttering eyelids caught the gist of Sooty's conversation. The new place was straight up the canal footpath. He did not know accurately how far but Mr and Mrs's son (on holidays from his boarding school) had cycled from this house to it that weekend when they had done the measuring. Then sleep became impossible as I felt it prudent to know all the details so I forced myself to keep my eyes open.

'The place has a long garden and then a little orchard with fruit trees good for climbing, that leads down to the canal.' Sooty was enjoying being the centre of attention, the font of all knowledge. 'The outside buildings, where you say you'd like to live, are near the back of the main house, behind the garage, nowhere near the canal. So there's no need at all for you to go by the water if you don't want to.'

Minnie laid herself down and relaxed at this. Then she said, 'I don't want to even see the water,' and although I thought she was being a bit melodramatic, credit was due to Sooty who refrained from questioning his sister's obvious fear. He must have thought about it though because a few seconds later he said, almost to himself,

'Well, I don't like it either but I'm a jolly good swimmer if I have to be. I bet you could too, Minnie,' but she shrugged and turned the other way. I went to sleep.

# CHAPTER 18

'They're stopping working – they're going for their sandwiches,' Minnie was digging me in the spine with one her forepaws. She repeatedly signalled, 'Wake up, wake up!'.

'As it happened I was waking anyway,' I told her crossly, my eyes already starting to open. But I didn't like being prodded with a finely sharpened paw and I hissed a bit to let her know. I hoped she wasn't going to make a habit of always rousing me just as I was getting off to sleep.

Sooty was nowhere to be seen as I stretched then curled back up into a ball – a trick I'd learned early on which seemed to straighten out all my joints after I'd been asleep. He came bounding round the corner of the garage. 'They've not gone anywhere,' he reported, 'They're sitting in their cab with flasks and food boxes. You'll have to be really careful that they don't see you go in.'

'Are we really going in?' Minnie asked excitedly. I just wished I felt more optimistic about it all.

'Are all the things in? All the furniture?' I tried to appear calm although my heart was thumping.

'Yeah!' Sooty nodded his head and waggled his ears for good measure. 'Mr and Mrs are just inspecting it. Then they'll give the men the OK, put me in that wretched box and we'll drive on ahead to the other place. Then I'll see you both there.' He was definitely enthralled by the whole adventure and kept darting furtive glances in my direction. Uneasy was a mild way of describing my feelings, but there was no choice. Not for the first time did I question the sense in leaving the cosy warm Aga behind at the farm.

'I'm hungry,' Minnie broke my train of thought.

'Food's all packed,' Sooty replied promptly. 'And there's certainly not time to catch anything. You've got to get going and NOW!'

Minnie jumped up obediently; it was interesting to see such an independent little puss rush to do her brother's bidding. I followed them along the side of the house under cover of the shrubs. Creeping past the munching men, warmly enclosed behind their high panoramic windows, we stopped only as we got level with the end of the giant ramp. Sooty, bravely I considered, said he would investigate the situation and told us to wait, so we crouched down and followed him with our eyes, all the time making sure no one else was about. His minders had gone back inside the house, presumably doing their final checks in searching for possible forgotten treasures. Very gingerly Sooty crept up the ramp and soon disappeared into the bowels of the wagon. Mr came out twice into the garage, scrutinizing every inch to make sure everything had been taken.

"What's this bundle of bed linen? Don't you want to take it?" he shouted back into the house and we heard Mrs clatter down the front steps and puff into the garage. "Ho ho ho!" her demented spouse bellowed. "That got you going, old thing!"

After a brief hesitation – obviously whilst the questionable humour sunk in – Mrs let out a shrill giggle. "That's not really funny," she spluttered laughing with him more loudly than ever.

'What a strange couple,' I looked at Minnie.

'But they're ever so kind to Sooty,' she said contentedly.

My doubts began to multiply. The continual prowling of salacious Sooty, the constant demonstrations of Mr's warped sense of humour, the deranged sounds of mirth that ensued from the weird couple – life was not looking so rosy. Sooty's head cautiously appeared above us, then he shot back down the incline, anxious not to be seen by the duo who had left the empty garage and had gone back into the house again.

'Quick!' he directed, 'Up the ramp!'

We followed blindly, and I dug my claws into the wooden surface as we streaked upwards, so as not to slip or slide. We all leapt up on to some chairs just inside the entrance of the enormous truck.

'Well!' Sooty's breath quickened. 'You're in. Now, where to hide?'

'Not right at the back – it's dark and claustrophobic.' Was this really me saying that?

'I agree, and there's more chance of you not getting out in one piece if you're right at the back. They don't seem to be too fussy about the way they fling the stuff about,' Sooty was definitely back in command now. 'There's the old man's fishing box over here - up on the table. It's got some tatty cloths in and netting at the front and it's just big enough for you two. The material will stop you from rolling about when you get moving.' He had done his reconnoitre well. 'Anywhere else where you will be able to breath and look out, you'll probably be seen. You can lie low and see out through the bits of netting – they're all loose so when you want to get out at the other end just pull the stuff aside and choose your moment to jump down. Doesn't really matter too much if you are seen then – you'll already be there.'

It all sounded so plausible and we were digesting it when the quiet was broken by Mr and Mrs shouting to each other in the front garden. Then Mrs called loudly, "Sooty, come on Sooty. Time to go for ridies!"

'Jump in!' Sooty instructed impatiently.

We both jumped the short distance from the chairs to the fishing box, crept in through the open end and sunk down on the cloth inside. Pieces of netting did dangle haphazardly over the front, so that we could indeed see everything that was happening.

"Sooty! Soo-ooty!" screamed Mrs in a determined manner.

We heard two sharp bangs as the men jumped from the front of the van and slammed their doors. Sooty scampered down the ramp, his claws stumbling between the slats in his haste.

"There's a good boy, Sooty!" chattered Mrs. "He always comes when I call him, don't you pet?"

We could hear the men talking to Mr and Mrs. Yes, everything was in, nothing had been left.

"We'll just secure her," the commander said as if readying his ship for a long sea voyage.

I held my breath and flattened myself down against the box floor. Minnie scrunched herself up and stared through the flimsy material, her eyes stretched up almost to her ears in order not to miss anything. Neither of us had envisaged our adventure taking such a twist when we had set out from the farm.

"Co-ey! Coo-eey! Are you there Mabel?" A new voice screeched above the hum of the traffic.

"Oh, it's Jean! Jean and John!" squealed Mrs, in fortissimo delight.

"We've come to see you off. We've come to wave you goodbye!"

"How kind – how sweet of you!" gabbled Mrs.

"Very good of you both," Mr joined in good naturedly enough, even though he sensed this farewell might cause more than a temporary delay. The other man, John, never said a word.

"They're just shutting the lorry door," Mrs informed the newcomers shrilly. "Everything's in!"

"Don't close it, don't!" shouted the female well-wisher. "I must just see how it's all fitted in. I've never been inside a removal van before." She somehow made it sound like an experience that no-one should miss. (Oh heck, I thought, they will be selling tickets next. Thank heavens we can see everything that's going on but they can't see us at all.)

"My - you certainly have got a big one!" she acknowledged to the head man, who suddenly felt an embarrassing need to study his shoes intently.

"We are just about ready to go," the remover warned, lifting his face but avoiding looking at his companions.

"Just a quickie! Just a second!" Before anyone could restrain her, the visiting Jean clattered up the ramp. "Oh, how exciting!" she shouted back over her shoulder as her skinny frame came into our view. "Oh, it's very spacious in here," she twittered, stepping off the loading slope and crunching one of her dainty tapering heels into the minute space between ramp and vehicle floor. "Oh my Gawd!" she grunted, wriggling her foot frantically, trying to free the shoe.

Below, the others went on talking.

"I think your, er, friend is in trouble," one of the men said, anxious to get the show on the road.

"My heel's stuck and it's a Jimmy Choo model!" she called insistently, loudly.

"Copy," growled her hitherto mute husband, just loud enough for us all to hear.

"Come and help me!" she screamed, and obediently, the removal men, the husbands and Mrs, stomped towards us, with Sooty following at a respectful distance behind. The whimpering, gesticulating woman then made her first sensible move by extracting her bony foot from the offending shoe. As everyone was offering advice as to the best method of freeing the thing, Mrs swooped on Sooty, gathering him up.

"No, no!" she admonished, "We don't want you getting lost in there, do we?" She shunted back down on to terra firma, firmly clutching her cat beneath her arm. She expertly popped him into the waiting cat box – a startling turquoise contraption on to which had been stuck a selection of silver and gold paper stars.

'Minnie, Penny – keep your heads down!' he screamed, yowling loudly to reinforce any eye movements he might have been flashing.

But no-one took any notice except Mrs who reprimanded, "Naughty Sooty!" misinterpreting his protest. "It's not too far. We'll be there in no time."

The ensemble at the head of the wide gang-plank was watching the woman, twisting and pulling at the shoe.

"I'll have to hop or I'll get splinters from this dirty old lorry," Jean, the one-bare-foot shouted to her audience.

"This is not a dirty lorry, Madam!" the foreman spoke up firmly. "It is cleaned thoroughly before every job."

"Well I am glad about that," she said menacingly. "And I hope there are no splinters. I do not want to have to sue for foot amputation or similar."

"Madam," the man replied with honeyed sincerity, "Our vans are not maintained in such a manner as to accommodate ladies who insist upon jumping all over them barefoot. Their main purpose is the transportation of goods and chattels."

"How dare you speak to me in that tone!" she rasped. "Tell him, John. Tell him how much my shoes cost!"

The fairly long silence, which met her imperious demand, was broken by husband John saying, "Cheaper than a foot amputation I should think."

Mr jumped up and down at the hilarity of this. "Let's just cut the thing off!" he spluttered. As Jean screamed, and lent heavily on the table that our box rested on, Mr chuckled and corrected himself. "I mean, cut off the shoe heel – not her foot!" he gurgled, but no-one took any notice of him. As our box hiding place wobbled on its table the shoe was momentarily forgotten when Minnie's wide yellow eyes were caught in the afternoon sunlight.

"Something is moving in there," one of the men said slowly.

Jean hopped on the spot. How dare something extraneous detract from her very own most serious crisis? "Nonsense! Now, what about my shoe?"

"It's an animal," said the most junior man slowly, addressing his colleagues. "I don't remember loading an animal. None of us would load an animal. It's against the rules."

"What animal?" Mr stopped his sniggering and gazed to where the man was staring - towards our fluttering camouflage.

"Are you conveying live animals in our truck?" the leader interrupted, staring cuttingly towards the round, bald, jokester. His tone indicated the possibility that an extremely serious crime may have been committed.

"No animals. This is nonsense, Sooty is in his box. Is Sooty firmly secured in his box, Mother?" Mr shouted, switching to his sensible, I-am-head-of-the-household self. He peered around the end of the lorry at Mrs whose large feet were planted firmly each side of the hideous cat container.

"Sooty's here!" she squawked, leaning forward anxiously. "Why? What is happening?"

On hearing his name Sooty let out an agonizing yell – presumably trying to distract the assembled company from discovering our predicament. On hearing Sooty's cry, Minnie retaliated by catawalling. As she couldn't see Sooty to converse with him a 'wall was the only way to inform him of our imminent danger. Our imminent danger swiftly turned into the termination of our proposed journey. Number One man lent authoritatively towards us and I flattened myself down on to the rags, hardly daring to breathe. Minnie sat up straight, blinking her eyes and staring out through the netting. 'Sooty will sort this out,' she told me confidently.

'Sooty is imprisoned in his carrier,' I replied coldly. 'You obviously have never been in one of the damned things otherwise you would know there is no escape.'

"Two little cats," John the mute observed, as he bent over and peered in at us.

"Never mind them. What about my shoe?" his wife snapped.

We all watched as the leader of the gang cleared his throat, preparatory to taking charge. "They must have stowed away," he said. "Come on cats!" He lifted the net and put his hand gently behind our backs. "There! Jump down from the table and trot off home down the ramp," he said in quite a forgiving voice.

Almost paralysed with fear I automatically obeyed, relieved to see that Minnie, albeit it half heartedly, followed me. I did fleetingly, pray that she would not relapse into one of her more farmyard ways of spitting, scratching and even taking a lump out of someone's neck or hand. But, I think she was too frightened to even think of it. One of the men busied himself straightening the fishing box, pushing it well back on the table, probably in case we might have ideas of sneaking back there. Minnie and I stood awkwardly at the bottom of the ramp.

'Try and get back up,' Sooty's look hissed from behind his cage door. I knew it was not even worth a try as the group at the top had all eyes fixed on us, even the one-footed Jean seemed momentarily interested to know what we were going to do next. Well Minnie gave them their money's worth. She streaked back up into the van letting out a piercing wail as she went.

"Get that cat!" bellowed Mr. "God knows where it's come from – where they have come from, rather." He turned to stare accusingly at me as I slithered into the hedge. "They are certainly not ours!"

Six pairs of hands competed for a successful grab but Minnie shot between table legs, over stools, by boxes and through spaces that even a mouse might have found challenging. Everyone tried to find Minnie. Furniture was moved clumsily from the exacting positions that the man had allocated it to, boxes were upturned, spilling contents on to the floor.

Although mesmerised by the pandemonium, I knew we needed help so I skirted the front garden and circled until I was in close range of Sooty again but away from the onlookers. By this time, thankfully, Mrs had galloped up to join the cabaret on the upper deck, leaving the way clear for us to talk.

'Shall I go up and help her get back out?' was all I think of suggesting. Although how could this be done? Anyway, why was I asking this common lecherous farm cat for guidance? He spat at me contemptuously (my turning away to have private thoughts had clearly not been soon enough.)

'Get up there with her,' he hissed. 'Sneak in and you'll get your free ride.'

'But they're taking the van apart,' I told him, 'Look at the way they are hurling things about to get at poor Minnie.'

Sooty snorted. 'Poor Minnie is a bloody sight more capable of taking care of herself than you are, my fine lass Penny. Just get in there and hide – that was the, my, plan anyway.' He fluffed his coat out and tried to stretch himself up to look as big as possible but it was difficult to look important when one's head is banging against the top of a cat carrier. I eyed him disdainfully.

'They will get her out,' I said softly.

'Not a chance!' he shook his head, then extended the shake to the rest of his body, not an easy movement in such a confined enclosure.

'The men will sort it, time is money,' he said logically. Almost as I digested this and prepared (against my will, naturally) to follow his instructions to re-enter the vehicle, the head man spoke up.

"Ladies and Gentlemen!" He might well have been acting as toastmaster at some gentile function. "Please!" Everyone stopped chattering and stood still. "If we empty the van to find the cat, the delay will cost you, Sir and Madam, dearly, as we shall undoubtedly be in overtime before we get finished at the other end – if, in fact, we can finish the job today before the light fails. Overtime is double time," he added pleasantly.

There was a silence as they all looked at Mr who immediately retorted, "Well, hey, we can always find the little rascal when we get there. We don't have to waste any more time looking now."

Mrs shuffled over to him. "But the poor pussy must belong to someone – we will be taking it miles from its home. It'll be lonely in a strange place." As she whined at her husband she darted an apprehensive glance into the gloom of the stacked furniture. Then, as if suddenly realising the possible extra expense that might be incurred, she went on. "I know – we'll come back and put an ad. in the post office here. Mrs Collins is sure to know if any cats have gone missing. She and her post office know everything that happens around here. Yes, it's not too bad. We can take care of the little soul until someone claims her. I've never seen it around here before, have you?" As she shook her head she looked questioningly at the others.

One-legged Jean said spitefully, "It's a stray. Yowling like that. Not a local cat, I'm sure. Alley cat if you ask me."

Sooty shot me a thunderous look. 'That's my sister you are talking about!' his bright yellow eyes screamed, and he screeched loudly for good measure. But no-one even looked in his direction.

"Right!" said man Number One. "All off the van please! I'll go into the cab and raise the back which should release your valuable shoe - Madam," his tone suggested just a hint of sarcasm. "Then I will rescue it and return it to you. Now, please, all down into the garden. My assistants and I will restore the contents to rightful places for safe transportation. It

154

should not take too long," he finished, glancing meaningfully at Mr to let him know that some double time might still be inevitable.

Everyone clomped down the ramp and stood watching as the men leisurely re-arranged the furniture.

'Get up there!' Sooty hissed at me and an instinct of self preservation propelled me on to the slope. A tabby or tortoiseshell, a black or grey may have had a chance of slinking up unnoticed but, no surprise, every, but everybody watched spellbound as I, the ginger no-tom, attempted to ease my way over the threshold.

"There's the other one!" shrieked hopping Jean.

"Two little cats," mused her husband again, scratching his head.

'Where are you Minnie?' my eyes asked into the gloom. I let out a loud meow, which came out as a shriek, just to let her know I was coming, but there was no answer.

Unaccustomed as I was to leaping and sprinting and generally avoiding danger, my legs just stood there as my eyes searched into the darkness of Mr and Mrs's furnishings.

'Minnie!' I yelled in my loudest verbose language but my cries only served to strengthen the resolve of my would-be capturers who once more converged on the vehicle. Knees were bent and hands grovelled along the flooring as the human contingent entered fully into the spirit of the hunt. I was the fox, they were the hounds and although I performed what can only be described as a mighty leap upwards – my intended destination being the top of an inelegant MFI self-assembly wardrobe – a sweating human hand grabbed at and caught, my left hind leg. I screamed, more with the indignity of it than with pain.

"Don't hurt the mite," cautioned Mr, for once not rolling about with mirth. "Quick! Get it back down on the ground and shut the van up!" Obviously a true cat lover to consider my safety, I thought. Or maybe he was counting up the minutes of possible overtime.

The removal man who was clasping my leg moved his hand deftly and grasped the scruff of my neck (from which grip, as all cat people know, there is no getting away). I was thus un-majestically removed from the removal van. The MFI wardrobe looked down at me with disgust. Standing in the middle of the driveway, the centre of attention, I consoled myself with the sure knowledge that if my take-off had been executed a few seconds earlier, my elevation to somewhere near the top of the van would have been assured. As it was, Minnie was hidden away safely, Sooty was secure in cat box and I was frantically washing myself all over, which is something that cats do when they feel deeply embarrassed.

The group was recovering from the excitement and gradually feet returned to the ground again. From somewhere inside the vehicle the head man operated the device which closed the back, whilst another member of the crew, who had remained at the top, extricated the rebel shoe. The ramp was lowered again and the man strode down waving his trophy.

"Your shoe, Madam," he said graciously, holding it out to one-shoe Jean. "It looks intact to me."

She snatched it, ungraciously, from him. "It certainly is not in tact!" She examined it as the others watched with mild interest. "Look at the heel. Some of the ly-lick has rubbed off. There's a bald patch where the ly-lick should be!" She brandished the shoe so that everyone could verify this.

"Let the men get on," her dour spouse intoned, openly bored to the teeth and wanting to get along home.

"Look!" she waved the chipped stiletto under her husband's nose. "Compensation, that's what I want!" she turned on the head man venomously.

"Write in to the company. The boss will sort it out," he said soothingly. Obviously he had been there, heard it all before.

"Compensation!" she repeated, savouring the word as she continued to study her shoe.

"Look, Jean," her patient husband said, "I will touch it up for you with some of my mauve boat paint."

"It's not MAUVE!" she shrieked, "It's LY-LICK! It's got to be done properly in Ly-lick. I certainly won't let you touch anything up of mine!"

156

And everyone nodded, firmly believing her.

Then the congregation stood in some reverence, facing the ramp as the soft drone indicated its final raising.

'What shall I do?' I turned to Sooty as the group was breaking up. The men were moving towards their cab and the neighbours were taking their leave of each other.

'You'll have to walk up the canal to us,' he said without hesitation. 'Not the way you came – don't go back under the bridge – go the other way. Just follow the towpath. It's not all that far.'

'Ten miles?' I whispered.

'Not necessarily,' he said comfortingly, 'That's only approximately.'

'But which is your house? How will I know when or if I ever get there?'

He shuffled about in his plastic cage. 'It's got a metal gate from the garden opening out on to the grass by the water. There's barbed wire along the top,' he explained carefully.

'There might be hundreds like that between here and there,' I spluttered. 'Is there any other way I can recognise it?'

He had a good scratch, then spun back to face me. Mrs was just swooping to gather up his carry handle. 'Just past the lock,' he muttered, 'You know what a lock is do you?' he was not being facetious I realised, just making sure, in the short time we had for this last minute conversation.

'I know what a lock is,' I retorted remembering, distantly, humanly, the enormous locks on the Thames.'

'Well, before you start, there's some food outside the back door – they've left it out there – their leftovers. Well, when you get to the new place there's a little wooden bench seat just by the lock, just before you get to our new house. Penny, you will come won't you? Penny....'

The turquoise plastic transporter swung into the air as Mrs hurried towards the car. Mr was encouraging his guests to leave.

"Don't want to incur too much overtime!" he joked, flashing a dark glance at the injured shoe. "We will be in touch!" He climbed into the car, which had been parked outside the front door, as the huge removal van edged its way tentatively out into the main road. Jean and John slowly retreated (well Jean hopped, leaning heavily on her husband's arm) past the front hedge to whichever near house they occupied. Mr carefully turned his car, just causing the front wheels to go over a tiny strip of his immaculate lawn, in order to drive out forwards. There was a cloud of dust and diesel fumes as the lorry pulled out into the traffic. Mr revved his car for a farewell Vroom out of his drive. I crawled out from my hastily sought refuge under the lavender bush and sat in the empty driveway between the gates.

Never, in either of my lives had I felt so alone. I shut my eyes tightly and prayed that Tina might appear from nowhere and scoop me up as she used to do. I wanted to be in her arms, cuddled and secure, loved and wanted. But no, when I opened my eyes I was still sitting alone in front of an empty house, the noisy traffic hurtling by the gate and the dark forbidding canal just a few yards behind me. When, I wondered, would the new owners be coming? With their dogs?

# CHAPTER 19

It didn't take me long to fully explore both the front and back gardens. At the rear of the building most of the space was taken up by a paved patio with three steps leading on to a small but perfect lawn. Around the edges there was a border, carefully planted with pansies and other winter flowers which I did not recognise. Having nothing better to do I studied the area at some length. Each sturdy little plant seemed to be precisely the same distance from its neighbours and each ran in a carefully planned colour pattern. Although I couldn't tell the exact hues, each group consisted of a dark one, a medium toned one and a light speckled one. I wondered whether this had been the meticulous labour of Mr or Mrs.

The shed at the end of the lawn was firmly shut and there appeared to be no loose panels that might have afforded entrance to this possible night shelter so I wandered back to the terrace. Outside what must have been the back door, stood a tall green plastic wheelie bin, its bulging contents preventing the lid from being closed down. All around the bin, boxes lent against the wall. These seemed to be full of books and other bits and pieces, each carefully covered with used supermarket plastic bags. Against the wall by the door a black bin liner held more undisclosed rubbish. Much more interesting, though, just past this, was a cardboard box lid on to which had been emptied various small biscuits, cut slices of toast, pieces of cake and some dry corn flakes. At one end of the lid-tray a cracked plate offered some baked beans, something strange-looking, that turned out to be scrambled egg, pieces of cooked tomato and bits of bacon. To my unmeowable delight, this tantalising spread was topped with a good handful or so of my very own favourite breakfast biscuits. Sooty certainly had fallen on his feet when he adopted his minders – they seemed exceedingly considerate people. When he told me they had put left-overs outside for any stray animals I really had expected to find just garbage. This was manna beyond my wildest dreams! Because I was afraid the new people might arrive at any minute, and because I was very, very hungry, my whiskers and paws didn't get so much as a quick lick before I started on my first course. About half way through gorging, the realisation hit me that this might be my last proper meal for some time. I toyed with the idea of moving some of the food and depositing it behind the shed for a future feed, but no plan of how to do this formulated itself and by the time I'd finished thinking about it there was only some congealed balls of egg and some very hard toast left.

Although I was extremely full and feeling very tired I set about giving myself what turned out to be a virtual bath – after all it was some time since I paid due attention to my appearance. I clearly remembered my human mother saying, "Cleanliness is next to Godliness. Never let your standards fall......" What did she call me? I sat up straight, very still, beside the bulging black sack. My tail twitched involuntarily and my whiskers wiggled. What had been my name? How could I so clearly hear my mother's voice from way back in my childhood, yet forget the name, my name, which she used at the end of her admonishment? My name is Penny the cat, I thought with a shudder. That is what I am.

Feeding and ablutions completed, the cloud of loneliness swam over me again. The wintry sun was sinking fast and a chill wind ruffled my fur up the wrong way. I turned into the breeze and tried to force myself to concentrate on what to do next. But my coat was becoming even more tangled and the gusts were swirling, piercing down into my ears and causing my whiskers to droop. It was a mini-typhoon, I decided helplessly when, as if to punctuate my thoughts, with a low howl the strong breeze suddenly carried the discarded dry toast across the patio until the pieces raced each other to bump, bump down the steps before finally catching and resting in the lawn. The unappetizing lumps of scrambled egg bounced over my fore paws and one of the plastic bags from the boxes swooped up into the air with the TESCO logo fluttering out like an aeroplane-towed advertisement in the sky. Low cloud was making the garden dark and I decided it was possible that the new owners of the house may not be coming that day after all. It would be too dark to unload the furniture vehicle. The next day maybe? Or when? Sooty had not known this crucial fact. It may even be another week, I told myself philosophically. As I huddled against the kitchen door, pictures of Sooty and Minnie arriving at their new home floated tantalizingly past my eye whiskers. What was going to happen to me? The cold was seeping into my bones and I felt so very tired. Then I remembered the little hole cut into the garage door for Sooty's convenience.

I ran around the side of the garage and as the first spots of rain slashed into my face, the small horseshoe entry beckoned in welcome. Inside, all the boxes, containers and other paraphernalia had gone but the dilapidated mat that I had scorned just a few hours earlier suddenly seemed like a comfortable cosy bed. Should a lorry or car with people (and dogs) arrive, then I would be ideally placed to hear it and have ample warning to evacuate. I curled up and was asleep immediately.

A rather small thin kitten poked its head through the gap in the door sometime during the night. The slight scuffle alerted me immediately. I feathered my eyelids so that I could see perfectly clearly, whilst appearing to be fast asleep.

The interloper called. 'Me! Me!' tentatively and just stood inside the hole waiting hopefully. Without hesitation I gave my particularly poisonous hiss (I do not take kindly to being aroused or in any way disturbed during my hours of slumber.) The scraggy thing belted away instantly and I could only assume it was one of Sooty's female admirers. Keeping one eye alert for a few moments I allowed the other to close firmly, feeling once again heavy and relaxed. Then I went back to sleep.

Rain was thundering against the metal up and over door when I finally surfaced, just as it was getting light, and there was an unpleasant stream of rainwater working its way towards my magic carpet. In an hour or so, if the rain kept up, the whole place would be sopping wet and flooded. Feeling vaguely hungry I wandered around the dry parts of the garage floor. No hidden feasts were discovered. An urgent call of nature demanded swift exit from my overnight hostelry and I stepped delicately towards the doorway. Although I managed a quite credible leap, my rear paws just dangled in the gathering stream. Standing outside, close to the house wall, and partly under cover of the overhang roof eves, I shook my back feet violently. To be obliged to have mandatory foot-wash at any time is an enigma for an animal but for a cat, so soon after awakening, it is inconceivable. Fortunately the monsoon had stopped and as I stepped out of my bedroom the wind seemed to have run out of steam. As I was dancing about, mentally bemoaning my misfortunes, my eye rested upon a small compact parcel of something, just laying inches from the garage door. Although having been carefully placed close to the side of the building, the furry surprise looked a little bedraggled where the water had ingressed. The deceased mouse's head and body were still in place but the discreet tell-tale teeth marks by its ears and one torn leg indicated the vermin had put up more than a token struggle. Brief investigation revealed that it was cold, though still fairly pliable – probable time of demise, a few hours earlier. But why? Why had some charitable benefactor thoughtfully delivered breakfast to my door? Smiling, realisation hit me. My poor thin and half-starved night visitor had caught and brought this nourishing gift for her black-haired beau. Sooty really was the cat's whiskers! I studied the still little creature for a moment or two; the colour of its fur reminded me fondly of my friend Monty the mouse. Its peaceful pointed face brought back happy memories. Then I ate it.

Just as I had finished relieving paws and whiskers of those infuriating little clingy bits that insist upon remaining to remind one of a hearty meal eaten too hastily, I heard it. It was the now familiar sound of a belching, spluttering diesel engine that can only spell disaster to a lone puss cat hoping to have spent a quiet day in a pleasant empty garage. And a car too, judging by the hooting of a rather shrill horn. Jumping away from the garage door I panicked and ran to the nearest cover – the lavender bush. Not a good choice as the plant shook off all its collected rainwater on to my coat as I squirmed amongst its dripping leaves. I contemplated making a dash for a more suitable hide but there was no time. Doors slammed and voices shouted to one another as my ginger head coyly protruded, being the unlikely centrefold of this soggy, drooping shrub. I spread my body against the damp earth but whatever I did with my head, it just stuck up like a very unusual specimen of flora. On the one hand this was useful as I could observe all that was going one but it didn't please me to know that I must have looked quite ridiculous. As the stalks stuck into my chest and the wet permeated my fur I attempted to remain calm and still.

Then the dogs barked. "Woof, Woofie, Woof!" and "Yelp, Snap, Grrh, Woof Woof!" Yes they were both there all right. Nice friendly creatures they certainly did not sound. A matter of seconds and they would discover that the picturesque antique-coloured giant sprig of lavender (with whiskers) was indeed one of their favourite play things. Drumming up all my courage I sprang out of my hiding place and sprinted back along the side of the garage towards the back garden. Desperate for some immediate safe haven I shot behind the shed, hoping the canines would not be able to squeeze through the slot I'd used. Cowering almost flat and completely out of sight, hardly daring to breathe lest this should give me away, I lay there uncomfortably for what seemed like hours. I needn't have bothered. The dogs must have been caught and tethered in the front area as they didn't even enter the back garden.

From where I had imprisoned myself I couldn't see or hear anything that was going on but I laid low, just in case. After about 15 minutes I braced myself and crept across the garden towards the back of the garage, keeping close to the side hedge in case I should need to dive away urgently. Nothing. No sound except the men of the van making unloading noises. Keepers and dogs were ostensibly absent from the front line. Walking around the inside of the house, no doubt, monitoring where every article was to reside after its entry through the front door. I cast a brief eye over the patio area by the back door just in case any surplus food from the night before should have escaped the storm. Not even a crust remained. It occurred to me then that maybe the dogs had been driven away in their car as there were none of the usual unpleasant sounds one had come to associate with these thoroughly unnecessary creatures. What are their uses after all? - working sheep-dogs or guide dogs excepted. They just make one hell of a mess, a lot of noise, moult or shake themselves everywhere and do a lot of yapping and prancing about like imbeciles. Suddenly, I shook my furry head in disgust. Was I really thinking this? As a child, as a girl even, I had always loved dogs. What was happening to me? But I knew. I was turning into a true feline.

Then I saw them. White with pointed ears and shifty darting pink eyes. Fortunately they were both on firm leads although they seemed to be constantly struggling to pull over their handler. The man was a tall thin elderly chap, slightly bent over at the shoulders. I momentarily feared for the safety of his balance as the two terrible terriers strained and pulled in opposite directions, as if this were part of a plot to overthrow their owner. Then their snorts and panting turned to a joint strangled yelp as they caught sight of me. Now pulling together they dragged and tugged at the poor old man until all three were hurtling in my direction. Never have I run so fast. Streaking behind the shed again, I frantically clawed at the roots of the prickly hedge to try to find a way through. Squeezing between the thorns and berries, the dark shiny leaves miraculously parted just enough to let me through. I glanced quickly over my shoulder to reassure myself there wasn't a break or hole in the hedging large enough to allow my pursuers to follow. But no, the brambly twigs were dense and closely knit along the full run of the boundary, in fact the thoroughly unpleasant hedge extended to either side of the garden. Then I remembered the dogs were on leads anyway with, I hoped, their elderly man still holding on to the ends.

I ran away from the house, over the grass towards the canal. There was quite a wide strip of undergrowth and weeds behind the plot, amply separating it from the towpath, but my progress was hampered by various obstacles, such as tree stumps and piles of refuse that had been dumped there. When I reached the path I sat down to gain my breath. The din of the white dogs barking and snarling faded as they were presumably led away back around to the front of the house or perhaps locked up in my garage. My heart was pumping too fast and I slowed my breathing and lay down for a moment or two behind a small clump of thistles which would hide me from anyone passing. There wasn't a soul about though and no movement whatsoever on the waterway. The only sounds of civilisation were traffic noises from the distant road and the occasional vehicle or bicycle which turned and crossed the bridge into the side lane.

Although the rain had stopped, the day was damp and dismal so I thought that after all the excitement I deserved just a short nap. Taking care to make myself as compact and unobtrusive as possible, I curled up and wound my tail around my extremities. I had a little trouble in getting comfortable on the moist ground and some startling noises escaped from me during my manoeuvres, due, no doubt, to the doubtful quality of my freebie mouse breakfast. But it only took about five minutes before I was once again in the land of nod (and, yes, cats do dream, quite vividly – my favourite seems to be - me as a human but having four legs and a tail and driving the most enormous red sports car. This does seem to be a recurring phenomenon. But it's quite interesting so I don't mind it.) Once again I was asleep.

Thud! Bang! Thud! Bang! Someone was beating a giant kettle drum by the side of my head, just about where my ears should have been. On and on relentlessly until I was quite wide awake. Jumping up I craned my neck forwards so that the world outside my clump of thistles swam into view. My normally alert eyes seemed to be refusing to focus as I searched about for the source of the noise. (I obviously hadn't enjoyed the amount of sleep which was essential to maintain the bright-eyed, bushy-tailed look, and was consequently doubly angry with whoever was making the dreadful racket.) No-one or thing was to be seen. A pathetic wedge of watery sun filtered between ominous looking clouds and as the thud thud sound became almost deafening I sunk down again behind my weeds. Then I saw, as well as heard, the culprit. The long steel boat was painted a bright shinning colour, probably red I guessed. And, I think, a dark green or brown maybe. It had a sort of sparkly (gold or yellowy?) lettering and figures on a side panel – I supposed this was its name or maybe the name of the owners. At the front (was it called the bow?) there was a huge V metal rail following the contours of the craft and protruding out over the murky water. There was a wide ledge around the inside of the bow which provided a small seating area. (This was being occupied by a large lady wearing dungarees, a sun vest topped by a fringed shawl and a tattered knobbly straw hat. She had draped herself expansively about the area, half laying and half sitting.) I sat entranced as the vessel moved across my line of vision; both of my eyes were now working perfectly normally. After the panel of writing, a quite large, partially opened window chugged past, showing a galley with kettle, crockery and other cooking implements neatly stacked on a surface. Then a sitting room area, with table and seating benches. In spite of my fear of the hideous diesel drumming, I wriggled forwards, uncaring of my vulnerability, because I was so interested in what floated by. Windows revealing bunks with cosy bedding carelessly crumpled, drifted away and, at the far end of the boat, a longer narrow window of frosted glass which I assumed must be a shower or bathroom. The roof was decorated with two long flower boxes which, even at that time of the year, housed voluptuous healthy flowers waving royally in the breeze. At one end of the roof a bicycle was firmly chained between the rails that ran along the sides. In the middle, near the short chimney stack, a pile of cut logs had been neatly piled so that normal slow movement would not displace them. The stern was rounded with another robust metal rail providing security for the helmsman or anyone else who cared to stand out there in the dismal weather. I watched as the man swung the metal tiller from side to side with nonchalance, as he sat on a stool puffing away at a curved pipe.

For all its racket the boat moved slowly and smoothly down the very centre of the water, well away from weeds and uneven grounds at the edge. As the sound faded in the distance, there was something almost tranquil about the floating home of the floppy woman in her sun vest and straw hat and her partner who was dressed for the elements in a shiny sou'wester beneath which protruded a bulky sweater. The canal was so much narrower that the ones I vaguely remembered from my past and in spite of the darkness of the muddy still water I no longer felt afraid. The passing boat had looked so cheerful with its colourful graphics and pretty window lights, almost like a small home afloat. As it disappeared into the gloom of the afternoon I suddenly wished I were there with those strangers instead of hovering uncomfortably on my damp patch of grass and mud.

Then, as I realised that Sooty and Minnie had now been at their new home for almost a whole day, it dawned on me that in almost 24 hours I had made absolutely no progress in my intended journey to meet them. All those miles to be covered and all that had been accomplished was sleep, feeding, hiding from dogs and yet more sleep. Pulling myself up to a standing position I stretched longways, bringing my nose forwards and aligning my tail to stick out way behind me. When I relaxed forwards again this showed that at least I had travelled a few inches along the track. Then I wondered about finishing off my nap. But there were still a few hours of light left in the day, though, and it wasn't raining so, I told myself, there was positively no excuse for not setting off, right that minute. I strode purposefully in the direction that Sooty had told me to take – the same way as the boat had gone, walking quickly and trying to avoid the puddles and the muddy ridges. My legs soon became covered with splatters and my tummy was wet and sticky where it brushed against the tall grass. As I trotted along (half hoping to catch up with the boat people) the sounds of the traffic on the road ceased and in the miserable silence I again felt so alone.

# CHAPTER 20

I squelched wretchedly on along the canal towpath, through pools of smelly water, across furrows of oozing mud and over high waving wild vegetation and grasses which were wringing wet and lethally prickly. Thorns stuck into the soft pads of my feet and crazy insects kept trying to blind me by flying straight into my eyes. My (always scrupulously clean) ears filled with bits of undergrowth and my nostrils were blocked by weed spores and loose floating debris. I was not a happy pusscat. I was dead tired and it became a momentous effort to work my feet along the uneven stony pathway but as the sky still showed some lightness I felt compelled to go on. If I went faster there might be a chance of catching up with the friendly chugging boat but even though I ran for a while there was still no sign of it in front of me. Cats (or anyone else without a wristwatch) find it difficult to determine the accurate time but it seemed I had been lolloping along for hours. There was no sun to help ascertain whether it was mid or late afternoon and although a church clock did strike nearby, I had missed some of the chimes before realising its significance. Anyway, could I even still count accurately? I checked my feet. Four. Tail? Yes one. So far so good. How many stupid birds sitting on that fence, just waiting for me to run and pounce? I never did find out as at that very moment they all took off, circling up in the dusky sky. Not so stupid, I admitted, but was rather annoyed as any one of them would have made a decent snack.

To cheer myself up I decided to search for a reasonable place to rest and perhaps stay for the night; surely darkness could not be that far away. Then, pangs of hunger tweaked at my belly. Although I hated the thought of water generally, there was something almost familiar about this narrow inland waterway and I hesitated to turn off my route and walk away across the fields to goodness knows where in order to find something to eat. Just around the next bend, I told myself, there was bound to be something. And there was – a small house, nestling against the trees, all on its own. As I came alongside the fence my eyes narrowed to give me better vision. Yes, what I could make out, even at that distance, was the welcome sight of pieces of bread and, joy or joys, what looked like lumps of fruit cake, put out on the lawn for (presumably) the birds. Squeezing through the palings with a delicate cry of warning (which roughly translates, 'I am a huge hungry cat'), what winged creatures there may have been waiting hopefully in the branches, were soon on their way. The snack was mine to devour as I thought fit. (I thought fit to swallow it down quickly before anything bigger than me came to lay claim.) There wasn't much but it adequately filled the hole in my stomach which had been responsible for the musical rumbling, belching and worse that had occurred during the latter part of my trekking. I really must try to eat regular meals again. My eyelids drooped and I sniffed around, desperate for somewhere to flop down.

Then I spied an ancient wooden building, leaning against the house at the end of the side garden and I crept towards it. By now the daylight was failing and the curtained windows of the cottage shut in any glow from electric lights. I felt sure it was some sort of animal shed – possibly pet rabbits (wonderful!) a pig or a place for outside dogs (I must be extra cautious). It was in complete darkness. Wrinkling up my nose against the pungent smells, I carefully picked my way across the hay strewn planks of wood which lay scattered around on the mud. Hoping the place was empty, or at least temporarily deserted, I investigated the little flap door at the side. Mistake number one! The sleeping chickens objected most strongly to my nose and whiskers poking into their bedroom and startled squawks and grumbles gathered momentum until the little building practically shook with clucking complaint and feverish fluttering. Reversing hastily I retraced my steps to the towpath, taking care not to walk too close to the edge of the silent water. So much for a night in eggland!

Forcing my legs to move forwards again, after a few minutes - with the house and its outbuildings well past me - a small stone bridge loomed above, just a few yards ahead.

Mercifully, at one side of the archway was a tiny stone shelter; just a small box-like affair but it had two sides, a roof and, fortuitously, a shelf about half way up the back wall. A large stone at the side, proved an excellent half way stepping up platform and within seconds I was perched reasonably comfortably up on the shelf, almost enclosed in a nest of dried leaves which must have blown in during the previous few days.

I do not even remember going to sleep but suddenly, white light pierced my fur and forced me to open my eyes. It was as if someone were shinning a powerful torchlight right into my face. But there had been no sound and there was no-one there. I was alone in my little place with the unseasonably bright sunlight bearing in through the open doorway. I stretched with relief. Once again it was time to get up. (It always seemed to be time for waking.) Jumping down on to the leaf strewn floor I stretched more thoroughly and did some of my Yoga exercises. I always find this helps in times of stress, when one's alone, of course. I could never have imagined Minnie taking it seriously enough to join in, though I had a feeling that Sooty might enjoy watching my endeavours with some interest. I shook myself thoroughly again to obliterate any loitering doubts about being reunited with the siblings. After searching for something to eat, my journey would start in earnest again.

Something to eat was not easy to come by along my route. Deviation, therefore, seemed necessary. As I trotted on, under the bridge and round a bend, a housing estate materialized and I knew that houses meant stores of food. Some of the gardens stretched down to the towpath and as I hurried by, each lawn and patio was scrutinized for some hopeful sign. But this was urban and no-one cared about stray animals, feral, wild birds or the like. Nourishment here was all tightly packed into freezers or being squashed into plastic lunch boxes to take to school or work. The more I thought about breakfast, the more famished I got. Creeping up the bank so as to have a better view of the backs of the tidy brick semi-detached food stores, there was nothing to encourage me. Handsome young men in dark suits clutched briefcases (full, no doubt, of meat and fish and other treats for their lunch) as they hurried towards shiny company cars. Small children swung brightly coloured satchels and back packs (full, no doubt, of cartons of cream and pieces of cake and cheese.) Housewives, having completed the early morning shopping, trudged in and out of their homes, unloading copiously filled crinkly plastic bags from their small car boots. Hope surfaced.

One such lady had obviously been delayed in her carrying in of provisions, as she had left the boot lid up and the remaining bags strewn about inside. The gardens of the houses were small and the driveways ended quite close to the canal bank. This particular car was conveniently low to the ground and the lip into the boot looked easily negotiable. I strained my neck as high as I dared and was rewarded to see, through the patio doors, the car owner, still in her long coat and clutching a carrier bag in one hand, chattering animatedly on her telephone. Seizing the opportunity, I sprang through the open staked fencing and raced towards the car, standing briefly underneath, by the rear wheel, for cover. There was no one about so I eased out and after making sure the coast was clear, I sprang up into the boot.

Waiting for a few seconds to make sure I hadn't been watched I set to and rummaged through the carriers until I smelt an interesting polythene bag, heavy and tightly sealed. My mouth watering, I clamped my teeth firmly over the tag and dragged it towards the lip of the boot lid. Letting go for just an instant to make sure that I was still alone, I gripped on again and pulled towards the edge. Then I lent against the bag, sliding it forwards until it silently disappeared, falling down on to the ground. I jumped down, landing alongside my prize. I re-located the tie-up tag, holding it rigidly between my teeth. The heavy load was awkward to carry so I staggered back to the bank somewhat haphazardly, dragging it behind me. Pushing, to roll it down the grassy slope towards the canal, I leapt ahead to make sure it didn't tumble into the water. Then dragging the cumbersome thing through the undergrowth I became impatient to get inside and eat the contents. I stopped

171

on a fairly flat piece of ground and started a concentrated attack with my teeth. Having encountered the human frustration of opening polythene many times, I anticipated difficulty. In this instance it was particularly troublesome, refusing to break, tear or puncture. When I at last breached it, pieces of the stuff stuck in my mouth and even attached themselves to my back teeth. But in front of me was the most delicious chunk of raw filet steak I could ever have imagined.

Glancing around, I carefully moved the meat further into the grass. Saliva dripped from my mouth as I turned it so that it was more easily accessible and so that I could eat in comfort whilst keeping an eye on the footpath. Then I attacked my unexpected treat with enthusiasm (probably an understatement, I think.). After a few minutes of steady chewing my jaw started to throb and my insides warned me to slow down. The steak was big and my stomach was quite small; it could only take so much. Even resting every few seconds didn't help. I was just too full up, too soon. (Minnie, where are you? You would see this off in no time. But there was no Minnie. Just a very bloated me.) I wondered about trying to take it with me for my next feed but its size and awkwardness would have hampered my progress and it would have got dirty and unsavoury by the time it could be eaten. Trying again, unsuccessfully, to nibble a little more I decided to give up and leave it where it was.

Then I heard and saw that I had company further along the path. A woman wearing a track suit, and her small shaggy hound were strolling towards me unaware of my existence. Thankfully, they seemed to be veering off just ahead, up the bank towards the houses. I quickly realised that if the dog smelled the meat, it would change course and dive towards my unfinished meal (and me). Holding the slice firmly between my teeth I backed up the bank, sliding the filet towards me so that it might be covered by grass and weeds, thus concealing from the nearby enemy any delicious odour. The scent was hidden just in time and the dog and walker continued their walk just a few feet away from me, heading towards their back garden gate.

The woman released the animal from its collar and it ran wickedly into the neighbouring garden, sniffing at the still open car boot lid. At that moment the supplier of my breakfast emerged from her back door, having finished her telephone conversation. She at once saw the dog as it cocked its leg against the back wheel (the same one that I had hidden beneath before making my jump into the grocery bags).

"Hey!" she shouted to her neighbour who was walking on, towards her own house. The woman appeared to take no notice of her errant charge. "Hey! Get your dog out of my garden!" the shopper called again, loudly, wrinkling her nose at the yellow stream that trickled from her car wheel.

"Sorry!" the other woman shouted carelessly. "Come on Tweedle! What a naughty boy!" Tweedle took no notice and continued his mission after which he stood on his hind legs to get a better view of the supermarket bags inside the boot.

"Get him out!" shrieked the first woman. By her tone I imagined the two ladies were not on intimately friendly terms.

"Tweedle!" his owner called opening her gate. "Come on, Good boy!" she patted the tops of her thighs provocatively and the dog turned and started to walk half heartedly away from the car.

The shopper rushed to her car and grabbed a handful of the carriers. "Damned dog!" she shouted after the disappearing animal which, from a distance, reminded me of the head of an untidy floor mop. Then she let out a piercing yell. "Your bloody dog has taken my meat!" she screamed, dropping the bags on the driveway.

The other woman stopped in her tracks. "What? How dare you!" she shouted back across the fence. "My Tweedle has been with me all the time, on his lead. Up until now," she added crossly. "How could he have taken anything? Don't talk so stupid!"

"Stupid!" The first woman pointed to her car. "Don't you call me stupid! I left the car for just a few minutes to answer the phone and your wretched animal has made off with my steak. Filet steak it was too! What a cheek to call me stupid! You will pay for this!"

The second woman started to lose her patience. "I tell you, the dog has been with me all the time. Anyway, fancy leaving your car open. Just inviting trouble whilst you jaw away on your phone." She said through her teeth.

"Well then!" the other retorted at the top of her voice, "If he was with you that can only mean one thing!"

"Are you calling me a liar AND a thief?"

"If the caps fits, wear it!"

"This is libel!" (Slander I correctly automatically.)

"And that is slander – to call me libellous!" the other said as if reading my mind, which pleased me no end. "And you will hear from my husband!"

"Oh Yeah! He certainly doesn't frighten me. I shouldn't think he frightens anything."

"How dare you insult my husband! You will hear from my solicitor!" the shopping lady shouted, intent upon improving her first offer. She bent to pick up one of the bags she had dumped on to the ground with one hand and slammed the boot lid down hard with the other. Unfortunately she just managed to catch the hem of her flowing knitted dress in the action and when she stretched to collect the other bags the ripping of material could be easily heard from where I sat guarding my filet in the long grass. "You bitch!" she cried in strangled tones, "Look what you've made me do! I've had enough of you! I will report you to the police, I will. You are a neighbour from hell! And that's where I wish you were! Hell!"

There was a short silence, then the other woman in the track suit burst out laughing and picked up her dog, and went into her house. I gazed at the shopper, now firmly attached to the car and wondered if she had keys or any way to open the offending boot. But she didn't seem to think of even trying. She gathered up her bags and strode towards the house, seemingly unconcerned that her skirt became shorter and shorter as the car boot claimed the larger proportion of her outfit. I lowered my head, to avoid the possibility of her spotting me and venting her anger my way, but I need have had no fears as she marched towards the door with her purchases. Bulging white flesh wobbled above lacy hold-up

174

stockings. Then, as her skirt finally disappeared, the lard-like stomach flopped above a little scrap of panty that cut cruelly into spare tyre and ample bottom.

I couldn't be sure but I think the lady was sobbing.

# CHAPTER 21

After all the excitement I felt a bit hungry again. Parting the undergrowth I tried a brief gnaw at the now soggy, muddy piece of steak. Because of the state it was in it was a very brief gnaw – more a tentative lick or two. I turned my back on the early morning adventure and continued along the canal towpath. The curtain of mist that hovered over the water depicted the probability of a fine day. As my paws negotiated a route around the puddles I lifted my head so that the morning sunshine caught my nose and whiskers. It is always pleasant to have one's foremost bits brightened and warmed in this way but, so far in my short cat life, it occurred far too infrequently. An occasional bird swooped overhead but apart from some dogs barking somewhere behind me on the housing estate, there was no sound. The stillness caused me to keep glancing apprehensively over my shoulder and I kept up a steady surveillance from side to side. The track stretched emptily before me but way ahead something that I didn't recognise straddled the waterway. Hurrying onwards I kept close to the grassy undergrowth which would act as cover if necessary.

The contraption in front looked like a huge wooden beam spanning the water in a sort of V shape. Iron handrails suggested this could be a walkway. As I got closer, the noise of rushing water became quite frightening. Then the grass gave way to a wide cobble-stoned path which sloped downwards and under a dark forbidding looking stone bridge. At this point the canal narrowed to only a few feet across with the sides being lined with sticky bricks and moss-covered stone boulders. Past the wooden walkway the water seemed to disappear. Creeping towards the edge, I craned my neck to investigate, taking care not to go too close as the swooshing sound of the water was extremely off-putting. Staring down the walls of black slimy stonework, I focused on the depleted water which lay many feet below, at a completely different level to the canal I had walked alongside. Swivelling around I saw that the little wood walk-bridge was atop of a pair of huge gates which prevented the canal water from cascading down into the reservoir below. The pounding sound was being made by water gushing through slits and holes where the sides of the gates had worn. On the opposite bank, behind the cobble path, a speeding stream seemed to somehow take water from the top of the canal behind the gates and let it out somewhere beyond a second pair of gates, at the other end of the basin. These gates were wide open to reveal the continuation of the canal on the lower level. This, then, must be a lock.

I comforted myself with the thought that this had not been immediately apparent because the ones I used to know were bigger, wider, and seemed completely different to this small narrow affair. Keeping as far away from the edge as possible I scooted down the path slope and under the small stone bridge which covered both water and pathway. On the stonework above the archway was fixed a metal plaque showing a number and there were some notices nailed at a lower height. How I wished I could read! Leaving the open lock gates behind I heaved a sigh of relief. It was good to be on level ground again with the sunshine and low swirling mists around me. Then I remembered what Sooty had said about his new home. By a lock. I stopped and turned my head from side to side, retracing my steps so that I could climb the bank at the edge of the stone bridge. But there were no houses nearby. And there was certainly no seat or anything to sit on. Anyway, this couldn't possible be the right lock as I know my journey hadn't covered more than a mile or so. So how many locks were there going to be before I reached my goal? Few, I hoped, as they didn't appeal to me one little bit. Thankfully there were no boats or people about but I could imagine the pandemonium if a boat, and its handlers, was passing through, or, worse still, if there was more than one vessel trying to go in opposite directions. Shuddering, I hurried on.

Because the weather had been so warm for the time of the year and there had been days of quite hot sunshine, the trees looked uncharacteristically colourful and virile. Although I had no idea of the actual date, I knew we were well past November 5th (Ugh – horrible memories!) and that autumn must be almost over. Branches that dipped into the water in front of me were still covered with leaves. Some yellow, some golden, some red. So many leaves and no stark bare brown branches as one might expect.

A flotilla of ducks bobbed towards me, taking no notice of anything except each other and their own reflections. I stared directly at them and called a cheery, 'Hello!' but I might just as well have been invisible. Clearly, not a Zoon amongst them as they paddled serenely past, quacking to themselves.

The canal straightened ahead and seemed to go on for miles in an endless line until it disappeared into the distance. The stillness of it made me remember paintings I had often admired in the National and Tate Galleries. I paused and sat down quietly for a moment to think. How clearly I could remember some of those paintings. How strange that I should positively link the picture stretching before me with Turner mistiness, with Monet reflections on water, and yet I still could not think what my name had been. Fighting the familiar feeling that a short sleep might do me good I struggled up again and bustled on in the sunlight. Then, quite without warning, the sun disappeared and the mist seemed to darken. Eerily the scene changed and I could no longer see the stretch of water in the distance; there were no more reflections of sky and trees dancing on the glassy surface. Instinctively my pace slackened. I wished then that I had somehow managed to bring some of the breakfast meat with me and wondered vaguely when my next feed would be. But, I had to admit, tiredness was more of a priority than hunger. Minnie had been right, I did seem to need rather a lot of rest.

Searching around for a spot in which to curl up and linger safely, the side of the path and the now steep bank were examined. The track was too open and unsheltered and the incline at the sides was too steep – if I lingered there and fell into a deep sleep there was distinct danger of a rolling cat and a big splash. Further on there might be a better place. Then I heard the low throbbing behind me. It was not such a loud chug, chug, as the earlier boat had belted out, more of a throaty rumbling tone; it was as if something big and well mannered were approaching. I checked each way up and down but could see no movement on towpath or canal so I turned around and walked back a few yards towards the lock, so as to have the advantage of taller side weeds and wild flowers whilst I was watching. Then I sat down tentatively, away from the water, near the grass at the foot of the bank, in order to see what was going on. Since my departure from the lock, movement had obviously taken place as when I stared back through the gloom, the huge gates at the bottom of the basin were firmly closed. The sound droned on from somewhere inside the lock. Curiosity got the better of me and I stood up, leaning forward as far as I dared. Straining I could see a figure running down the slope from the bridge. He shouted and another person, out of sight, laughed loudly in reply. The man turned and strode back up to the lock. There was a grinding sound of metal being turned, then the gates swung magically apart. My stare was fixed towards the opening. My eyes nearly popped out of my head and I jumped up and shook myself all over to make sure this was not a dream.

Gliding out of the lock, slowly and sedately, beneath the old stone bridge, came the bow of the most beautiful boat. The front rails were encrusted with little white lights, and glowing stars glistened from behind the small front glass door and the long windows either side. The throb of the engine subsided to scarcely a heartbeat and the shinning apparition slid towards where I stood rooted in wonder. All along the roof rails, tiny flashing fairy lights seemed to chase each other around and around, and in the centre of the roof a worded message was picked out in a bright glow. (Oh, what did it say?) There seemed to be so many windows in this massive craft and each was lit with sparkling shapes. The whole silent vision was almost ethereal. As the boat passed by, scarcely moving, the windows gave way to an opening, obviously the main entrance. I could see no one or nothing in the spacious open-sided central cockpit except slatted bench seating and the garlands of leaves and berries that hung from the roof. Small twin doors opened into the main accommodation and another entrance went the other way into the smaller quarters at the back of the boat. Here again, windows were lit extravagantly and the aft rails were encrusted with more little white lights. Behind the enclosed rear part of the vessel there was an open cockpit from which the helmsman steered his course, using a magnificent varnished wooden tiller, decorated with gaily painted flowers. The young man stood on a slightly raised platform as he gently swung the handle over to bring the glittering spectacle alongside the bank. The other man, also little more than a boy, came running from under the bridge. "Make her fast!" shouted the helmsman, throwing a rope. The other deftly caught the end and secured it to a white mushroom shaped bollard at the edge of path.

Suddenly, feeling very vulnerable with this flashing, illuminated contraption parked right in front of my nose, I edged backwards into the damp waving weeds and nettles. Then, turning my head, I saw it. In the ample space, behind the man driving the boat, stood the most glorious spruce tree. The branches of the conifer (which was firmly embedded in a large shiny ceramic pot) were subtly dressed with pinpoints of lighting, and minute packages and parcels swung from glitzy wires. Around the foot of the tree, larger wrapped boxes were randomly placed and balls of something that reminded me so much of snow were scattered around the pot. Then it hit me! It was a Christmas Boat! But why? Yes, it must be getting on towards the festive season. But why would anyone want to decorate a boat in such an excessive way?

As the man on the bank jumped into the stern of the boat and he and his companion disappeared inside, I made my way gingerly forward towards the water and the lights. After a few moments, to gather my thoughts, I stepped cautiously alongside the moored craft, gazing into the large rectangular windows. Instead of bunks and seating and bedding I was amazed to see rows of fixed tables and bench seats covered with tapestry cushioning. On each table was a candle with its holder dressed with holly and flowers, but these were not alight. Of course! A restaurant boat! They had had these on the Thames, I knew, but they were bigger, wider and took many revellers on long summer evening dinner trips – some even holding supper dances and discos. This was very different but, yes, definitely a floating eating place. As if to reinforce my discovery, from somewhere at the rear of the boat came the delicious smell of cooking. Not just cooking, but cooking fish. My nose automatically lifted in the air and my feet made their way towards the long rope which tethered the Christmas Tree end of the boat. This, I decided, was the part of the boat in which the real business was conducted. The galley!

One of the men poked his head through the doorway. I would have backed away except that he was holding a dish in one hand and a pint of milk in the other.

"Hey Cat!" he called, "Want a drink? C'mon – it's fresh milk!"

I reversed swiftly into the grass, just leaving my head showing. The smell of fish was overpowering but I kept my slanting eyes on the fellow with the drink offering. He leaned over the side of the rear cockpit and set the dish on the hard bank, pouring from the bottle at an exaggerated height so I might confirm that it was, indeed, milk.

"C'mon!" he said again, turning away to go back inside.

Left alone I fixed my eyes on the saucer, then checked the towpath again. Then, much against my better judgement, I sidled towards the boat. Milk! How delicious it tasted! Quickly I drank it. If I had nothing else this would see me through the day. The man put his head out of the cabin again and backing away slightly I gazed pointedly at the empty dish.

"Second course coming up!" he said smiling. "I bet you can eat some fish. Won't bother with the chips for you!"

He lent over the rail and picked up my empty dish. Stooping inside he brought out another plate. For a few seconds he cut and chopped with a spoon, spreading the meal to let air get to it.

"Bit hot. Wait for it to cool. There's a good cat." He carefully laid the plate down by the side of the boat, just there in front of me, but I didn't move from my cover point.

"Don't worry," he said reassuringly," I'm not stopping to watch you. Got my own to eat, Matey."

He disappeared once again, this time closing the small door behind him. I was alone on the towpath and so very close was a feast of warm, cooked fish. All instincts warned me this was a dangerous situation but I did what Minnie would have done. Without a second thought I sprang forward and systemically devoured my early lunch. I ate so quickly that my stomach complained by burping loudly, but there was no one to hear so I wasn't embarrassed. Licking the plate as clean as I could (by that time I was rather full again and it was a bit of a struggle) I recalled Tabatha saying one should leave one's eating implements as tidy as possible. As a show of gratitude, I supposed, or maybe to save washing up.

Slowly making my way to the back of the path I washed thoroughly and deliberately, taking care to check behind my ears and under my tail (places which sometimes get missed in a rushed ablution.) Then I knew I must rest. I walked slowly on (or more accurately, staggered) for no more than a few steps before flopping back into the straggling, dying wild flowers. As my eyelids clamped closed I prayed I was out of view and that my smelling of grilled fish would not attract any passers by. Carelessly I allowed myself to drop off to sleep immediately, disregarding the golden rule that one eye should always remain partly open, on guard for a while.

When the insistent drone of a near diesel engine roused me again, the sun had completely disappeared and the day was turning to dusk. With both eyes now fully alerted I watched a smaller narrow boat coming towards the still open lock gates. A man and a woman stood in the stern, the woman steering and her partner shouting instructions.

"Bring her in here, just behind the big boat!" he yelled at her, although she was only a few inches away from him. "Get as close as you can without hitting it," the man said loudly as the poor woman visibly deliberated whether to push the metal bar towards her or away from her.

"Can't we just go straight into the lock?" she suggested hopefully, "It would be much easier than trying to stop here. Then we could tie up when we're through when there won't be another boat to avoid crashing into."

The man wasn't having any of this. "Rubbish!" he shouted back, "Pull the thing over and I'll jump ashore and tie us up,"

He clutched a coiled rope clumsily to his chest. If he jumps now, I thought, he will get awfully wet. There was a lot of canal between him and the bank. The noise must have disturbed the men in the restaurant boat (the very kind men that had fed me, I amended mentally). As I watched, they both clambered from their craft on to the bank.

"It's OK!" the younger one shouted to the couple. "Throw the rope, I'll make it fast for you. Cut the engine!"

Sensible fellow, I thought as the smaller boat was approaching at a startlingly rapid rate. He was obviously concerned about the wisdom of expecting the vacillating female to magically bring the thing to lie snugly behind his boat without even a touch.

"Oh, Thank you!" she piped as the man threw the rope to the bank.

Even though the engine had stopped, the metal hull hurried on and the mis-thrown rope snaked along the path before dropping into the canal. The younger Christmas-boat man was quick off the mark though and shot his arm down in the black cloudy water in time to grab the painter. His mate seized his other arm and pulled him upright and they both pulled backwards on the rope to bring the incident-waiting-to-happen to a standstill.

"Well, done!" shouted the woman.

"Yes, jolly, well done!" echoed the relieved man.

When the smaller narrow boat was tightly secured, the couple lent over their aft rail. "Come and have a drink?" the man shouted to his young saviours. "It's not cold we can sit out here. What will it be? Whisky or beer?"

"Well," hesitated the younger man, "That's good of you, but.."

"Rather!" interrupted the older of the two. "We'd be delighted. Thanks. Beer for me. And for Robbie. Thanks!"

Robbie and his friend climbed into the boat, sitting themselves on the padded side benches. The woman dived inside and reappeared with bags of crisps and nuts which she poured into a large, sectioned lead crystal dish.

"Cheers!" the man dumped a box of cans of lager on the floor and helped each of his guests to one. "Beer, Love?"

"No, I'll get my own. You carry on. Crisps, everyone?"

She disappeared again and came back with a tumbler almost full of amber liquid.

"It's got dry ginger in it," she told her husband defensively.

There they sat, munching and drinking and talking and I could clearly hear every word. The first thing I noticed, after all the excitement, was that the beautiful lights on the big eating boat had been turned off. In the gloom of late afternoon it stood creepily – a silent black outline. There was no lighting in the lock and I could only just make out the gates.

"You've got a big boat, there," the man was saying conversationally. "Do you live on it? Is it a work boat?"

"Yes, it's nearly 72 feet long and she's definitely a work boat - a floating restaurant, as you would see if the table lamps were switched on. You know, we take people out on Sundays for a Sunday lunch cruise. And in the evenings, Thursdays, Fridays and Saturdays we do a shorter trip before we serve a carvery meal. Believe me, it's a hard-work working boat!"

They all laughed.

"Sounds fun!" the woman said, having downed half of her drink. "But it's winter now – do you still get customers. I thought it was only a summer thing."

"You're right," Robbie said, nodding. "We operate all through the summer, then we break but start again just before Christmas. We don't actually go on a trip in the winter but the attraction, we hope, is the novelty of a special Christmas menu afloat. The boat's all heated, so it's fine. Then we stop completely until the spring. What we're doing in the run up to the Christmas is advertising. We go up and down the canal between the towns, stopping at populated areas and putting out our advert boards and leaflets. That way we hope to get bookings for the whole holiday period. That's what all the lights are about, even though you can't really see them now," he added.

"Is it your boat, or do you just run it?" the man asked, interested.

"Well," Robbie stopped.

"Well?" the man persisted.

"It was ours. But, well, you tell them Ben."

Ben reached for another can of lager. "Well," he said, "It was ours – we'd taken out a mortgage on it, but business wasn't too good. The credit crisis just finished us off. I mean, we both have temporary day jobs during most of the year as well but, well, we're going to have to sell up to pay off some debts. Not many," he added hastily, "But we don't like owing. Not fair to the people who have had faith in supplying to us. Some of them took quite a chance. We're young and have little business experience. Just that Robbie is a bloody fine chef. Sorry, er. M'am."

He swigged from the can and I crept forward to get into a better position.

"Do you have books, accounts?" the older man asked, putting down his drink. "I mean, you must have gone into the viability of it all before you started."

"Oh Yes!" Ben said quickly. "I did a terrific business plan. Getting money from the bank was no problem. It was all going very well, gradual but well, until this summer. We were even going to open as a winter time evening coffee shop, moored along the quay in Stone – that's our home base mooring. Of course, we have to lodge her elsewhere when we are not actively doing business – a sort of winter storage tie up. We had such plans.."

"Well," interrupted the woman, draining her glass. "Although I have no idea of how to steer a boat, I am in marketing and I have got one or two quite major successes under my belt. We specialise in sussing out good ideas that need exposure and nurture. But my husband is the entrepreneur."

She smiled at him and he stooped inside the cabin for another carton of lagers.

"What I suggest," he said carefully. "Is that you, Ben and Robbie, show Claire and me – I am Robert, Robert Howes, around your restaurant and tell us more about it. How many people can you seat, for instance, and what legislation do you have to abide by – things like that."

"Yes, well," Ben came in, "We can do about 12 covers – not many but it's comfortable and for that many we have to have periodic checks. This is for the licence. Everything's above board," he finished hastily.

"I am sure it is," Robert nodded. "I do have quite a few business interests and am always on the lookout for others. Corporate entertaining is the big thing nowadays. It could well be that some of the larger companies might be prepared to offer a retainer for periodic use. They're always asking for unusual venues. Yes," he collected his thread and continued, "Yes, I suggest that you show us your operation, your boat, your books perhaps, and we sample your cooking – it will soon be dinner time and you haven't started to have visitors yet, have you? We will certainly pay for anything you use for the meal, cash, of course."

There was a silence. Ben said slowly. "That's really good of you and interesting. But we don't know you, who you are. I'm very inclined to jump on you with joy, but we don't know you. Certainly, we'll cook for you, or rather Robbie will, but, well, showing you accounts and things…"

The man smiled. "And right you are to be wary. We could climb aboard your boat and hijack it." Then, more comfortably, he added. "Here is my card. Phone the number and verify me. Better, still, phone the local Chamber of Commerce and check. Or my bankers – I'll write the details on the reverse of the card. Claire – get yours and some bumf about your company. You'll be sure to have heard of them and, somewhere on the stuff is a delightful photo of Claire (taken about 10 years ago!) to prove that she owns the outfit."

"It was not 10 years. Sauce!" she shrieked, waving her empty glass. "How about another? Oh, don't bother yourself. I'll get it!"

"Well?" the man looked from Ben to Robbie, his brows arched in question. "You can check up on us and we can talk again later if you want to take it further. But tonight we will eat and maybe just talk a little about the possibility."

"No 'maybe' about it," Ben said decisively having scrutinised the cards and literature that Claire had put before him. "We can eat in about 40 minutes after we leave here. Are you allergic to anything, by the way, or have any dietary or taste dislikes? No? Good. Leave the choice to us then. Cash before food, though," he finished slyly.

The older man dug into his pocket and brought out a roll of notes. "Couple of hundred do you?" he asked casually, peeling the appropriate amount from his wad. "But I will expect a good wine included. You do do a good wine, I hope?"

Ben and Robbie gulped in chorus. "We do an excellent wine," Ben said steadily.

"There's just one thing," Claire said slowly. "I do hope you will switch on all the lights for us. You will, won't you?"

"We most certainly will," Robbie assured her.

Then Claire asked, "What do you think of our little boat? We've only had it a few weeks. Step inside and see what we have had fitted into such a small space."

They all disappeared through the little door, clutching cans (and, in Claire's case a refilled glass of whisky.) I moved away from my cover and looked closely at the smaller boat. It was indeed immaculate with extensive carvings and paintings adorning its sides and roof. The glass windows were frosted in the corners and the curtains, and what furnishings I could see, looked luxurious and expensive. There was obviously some money here, I thought. After about ten minutes they all appeared again and deposited their now empty cans in the carton on the floor.

"Absolutely brilliant!" Robbie said, whistling.

"Yes, I love the mahogany doors and cupboards," Ben nodded. "I suppose it must be great to have everything done to order. You can have exactly what you want where you want it."

Both boys looked wistfully back into the cabin area.

"Well," Ben drew himself up, ready to jump ashore. "We'd better get started on the meal and we've some tidying up to do as you'll want to look over the boat first. We've an early start tomorrow – got to get up to the next village as soon as possible to catch people on their way to work. Then on to the town so as to have the lights on at lunchtime and again when the mums are going on the return school run and when the workers start home again." He smiled at the couple. "Let's say aperitifs in 40 minutes – dinner will be about an hour and a bit from now. That will give us time to clean up."

The visitors climbed on to the bank and headed towards their boat. Claire collected up the carton of empty cans and Robert Howes gathered the business cards and leaflets that were strewn about. Then they went inside and I was left sitting alone on the towpath.

"Hey!" Robbie turned as they climbed aboard. "Cat is still here with us. You're not still hungry are you?"

I emerged further out of the grass in a gesture of goodwill. Having fed me he was entitled to a good look at me and I was still immaculately clean, having hardly moved since waking.

"Anyway," he went on good naturedly, "We're cooking a special just now. Stick around and I'll pass some out to you before we sit down to eat."

"Come on!" shouted Ben, appearing in the deck area amidships. "Give me a hand with this!"

I shuffled back to cover again as together they fixed a wide safe-looking gangplank on to the side of their boat. The other end was wedged firmly into the canal side. A handrail was fitted and a roll of, presumably, non-slip matting was laid. Spotlights were switched on which illuminated the entrance handsomely. This, then was where the paying customers boarded and very professional it looked, too, I thought.

The offer of an evening meal was very appealing and I tried not to think about the distance of the walk that loomed in front of me which had hardly been started. During the last day or so it was doubtful if I had gone much more than half a mile; at this rate it would take years to get to Sooty's. But one had to eat (and sleep) to keep up one's strength for things like long journeys. Having convinced myself, I settled back in my little nest amongst the wilting flowers, which by this time, thankfully, were quite dry. I really must not allow myself to drowse for too long.

It seemed only seconds later when I heard, "Cat! Cat! Are you there? Want some dinner?"

It was by then pitch black and the big boat in front of me was fully lit, looking, once again, like something from a fairytale. "Cat?" called the voice again and I rushed forwards, completely indifferent to any evils that might have lurked.

This time it was chicken, in a rather nice creamy sauce, and as he gently dropped the large dish down on the bank Robbie said, "I didn't think you'd be far. It's not too hot. Sorry it's a bit late but we got talking and ate first. They've gone now and we were just turning in and I remembered you."

"You talk daft to that cat," Ben said beside him, but he said it in a nice way and I wasn't in the least bit frightened of going right up to where they leaned over.

"Do you think it's a stray?" Robbie looked down at me as I started to select which pieces I would take first."

"No." Ben shook his head. "No chance. Its coat looks good. It's been cared for, that cat. That's no stray."

Robbie studied me as Ben went back inside. "You're a nice cat," he said thoughtfully. "We could do with someone like you on board. Good mouser are you?"

'I am the killer of a Leader Rat,' I wanted to shout proudly, but, of course, I couldn't as I had a mouth full.

"Well," he went on chattily, "If you're still around in the morning you can come with us for a ride. We'll be back down here in a couple of days, then you can go home if you want to."

He had a nice smile and I felt I trusted him completely. Yes, I decided as I chewed and swallowed (trying to purr at the same time to show my appreciation). Yes, I might well be around in the morning. (Really must not sleep too long, I told myself sternly.) To live on a food boat, warm and comfortable, even if it was just for a little while - this couldn't be bad. And they were going in the direction I was going. It certainly would be better than all that tiresome walking in the wet, and it was getting very cold, particularly at night.

# CHAPTER 22

Unbelievably, I was awake before dawn – or rather, just as it was getting fully light. My night's rest had been spoiled by my waking abruptly at frequent intervals. This was probably due in some part to the discomfort of my dampish nest in the undergrowth but the main cause was that I was terrified that the lit-up eating ship would sail without me if I overslept, as I frequently did. But I had disturbed myself unnecessarily. In the sharpening morning light, the stark outline of the barge was imprinted on the skyline. As I stood up and stretched, carefully moving each leg in turn to dispel stiffness, the comforting lights from the back windows cast pools of yellow on the muddy path. There were sounds of movement inside and a radio had been turned on. Washing quickly I reviewed the situation in the cold light of day. (Or rather, just before the cold light of day.) What had sounded exciting and tempting when I was happily full of food last evening, seemed less attractive and downright risky now as I stood eyeing the water being whipped by the wind. The noise of these boats frightened me enough, without the thought of being in actual movement upon water in one of them.

How do I enjoy being in a car? I asked myself. Cosy and safely secured? I hate it! And how do I feel about cold, wet, slimy water. Ugh! It was madness to even consider this stupid idea. And anyway, how would I get on to the boat? Robbie (or Ben) would have to carry me, I supposed (I loathed being carried). Or would I be expected to jump - jump from a slippery bank up on to the open back cockpit, avoiding the various ropes and rails and other obstacles? And over a narrow strip of water which widened alarmingly as the wind moved the boat? It was all impossible. What, I questioned my sanity, was a few miles hike in the wind and rain, without food, shelter or company compared with all these hazards? The only up-side would be constant food, warmth, comfort and someone to stroke and talk to me, plus the added bonus of being transported nearer to my destination. Put like that, I decided, it didn't sound too bad. Not too bad at all. I could find somewhere to sit away from the engine, away from the noise. There would be no need to ever come out of the inside part so the water would never be near to me (and the sides of all the open parts were very high.) The boats only go quite slowly, so there would be little movement; really the only problem was – how to get on the thing. Satisfied that I had talked myself back into it, I paced up and down the grass alongside.

The centre gangplank was still down but the hand rails had been dismantled. All other bits and pieces that had stood on the bank had been gathered in. The mooring was tidy, ready for departure. The freshening wind drew the boat in and then pushed it out from its tethering posts, slacking and tauting the ropes, but the rigid gangway remained firm. One of the men, I couldn't tell which, jumped ashore and ran past where I crouched, to the bow. He expertly untied the rope and threw it over the front rail, then he ran back to the stern.

Hells Bells, they were going without me! Impulsively I streaked up the centre gangplank although by now this was also moving about from side to side.

"'Plank's still down!" the man ashore yelled and almost as I jumped clear on to the boat and scooted under the slatted seating, Robbie appeared and started to drag the board in.

I sat petrified as the dull thud of the engine started somewhere beneath me. There seemed to be a lot of shouting and rushing about and then I knew we were moving – floating away from dry land. The very thought made me feel faint. What had I done?

"Mind the governor's boat!" Robbie sang out from somewhere nearby and I guessed we were inching past the lovely hand-built boat where Robert and Claire were no doubt still sleeping.

The engine quickened slightly but we had stopped weaving and turning, and going in a straight line really wasn't so bad. Relieved that the prospect of immediate vomiting was receding, I opened my eyes and allowed my head to move slightly in order to examine my surroundings.

"Blimey!" Robbie shouted as he bent to the deck. "It's Cat! Christ –I'd forgotten all about you!"

I stared at him coolly. 'Yes, I know,' I told him through slitted eyes. 'You did not give me a single thought, even after all those promises you made.' For some reason I felt deeply hurt. If it had been possible to escape back down on to the bank I would have done so.

"Hey!" he called to me, bending right down so that his hand would reach into my hiding spot. "C'mon out."

He gently stroked the top of my head but I scrunched up against the side. No way was I ready to forgive such an oversight on a tentative stroke of fur.

"C'mon out. There's better places for you than that. We'll make you a nice box near the heater. C'mon Cat!"

I stayed firmly where I was. He was undeterred by my hard-to-get tactics. "OK. Suit yourself." He turned back into the rear room. "You'll come out when you want to. Breakfast in 10 minutes. I'll leave the door open - just wander through when you feel hungry. You're an independent old Cat aren't you?"

He stood on tiptoe and shouted back over the roof to Ben, who was steering the boat. "Guess what? Cat's here! Came on its own. Must have climbed the plank."

I heard Ben laugh as Robbie bent his head down and disappeared into the innards of the boat. From the open door wafted warmth and within a few minutes, the unmistakable aroma of eggs and bacon cooking. How could a cat stand such bribery? I couldn't, so with as much dignity as I could muster, I strolled nonchalantly in through the open door.

"Bacon and sausage OK for you?" Robbie didn't even look up from his cooking as I sidled past him. "You and I eat first, then I'll take over from Ben whilst he has his."

I looked up at him as he served out our breakfasts. He sat at a tall bar surface which ran along the side of the galley. My dish was placed near his feet. We both ate in silence (well, not really silence as he made quite a lot of noise.) Then he said, "Ground rules, Cat, otherwise Ben will get on his high horse. This is the galley," (yes, I had already worked that one out)

193

"And our cabin and wash is back there, aft, just before the Christmas tree. These, and the open bits at the back and in the middle are your allowed places. When there's no customers, like now, you can go where you like, but when we're in business you stay in your allowed places."

Then, as if I were some kind of idiot he pointed firmly to the back and waved his arm around the galley. "Yes!" he said, nodding like a maniac. He then stretched out his arm and pointed towards the dining part. "NO!" he growled, shaking his head like something possessed.

'Right, I just about get the picture.' I nodded politely, to show my understanding of the situation and he laughed. "Well, I hope you do understand, Cat, then we'll all get along fine. We once had another moggie that was an absolute pain. Kept begging in the dining room from the punters whilst they were eating. Howled, it did if they didn't drop something down for it. Even clawed at some woman's posh dress – ruined her hemline, it did. That one didn't last long, I can tell you," he finished darkly, wiping around his empty plate with a hunk of bread. I hoped he wasn't going to elaborate as to what had befallen the unfortunate feline.

'I will keep to my places,' I answered him with my eyes, but, of course, he couldn't see my words of acquiescence. I wondered vaguely why he referred to cats as 'it' but supposed this saved possible embarrassment all round. He stood up and started to cook again, presumably Ben's breakfast.

"And," he turned back to me and I looked up obediently, although I was agitated that he wouldn't let me finish eating in peace. "I don't advise going up on the roof – not until you've got your sea-legs. Can get quite slippery." I shuddered as more bacon started to sizzle. Nothing in the world would have induced me up there anyway.

When the breakfast was put in the oven to keep warm and Robbie had disappeared to the back (sorry, aft) I investigated the galley, then moved through to the double cabin which, although somewhat cramped, had two comfortable looking tiered bunks, small drawer chest and small wardrobe built into the sides of the boat.

As Ben passed down the narrow passageway towards his breakfast, I poked my head around a half open door into the last room (before the back cockpit opened out). The wash room was tiny, but had basin, WC and a hand held shower unit. Small but functional I acknowledged. Outside I could hear Robbie singing as he guided us along at our leisurely and not too noisy pace. I looked longingly at the crumpled, rumpled beds –inviting and snug, but decided it might be better not to invade these uninvited. Back to the galley I trotted, to renew my acquaintance with Ben who was demolishing his meal at breakneck speed.

"Ah Cat," he said, a little egg yoke running down his chin. "No going in the diner when the customers are on board. In fact, not beyond the galley."

'I know, I know,' I told him, but sat listening intently with my head on one side to look as if I were engrossed.

"Mice," he said firmly. "If you catch, and feel you must eat, vermin, do it away from me. If you do catch any, better just leave them where we can find them. I'm not partial to finding half eaten animals in my boat."

'But Robbie asked me if I was a good mouser,' I protested silently.

As if reading my thoughts he went on (whilst scrubbing a doorstep of bread around his greasy plate) "You don't have to catch anything – just walk around and look as if you could if the need arose. Sort of deterrent, you are." Well, in neither of my lives had I ever been referred to as 'a deterrent'!

"We'll have to get you somewhere to sleep. A box or something but I'll leave that to Robbie." He stood up, anxious to retrieve his captain's responsibilities. "Oh," he remembered, "We'll fix you up a litter tray outside by the Christmas tree, under the canopy. Don't want you jumping ashore and falling in or getting lost."

Then he was gone, leaving me alone in the middle of the galley. What really nice chaps they are, I felt. What a pity Tina isn't here too. I congratulated myself on landing in such a great set up. The rain started to patter down on the roof as I curled up in a tight satisfied ball by the cooking stove. Happily I

195

decided that my stay could last for forever if it were up to me. But the reality I wondered, was just how long? My eyes started to close.

They were discussing time scales when I came to at lunchtime. The engines were idle, we were tight against the bank and no one could possibly sleep through the smell of steak and kidney pie or the wonderful sound it made when it was plopped out on the plates.

'Meow!' I said brightly, stretching.

"Yeah, Yeah!" Robbie said, "Already put yours out – it's cooling."

I reflected on Ben's conversation earlier. How could any cat in its right mind want to catch and eat scrawny mice when cordon bleu grub appeared in their dish so regularly? But time – they were discussing time and I listened carefully. Four weeks until Christmas, all of which would be working weeks. After only a few more days of floating advertising and flashing lights, reservations would be taken up and the restaurant would be full of revellers having a good festive time and (Ben hoped) splashing their festive money about. Robert and Claire had apparently made some business offer, and suggestions for immediately improving the cash flow included working extra nights in the run up to Christmas. Not only the Thursdays, Fridays and Saturdays, and Sunday lunches, that they worked in the summer months, but Tuesdays and Wednesdays as well. This, it had been agreed, would not be too difficult as only one set meal (turkey, naturally) was being offered with one fish/vegetarian alternative plus the usual Christmas pudding or fruit salad.

"So," Robbie bent down with my lunch dish, tickled my chin then straightened up again. "Four weeks of hard work. Let's run through it again. They come aboard, aperitifs, food, coffee, chocs and liquors and finish. No canal cruise trip included this time of the year, nor sitting outside for drinks. Same thing, same place the next night, according to reservations, or on to the next venue. We'll work out, in advance, our turning at winding points, so we can offer a choice of dates either on the outward journey or on the homeward trip."

"Yep," Ben agreed, starting on his lunch. "Our forward planning is now up the creek due to the extra days. Still, won't take long to rearrange it all. It's stocking the provisions that could be a problem. Still, you can always get on to Freddie or one of the others to deliver to wherever we are going to be. I'll stock up the liquor side in town, or, again, they'll deliver if we run short. It's only a matter of a few miles, for them."

He broke off to concentrate on his pie and after a few seconds of companionable munching, Robbie nodded and continued. "The bookings we've already got can be slotted in and if we come alongside early enough, with all lights blazing, we should pick up a few passing customers on the day – we always have before. By adding the extra days we should accommodate anyone interested and not have to turn people away as we did last year. We'll have to ink in the blanks on the leaflets for the extra dates, but we've got plenty."

It all sounded so busy, how I wished I could have helped, but in the rush of the next few days I learned when to make myself scarce and when to take to my bed (a very clever box, cut to just fit me, lined with a comfortable cushion.) Only once did I venture into the no-go-areas – just to see what they were like, but never up on the roof. Having got used to the thud of the engine and the sometimes slightly rocking movement, life was more than comfortable. The afternoons were the best time as when the men were busy talking to people and giving out leaflets, I sat in the open centre cockpit, beneath all the lights, washing and stretching and generally being a poser.

"Oh, look – a cat!" stupid humans would yell as if they had never come across one before.

"Ah, yes!" Ben or Robbie would say something like, "Ship's cat – keeps the place spic and span. That's one person who will certainly vouch for our catering, won't you Cat?" and I would preen myself and purr and maybe roll over, then everyone would laugh and the women would lean over to stroke me and the men would receive their instructions. "Well, go on! Let's book. Which night shall we come?"

197

And so, I reckoned, a lot of the bookings were down to me. Ship's Cat became a number one attraction, particularly since Robbie had fixed me up with a collar that flashed on and off. (Not something I would have countenanced under any normal circumstances but, well, it made me feel I was doing my bit.) Incidentally, I never did actually see a mouse the whole time I was on board so maybe Ben had been right and a deterrent was all that was needed.

One woman did say menacingly, as her husband obediently handed over his money for reservations. "I do hope the cat – beautiful though he is – will not be there when we dine. I don't allow the animals near me when I'm eating at home."

Ben had flashed his most provocative smile. "Madame, believe me, Cat is a worker. It definitely is not allowed in the guest rooms."

Aside, Robbie had added, "And I don't suppose you let anyone else near you, eating or otherwise."

Yes it was all in a day's work.

# CHAPTER 23

Life aboard a narrow boat is interesting. Probably not in just any old boat but, for a cat, a restaurant boat certainly was the tops. Lots of food, absolute warmth and petting whenever I cared to allow it (especially from Robbie who obviously adored cats and probably any sort of animal.) During the day we chugged up the canal for a few miles and then we would stop and do our publicity bit and then on to the next place. It was all quite exciting. Most of the time it was enjoyable but there were some awkward moments.

One that will stick in my mind for ever (however long that might be) was one dark evening when we were moored with our usual flamboyant display. School children had long ago been led home to do their homework or, more likely, to watch TV, and workers had either hurried past to their houses or had stopped and collected a leaflet. Few people were about and Ben had just decided to secure for the night. From nowhere, it seemed, a huge woman in a flapping flannel trouser suit appeared on the pavement by our little table, set out at the bottom of the gangplank. At the end of her pinstriped arm, a heavily gloved hand dragged at an equally dumpling boy who could have been any age.

"Come on!" she snorted at him as Robbie and I lounged in the centre cockpit, leaving Ben to deal with any latecomers.

The woman pulled at her offspring as she strained towards our display board and stack of brochures. Under closer inspection, beneath the lights, the over bloated child reminded me of someone my mother used to call Billy Bunter – fat, grubby and wearing a school cap and - in this cold weather, would you believe - short trousers. His socks had slipped down and wrinkled around his muddy shoes and he held what looked suspiciously like a catapult in his other hand. I half expected him to say, 'Won't!' but he said, "Why must I?" which was pretty close, I thought. Then miles behind them wandered a tall, thin, ragged man, looking very reminiscent of a second class scarecrow; he was also summoned.

"Henry!" The woman had a remarkable voice. An ex-actress or out of work contralto I guessed. No ordinary mortal had a voice like that. "Henry!" she repeated, just in case he might have missed the first address.

Henry didn't reply but the boy chanted, "Why should I go on a boat? Can't we eat in a caff?"

"Café!" his mother corrected. "And no we can't. It'll be a treat to eat on a boat. Don't you think so Henry?"

Henry did not appear to have any views on the matter and remained his mandatory four paces behind the boss and boss heir-apparent.

"When shall we book for?" she asked loudly as if wishing to impress anyone who might possibly be listening. Then she lent towards Ben and whispered, "Do you give a discount for the over 50's?"

Ben shook his head. He was used to being asked for discounts. "I'm so sorry Madam, but we do not give discounts," he gushed in his best we-only-have-a-few-places-left voice. "Our floating Christmas extravaganza is so popular that we are usually fully booked before we start. Owing to a cancellation though, we could just about fit the three of you in for – well, either the Thursday or Friday that we are here in this area."

Madam drew in breath and I feared the full impact of her dulcet tones, should she decide to pursue the matter of a concession price. Ben, bless him, was one jump ahead. "Why do you ask me about discounts, Madam? This is a mystery. Surely not for yourself? Or maybe," he lowered his voice dramatically, "Maybe for your gentleman friend?"

Madam hooted with loud laughter, and her ample shoulders shrugged up and down in an exaggerated manner. "Oh well," she agreed, with good humour, "It's always worth a try. OK – How much then, for the two of us - he's my husband, difficult to understand I know, but between you and me, I'll never know what possessed me – and the boy?"

"Don't want to go on the boat. Can't we go to a cyber caff?"

His mother shook off his hand abruptly. "Silly boy!" she smiled benignly at him as he rifled through the advertising matter which had been neatly stacked. "There are no cyber cafes here – that's only on television."

"They have 'em in Liverpool. Daryl says they have 'em in Liverpool. They have 'em everywhere."

"We are not in Liverpool. That's miles away. And they do not have them here. Even if they did, that's not something I would like to go to." The woman said haughtily. "Well," she demanded to Ben, "How much? Surely it's cheaper for the boy? He won't eat as much as an adult." (By the look of him, I thought, podgy Billy Bunter would have little trouble devouring a horse. She might certainly have stood more chance of a reduction if she had cited her scraggy husband.)

Ben handed her a leaflet. Even I knew he had given up on this one.

"The prices are all on there," he said reasonably as he started to stack the papers and cards into neat piles, ready for their night time captivity within restraining elastic bands and large brown envelopes. Ben had expected (or I think, from his expression, hoped) that these difficult prospective customers would turn away and leave us in peace. He nodded to Robbie, who prepared to raise the gangplank, but suddenly Madam let out a whoop of delight (I assumed it was delight) as she spotted me, laying near the edge of the centre cockpit.

"Oh, will you just look at that cat! Isn't he lovely?"

I stretched and rolled over to give my audience a better view – after all, this was part of my promotional duty. Neither she, her husband or son paid any attention; the boy wrestled with Ben for ownership of the pile of catalogues and the man examined his dirt caked shoes with a deep frown as if he was surprised to see them in such a state.

"Come here!" The trouser suit lent across the rail and made a grab at me. Unfortunately I have never perfected the knack of leaping up and away to avoid such abuse, from the laying-on-the-back-and-waving-legs-in-the-air position. I was doomed to be captured by those enormous hands and chubby sausage fingers. My claws were facing the wrong way otherwise I could have dug them into her flesh or at least grappled with her frizzy grey hair. All I was able to do was to yell at the top of my voice. Both Ben and Robbie reached out towards me.

"Cat doesn't like to be picked up!" Robbie warned ominously but the damage had been done.

My screams and wails increased as I was virtually a prisoner; she lifted me from the boat by my legs so that I was upturned toward the black sky and I could hear the boy laughing cruelly.

"What a lovely pussy!" the mad woman carolled waving my inert body in the air.

"Put that cat down!" Ben instructed, customer manners forgotten, but she held me even more firmly.

I swung my head giddily to the side and saw the husband stamp his feet and start to walk away. Robbie ran down the gangplank but there was little he could do as we both knew that if he grappled with the brainless harridan I would be torn apart.

'For God's sake turn me the right way up!' I screamed. Cats hate to be upside down. Surely she must know that or maybe she was just being vindictive because she hadn't won a discount.

Then suddenly the fat boy sprang forward, towards his cavorting mother, and he grabbed my tail which was lolling down towards the ground in a most unseemly manner. And then he pulled it. He pulled it so hard that I was shocked into silence. But as my mouth shut, a reflex action somewhere inside me (over which, I promise, I had no control whatsoever) caused another part of me to operate rather violently. Without any warning, from somewhere near my tail spurted the most unexpected burst of a most unpleasant smelling, lumpy river of matter - obviously my well digested lunch. As if this spontaneous act, that completely startled everyone, wasn't hideous enough for me, the accompanying embarrassing woopy-cushion-type noise cemented my disgrace. I have never, ever felt so bitterly ashamed in my life (or lives). I certainly did not deserve to ever be a human again or even carry on being a cat. In my complete lack of self control I had behaved as the lowest form of animal, whatever that was.

For the following seconds it was as if time stood still. I was aware of a brief silence during which both Ben and Robbie stood as if rooted to the ground. The boy stared wide eyed at his mother, who remained immobile as a statue, still holding me aloft, as the warm liquid trickled from her shoulders down on to her ample bosom. Then she screamed a scream that would have ended all screams – and she dropped, or rather, flung, me into the canal.

This was the day I realised that, yes, I could swim and, no, I did not like it.

Yes, this was a day I never forgot. I felt marginally better after the boys had fished me out and dried me on an old towel. (All their towels were old but some were particularly disgusting, like this one - hard and holey, not like Tina's beautifully soft and fluffy ones.) Humiliated and cowed I hid beneath the slatted seating in the open centre of the boat. In spite of Ben's reassurance that he would have acted in exactly the same fashion (given the unlikely event of his tail being yanked out) I still couldn't believe his retaliation would be by squirting poo at a customer. I stayed put. Robbie tried to coax me back into the galley by banging my dish with a fork and shouting, "Food!" and other extremely nice things that made my whiskers twitch, but my feeling of remorse compelled me to remain out of circulation, for a while at least. Anyway, the thought of eating anything made me tremble at the possibility of my rear-end activating itself again without permission; I hoped this was definitely going to be a one off. As I curled up in a shivering, clammy heap, sleep, not surprisingly, eluded me. Visions of the dreadful female and her vile son reappearing to take revenge, haunted me. Every time a car went by, I feared that swarthy men in dark uniforms were coming to collect me. I nudged further backwards on the uncomfortable boards. Men, who usually, I remembered, had rotating blue lights on top of their cars. Then, frantically, I searched my muddled mind for the name of these troops who took villains like me away. They were officers – I recalled people calling them Officer. But no, their real title evaded me. It was gone. The name I was searching for had vanished, probably for ever.

I started to accept the depressing realisation that this sort of thing was happening to me daily now. My mind and memory were becoming numb and although wrestling with the blockade at every opportunity, I knew I was truly becoming Cat. Now my real, and only, name was Penny, and the only memories I was able to hold firmly were my cat-life memories, though it was faintly comforting that nothing would ever erase the good times I had had with Tina. Laying miserably under the dripping seats I could easily think of Tabatha and Gull and Monty Mouse and the horrible children at the farm. But, before that? Before that there was nothing. Vaguely some instinct reminded me that I wasn't so good on heights but nothing really tangible. Why then, I asked myself, did useless things like Billy Bunter, Dick Whittington and other nonsenses pop up without being sought? But there was no answer and constant human contact only served to remind me of my differences. The only way of lessening my distress, my intuition hinted, would be to find another like minded Zoon as soon as possible. That way the problem could at least be discussed and my anxieties shared. Then I must have fallen asleep.

The next morning we were away early. Today, I heard Ben say to Robbie, was to be to the final destination before turning back down the canal to start the actual business of restauranting. Today was to be the last day of promotion. Then the real work would start. The morning was dull and misty and we made just one stop, at lunchtime, at a small village, well, really only a handful of houses, a church and a pub. Robbie and Ben disappeared (to the pub) to talk business. I quite liked these absences of the management as it left me completely in charge of everything. During one of these times I adventurously made my way up to the roof and investigated its length and breadth in detail. Nothing really interesting, quite disappointing in fact. Not a jaunt I would repeat unnecessarily but at least it meant I had covered every inch of the ship.

Then we were on our way to our very last stop. Amazingly I had thought little of my real reason for being on the canal. The long walk to find Minnie and Sooty had been pushed to the back of my mind with all the excitement of being an integral part of a business enterprise. But now, as we were nearing our final destination, which would be the nearest we would get to where my friends may be, a decision had to be made. When we tied up that evening, would I abandon ship and continue my slog in their direction to locate them, or would I stay where I was for the next few weeks and remain as part of the crew? When the promotion trip reached its furthest point, we were scheduled to turn round and go back to our home port at Stone. There we would load supplies and repeat our journey all over again but this time as a serving restaurant. We would stop at all the places where we had taken bookings until we reached this end-of-route turn-around place. The boys had been looking forward to this, the outcome to their previous weeks of planning. They would be plying their trade – cooking and serving Christmas meals to those customers who had reserved places.

As I turned this over in my mind (after a rather heavy lunch of stew and dumplings, followed by a trial run of Christmas pudding and cream) I realised that I could defer my decision for a while longer. When we arrived at our last point on the cut (yes, I was learning the canal lingo) this would be where we turned before starting our return journey. Then, and only then, would I need to evaluate the promise of tantalising comfort for another week or so on the boat, against the possibility of meeting up with Minnie (nice thought) and Sooty (apprehensive thought) for a prospective long term home, in an outhouse with the chance of food being thrown in occasionally.

I shook myself and exercised my whiskers. (By moving them periodically, the muscles in my face remain alert and stop my neck from drooping. Not a vanity thing, more of a healthy attitude to keeping oneself fit and trim. As everyone knows, a cat's width is measured by the breadth of its whiskers. If whiskers go through an opening without touching anything, then body will follow easily. A droopy jaw line and misaligned whiskers could, therefore, lead to catastrophe.)

Then, a few hours later, as Robbie made fast our ropes, I was confronted with my dilemma, earlier than I had expected.

# CHAPTER 24

We moored just below a lock. Nothing unusual about this, there was always a lock, every few yards, it seemed. But as the ropes were wound around the little tie-up mushrooms a strange foreboding seemed to emulate from between the tall, black, closed wooden gates. I felt a sort of ESP, a premonition - a 'something unpleasant is going to happen' feeling.

"Are we going through?" Robbie yelled above the din of cursing water.

"Might as well," Ben shouted back over the roof. "There's one coming down so we can use her water. We need to be on the other side to turn. Winding point's only up a bit."

Robbie nodded in agreement and stopped coiling the rope. Instead he just held on to it after one or two turns around the white metal holding post. "Yes, it's better up above," he shouted back, "Nice flat paved path, if I remember. More conducive for the punters!"

They both laughed and I grinned to myself as I lounged on the bow seat at the very front of the boat. I quite liked to sit up there as it was an extremely advantageous look-out point. From my safe perch I could hiss at ducks and swans and meow enticingly at passing dogs. Frightening the birds who landed unsuspectingly on the rails was the best part though. The smaller birds, that is. Once, I remember, a bad tempered looking rook landed precariously on the end of the roof and I foolishly leapt up to grab at its wings. Slithering dangerously, my body swaying out above the water below, I just managed to hang on by my toenails whilst the dratted creature flew off, laughing – Haw, Haw, Haw! Another disaster narrowly adverted.

In the early days of my marine life I had been extremely frightened by the negotiation of locks but now I was an experienced Ship's Cat I would no more dream of disturbing myself during lock time than consider taking a voluntary dip in the muddy, smelly water. (Ugh! Memories of the fat woman with the loud voice and her bloated son, forced my mind to change subjects, quickly.) I sat firmly, courageously, posing, as the boat entered the lock and gracefully rose with the water.

Being the first of our little team through a lock filled me with a kind of pride. Leader of the pack, that's me, I thought. I could see everything we were approaching before anyone else. And then – there it was! A little wooden bench seat set slightly back from the canal, beyond the upper part of the locks. (But at this time of the year, of course, no one was sitting on it, using it.) But a seat next to a lock – this certainly rang a bell. Then I remembered. Sooty had said, a wooden bench just above a lock. I swivelled myself round and scanned the banks. What I was looking for was a gate with barbed wire across the top of it. I searched with my eyes as wide as they could open. Just trees and bushes, widening out on to a winding paved path which led alongside a large car park and a pub entrance. Good place to moor for catching passing trade, I thought smugly, pleased that even my thoughts were entering into the spirit of things. There was no wire on any of the houses on this side of the water, I noted with a strange feeling of relief. (Why relief? Didn't I want to locate Minnie and Sooty?) Then, turning my head slightly, I saw the little bridge, just above the lock, and houses on the other side, the gardens of which sloped almost down to the water. One, the nearest to the bridge, had vicious looking barbed wire nailed across not only the tall iron gate, but all along the rear garden wall. There appeared to be no proper footpath between the wall and the water but a well worn dirt track ran between the properties and the top of the slope down to the canal. A track, it appeared from the scattered debris, that was well used by playing children and pedestrians of all ages. Even from that distance I could make out the tyre marks of mountain bikes and a larger set of ruts that suggested a small motorcycle or scooter had passed that way recently. I sat up to examine the area more thoroughly, wondering why I didn't feel elated, overjoyed, actually beside myself, on being brought so comfortably to the very spot I had been making for.

It was getting dark and my earlier doubts crowded back. I considered again the three possible choices. Should I get off and go to find Minnie and Sooty and tell them that I would be back with them in a week or so? This didn't seem very friendly. It was like saying, I've had a lift here in the lap of luxury and would like to enjoy it for a while longer but will come back when my luck's run out. The second choice was not to seek them out now but to continue back with the boat and take pot luck in finding them when we returned for the final time. (Could be difficult – something may prevent the boys and the boat from coming back or the house I was looking at may not, after all, be Sooty's). The last choice could be to leave Robbie and Ben right now and go to find my friends and stay with them permanently – and not go back to the boat. Absolutely impossible, I told myself. Who would act as a deterrent to the rodents on the Christmas celebration voyages and – more importantly – who would eat up all those delicious scraps? This was a chore I had been anticipating with some relish for days now. No, I decided. I would consider the matter again when I'd had a good sleep.

My sleep turned out to be so good that I didn't waken in time to join in that evening's promotion of our business. When I eventually stirred, the lights had been switched off and Ben and Robbie were tucked up in their bunks. Tomorrow we would go on to the winding point, turn the boat around and start back down the canal the way we had come. Having stretched, done a few perfunctory exercises and lapped at the saucer of milk they had left out for me, I trotted down the centre of the gangplank to the shore. When we moored in what Ben termed a rough neighbourhood, the 'plank would be drawn into the boat but when we were somewhere that respectable punters might pass during the late evening, the box, which surrendered only one leaflet at a time, was left for prospective customers to help themselves to our tasty details. On these occasions I would take the opportunity of going ashore myself, although I never went far from the boat. This, then, was obviously a reliable neighbourhood and somewhere we had so far failed to fill all our places because the leaflet box was still there.

I was getting used to the routine. When the dining spaces had all been allocated for the boat's return trip, Robbie and

Ben would take themselves off to the nearest pub for a game of darts; I, then, was left in complete charge. It was quite a responsibility, I reflected. It was a big craft to keep an eye on and it meant patrolling continually from end to end (pausing only for visits to the galley to quell frequent hunger pains.) But tonight, I told myself, there was no need for my security role as my companions were aboard. I sat for a few moments at the bottom of the gangplank next to the little publicity box, which was firmly chained to the boat's iron railing. (Ben took no chances, even in a respectable area.)

I stared across the water to where the house lights opposite picked out the metal gate with its halo of spiked wire. Making a considered decision, I picked my way carefully along the path towards the bridge. I would seek out my furry friends and see how things were with them and take it from there. There were few vehicles in the pub car park and no sign of anyone moving about and although the street lights blazed away, the place looked desolate and abandoned. I kept out of the light just in case someone unfriendly should appear or a stray canine might pass by; I had enough to worry about without any extraneous encounters. As my paws crackled crisply over the frosty grass I hurried towards the bridge. I covered the ground to the house in no time and, squeezing through the iron struts of the garden gate, I could make out a stone building just beyond the fruit trees inside the garden, a short distance from the main house. This must be the outbuilding Sooty had mentioned. It looked as if this was the right place then. I hesitated outside the low structure, which looked like an old garage and peered in through the open door. There was little light inside and I could see nothing except blackness and the shape of some large boxes and bins. Taking a chance I gave a small controlled meow – the sort of communication one uses when one is unsure of who or what might be around. I was a little surprised that neither Sooty or Minnie appeared, particularly remembering that Minnie had vowed she would definitely live in the outbuilding.

Maybe it wasn't the right house after all. Maybe she never actually got here in the removal van. Satisfied that there was nothing of interest in the immediate vicinity, I made my way towards the house. Sooty had not exaggerated. It certainly looked big and imposing and, just as he said, the garden was quite spacious. I skirted about the edge, for safety's sake, and crept towards what looked like the kitchen door. There were two pairs of boots outside under a small canopy, and an umbrella. The door was firmly shut, of course, but there was an old chest of drawers standing just outside the canopy, beneath a window. Calculating carefully, I sprang up, conscious of the probability of my feet slipping on the frosty surface but, no, all was well as I landed and I inched forward to press my nose up to the window. This was indeed the kitchen. A dim light shone into the room (from a hallway or landing possibly) and I could make out a long table with wooden chairs tucked neatly beneath. A large cooker stood alongside what appeared to be various clothes and dish washing equipment and a menacing black stove – it looked like a old  wood burner to me – glowed in the corner as it released its last glimmers into the room.

My alert eyes were taking in sink and cupboards and fridge (where food might be) when suddenly into focus drifted a large brown fur igloo-type cat basket, with a beautiful inviting quilted lining. Standing to attention and leaning forward so that my nose really did flatten against the cold glass window pane, I scrutinized the igloo. Inside (no doubt warmly, comfortably ensconced) were two figures. A black cat and a grey cat. Sooty and Minnie! Minnie – in a house! Narrowing my eyes, I satisfied myself there could be no mistake. It was definitely them. I shuffled back on my uncomfortable perch. Yes, this was the right house after all. Minnie and Sooty were here; so contented and happy that they did not even sense, smell or hear me at their window. (I pride myself that I would abandon sleep automatically, should a foreign creature come within yards of me. I would have known, without any doubt whatsoever, if someone had ogled me from a window just a few feet away.)

Sighing, I had to admit that they looked absolutely peaceful together. But what was Minnie doing in a cat bed – let alone a house? She definitely had said.... But here she was cosy and cared for. And, if I appeared? What would happen to me? It was doubtful if the trusting family would accept yet another mouth to feed. More than likely I would be shooed away and left to fend for myself. (I knew that Minnie and probably Sooty would take pity and help me all they could but I also doubted very much if Minnie would abandon her newly acquired life of comfort just to be with an old friend.) I sat on my frozen chest of drawers, desolately gazing in at the enviable scene. Minnie would be stretched two ways if I made myself known. She would feel, I assured myself, that she wanted to be with me, of course. Sooty too, no doubt. (This sent a shiver down my spine.) But maybe not? Suppose they didn't want to know me, after all? Did I really want to hang around to find out? I turned slowly, being careful not to slide. Springing down I gave my body a good shake. Let's get back to my boat as soon as possible! There, I had comfort, warmth, companionship – so what did anything else matter? Well, now there was no decision to be made. Not yet at least.

I strutted back towards the gate. It was status quo, I comforted myself, for a week or so more. And then what? Striding on I shook myself. (It's not easy to shake and stride on, but I managed.)

Passing the old garage building once again I heard a sound. I wasn't feeling particularly hungry, more unsettled and a little angry at what fate had thrown my way. If it was a mouse it might be fun to engage in a brief hunt and then torment the thing. Someone ought to pay for my plight, I acknowledged. Yes, it was definitely some creature that was just begging to be trapped and caught. I eased myself in through the doorway and the sound came again, so suddenly that it made me jump. Whatever it was, sprang down and shot outside and, as it must have been resting on the spring mechanism, when its weight was released, the big door swung closed. I was the unfortunate one who was trapped.

The complete darkness imprisoned me and even my good eyes could still only make out vague shapes. But where I stood (or rather, crouched) was engulfed in warm dry hay. The smell was comforting and I suddenly felt tired. There was nowhere to go, nothing pressing to do so I decided to have a nap. Getting out of the place could be put off until morning. Just an hour or so, I promised myself.....

As so often happens with me (though I hate to admit it) I did sleep rather a long time. Watery, wintry sunshine was fighting to penetrate the stained glass window high up in the wall. (Not really a stained glass window as one is familiar with in churches and such places – more the result of someone having done some paining carelessly. Anyway, you couldn't see through it properly.) After my stretches, a few twists and turns and a quick look around what was, in daylight, an extremely uninteresting place, I made for the door. It was quite firmly shut. The window was quite firmly shut too (probably stuck with paint). The floor was stone and there were no gaps in the thick walls. There was no easy way out. In fact, there was no way out at all. Being quite phlegmatic (as I can be on some occasions) I told myself there was nothing to do but sit and wait for some external force to release me - someone to open the door or, less likely, to break a window. So I sat quietly for about two minutes before my patience ran out. Washing abruptly, I realised I would have to form a plan for escape. Then it dawned on me that I was getting hungry. Nothing stirred. Not a mouse, a bird or even a sizeable fly. I was alone in this comfortable, warm, sweet-smelling-hay place. Squinting up at the window I realised the sun was high – quite high – in the sky. Which meant it was late morning. And what was happening in the early morning? The boat was going!

I paced up and down, bits of hay sticking between my claws. They would have set sail (well, not exactly set sail, but, certainly got going) at first light, or at least after a good breakfast – breakfast! I could almost smell the crispy bacon and the lovely rich aroma of baked beans in tomato sauce. How I used to enjoy my baked beans!

Prowling around the room I fought to keep calm. If I left now and hurried I might still catch them. But no, possibly once they realised I wasn't aboard they might wait. Search for me even? On the other hand (the more likely hand) they would not necessarily miss me for some hours, assuming me to be curled up asleep somewhere out of sight. I tried to work everything out logically. It wouldn't take them long to reach the winding point where the boat would be turned around for its homeward journey. They would then chug back past last night's mooring. How much time would this take? Looking up again at the position of the sun filtering between the magnolia coloured paint streaks in the window, every instinct told me this would probably have been hours ago. Why had I stupidly slept for so long? But even if I had woken up, how would I have escaped from this building? And how was I going to escape now? Then the thought of Minnie and Sooty discovering me cheered me slightly. But they didn't come. I got hungrier and colder during the long day and it started to get dark again.

Then someone opened the big wooden door. Who or why I will never know. As the footsteps crunched outside and whoever it was stopped to turn the handle I hunched down, ready. As the door swung open I sped out, dashing through the grounds down towards where I knew the canal was.

Galloping along the track and over the bridge, coming again to the car park (which was now filled with vehicles) and down the paved area to the water. There were no boats there. Not caring if I was spotted I collapsed in a miserable heap on the towpath. Just feet away were the holes that our mooring stakes had made – alongside the commercial mooring posts. Gulping, I recognised the marks that our gangplank had left. Our gangplank? Shaking my head viciously I knew that 'our' might be wistful thinking. If the boat and Ben and Robbie had gone without me what was I to do? I shuddered and shivered and crept back into the weeded bank. Surely they would come back when they realised I was missing? But I knew their schedule was tight, with little time for hanging about. I knew also that long boats cannot be manoeuvred around easily. More likely, they might have thought that I had just gone off, decided to go to somewhere else. Which was exactly what I had been contemplating, thinking about. Was this, then, what my mother had always referred to as 'poetic justice'?

I sat and thought, and got colder as the late afternoon turned into evening. And because I was so cold and hungry and miserable and too full of misplaced pride to throw myself on the mercy of my erstwhile friends – and I still half hoped the restaurant boat might re-appear - I found myself drawn towards the pub by the car park. If I sheltered there, somewhere, I could keep one eye on the mooring place. (And it was a lot nearer than the house where Sooty and Minnie were no doubt curled up in luxury.) The big yellow lit windows seemed so appealing in that they promised heating and food and drink. I sidled towards the building. Sneaking into the covered porch I forgot about keeping watch on the canal and when the door opened I scurried inside the pub. The hallway was warm and under the radiator seemed a good place to hide and thaw out. As I crouched low, close to the skirting board, my paws discovered a bag of half eaten crisps. (Not my first choice in good eating, but I was starving.) Several women stopped and stroked me (the men pretended not to see me) and one lady even went back inside to the lounge where she had had her bar meal and reappeared with some chicken pieces wrapped in a piece of tissue. I purred exceptionally loudly and rubbed myself against her smart dark trousers to show my gratitude.

"You're walking rather gingerly!" spluttered her young male companion, who doubled up laughing at the sight of her one fluffy leg. (I inwardly cursed Robbie and Ben for not ever grooming me. How can one possibly maintain any reasonable standard when one moults indiscriminately all the time?)

But the girl took it in good part and patted me and they left me to enjoy my dinner.

Then there was a commotion inside and the double glass doors from the lounge were flung open wide. A short, stocky unshaven old man was being ejected.

"Now, get going Jim!" a voice from inside the crowded room shouted, "An' don't come back until you're sober!"

Clearly, there was some force behind Jim's assisted departure and as he sprawled, attempting to keep his balance, his muddy boot struck me in the side. I screeched with pain and ran outside, through the hall door which had stuck temporarily ajar. Jim stumbled after me. If I had expected an apology I was unlucky. He kicked out at me and swore rather expansively. Crouching and spitting I decided that this was not a nice old man. Then, before I could manage any further disagreeable thoughts about him, he stooped and deftly scooped me up, pushing me into some kind of smelly coarse canvas bag where bits of bones and some screwed up papers swished about. Gripping the material frantically I retched as he swung the contraption up over his arm, banging me uncomfortably against his back. I shouted my protests as loud as I could. But the man ignored me. Screaming for someone to help me I realised then that I was Jim's prisoner.

# CHAPTER 25

"Buffin cat!" he rasped as he bumped down the pathway, jarring my poor body against his stronger frame.

'Help! Someone help me, please!' I blinked to myself.

"Buffin pub!" he added for good measure. He continued stomping and weaving his way, muttering to himself. I clung on as tightly as I could in the blackness but I was still jostled and banged about. The cloth was thick and black and there were no holes or places to look through. The opening seemed to be shut by some draw-string which gathered in the fabric and crinkled it in somewhere above my head. I tried to turn my neck or move my body as we padded along but the continuous movement of the sack just shook me back down again. Then I heard rushing water. The lock! We must be back near the canal. A terrible thought washed into my head with the familiar sound. Surely to God he wasn't going to throw me in! How I wished I had gone in to see Minnie and Sooty, even if they had disowned me and told me to go away. At least I would be alive and not be on the verge of being drowned. (After the episode with the fat woman and now this, I seemed destined to end my cat life by being submerged.) I stirred around and attempted to claw my way to the top of the bag but the neck was closed tightly and the weight of my movement made sure it held firmly that way. Old Jim still walked on, trudging heavily and occasionally stumbling. Once or twice I felt him kick out at something in his path. He stopped and turned sharply, seeming to walk away from the noises of the lock. We were obviously, thankfully, making our way unsteadily down the towpath away from the gates, away from Sooty's house.

"Buffin boat!" Jim said, almost conversationally, the aggression disappearing.

Boat? Did this mean he was from a boat? My little heart started to pump quickly, hopefully. But which way was he going? Could it possibly be that he was going the same way as

My Boat? This question was immediately, conveniently, answered.

"Buffin lock!" he said stopping suddenly. "Thank Gawd, don't have to go through. Buffin lock! Thank Gawd, done it!"

Yes, Yes, I reiterated. Thank Gawd indeed! So his boat was going the right way. My mobile prison was flung down on to the sharp frosty ground. My poor bones reverberated with the jolt but I scrambled frantically to try to find the opening, amongst the squalid bits and pieces that stuck to the material. But Jim was too quick for me.

"Buffin bag!" he said reasonably, "Buffin boat!" he added.

Then the bag was gathered up and swung with a breathtaking whoosh into the air. Then it banged down again on to something very solid.

"Into the buffin boat you go, buffin cat!" This was my initiation into the vessel, Swan the Third.

There was a thud as he stepped aboard and the craft rocked and swayed frighteningly. Something metal was knocked over and clattered on the deck nearby and I and my bag were literally dragged down a couple of steps and pulled over what must have been the floor bar of a doorway. My sore legs tried to connect with the ground beneath the material but he tugged me along so roughly that I just rolled about like a rag doll. I heard another door open and Jim slid the bag and me along the floor until we hit a wall (sorry bulkhead). The door crashed shut. Somewhere outside a voice shouted through the night.

"Ahoy! Is that Jim of the Swany-Third? Well, mate, what time do you call this? Thought you was going off this afternoon."

Jim cleared his throat noisily. "Right you are, buffin right!" he yelled back. "Got held up in the Arms. Got talking, buffin talking,"

"Don' you mean drinkin?" laughed the other voice.

"Never you buffin mind," Jim retorted, snorting. "I'll be off afore you wakes in the mornin' - you see. You buffin see!"

There was some laughter from the other boat then silence. My captor then shuffled away and after a few moments the quiet was pieced by the unmistakable sound of a stream of liquid hitting the canal surface. From the grunts and sighs of release I surmised this was my host, relieving himself over the side into the canal.

"Buffin tired!" he muttered loudly to himself, then I heard a heavy thud and assumed he had fallen to the frozen deck where he must have gone to sleep. I waited a short while to be sure he would not come barging back in but there was no movement. After a brief lick at my sore places I got down to the task of systemically scratching at the folds of the bag until I felt the top cords start to loosen. Prising the neck of the material apart I crawled carefully out and zoomed my head around the cramped little room.

Somehow I had expected to find this was a plastic boat – the sort weekenders use – but no, it was a proper narrow boat. Through the gloom it looked more like a wooden construction, not metal as My Boat had been. This was considerably older too, I was sure, judging by the musty smell and the uneven sides where wood had peeled away, leaving indentations. There was nothing in the cabin except logs. Some were in bundles, some were just lying around on the floor. This is obviously some sort of work boat, I told myself.

As I sat there two small mice strolled out over a bundle of wood. Absolute cheek! A swift leap, an accurate pounce and slight movement of one paw and I had them both. In my agitated state I was in no mood for games so I just ate the fanciable bits and left the carcass's in the middle of the floor for Jim to see and appreciate, if he was ever in a fit state. The door was firmly closed and all I could see through the small round side porthole was the white frost covered bank bobbing up and down drunkenly in the moonlight.

Turning, I was amazed to be confronted by not two but three more quite sizeable mice, actually strolling across the floor boards, just feet away from my tail. 'Scat!' I hissed but they just stood and stared, obviously never having seen a vicious animal like me before. They continued their walk, disappearing behind the piles of logs. Normally the matter would not have rested there but I really was feeling full. (Pieces of chicken, crisps and now two young mice made me feel definitely bloated and, believe it or not, more than a little tired.) As there seemed no way out of the room there wasn't really much I could do about my predicament so I decided to rumple the cloth bag to lay on it. It would make an adequate bed for my aching bones until I worked out a way of escape. (I always seemed to be forming plans of escape lately.) Abandoning the idea of making a plan just then, I curled up gently, trying to lay my bruised self as comfortably as possible. Then I had no trouble in dropping off to sleep. It should have been a good long sleep but every few minutes, it seemed, something rustled, shuffled or squeaked. My one slitted eye confirmed that the place was alive with vermin. There were probably rats too, and worse. I had heard stories of things that live in and by canals and rivers and the prospect of sharing quarters, even temporarily, with any of them made me shiver. I was a domestic, home loving creature who enjoyed civilised cuisine such as personally cooked meals, tasty leftovers and fresh milk - preferably cream. Mice and the like were only consumed out of dire need, and rats? Mmm! If they came in numbers they would probably tear me apart. Somehow, though, I managed some sleep, hoping that sometime the following day Jim might shake off his drunken stupor enough to release me or at least to get the boat moving down the canal towards My Boat. But, I reasoned in my half awake state, the old man could well be out of action for a day or two.

I sighed and got up, turning slowly and laying down the other way around on my still warm makeshift bed. Then I heard the engine start. It spluttered and banged into action. I scanned the little porthole, but it was only just starting to get light. Who had started the boat? Certainly old Jim would be still lying on his frozen deck. Maybe he had passed away during the night of hypothermia, and someone else had taken over. Then his melodious tones broke into the early morning.

"Buffin boats all tied up too close!" he shouted into the crisp air. "Get yours further orf next time!" he yelled as I felt movement away from the bank. "An' I said I would be away afore yer!" he really hollered these last few words.

"Ger Orf, you stupid old Swany-Third!" the voice of the previous evening bellowed back, "No wonder old First and Second Swans gave up! The way you drive this poor old crate – it won't last much longer. How's the 'ed this mornin'?"

The same dry laugh chopped through the stillness as old Jim shouted back. "Buffin nuisance, you are, don' know how they let you on the cut. Buffin menace to shippin' you are!"

I felt our nose turn outwards and the sudden forwards lurch of departure almost rolled me off my lumpy piece of cloth. We were on our way, going in the right direction and I had not (yet) been heaved into the canal. I washed as best I could, carefully avoiding grooming behind my ears because, as everyone knows, cats only wash behind their ears when they mean to stay in a place permanently. And I had no such intention. Then I sat down, patiently awaiting my anticipated release. Surely he would have to come in here sometime? As we gathered speed, heavy footsteps sounded outside as Jim, no doubt, was collecting and stowing loose ropes before he took up his position to steer. I had no idea of the size of the boat but if my little room was anything to go by it was fairly small. As the patch of sky outside lightened it struck me how warm everywhere seemed to be. Concentrating on the steady thump, thump that shook the craft I realised that this was no modern style engine mounted unobtrusively beneath the flooring; the sound came from behind me and I could really smell the warmth rather than just sense it. Then, without warning the door was kicked open and the tattered arm of Jim's jacket curled in. I edged towards the opening just as his bony fingers closed around two small rough cut logs. Then his whole body appeared and he kicked out towards where I hovered.

"Get back, Buffin cat!" he greeted me, pushing the door to again. "Can't move the buffin boat, get the wood and watch out fer you. You stay! Catch some of these buffin mice!" He stooped to pick up more of the loose wood that rolled about the floor. "I'll not feed yer," he promised menacingly. "Yaam buffin here for keeping the mice down!" he added, just in case I might be suffering some misconception of his hospitality. "An' don' crap all over the buffin place. Do yer business in the corner back o' the wood. I hose it when wood's gone."

Well, I thought, he had made that fairly clear, though from the state of the place it was obviously some time sine the last hosing down.

"An' don' yer pee on the wood, else can't sell it. Buffin wood!" he finished in his customary manner.

As he pulled the door ajar behind him and squeezed his considerable bulk through the small space he kicked out brutally in my direction to oppress any move I might have thought of making. Just then, the piercing, warning wail of an oncoming vessel suggested that Jim might have neglected his post for a fraction too long and I slunk down, awaiting the collision which surprisingly, never came. Shouts were exchanged and the sound of boat hooks, or similar, thudding against our roof were quite discernible above the row that the two revving engines were making.

"Buffin boats!" Jim muttered to himself when danger had passed and things became relatively quiet again. I realised then that he was quite close by me and, from the various sounds that were being made, it seemed that whilst he steered the Swan he was taking his hands off the tiller periodically in order to throw wood into a stove; probably on the other side of the partition that separated us. I could hear the damp timber spit and sizzle. This explained our erratic wandering progress and also the welcome heat. Grudgingly I had to admit that the old man must have his hands full, manning the boat alone, keeping an eye on the engine (wherever it was) and feeding the heating stove. Full of liquor and possibly with a thick head, he certainly had his work cut out but, I came to the conclusion, he probably had had many years experience of it all. So, I mused mournfully, I was to be an involuntary vermin catcher, reliant only on my kill for nourishment. My tongue made long desperate swipes along my tail to the tip – a gesture cultivated by many cats when something rests heavily on their minds. I knew I just had to get out somehow.

The morning was blessed with sun again and the little cabin room became reasonably light. There were no signs of my small hairy companions, save their hard curly black droppings strewn across the floor. (It appeared that their toilet arrangements were not as stringent as mine.) So, old Jim sold logs for a living. Presumably the tied up bundles were for trading and the motley odd bits and branch ends that bumped against each other were for powering the Swan's heater system. Looking around it figured he would soon be taking on more as his stock was pretty low, unless there was an additional storage area. There was no point in sitting waiting for this possible reloading stop though; it might not be for ages. I couldn't stay for that much longer. There must be some way to get out. Springing up on to one of the wood piles I squinted through the small porthole. The bank scenario had been replaced with buildings that looked like disused factories, and scrap metal was littered about by the footpath. Railings and brick walls obscured the view from time to time, as we swished along, but sitting up there was marginally more interesting than shuffling about down on the floor. We passed people walking and a dog or two. Cows in a field reminded me of when Minnie and I had made our journey together. This filled me with remorse again about not having gone in to see her and Sooty. Before I could dwell on this, the Swan headed unexpectedly towards the side bank and her speed decreased quite abruptly. Apparently we were going to stop. As old Jim jumped from the boat, his bandy legs flew past my window and I watched as he tried to hammer a stake into the relentlessly hard ground.

"Buffin ground!" he cursed, throwing the stake back into the boat.

After a brief glance around he tied the fore and aft ropes to dangerously leaning tree branches. I half expected him to remonstrate 'Buffin trees' to the shrubs but he was surely appreciative of their help as he said nothing. He trudged up the slight banking and squeezed himself through a break in the rusting metal fence before heading towards a sign which swung crazily in the wind outside a bleak solitary building. I couldn't read the sign but a horse's head grinned garishly down as Jim pushed his way between metal barrels to the door of what was obviously one of his regular watering holes. I shuddered. How he could manage any more after last night's episode was beyond me. Then I remembered, fleetingly, how I had drank Tina's wine and vowed never to drink again. Those had been the days, they certainly had. I sniffed and shook myself. Positive thoughts only, I warned.

As old Jim downed his pints, or whatever, the boat became colder. I moved from my viewing position back down on to the floor and sought out my black bag. Dragging it across the boarding between my teeth I tried in vain to shake it from side to side. If I could dislodge its doubtful contents the thing might be pummelled into a more comfortable resting place. The bones and other rubbish did not budge so I moved the material about and shuffled it up into a sort of cushion, trying to keep its lumpy contents out at the edges. In my efforts to clean and freshen my bed I had, in fact, made it messier – the nasty little do's of the mice now clinging and nestling in its folds. As it was getting very cold indeed I did some brief exercises to keep my circulation going and then burrowed beneath the cloth and succeeded in making a short tunnel in which to snuggle. I was tempted to go right inside again but was afraid that either the bag might be picked up and again render me a mobile prisoner or that the meat sticking to the bones might have gone off completely and present a danger to my health. I lay shivering in my shroud, for once completely unable to sleep.

Then I heard low voices on the path beside the porthole window. I strained my ears but couldn't make out what was being said. There seemed to be a lot of murmuring and shushing and then I felt the boat sway and heard light footfalls as someone climbed aboard. Keeping my body well concealed inside my bag-bed, my ears and nose quivered in an effort to make out what was happening. One thing was for sure. It certainly wasn't the return of old Jim.

# CHAPTER 26

The boarding party was quiet and efficient. My door was opened softly and a voice whispered to its companions, "Nothing, only wood."

I was tempted to leap over the logs and make a run for freedom through the small door space but caution warned me to wait. More than one human standing so close to the exit could inflict serious damage to a hurrying pusscat. I could see several legs, and a face was peering in. After a quick look around, the door was closed again. Drat! My chance had gone. Footsteps sounded faintly as the boat was examined by the newcomers. This did not take long and three voices spoke lowly, just the other side of the wooden partition. Whoever was there must have lent up against the door as I could clearly hear what they were saying.

"The old bloke will be in the Horse's Head till mid afternoon at least. It's his habit. But I'll try to keep him there 'til evening." A man, who sounded quite young said, his voice barely above a mumble.

"Are you absolutely sure?" Another man, much older, questioned gruffly.

"I'm sure," the first voice said more firmly, "I've cased this thoroughly, trust me. You can be miles away by the time he gets back. He'll be so out of his skull that he'll probably forget where he left the boat anyway. I can tell you he's spent more than one night in that old 'bus shelter up there."

"How do you know all this?" hissed the first.

"I told you, I've researched it well, trust me," the younger voice said. "In the next few miles you've got two junctions – he'll never know which way you've gone."

"You can't go very fast in one of these to get anywhere quickly," a woman's voice interrupted in a low drawl. "And is it really worth all the aggro? And money?" adding in a wheedling tone. "The boat's not worth all that much."

"This boat, I assure you, and as your gentleman friend well knows, is a gem.' The young salesman said earnestly.

"One of the last timber built craft which, until the last couple of years when the old man took it over from his cousin, has had every care and attention lavished on it. Once you get it in your place, under cover, it won't take long to put it to rights." The young person went on almost casually. "They really built them in those days. It will be an enthusiast's dream. You'll be able to turn it around – no problem, trust me. You agreed how much you normally have to do to a boat in order to get a reasonable return. For half the work, on this little beauty, you'll be getting twice the profit. Can't lose. Solid elm bottom. Will go on for years, not like these steel ones that need patching up every so often. As you well know," he finished, for good measure.

One of them coughed energetically. "I would suggest," the older man spoke again, clearing the phlegm from his throat. "That you come some of the way with us before we settle up with you. Although we had a quick look round her with you when the old bloke was away on his last drinking spree, we didn't go over it in detail. We want to be sure we haven't paid handsomely for a lame duck. We need a trial and we need to know we can get it away to…well, where we are taking it."

"You don't need any trial. The boat works 7 days a week 365 days a year. What more proof of reliability do you need? You know you'll never find another deal like this. You'd be mad to pass it up. There's no danger at all." the young voice went on arrogantly, "Anyway, I've got to go back to the pub and make sure the old blighter stays in the bar, preferably until closing. When it's dark he won't even try to get back to his boat. By morning you'll have sunk without trace, as they put it. Anyway," he continued, "I don't want to know which way you're going. For all I know you may even be intending to winch the thing out and have it towed away. You said you have somewhere to take it to but I just don't need to know the details. You're getting it at rock bottom – I'm practically giving it away!"

"Hardly yours to give away," the other said drily.

"I bet you're familiar with all the boatyards and marinas for miles around, you could easily find out where we've taken her. You're a local lad, not strangers like us." The woman said evenly.

The older man cut in sharply. "That's right, you, give him all the gen. about us. The deal was, he finds us something, we pay. Nothing more. So button up, there's a good girl!"

"I'll untie you," the young voice said, relief sounding in his voice. The boat rocked slightly as he moved about. "No locks for miles in either direction – just make way as fast as you can. There's nothing about these days, the cut's empty. You've got at least five hours clear in front of you, trust me."

The other man grunted and from the swaying movement I gathered that they all must have moved to the side of the boat. "How much did we say?" he asked grudgingly.

"Six grand - cash," the young voice said precisely. "And a real bargain. Worth at least ten times that. And you've got a full tank, I've checked, with spare can for'ard. A real bargain!"

"We're taking the risk," the woman pointed out.

"No risk at all," the younger man replied smoothly. "You'll be wherever you're going in no time. You told me you worked it out. No, no risk. Just got yourselves a little goldmine. Anyway," his tone became treacly. "You know where to find me if you need anything else. Equipment, day boats, times and dates when residential vessels are left unattended – some of these old dears have some very nice stuff stashed away.."

"I am not a common thief!" spluttered his accomplice. "I'm not into taking old ladies' jewellery."

"I could do with something nice," the woman whined plaintively.

"Shut it!" snapped the man, then, "Here's your money. And," he added darkly, "If we're followed or if anything goes wrong in any way, as you say, we know just where to find you."

"Nothing will go wrong. Trust me. Just get off quickly and get it under cover and keep it there for a while. I know about the old bloke. He's had heart attacks and a stroke. He's not long for this world anyway. He'll be gone by the time you get the boat all sorted. How many grand will you sell it for then? And, talking of money and profit - what about some expenses?" he demanded, quite loudly, I thought. "I'll have to buy him ale all day and some mushy peas and chips…"

"Not a chance," the woman said sweetly. "See you again, though - possibly."

The boat rocked and swayed and nothing more was said. The engine was started and, strangers though they may be, the hijacking couple were well able to handle the boat efficiently. We practically sped along, going steadily and straight – none of old Jim's weaving from side to side. I sank back into my cover and wondered when and if they might open my door. Starting to breathe deeply and feeling my body relax down, I was very nearly allowing my eyelids to feel heavy.

'What's your name?' a pair of dull eyes asked, peering under my tent-like hood. (It was a good job I hadn't really been asleep otherwise I might have missed this encounter. As it was my slit eyes had been on the verge of drooping.) My head shot up and the black material slipped away, down my neck. Some type of rodent was confronting me. It looked like a cross between a very thin low-slung rat and a misshapen spineless hedgehog. Or it could have been a flattened squirrel.

'What are you?' I narrowed my eyes to assume an expression of strength should this be apposite. The strange creature could have even been a vicious snake with a fur coat on (unlikely, as there were also little feet protruding and a tail.) 'Well?' I demanded again.

My visitor backed off but kept its misty eyes on my face. 'I asked you first – what's your name?'

Then I felt a rush of happiness. Another being! At last! Something I could talk with! 'OK!' I said, smiling as much as I could manage, just in case it should get fed up and disappear, 'OK! My name's…' God! Don't say I've forgotten my name, my cat name! No, of course, not. 'My name is Penny,' I said hoping the visitor would put the pause down to strategic timing on my part. 'And,' I repeated quickly, 'What, and who are you? And what are you doing in my… er.. .this boat?' I shook the bag from my back and gave myself a casual wash. Never having been one to greet guests straight from a nap without some sort of tidy up, I didn't want to overdo it as this may have construed more importance than was called for on the occasion.

'I'm a water vole and I live in a hole,' the thing said poetically. 'And my name is just, Vole.'

Oh yes, I thought, turning away so as not to offend. One of those. An animal that no one ever bothered to name. Only the wanted, the hierarchy, were given identification, I thought smugly. The others just assumed the title of their type, except, of course, those who were intelligent enough to acquire or make up names so as to get on in the world.

'If you live in a hole, what are you doing here? There are no holes here, I hope.' Noting that Vole looked quite small beside me when I stood, and that he had noticed this too, I could afford to joke. He was certainly not going to be a threat to me although I would keep clear of those nasty little teeth he kept sticking out when his eyes spoke.

'I am a Zoon, and I have been abducted on this boat,' I boasted. There is no point finding someone to talk with if you can't impress them.

'I'm a Zoon too,' he said immediately, relaxing somewhat. 'Abducted? I haven't heard that word for years,' he mused thoughtfully before continuing. 'But I suppose I was, as well. Abducted, I mean. I climbed up the side bank earlier to get some bits of lettuce that were laying about and I slipped over the edge and fell into the boat. Before I could work out the best way to get back to the grass – I live on the bank, as you must have guessed – before I could do this, the engine started. Frightened me to bits, absolutely, and..'

'Yes, Yes,' I interrupted his narrative. Would he ever have stopped otherwise? 'And now you are an unscheduled passenger too.'

'Unscheduled?'

'Yes,' I replied importantly. 'I was abducted, taken prisoner, before the vessel was hijacked.

'You mean, these people, aren't the owners? It's not theirs?'

'It is not theirs,' I confirmed.

We sat in silence for a few moments, listening to the engine which seemed to have adopted a more rigorous tone.

'We're going quite fast,' he observed. He wasn't so stupid, this vole. 'Too fast,' he said. 'There's a speed limit, you know, if anyone goes too fast it makes big waves, makes it dangerous for other boats, particularly ones that are moored, though at this time of year, there's not much traffic and..'

'Yes,' I said loudly to shut him up. Were all voles so chattery, I wondered. 'How long have you been a Zoon?'

'I don't know,' he said quietly. 'It's so long ago that I've forgotten. I forget most things now. I can't remember much of my other life at all so I suppose I must be getting on and...'

'YES!' I flashed at him.

'How are we going to get out?' he was off again.

'How did you get in, into this room?' I countered, half hoping he knew of a secret way.

'I've been behind the logs watching you,' he said snidely. 'Was outside to start with, then came in when they opened the door, when the three were looking in. Didn't want to risk them seeing me. They didn't look good people.'

They couldn't be worse than Old Jim, I thought. I watched Vole stretch and settle down. I gave myself a good shake, then started to wash properly (still assiduously avoiding the spots behind my ears.) I certainly needed a good clean as my coat was beginning to smell, which, given the circumstances, was not surprising. I smiled to myself as I remembered Tabatha (and my mother) going on about keeping up standards. On the one hand I was exhilarated to be speeding towards my own, the restaurant, boat, and out of Old Jim's clutches, but on the other hand I was fearful of the unknown. What if the thieves were cruel and unkind and hated cats? How I wished once more that the lure of those extra days on the restaurant boat had not influenced my intended reunification with Minnie and Sooty.

'They will open the door soon,' Vole said thoughtfully. 'They will need logs for the stove otherwise we'll all freeze to death.' This made sense but I wasn't holding my breath. At best, we (well, I had to include Vole I supposed) could dash out when the door was opened and chance being able to make for safety. At worst they could discover us and beat us to death. As I had been staring at Vole, he picked up my gist.

'How would we get to the bank?' he asked sensibly. 'I'm too little to jump far, though I'd quite welcome a swim. But you? Unless we were close in, you would get very wet and I don't believe you would like this.'

We exchanged thoughts in this vein for a while until the engine started to noticeably slow down. The rate of chugging decreased and the steering seemed to change direction.

'A lock maybe?' Vole suggested.

'Or a junction,' I put in. 'Maybe they're turning to change canals. I heard them say there were no locks.'

'Ah!' my companion said knowingly, 'That was the youngster who said that. He would say anything to make a few bob.'

'Bob?' Oh yes, before decimalisation. 'You remember that? About bobs?' I asked with surprise.

'I can remember some things. Important things,' he stated. 'But not the things I want to remember, things like..'

'Right!' How many other useful conversation-stopping phrases would I be able to conjure up?

'That young man is well known where I come from. Well, where I came from,' he finished sadly.

I turned away from him. It was true, we must have covered several miles from the Horse's Head and maybe more from the bank where Vole lived. Could voles run or might he swim back?

'Yes, we are definitely going into the side,' he said, perking up. He was right. The engine stopped completely and the boat swung sideways, obviously someone was yanking it towards the edge of the canal.

"Get a move on!" the man shouted and his legs came into view through the porthole.

"Coming!" shouted back the woman.

There was little fuss. Within seconds we realised we were securely tied up alongside.

'I'll just clear us some loose logs out," the man shouted again and our door was opened. The fellow was either careless or in a hurry as he did not notice us sitting towards the far edge of the little cabin. He picked up some wood and threw it in a bucket which swung from his arm.

"That'll do," he muttered and strode out, leaving the door slightly open. "I'll stoke up the stove immediately we get back. Not locking up - won't be long," he yelled to the woman whose footfalls were already receding into the distance. He plonked the bucket down somewhere in the cockpit with a loud clang and moments later sprang off the boat.

"Hang on, wait for me!" he called.

"Just need fags and the loo!" she sang back.

"Right! I'll do the drinking water, just in case. Don't think we'll make it before dark, might need a stopover for a few hours and get going again at first light."

"Well, I'm not spending the night on that, not in that state," she said loudly, clearly having backtracked towards him.

"OK, We'll find a pub if needs be but we should make it. As soon as it gets dusk, we'll put the temporary cloth signs over the side panels so no one will recognise it."

"Why not now?" she questioned impatiently, "Then if someone sees us, it won't look like the same boat, the one they may be out looking for."

"I told you," he said slowly, "If we're stopped now we just hired it for a couple of days from that nice young Martin Thomas. Don't fret – I marked all the notes we paid him, well traceable they are. Our friends will sort him out – we won't lose any money over it. We know where he hangs out – anyway he'll still be in the Horse's Head until closing time I shouldn't wonder, earning his keep." He chuckled. "In an hour or so we'll be far enough away to change the side logo's if we need to, but we might just make it back to get under cover by then. No worries either way."

She started to walk away from him again, humming to herself. Then we heard him running to catch up with her. As one, Vole and I hurried from our room, and through the tiny living room with the singing stove. The afternoon light clearly seemed to upset him as he seemed to struggle to maintain balance. (Were voles blind like moles, I asked myself. I had read somewhere, sometime, that they only ate plants but knew little else about them.) He was first off, clattering up onto the bucket of logs and then gingerly stepping on to the wet rim of the boat. I watched, envying his courage, as he crouched down on to his stomach and made a spectacular leap. We were right alongside, with all three ropes pulled quite taut, leaving no room for movement. In fact, the side of Swan the Third was wedged tightly against the grass. But, somehow Vole missed. His heroic jump to safety ended with a gentle splash and for a second his small head bobbed up and down before his body streaked over the water in a graceful line. My attempt was more successful and my paws landed in almost perfect fashion.

'What are you doing in there?' I lent over the edge of the bank, watching him cavort about making icy ripples.

'S'wonderful!' he spluttered. 'Just great to be back in the water. I miss it so much when I'm away for any length of time I feel ...'

Fortunately he turned away and I was saved the report on his current feelings. I shook the dirt from my legs and looked carefully around. This was indeed a junction with the canal stretching in three different directions. Boats were moored in a line nearby and banks of boats, two or three deep, were tied up in a hollowed out marina. There was a large car park and boathouses and other buildings along the water's edge. This was hire craft country, I told myself.

'Can you read?' Vole asked climbing the bank deftly.

'No,' I said shortly as we both stared at the little wooden signpost.

Two canals were going towards places with long names whilst the third pointed to a lesser place.

'Which way did we come?' he asked, scratching his head. (I really did wish he would hide those teeth. They weren't at all pleasant to look at. Even though he spoke with his eyes, his mouth kept opening and shutting as if contributing towards the conversation.)

'We came this way,' I said firmly, nodding my head towards my uneducated guess.

'No, I don't think so,' he argued.

'Well, look at the direction the boat is pointing and we definitely did not turn all the way around. So it's not that way. It's either that one or this one and I emphatically think we came down that way.' Even so I wasn't sure and neither was he. He was willing to take a chance though on the one I'd selected.

'I'm starting for home,' he said, his nose quivering with excitement. 'My family is at home. It's a big family, you know. There are children there I have to tell stories to and..'

'Your children? Or grandchildren?' I enquired, more to quell his flow than because I really wanted to know.

'Who knows?' he said nonchalantly. 'Who knows whose children they are. But there are a lot.'

There was no point in pursuing this further so I said, 'Are you going to walk or swim?'

'Bit of both,' he said, already setting off in the direction we almost agreed we had come. 'But hopefully, catch a ride if there's anything going that way.'

'It could be an awful long way,' I was quite amazed at his nerve.

'Absolutely,' he agreed. 'But there will be folks all the way along. Some will be Zoons so I can ask. All I need to know is where the Horse's Head bank is. Someone will know.'

He seemed happily determined so I called after him 'Well, goodbye then! Thanks for your company!'

He waggled his head at me and turned briefly.

'Goodbye and good luck!' he stared back at me in a final gesture of farewell and then disappeared into the long grass.

# CHAPTER 27

Which way? What to do next? I was still fairly sure of the direction we had come but whether to climb back into the Swan and hide somewhere on the deck until we caught up with the floating restaurant was another question. It was just possible that the Swan might not be going along the same canal as My Boat, and although I sprang up on to a length of fence, there was no movement to be seen anywhere ahead on the three waterways. I slithered down and sat in the wet grass. A decision would have to be made soon as the thieving twosome would be back any minute. Gazing desperately around for someone I might ask I tried ducks, birds, two cows looking over the hedge and a couple of sheep grazing on a vegetable plot opposite. None were Zoons. They just waggled their ears and carried on with whatever they were doing. Eventually a rather stout donkey ambled up to the cows.

'Problems?' he blinked his black eyes in my direction.

'Oh Yes! Thank goodness!' relief flooded through me. 'I'm in a hurry to catch up with a big, very long narrow boat. It's a floating restaurant. There are lights hung all over it, though they wouldn't be on now I don't suppose, and Christmas decorations at all the windows. And a Christmas tree at the back. Have you seen it? Which way did it go?'

'Nay, Nay,' he shook his head sadly. 'Not seen anything like that today. Was it today it came?'

'Yes, of course, today,' I snapped, disappointment taking over from hope. 'It must have come past, it was ahead of us. I came down on the Swan the Third – this one just here.'

'Oh yes?' he nodded conversationally.

'Yes. It's been stolen and I was kidnapped and locked up in it.' I gabbled on.

'Oh yes?' he said in the same morose, slightly disbelieving tone.

'Yes!' I stormed. 'But I need to get back to my boat.'

'What's wrong with this one? How many boats do you want?'

Was he being intentionally sarcastic, I wondered angrily. All this was wasting time.

'I need to find that boat – the big one,' I was throwing myself on his mercy. Please help me, I begged silently.

'Nope,' he shook his big head again. 'Not seen anything like that. Been awake all day too,' he said as if there were something to be truly proud of.

Exasperated I said, 'Well it must have come this way.'

'Unless it pulled in somewhere,' he said logically, still shaking his head. (I think he might have had fleas or some other irritant as he seemed to need to shake his head a lot.) 'But then you would have seen it as you went past,' he reasoned in his dull voice.

'I would not,' I hissed, 'I told you, I was locked up.'

'Ah,' he nodded his head this time.

'It must have come this way. Have you been over the other side of the field? Might you have missed it going past?' If nothing else I was anxious to eliminate one of the canals.

'No. Nothing has gone past going any way today,' he confirmed again.

He twitched his long ears then flattened them sideways. By instinct I knew this meant his departure was imminent.

'Please!' I started, 'Are you really sure?'

This time he shook his head so violently that his shaggy mane ruffled, but his ears went back up to their rightful position. 'Told you,' he repeated, 'Nothing moved. And it won't,' he promised. 'Cause there's going to be a thicker frost tonight. They say the cut will be frozen over in places.'

'Who says?' I demanded, this piece of news adding to my despondency.

'Hire folk. And they know. Nay, nothing will be moving for a day or so. You'd best find somewhere in the warm to go.'

'Canals don't freeze over.' I said with more certainly than I felt.

'Have it your own way,' his ears flattened again. 'I've heard tell of 1917 when they froze over for days and days. Some folks can remember the time well. Nothing moved for weeks. This one's coming could last anything up to 10 days, so is said.'

He tutted loudly and bared his browning teeth. Then he shook his head again.

'Restaurant boats, lights and Christmas trees and kidnapping and boat thieving. Whatever will you think of next?' he muttered as he started to turn away. 'I'd get back on to your jail boat if I was you,' he said, 'I'm off to my old barn. Warm there. Nay.'

He then trumpeted a resounding 'EEE ORR!' and trotted away at an unexpectedly rapid rate. Further communication was halted and I watched him break into a show-off gallop towards a building in the far corner of the field. The two cows, who had witnessed our exchange with curiosity, continued munching and waggled their ears.


"Going to be a sharp one. Got to get there tonight. Fortunately it's going to be a light evening. No more stops." The man and the woman were returning. She carried a plastic bag and he held a white polythene water carrier. She said something I couldn't hear and he laughed. "Well, we'll just have to make do with the snacks we brought. I'll buy you celebration eats and some champers when we get this lot out the way."

"I should think so too! Why I let myself be conned into this I'll never know." She grumbled as they approached the Swan.

"Money!" he said swiftly.

My mind churned. If I stayed here I could shelter in one of the boat building houses or a better place if I could find one. If I jumped aboard I would have to chance finding a hiding place but at least I knew it would be warm and there might be a chance of some food or, at the very least, plenty of mice. If the canals froze no boats would move (donkey had been right about that much.) But what of Ben and Robbie? How could they do their business if they couldn't move their boat? Shrugging, I focused on my more immediate problems. The prospect of spending the rest of the day and a freezing night in a boat shed surrounded by water and ice where it would be too cold for mice or any other right-minded food to be wandering about was not attractive. As the man climbed on to the Swan and the woman started to untie the aft rope, I crouched and sprang up. The engine began to throb and the nose of the Swan headed out into the middle of the canal as I slithered down the steep steps, keeping well to the side so that the man wouldn't see me. The sun fought its way through the thin clouds and for one brief second I felt its warmth.

There were plenty of hiding places. Old Jim was probably the most untidy human ever and clothes, receptacles, boxes and other rubbish littered the outside and the passageways inside the boat. The man, at the back end, was steering and looking intently at maps that were strewn on the hatch cover. The woman was somewhere in the front of the boat. For the first time I studied the layout, which was easy as they had conveniently left all doors swinging open. At the back was a small cockpit where the business of steering was conducted. Then a tiny living cabin which housed the stove that made everywhere lovely and warm. Next was the inside wood storage room where I had been captive; this was no bigger than a large cupboard. Then, the other side of a thin partition was the place that housed the diesel engine. Trotting down the passage past this I came to an open deck area where more wood was stacked; these piles were partly covered by old greasy-looking pieces of tarpaulin. I quickly skirted this section, as it was freezing cold out there, to reach a little door which was firmly closed. I supposed that the woman was sitting somewhere inside comfortably, although not so warmly as she would have been in the rear cabin.

I cautiously made my way back to the engine room which was warm and had a nice friendly smell, although it was terribly noisy. There were piles of cloth and sacking scattered around on the floor and I crept beneath one gratefully. A short nap was required, after which I would hunt for a mouse to eat – not an appetising thought but, in an hour or so, this would become a requisite. (The couple did not look the sort who might leave any delicious scraps laying about.) In spite of the constant bang-bang of the diesel, I managed to drift into oblivion.

Curled up and fast asleep I dreamed that it was getting very, very warm. Very warm - in fact I was sweating and my fur was sticking to my skin. Surely this was more than an uncomfortable fantasy? I opened both eyes wide and my neck hair shot up vertically. Something was wrong. The engine was still clanking away and everything looked as it had before. The door into the wood store was still swinging open and I could see that it was still dimly light outside. But there seemed to be a strange feeling to the place. On the bulkheads at each side of the engine room, in the sides of the boat, were narrow shutter doors. One was tightly secured but the one on the other side of the boat, had become unfastened and banged back against the outside of the craft. I jumped up on to an upturned can and standing on my hind legs, stretched my front paws up against the bulkhead. There was a ledge just below the open window space but I didn't climb up because it was only a narrow shelf and could be a dangerous place to perch if there was sudden unexpected movement. With a little stretch upwards, I was able to balance on my can enough to clearly watch the bank and greenery creeping by as we made our way past fields and the odd house or two. Everything looked normal outside so I got back down on to the floor and performed a mini wake-up wash. It really was so warm, unnaturally so.

Then suddenly the engine died and the man clambered from his steering seat. He clomped through the wood store room and into the engine room. I pressed my body down onto the flooring but he didn't look in my direction. For a brief second he surveyed the silent machinery and I could feel the boat sway as it was no longer under power.

"Where are you? What's that smell?" he shouted, presumably to his female companion. "Marilyn – where the hell are you?"

In the front cabin? I suggested with my eyes, but you would think he could have worked this out for himself. Where else would she be? By then I was thoroughly awake. And, yes, there certainly was a smell. Not just a smell – my sensitive ears picked up a distinct crackling sound.

"Bloody Hell!" the man shouted rushing through the half open door to the outside cargo store. Cautiously I followed him taking care to keep well back.

"Marilyn! Marilyn!" he thundered desperately, running past the open storage area. He stopped suddenly as a small flame flared from beneath the door of the front cabin. The man seemed rooted to the spot as the flame licked up the edge of the door frame and the door started to blister and spit. I crouched down petrified that the great fangs might reach out to me.

"It's a fire!" he yelled frantically to no one. "We're on fire! Her and her bloody fags! Marilyn! Open the door! Marilyn!"

His voice was hoarse as he hesitated outside the door. Taking a handkerchief from his pocket, which he wound loosely around his fingers, he tried to wrench open the door but the wood was stuck and no amount of yanking at the catch would free it. The singed cloth fell from the man's burnt hand and he shook his arm about agitatedly, cursing loudly. Inside, the place must have been an inferno; the poor woman would surely have been burnt alive by now. My mind was whirling. If he had managed to force the door open, the draught would fan the flames and they would devour the whole of the Swan in moments. I stood rooted to the spot as he rushed back past me, returning seconds later with the bucket. Like a thing possessed he leant over the side and then pulled the slopping pail back on board. He threw the contents at the blackening door but it was a waste of time. The boat was floating in towards the bank and the boat was well and truly on fire.

Why was I standing here in the deep, open part which was filled with burnable timber? Get out! My inner voice demanded. I must get out! Fleetingly, remembering the agony I had suffered at the hands of the terrible children at Guy Fawkes, I didn't dare even contemplate being trapped in that boat. Streaking back to the eerily quiet engine room I jumped up on to the can again. This time I made for the shelf below the open window. Fortunately it was this side of the boat that was closest to the bank. The bank and grass were almost outside my escape hatch. I hesitated only as the boat leaned in and then drifted out into the water again. Then I heard voices, coming from the pathway opposite.

"Use your hook! Fend her off!" someone instructed and there were more shouts that I couldn't hear.

"Keep her away from the other boats!"

Panic sounded in his words. The crackling behind me gave way to a splitting, splintering sound and as the old boat burned it seemed to sigh and sing in a mournful rhythm. An anthem of farewell, I felt.

"Get more hooks from the boats at the lock!" the same voice was taking charge from across the water.

More shouting but still the bank my side was just too far away. So what? I knew I could swim (nasty, nasty thought) and I also knew I could burn – very quickly. There was no choice. Taking a mighty, deep breath I balanced on the ledge and crouched carefully in preparation for my greatest spring ever. But I just dropped into the muddy, freezing water. The boat swung out again into mid stream and away from me, towards the opposite side of the canal. Several clanking sounds confirmed that something had connected with it and was holding it more or less steady. Through the piercing cold ripples that engulfed me, it appeared that someone on the opposite path was pulling the blazing mass slowly forwards; this was good as it cleared the patch where I was splashing about, trying furiously to remember what movement should be made with my arms and legs. I must have been in great shock as I don't recall anything after hitting the water and realising I was drifting somewhere towards the stern of the burning Swan. Lifting my head, my eyes confirmed that the fire had spread, and at least half the boat was surrendering to the hungry flames. As my ears and eyes filled with the dirty water I wondered fleetingly if the man had also managed to escape. Then - blackness.

The world went dark and the shouting and screaming from the attempting rescuers drifted away into my present nightmare. But this time it was not the discomfort of feeling so hot and stifled that pummelled my subconscious. This time the horror was cold. I was encased in a solid block of ice. I had frozen to death.''

# CHAPTER 28

But I had not frozen to death. Or if I had, my new life was starting exactly where the other one had left off. I was laying half in and half out of the Arctic water. Every part of me from my ribs downwards disappeared into the mud and as there was no feeling I wondered if my back legs were still joined to me. My upper torso was wedged amongst a clump of dead sopping weeds. With some difficulty I lifted my head and turned to look sideways. Just a few yards away, on the opposite bank, was a gaudily painted, very small, home-made boat. No one moved on board. Further down, just above a lock, was a long narrow boat, seemingly on a permanent mooring judging by the equipment and various chairs stacked alongside. I could just make out the tops and chimney stacks of other barges and cruisers moored down beyond the lock. I fought to hold my exhausted head steady, my smarting eyes covering the bank in slow motion. Between these two nearer clean, bright craft was a dark, smouldering carcass. The bed of the hull rose shallowly from the canal and some resilient stanchions and pieces of infrastructure stood black and proud above the crumbling remains of the Swan the Third. Although I had no fond memories of my recent journey I felt a wave of sadness. What had once been a functional, handsomely crafted vessel now lay still and useless.

Distant voices from unseen people wafted up from below the lock gates and as my head dropped back on to the grass a siren sounded urgently. Would both the man and woman be in the back of the ambulance or would Marilyn have already been burnt to cinders along with her fags? I concentrated on breathing deeply but each intake was a struggle. If I wasn't already gone I certainly was well on the way, I acknowledged philosophically.

Just as my eyes were closing, two quite large white paws planted themselves within inches of my shivering nose. Just what I need – a nasty small white canine to stand and sneer at my sad situation. Obviously it had come to watch my demise.

It certainly wouldn't chase me as in my state I was completely unchaseable and only foolish dogs would consider risking the harm that could be metered out by a stationary cat, I told myself hopefully. I just prayed it wouldn't observe that I was incapable of even lifting a paw let alone inflicting any harm. By opening my eyes just a fraction further, two rear legs came into view through the strands of grass. Not a dog, after all. A large white cat! I stared stupidly up at my observer, my eyes rolling as I fought to concentrate and to not drift off into oblivion. The huge round green eyes stared back and there was a suggestion of a smirk around the whisker area.

'What's so damned funny?' I flashed. 'You wouldn't look at me so mockingly if you knew what I've been through. I've had it up to here!'

The eyes gazed down unblinking.

'Go on!' I spat hysterically as my whole body shook with the cold, 'Look all you like! I, who once was a successful person, good at English, had my own roof garden and,' my muddled mind meandered, 'And a champion bungee jumper!' I sobbed inside and dropped my head in anguish. My cat and human thoughts were all mixing; nothing made sense. I lifted my neck bravely, determined for one last assault. 'So don't stand staring at me! Go and waggle your stupid white ears somewhere else!'

As my chin dropped onto my matted wet chest my voyeur moved forward and squatted down beside me. Although my eyes remained tightly shut I attempted to wriggle away. My legs would not budge and my arms had no strength. I lay there quivering and, I realised to my embarrassment, making pathetic little squeaking noises.

Without warning, the nape of my neck was tightly clamped and my bedraggled little frame was dragged upwards, out of the mud and away from the water. Suddenly I could feel the undergrowth catching against my back and legs as I was pulled along – so they weren't paralysed after all. The surprise of being forcibly moved, opened my eyes instantly. But as my head banged up and down all I could see was my disgusting mud-caked stomach and those sad hind legs sticking out like stiff twigs. Then I remembered that this was how my cat mother, Lady Penelope, had carried me when I was tiny. After bumping me over weeds, stones and pieces of wood my transporter chose a smooth sheltered piece of grass on which to release me. Struggling to my feet I turned to confront those green eyes again. Before I could say a word he murmured, 'Bungee jumping eh? So that's what started it all!'

I suppose it was surprising that I hadn't for an instant considered he might be a Zoon. My frame of mind and my complete inability to move even a muscle had stopped all logical thought process. 'So you can talk. Not just waggle your ears.' I said haltingly.

'Yes,' the stranger said briskly, 'And I can see that you are in no fit state to do anything.'

'I am in rather a mess.' I admitted shakily. 'But I had to jump in, off the boat. It was burning..'

'I know,' he interrupted, 'I know all about the boat. I saw it all happen.'

'Did you see me jump in?' At that moment it seemed imperative to prove that I had some spirit, that I wasn't just a drowning stray.

'No I did not see. But that was a very challenging thing to do,' he said nodding.

Challenging would not be the word I'd have used but it mollified me a little. 'Thank you for pulling me out.. well, anyway, thanks!'

He briefly shook his spotlessly white body and then his front paws which had some of my mud adhered to them. I noticed that he had an almost circular black patch of fur on his chest and, as he shook, another smaller round patch in the centre of this back. I had never seen marking like that before.

'When did you last eat or drink?' he questioned, starting to clean his paws.

I managed to stand up without falling over (as I had expected to do) and made a brief, unsuccessful stab at licking my repulsive, smelly coat. The enormity of the task defeated me after a few seconds and I sat down again abruptly. 'Hours ago,' I said wearily.

'Firstly then,' he started in a workmanlike manner, 'We need to get you to a saucer of something even if it's only milk. Hopefully, at the same time, to get your fur wiped. Then you will feel more like washing.'

'How and where?' I whispered. I felt so weak that I almost wished he would leave me there.

'Come!' he said stretching. 'Follow me. We will go to the eating place. It is only just a few steps along from here – see just past those tall conifers?'

'Eating place?' I asked dumbly.

'Yes. It's a restaurant at lunchtime and on weekend nights and a café during the daytime in summer. By now,' he looked briefly up at the moody sky, 'They will have cleared from lunch and there will be milk and some food for us.'

'They might chase us off,' Even my words seemed to shiver. (Or even be cat catchers, or own a pack of wild dogs or set the place on fire.)

'Don't worry,' he replied soothingly. 'They know me well. I usually drop in at this time of the day. It's a bit later today, due to all the excitement. But they all came out to have a look and help. The family and the helpers.'

'All the excitement?' I shuddered.

'Yes. There's not too much excitement round here. Can you manage to walk? It's not far or I can carry you?'

I stood up immediately. 'That's very kind of you,' I said formally, inwardly dreading the thought of once again being bounced along the muddy, stony bank. 'But I'm sure I can manage. If we take it slowly,' I said as an afterthought.

Of course, then I realised why my lifesaving lift had been so uncomfortable. When a mother carries her kitten she is big and baby is small enough to swing easily from side to side through the air. Although the white cat was a large, strong specimen, I certainly was not just the size of a newly born kitten; this, then, was why my parts had caught painfully on passing pebbles, sticks and other obstacles.

Slowly we made our way past where the bright home-made boat was moored on the other bank, and on towards what remained of the Swan the Third across the water.

'Must have been a solid, well built boat,' he observed as we halted opposite to where the blackened mass was reflected funereally in the now still canal. I nodded miserably; all my energy and what spirit was left, being channelled into this short walk, which seemed like a marathon.

'Those people live on this boat,' he said, changing to a happier topic and looking across to the longer narrowboat. 'All the year round. Even now in this cold. Mad!' he said with feeling. 'They're not here now. Down past the lock with all the others. All the services were there to deal with the...'

'Excitement?' I finished with some resentment.

We walked in silence towards the house which served food. The white cat led the way along the side of the wall to the front porch.

"Hello William!" a woman in an apron stood in the entrance doorway. "You're late today. Well, hello! And who is this poor thing? Looks as if you've been in the canal."

'I have,' I told her, trying to hold myself up but the drying mud was sticking my fur together and I couldn't straighten my body. My escort, William, preened himself and rubbed against the woman companionably.

"You lovely thing!" she said effusively, "Want some milk? And I'll find you a little something, shall I? Does your friend want some too? I'll see what there is. Go round to the back door."

Obediently William, and I, following closely behind him, retreated along the side house wall again, through a small gate to another door. This was immediately opened by the same woman.

"Here then, milk first." She turned to a spacious open sided building adjacent to the main house and placed a large china dish on the stone floor, which contained enough milk for us both.

William set about his drink with gusto but I lapped hesitatingly. The liquid seemed to warm my mouth and throat though and after a few snatched gulps I started to feel a little better. Another dish was set down, filled with pieces of cooked meat and some vegetables. Again, I started falteringly,

247

chewing spasmodically and then resting but my rhythm soon increased to a steady lap, crunch, lap. William gallantly slowed down his rate of intake, giving me time to catch up and help finish the meal but I was soon full up. I just wanted to sleep. But no, I scolded myself, something must be done about my appearance. The building, in spite of not having a door, was warm and out of the wind and quite homely I thought, but William seemed puzzled. 'I usually go into the back kitchen,' he said, looking around the open fronted room.

'It's because of me,' I knew at once why it was. No clean person would want a weather-infested mess like me in their home. William leaned forward and licked my head between the ears. It felt so good, but he stopped because I think it made him feel sick. He tried again two of three times in short bursts and eventually I could move my ears as normal. Then the woman appeared again.

"Poor little thing," she said cooing down into my face. She held a piece of paper towel in one hand and with the other she held the scruff of my neck. (This very useful piece of cat was being fully utilised today, I thought. But she was no doubt ensuring that I did not dish out a spiteful scratch in return for her ministrations. I must have looked such a disreputable wreck that I couldn't blame her.) Slowly she stroked the dirt from my coat and wiped my legs. I tried to struggle (no one likes to be rubbed down with a piece of paper towel, however gentle the masseur) but eating had used up all my power and I was like a limp puppet in her grasp. "There!" she said, letting me go. "Much better. Now you get on and clean yourself, there's a good cat. And keep away from the water!"

'Yes, indeed, I certainly will try to.'

William offered suitable noises and gestures of gratitude and the woman collected up the dishes and hurried away into the house, carefully closing the back door behind her.

'We can sit here awhile if you want to,' William said kindly. 'You can recover then. They don't usually come out the back once lunchtime's over. If we keep over there to the side we'll be out of sight anyway. Or we can start for home.'

I blinked, fighting to stay awake. 'Home?' I squeaked, not understanding.

William inclined his head slightly. 'Yes,' he said quietly, 'I do have a home. Not far from here but I think it would be too much for you until you have rested awhile.'

'Home?' I savoured the lovely word. 'Might I? May I? Well......'

William sat down beside me but not too close. (I didn't know whether this was because I smelt bad or if he was simply respecting my space.) 'You can certainly stay awhile,' he said slowly, 'I know my mistress and master would not turn you away. But I can make no promises about the future.'

My face must have reflected how woebegone I was feeling as he hurried on, 'But even if you cannot stay with me, there will be a place for you somewhere up at the house – the Mansion House,' he finished grandly.

'Mansion House?' I repeated like a parrot.

'Yes,' he said gravely. 'Mine is not an average home nor, indeed, is the House. It is all steeped in a great history. But you do not need to know all this now. Here – come over here, under this seat, these sun chair pads make a comfortable bed. I have used them many times for the odd snooze. You rest and I'll keep watch. Just for an hour or so, mind. I would like to get back home before it gets really late.'

I shuffled over to a damaged wicker seat which stood by a pile of folded up white plastic chairs and their cushions. The wall opening did not take up the whole side of the lean-to building and this corner was sheltered from the elements and the floor was warm and dry, if a little dirty. Flopping down on an old discoloured cushion, my eyes closed at once. I sensed, rather than saw, my white knight (with his black blobs) take up a position of surveillance a few feet away. 'Don't you want to sleep too?' I managed, just before I started to snore. But I never knew if he replied.

# CHAPTER 29

Then the next minute he was digging his white forepaw into my neck. 'Come on, Friend, time to get up.'

'Already?' I stammered. Surely I had only just laid down?

'Up!' he levered my shoulders off the cushion, then backed away sheepishly. 'I don't usually prod people like that,' he apologised, turning in embarrassment to wash his own shoulder quickly. 'But we really must get on home, before it gets too dark.'

There was that very special word again – home - and it had the desired effect of making me positively spring from my temporary bed. I gave myself a good shake and, reassuringly, little pieces of mud flew away from my fur. With some remorse I noticed that the sun chair cushion was now even more discoloured.

'Always better to deal with when it has dried a little. You might be able to wash your face now,' he suggested.

Without more prompting I set to on this quite unpleasant task but after a few moments my eyes, whiskers, nose and ears were clean and free from unsavoury sticky matter. My face felt normal once again.

'That is excellent!' he encouraged, but deterred any further cleansing attempts by hurrying to the wall opening. 'Come!'

So I followed him out into what was left of the dim day.

'You look so much better now,' he chatted as we walked steadily across the garden.

I did feel much stronger but he considerately slowed his pace to accommodate my smaller stride.

'It is not too far but a bit complicated,' he explained. 'We don't go down to the lock, we will turn here, out through the main front gate of the restaurant.' We trotted sedately through the wide open gate and past the glassed menu panel which was set into the wall. 'Now we walk over the bridge.'

This was easily wide enough to take light traffic but, William informed me, was only really a bridleway because it did not go anywhere. 'It just leads to the lock and the river,' William said, slowing again so that I might catch up. (I dreaded to think how fast his normal strolling pace might be.)

'River?' I tried to keep my thoughts from shaking.

'Yes. The river flows just by here, very close to the canal. This is why we have such floods sometimes.'

Negotiating the canal bridge was no bother – the surface was as smooth as a road and the side walls were high. But at the other side, the road narrowed sharply as it turned towards the river. Tall reeds and grass and trees lined the banks. What a popular spot this must be during the hot weather.

'Right, now!' William said positively, as if he may have been expecting some argument on my part. 'We now go across the Essex Bridge. This old bridge spans the confluence of the Rivers Sow and Trent and is the longest stone packhorse bridge in England.'

'Is it? How fascinating,' I stuttered, my eyes fixed upon the low narrow structure whose side walls could barely be much more than a foot high.

William seemed flattered by my interest. 'They say that the Earl of Essex had it built for Queen Elizabeth 1 – it boasts fourteen arches.' We were now at the start of the bridge and through the screen of waving  grasses and leaves I could see the rushing rivers swirling about. 'It's certainly a long bridge,' I murmured, trying desperately to blot out the instant vision of the one I flew from, with the insecure harness around my human body.

'Yes,' he went on, seemingly oblivious of my distress; or maybe he understood, and this was why we were having this almost historical lecture. 'The site is much older than that. Before this bridge was built, there was an original wooden structure here. Imagine that!'

I was willing my mind to divert from imagining anything to do with bridges and heights, particularly those over large rocks. What I did try to focus on was living with Tina in her cosy home, or being on the restaurant boat with Ben and Robbie – especially Robbie who had petted me and yet made me feel important enough to be part of their small busy team. But I couldn't obliterate the thundering of the river below me.

We were now over half way across, past the point of no return and I scurried to keep close to William's magnificent tail, whilst trying not to think what my own tail must have looked like at that moment.

'I don't like this bridge much, in spite of it being old and famous,' I said clenching my teeth to stop them chattering. The frost was already thickening on the grass ahead and the cold was eating into my bones again.

'You will get used to it,' he retorted cheerfully, 'Not much further. See that building over there? Just beyond the river's edge. Well, that's my home.'

I stopped walking and rested briefly, and lifted my head to look. Just then two cyclists pedalled threateningly towards us.

'Quick! Into one of the side points!' William directed and we both darted into one of the tiny jutting out points that were dotted along each side of the bridge. 'Passing places for the old packhorses I understand,' he told me.

Having flattened myself against the rough walling I was pleased to note that yet more mud had dropped off me. My coat certainly felt lighter and I was starting to feel more like my usual self again. I had a brief shake as we walked the last length of the aged and, for me, frightening bridge. A cloud of dried dust flew into the air.

'You look much, well, cleaner,' approved my companion who stopped for a moment to scrutinize me. 'Almost appealing.' He had a smile in his eyes which gave me an agreeable, appreciated feeling. 'There! My home!' he said happily.

The narrow roadway from the bridge passed in front of William's house, going on into the distance with open fields each side. A second narrow track branched off through some padlocked iron gates, along the side of the house, disappearing between the most beautiful trees and shrubs I had ever seen. The early frost had whitened the foliage and the sweeping branches and trailing boughs cast an enchanting spell across these magic woodland gardens.

'What a place!' I breathed as we stopped beside the tall gates. There was an official looking notice fixed to the gate post, but, of course, I couldn't understand what it said. 'Surely this is not your house and gardens?' I looked carefully at the one storey stone cottage. Really it was a bungalow I thought. An old bungalow. Possibly built around the same time as the river bridge.

'This is my house,' William affirmed, 'But the gardens, apart from a small piece around it, belong to the Mansion. You see, I really will explain later, but this is a sort of gate-house to the main building, which, if you come over here and look through the fencing, you can see across the field. There!' I looked across the grass. 'That is Shugborough. That is the Mansion House. It's really mainly a museum now, but there is a shop, tea room and even a farm with some weird looking animals and...'

And he went on but I looked away again, over the grassland to the giant white building that rose majestically through the gloom, amidst the meadow, gardens, and trees.

'It is rather elegant, don't you think?' William asked, almost as if were personally responsible for the estate.

'I've never seen anything like it before,' I responded wholeheartedly. This was not quite true as long ago my parents had insisted on compulsory culture for me and my sisters. Every other weekend we would spend our precious out-of-school-time being dragged around 'places of interest' which, because of my mother's love of antique furniture, involved numerous trips to stately homes and establishments such as the one I was now admiring.

'It looks particularly resplendent with all this whiteness and the big Christmas trees illuminated, don't you think?' William said twitching his tail.

I gazed at the little lights that adorned the trees standing like sentries at either side of the front doors, above the flight of entrance steps. 'It looks like a picture,' I agreed honestly, willing myself to stop shivering.

'Well, now, young lady - I can't really call you that – do you have a proper name?' He asked as if he feared it might cause me some discomfort if I turned out to be nameless.

'Of course I have a name,' I said harshly, not least because I was freezing cold and needed to be somewhere warm pretty quickly, the threatened hypothermia having been superseded by a promise of frostbite. 'My name is Penny.'

'What a nice name,' he said pensively, as I begged to myself, please, no more talk. 'Come inside,' he said, 'And meet my family, my master and mistress.'

Normally I would have questioned these quaint titles he used for his people but I was gradually getting used to his rather old fashioned terms and way of talking. As I walked silently just a step behind him (as is the courtesy custom when someone new is offering hospitality and friendship) I flirted with the idea he may be descended from a human of high birth or even, perhaps royalty, particularly living by a Mansion House. Just what had he been in his human life? I wondered. Even his eye talk denoted articulation and he was definitely a gentleman (unlike some Sooty types I have known.) His consideration and manners had become very apparent during our short acquaintance and he had taken no liberties or advantages of my unhappy situation. That is, apart from physically pulling me from the canal and attempting to wash my head. But this, I assured myself, was what any cat would do for another and did not indicate familiarity in any form.

I smiled to myself as I carefully followed him through a gap in the iron fence railings where someone had removed a paling to make the opening wider. There was no other apparent entrance to the house or the narrow roadway apart from the locked gates. When we had squeezed through on to the damp grass we wove our way around the building to the back door. I felt a little apprehensive at barging my way into someone else's home, but, after all, I had been invited by William. I just hoped his people were kindly and would at least let me stay for the night.

His master and mistress were surprisingly young. As the puss flap clanked behind us I had expected to be confronted by a middle aged couple but instead a young woman came forward to greet us (or rather William).

"Where have you been William? You're late coming in." she said almost echoing the earlier words of the woman in the apron at the eating house. "And who have you brought home?" She did not sound at all angry or put out that I was trailing along behind her handsome cat, looking, literally, like something the cat had brought in. "I've been in from work, hours," she chuckled giving William a light pat and me a shy smile. ('This is an untruth,' William signalled me playfully, 'She never gets in before four o'clock.') "Anyway, He won't be long. There's not much he can do in the gardens this weather."

He, William explained as we settled ourselves on the long kitchen rug in front of a coal burning grate, is the chief gardener for the Shugborough Estate. ('They are called managers or something now, but that is what he is.' William pointed out.)

"You get yourselves warmed up. Your little friend looks in a bit of a state. Been too near the river have you? I'm just going to take a shower and change. Dinner in about half an hour," she promised swishing from the room.

'What a super minder!' I said with feeling, laying down and turning my back towards the glowing lumps of coal. 'What a lovely home!'

William looked pleased at my praise but sat stiffly at the other side of the mat.

'Do I smell very nasty?' I looked at him slyly.

He shuffled his feet and twitched the tip of his tail. 'No Penny, you do not smell at all, not nasty anyway. But I'm not used to having a, well, someone else with me. I am very much a loner. Friends I have, mostly up at the Mansion and in the surrounding cottages over the bridge, but no-one has been in my home before.' He said this so soberly that part of me itched to laugh.

'I am honoured,' I said, trying to effect seriousness and looking down at the fringes at the ends of the rug. (I would have a go at these later, I promised myself).

'You are a nice, well brought up young lady and I want you to know that just because we will share a rug and possibly a resting place, I hope there should always be a deep respect between us. But we can be really good pals,' he finished lightly, quickly washing his paw to divert my attention from his rather pompous speech.

Pompous? No, more dignified, I decided, wondering absently what age he might be. Quite a lot older than me, probably old enough to be my father? Ah yes, a father figure.

But we did not share a resting place, as William had put it. We lazed on the rug until Mistress appeared, rosy faced and clothed in a long embroidered housecoat. True to her word she served us dinner, in individual saucers. A large tin was opened and the contents shared between us. (Lately I have been spoiled with rather more succulent fare but this was decidedly better than starving or the alternative of wild vermin.) A communal saucer of milk was put down before the rug, but I couldn't eat much of the meat in jelly and I just did not feel like anything to drink. William excused himself to go urgently into the garden and, after a few minutes I followed his lead and exited via the cat flap. I finished my business quickly and hurried back into the warm room. Mistress was flitting about the kitchen, clattering amongst saucepans and dishes, so I lay quietly out of the way at the side of the room. When the back door swung open a tall man, undoubtedly He, strode in, with William at his feet.

"Wellies!" Mistress called across the room to him, eyeing the muddy puddle that was forming on the tiled floor. The man reversed speedily back through the doorway and reappeared almost instantly in his stocking feet. William ran across and sat quite close to me.

After the expected "Who is this?" type of remarks and suitable replies from Mistress, William and I were left to our own devices although the young woman did give us both a friendly passing stroke as she walked through to the hallway. They ate their meal in a small dining recess off the kitchen whilst William talked and I tried, with some success, to wash myself.

256

'It will take a few days before you look immaculate again,' he said knowingly. 'Benjamin was like that for nearly a week, and his fur is not as long and luscious as yours is.'

I shook back my head and felt rather pleased to have my poor lank coat described as luscious. 'Who is Benjamin?' Not another cat, I hoped.

'Benjamin Rabbit,' William clarified. 'He lives in a cage on the table outside the back door; under the porch. Didn't you see him as you went past?' I shook my head. I hadn't known many rabbits but had heard they made tasty meals. If one could catch them, that is. I had also heard that they are rather fast and very good at not being caught.

'Do not even think about it,' William cut into my contemplation.

'Why? Is he a pet rabbit?' I asked, even though this would not have put me off if I had been determined. A rabbit in a cage presented both an attractive food proposition and the intellectual project of working out his release – so that he may be chased.

'Not a pet,' William said firmly, 'But an untouchable. He badly hurt his back foot, got it caught in something nasty on the estate, and when Master found him he was nearly dead. He brought him home and they fought for days to save him. She fed him with a baby's bottle even.' He stopped as if considering something. 'Benjamin is a very lucky rabbit,' he said. 'Anyway,' William shuffled himself to be more comfortable. 'That is why this is a complete no-go area for both of us.'

Mistress appeared with a small but comfortable cat bed, which had a red fur cushion and splendid red and green tartan sides and lining.

'You can curl up in here together,' she suggested but William stood up and walked away, sitting down pointedly in the middle of the floor.

'Oh, I see,' she observed, 'Not that friendly yet, aren't we?' She chuckled to herself and ferreted about in a tall wooden cupboard. 'Here! Your guest can use this pillow. It's feather filled so it should be soft but the cover's a bit tatty.'

She could well have added that it suited the particular tatty state of my coat, but she was tactful enough not to.

We all went into the small sitting room and watched a quiz show on television. There were no invitations to sit up upon knees but as there was a small fire in there also, it was quite comfortable to sit on the carpet for our viewing. Although William was a pet cat he was treated almost as another adult. No one spoke silly baby talk to him or rushed to tickle or pick him up; I should be quite happy if this same arrangement were offered to me. I was sure it would somehow it made me feel more grown up. After a short evening Master put the fire out.

'Now he will lock up the house and pull the outer porch door almost closed and clip it so that it cannot bang open or closed. There will still be enough room for us to get out should we need to and it will be warm enough for Benjamin so that he does not freeze, though he always has lots of warm hay.'

I followed William into the kitchen and we sat on the rug whilst Mistress rinsed the dishes. 'They have to get up early for work,' William said in case I might wonder why bed time was so soon. When the lights were switched off and we had been companionably bade Goodnight, William said gravely, 'You take the bed, I will sleep on the cushion.'

I was going to argue – it was good enough for him to take me to his home without expecting him to give up his bed for me – but he was already settling himself.

'Thank you William,' I said softly in the dim light, 'Thank you for everything you have done to help me today.' As I snuggled down into the warm cosy basket I realised that I was starting to sound as serious as he did.

# CHAPTER 30

The first few days in William's house were bliss. As he had predicted, it took longer that I had expected to get back to feeling like a regular cat again. William was considerate, if somewhat distant, and I was left on my own quite a bit when he disappeared on his various walks and errands. Both the Master and Mistress went out to work and neither came back to the house at lunchtimes. The routine of the household had been spelled out to me. The husband had his lunch up at the Mansion House with other employees on the estate and his wife worked somewhere in a town nearby and did not usually return until late-afternoon.

My mentor, William, seemed to have several calls upon his time. He regularly visited certain other homes and shops in the village and, I understand, liked to put in appearances at the local store and post office, in addition to his afternoon attendance at the restaurant house. He told me he felt obliged to appear at any event that was being staged in the village, be it car boot sale or church bazaar. He let slip quite early on that he took immense pleasure in meeting the younger children as they came out of school. (I think he got a lot of attention and the occasional crisp or piece of chocolate.) He genuinely doted on kids, recounting little incidents that had occurred during his duties at the school. On reflection, it seemed that he might be extremely happy - and unbend a little - if he were part of a lively young family. I wondered if there was any chance of this ever happening in his home.

My first night there, and most of the following day, I spent asleep or dozing. It was very conducive to relaxation – curled up in the warm bed or stretched out on the rug. The kitchen fire was one of those that when no-one is home, the little glass gates are closed in front of the burning coals. This made little difference to the constant heat that was projected from the grate, in fact, when I was on my own I felt quite safe, knowing that nothing could spark or jump out at me. Lazing on the rug I examined the empty cat bed. It was an awesome, completely masculine affair and I wondered vaguely whether William was descended from, or perhaps was, a Scot. After all, William is a Scottish name, he sported a tartan bed and he could almost be described as dour. I made up my mind to tactfully ask him about this when the moment was right.

Apart from hasty visits to the garden, it was too cold for me to venture out on that first day – I would do this later when I felt one hundred percent recovered from my ordeal and when my coat was fluffed out normally again. So I stayed indoors. This gave me a great deal of time to think. Not that there was much to think about except that how lucky I was to have landed on my paws, so to speak.

The next morning, I was feeling a lot better. More myself. After William and his people had departed, the most pressing thing I must do, I decided, is to investigate the rabbit – Benjamin. I was intrigued to find out more about him. This wasn't something that could be done casually as I strolled past, as he was perched up quite high on a table and I couldn't see him properly. I was also a bit annoyed that he seemed to have no interest whatsoever in coming to the edge of his cage to have a look at me. I managed to climb up on to an old stool out there and was able to stare into his den. Flashing hypocritical messages of introduction and goodwill brought forth nothing except some brief ear waggling before he turned and flattened his bob tail against the wire netting to demonstrate his feelings on the matter.

As I was completely wasting my time I got down and went to explore the garden. Very small and nothing to get excited about. But beyond – the grounds beyond displayed the inviting sweep of lawns, clumps of shrubs and bushes and, I could clearly make out the trickle of a harmless stream. Giant, very old, trees guarded the grounds and the next generation of smaller specimens vied with their elders for any available sunlight. Careful planting, though, ensured that they could all be seen and admired by the passing crowds of visitors who roamed the pathways during the summer months.

During those early days William remained friendly, helpful, yet almost detached. I wanted for nothing; I had every comfort. He examined my bed regularly to ensure it was not crumpled or rucked up. He saw to it that I was warm enough and that I had food and drink. When we watched television he gave me the best viewing place and always waited until I had been out at night, before he relaxed into sleep. Although he very rarely stayed in all night, he took care to move about noiselessly so as not to disturb me. He made sure that I knew, and abided by, the rules of the house, and constantly enquired how I was and if everything was all right for me.

On the second night (it was particularly cold and even the kitchen was chilly) I had sheepishly invited him to share the comfortable bed, which was out of any draughts; I didn't like to watch him languish on a flattish pillow. But, no, he was adamant that he was happy where he was. Apart from feeling guilty, I had a sense of failure, of not quite making the mark. Having been used to the cat-calls in the farmyard and Sooty's underlying attentions, it rather shook my ego to find that William regarded me simply as a stray animal. One he had rescued from the canal and who, I feared, would be deported, once fit and well and when the weather stopped freezing. Reasoning along these lines made me realise the vulnerability of my situation. Master and Mistress would not keep me indefinitely – why should they? And if William was so spectacularly un-enamoured with me there was no reason to remain anyway. There was little I could do about earning an extended stay, I realised miserably. But on day four, my chance came.

I didn't set out to become a hero or to carve a niche for myself with this nice family but an opportunity presented itself over which I really had no control. It was a spontaneous, sudden occurrence.

Sunday morning is when Master and Mistress are both at home and, consequently, William curtails his travels in order to be with them. Mistress was feeding and cleaning Benjamin and, for once, it wasn't quite so cold. I sat and watched as there was nothing better to do. Benjamin was hopping to and fro and generally enjoying the attention when the front door bell rang out loudly. Mistress slammed his cage door and ran to see who was outside. But the little lock on the cage did not click shut and the large wired gate slowly swung open again. As I sat on the back step, washing, I could hardly believe this was happening. This luscious looking rabbit was sitting there just inches from me. Mmmm!

Then I shook myself and took a deep breath. Not on! I told myself severely.

When the stupid animal moved forward and stuck his head out of the hole I shouted to him, 'Get back, you daft thing or you'll fall out!'

Not only out, but down. A broken neck on top of already nursing a bad leg, I thought to myself, wouldn't do you any good at all. After a couple of ear waggles the bundle of mottled brown fur inched forwards even further.

'Go back!' I yelled, hoping that William would appear, but I knew he was way beyond the garden boundary.

The rabbit fell to the ground and I was astonished that it was still all in one piece. Sensing its unplanned freedom and probably smelling its companions in the near undergrowth, the furry lump tried to limp across the porch, dragging its poorly leg as best it could. Normally a decisive being, I had no idea what to do. I started by standing up and watching the painful progress. 'Don't go outside,' I implored him, 'Anything could get you. Possibly a cat.'

Even though I stared piercingly at him as he stumbled past me, my look fell on blind eyes. I was a good mind to jump on the silly thing and teach him a lesson, to sink my teeth into his neck, just behind the ears, so deliciously laid back, silky and enticing. Why would no-one appear when you wanted them to? The rabbit reached the outer door and wriggled himself out on to the path. He continued his laboured trek down the centre of the garden and then on towards the copse at the other side of the fence. Beyond that, I knew, lay the river.

'Not that way!' I warned him, but on he hopped - with a limp.

Then Mistress came back into the kitchen. I heard her gasp. "Benjamin! Where are you? Oh my goodness, the door's open. Benjie, Benjie!"

She knelt on the floor searching under the table and behind the stool. I trotted to the door to show her the route her patient had taken. "No!" she screamed at me. "Don't you dare chase him! Benjamin stay where you are!"

I stopped moving and sat down just outside the door to prove that I was in no way involved in this escape plan. She nearly tripped over me in her haste to reach the rabbit before he reached the cover of the wood. Then, suddenly, from nowhere, came an exceedingly loud "Grrrrrh!" followed by an extremely low pitched and masterful, "Ruff! Ruff!" The glorious coat of the red setter, as it streaked into the small garden, under the fencing by the trees, was just a blur. The rabbit screeched to a halt and stood as if stuck to the spot.

Mistress exacerbated the volatile charade by shouting, "Shoo! Get off! Go away!" which the dog did not like at all.

I was tempted to retreat stealthily inside to safety before my presence was discovered by the interloper. The dog slowed and stopped in its tracks, looking with disdain at Mistress who was standing waving her arms about. The rabbit gazed at them both wondering which might reach him first. The woman observed the bared teeth of the intruder and wasn't sure whether this display was for her or for her animal. The rabbit saw the teeth and was petrified rigid – he knew who they were aimed at. I knew that in one split second, the dog would have the rabbit, and the woman would lash into the dog and would probably be badly bitten for her trouble. Then they would all notice me, just standing there like a goof, watching.

I stood up, arching my back and fluffing out my fur until I must have looked absolutely enormous. Enough to scare the living daylights of anything, I lied to myself confidently. Letting out the loudest wail I could manage, in these terrifying circumstances, I walked steadily, John Wayne style, over to where Benjamin was cowering. His eyes were glazed and not a whisker moved. The big dog turned his attention from the woman to me and in my haste not to provide too easy a target, I backed into the damned rabbit and nearly overbalanced.

'Get back!' I attempted, Zoonlike, into the dog's wicked eyes, but he didn't even bother to waggle his ears. (Well, it was worth a try.) I clung firmly to the ground, subconsciously sharpening my claws, and spat forwards for all I was worth. With my back curved up as high as I could possibly manage, I rolled more venomous spit around in my mouth and got ready to hiss like I've never hissed before. Then I screeched very loudly. Then I yowled, and spat, and hissed, raising both front paws menacingly, with claws extended, ready to spring at the dog if he moved towards us. (I have to admit that I was simultaneously eying the nearby woodland with a view to hasty retreat if the thing flew at me.)

Miraculously, at that precise moment, William appeared from the bushes. Immediately taking in the situation, he sped towards the large animal. He also hissed and spat and we wailed in chorus. The elegant creature turned from side to side, now encircled by the woman, William and me, with Benjamin forming a useless fourth on the boundary.

"Get out!" the woman came to life and caught hold of a garden hoe which was leaning against the wall. "Clear off!" She brandished the pointed metal in the direction of the dog's face and William and I continued our verbal attack reinforced by much waving of drawn claws. The hissing and spitting and snarling and shouting was watched by a fascinated rabbit. The dog decided wisely, that he might be in a no win situation. Barking loudly he disappeared into the wood as quickly as he had come. Mistress threw down the hoe and scooped up the hypnotised bunny and William and I strolled to the side of the garden where we unanimously decided to have a quick wash. Master crashed into the scene, as he rushed in from the front garden to see what all the commotion was about, just in time to see his wife reunite the rabbit with its cage. Only then did its ears and whiskers show some signs of life. Mistress was in tears and William explained to me that she tended to be a bit stressed out lately.

"Did that stray cat get at the rabbit?" The Master asked at once, taking a hard look in my direction.

"No, No!" she protested, checking to make sure the wired cage door was securely locked. "That little cat was wonderful! I didn't shut the cage properly – the boatman was at the door –

and Benjamin escaped. But that little cat.." she broke off in a fit of sniffs. I found this singularly embarrassing, but I had to stay put, of course, to know the outcome. William grinned at me but said nothing. "That little cat," she went on beaming over at us, "Saved Benjamin's life. She actually went for the dog. Screeched at it and hissed and spat. Oh she is wonderful!"

'William helped a bit,' I put in, pretending to be fully engrossed in freshening the spot behind my ears.

"Special dinner for you!" Mistress gained her composure and lifted her head, all smiles now. "You and William will have something special!"

"Well, if she's that handy around the place, maybe we'd better keep her," the man said putting his arm around his wife.

I glanced across at William just as the woman said his name. "What say you, William? Would you mind having a guest for a bit longer? She might keep you in order and stop you wandering off so much,"

They both laughed and William said quietly to me. 'I would really like you to stay but I would ask you – may I possibly come back with you into my bed?' I stretched and purred a little, not knowing quite what to reply, when he added, 'I don't mean that exactly how it sounded, you know. It's just that the pillow is not too comfortable, and the bed is roomy enough for us both, I mean we can always sleep back to back. And if you decide you don't like the arrangement we can always revert to how we are now..'

I smiled at him and lowered my head coyly. It would probably take years to find out if this kind, attractive, companionable guy might also be affectionate. But as I had a more or less permanent home now, there was no hurry.

# CHAPTER 31

Now that I was officially accepted into the household, things changed slightly. William and I shared the comfortable, spacious, tartan bed (platonically) and with each day we became closer in mind and spirit, if not in body. I was presented with my very own eating equipment – a plastic two-sectional dish (a revolting lemon I think – yes, even with my spasmodic colour recognition the thing screamed at me) and a multi-pattened waxed mat on which to stand it. (Essential for catching those occasional drips and dribbles that will occur at feeding time.) Appreciative though I was, the clashing sight of my ginger fur against my dinner apparatus must have been a sight to behold. I can only imagine that Mistress Megan Morgan had little colour sense. (I would much have preferred the stainless steel macho model that William used but I supposed it was his due to have something distinctive which denoted his seniority in the house.)

Megan and Di Morgan were good caring owners. I had eventually voiced my objection to referring to them as Master and Mistress although, even after a prolonged debate with William on the matter, he said he saw no reason to change what he felt to be a respectful title. He did explain that as they, Megan and Di, were 'from across the border', he was merely following the Welsh cat tradition of using this courteous address. He referred to 'across the border' as if it were hundreds of miles away instead of a ninety minutes drive up the road.

During those first few days William and I had discussions on many things. I told him my story and he gave me snippets of his life. He was very definitely an individualist who treasured his privacy, so I was careful not to pry; he would divulge what he wanted to when he wanted to. William went about his daily routines and if I had expected that after my initial welcome he might extend an invitation to join his social programme, I was disappointed. I meandered about in the house and garden, occasionally wandering into the wood and

266

down to the riverside but this made me uneasy on two counts. One, that I might again come across that unpleasant red setter or another similar threat, and two, that I might somehow slip into the galloping river and be swallowed up for ever. I trotted up the lane several times and surveyed the Mansion House from a safe distance. It was a most commanding sight and I longed to know more about it but I didn't dare go too close. William had told me that it was now owned by the National Trust although the local county council administered its organisation. This included responsibility for opening rooms to the public during the summer months, running the car parks, café, shops, hiring out rooms and grounds for functions and generally endeavouring to balance the upkeep of the estate with the income generated. When my confidence grew, I casually made my way up the wide pathway that led from the locked iron gates, past our cottage and into the gardens of the House. Winter, as William had explained, meant that the estate was closed to visitors. This was the time for maintenance, redecorating and alteration. Many jobs there were seasonal – in the café, shop, the guides - but the office and administrative staffs were permanent. These were county council personnel who negotiated the long drive from the main road, through the rhododendrons bushes, in all weathers. From the amount of vehicles parked there, even out of season, I was glad that the main entrances were not from the village or anywhere near to William's house. I didn't like traffic at all. Peering past the trees I often wondered what drew people to come to work in such an isolated spot. I remembered, fleetingly, how I used to get such a buzz from going into the City and being part of the hustle and bustle of the busier suburbs. I should have loathed to be shut away out here where there were no life or shops to walk to. Perhaps the attraction was the aura of being in such special historic surroundings. If William were human I could imagine him revelling in working in such an environment. But maybe it all came to life and was fun in the summer, when visitors and tourists from all over the world spilled out from tired coaches, and schoolchildren arrived by the hundreds. (William's description.)

During Megan and Di's daily absences (and William's too) there was limited chance of conversation or companionship with anyone else. Although the path from the packhorse bridge alongside our home was a favourite route for dog walkers, very few Zoons seemed to come that way. Those who did were dragged past where I sat hopefully, under the small front porch, and if they did pull on their leads in response to my greeting they were hauled away in haste by suspicious owners – no doubt themselves longing to get back to their fires and central heating. I got used to hearing the fatuous remarks that came floating through the railings, such as, "Come away! That looks a really vicious cat. It will tear you apart!" (Usually to something like a German Shepherd or Staffordshire Bull Terrier.) Or, equally amusing, "Now don't go and tease the kitty. You mustn't frighten it!" (Usually to a bit of fluff at the end of the tiniest leash, that resembles one of those special dusters for cleaning behind radiators.)

In my boredom I even attempted one day to recruit the dizzy Benjamin as a friend. 'Hello!' I tried in my most cosy manner but the idiot just turned his back on me as he always did. (Did he not appreciate that I had saved his useless life?) I even meowed at him but he still wouldn't turn around. Spitting and hissing up at his pom-pom tail had more effect as on that one occasion, he slowly turned to face me. 'Ah that's more like it!' I tried again. Although I knew he couldn't understand me I really did strive to look and sound companionable.

He gazed down with vacant unblinking eyes as I switched on my most endearing smile – I would have purred but thought this may frighten him and cause an instant about-turn again. We stood staring at each other, both of us completely stationary.

'Me-ow,' I said moving my head a little.

He stood stock still.

'Meeeow!' I repeated, a little louder this time.

Almost as if he were showing interest, one long silky ear flopped forward, lazily poking out of his wired cage. So, I thought, now that I had his attention I would really put the wind up him. Screeching and yowling and jumping up in a vain effort to get my claws into his cage forced him to back off in a shuffling movement. He then jumped rapidly backwards, (I hadn't realised rabbits can do this) leaving his forward projecting ear tangled in the chicken wire that covered the front of his pen.

'You're stuck, old chap!' I told him with glee as I subsided to the ground, defeated in my attempts to get at him, but triumphant at the discomfort I had caused.

He shuddered away, crouching against the back wall of his enclosure. His long body stretched across the cage, but the errant ear was firmly fixed to the front wire.

'Can't get it out?' I tormented but, naturally, being a simple soul, he ignored me and twisted his dozy head around so that the captive ear pulled on the mesh and started to bleed. Little blobs came swaying down to where I stood then it started to drip more substantially. What an imbecile! This twit did not deserve to live he was so barmy. If only I could have got to him! If I could have leapt up to the grill! If I could have taken hold of that languid, limpid, lovely ear sticking out alluringly in my direction. If? But I couldn't. The jump up to the table was beyond me. All I could do was sit below, watching the daft bat twist and turn to try to free himself whilst the steady flow of his blood made a pattern on the back porch flooring.

'What has happened? What are you doing?' William asked as he loped in.

'Just observing our half-witted friend,' I replied with a smirk.

'Get inside!' William snorted crossly, 'Haven't you had enough to do with that rabbit? Let him alone.' I opened my mouth to protest but William puffed out his beautiful white coat and leapt easily up on to the rabbit's table.

'Shove your gormless ear in,' he told the stupid Benjamin, who shunted further backwards, yanking his ear into an even more painful position. He started to make strange squeaking sounds. William balanced precariously on the edge of the table and poked his immaculate paw into the cage, gently releasing the long silky lobe from its entanglement. 'OK Benjie, you're free again!' he exhorted, sliding from his unsteady perch.

Down on the floor again he turned to me. 'I would leave that object alone if I were you.' he said rather sourly. 'You do not seem to be able to get on with him.' His eyes fell pointedly to the small circles of blood that had formed on the stone floor.

'It wasn't my fault he got his ears in a twist,' I muttered, 'I only tried to be friendly, I was bored.'

'Well, from now on you won't be.' William said decisively. 'Tomorrow I will start and introduce you to the village. You have been here resting long enough now.'

Although I was pleased that at last I was to be included in his activities, it sounded more like a punishment, rather than a straightforward gesture of friendship. But thankful for small mercies, I gulped and said, 'Thanks William that will be really nice.'

As we ambled inside the house I couldn't help glancing back at the hutch on the table. That dratted rabbit, Benjamin, seemed to be in control of my life. In spite of the fact that I hated him, he appeared to be able to turn on some goodwill for me whenever I needed it, even though we could never communicate with each other. It was he, indirectly, who was responsible for me being accepted by the Morgan's and now he again, was instrumental in William inviting me to join the local social scene.

'But it will mean you crossing the bridge,' William informed me as we were having dinner that night. 'And I know you're not keen on that.'

'Oh, I don't mind,' I told him airily. (Killer of Leader Rats and Saver of Rabbits can certainly conquer a bridge, I pep-talked myself.) 'Are all your friends over the bridge?' I asked conversationally.

Some were at the Mansion House and there were a couple of nice strays over at the Estate farm, he told me, and then he stopped, hesitating for just a few seconds. 'There is one special person I will introduce you to,' he said quite firmly, 'As it is important that you two meet. That is Anson.'

'Anson?'

'Yes, Anson is the most magnificent cat I have ever known,' William said slowly, almost with reverence. 'So sweet, kind – a beautiful person. Intelligent and thoughtful. You will love Anson.'

Well, after a build up like that, I thought tartly, I'm not so sure. 'Lives at the big house, does he?' my look asked casually.

William nodded, cleaning his whiskers. 'She certainly does,' he said almost whimsically.

Another woman! I felt deflated, inferior and, yes, more than a tiny bit jealous. 'Is she really that perfect?' I tried, hoping he would laugh and dispel this nasty negative feeling I had.

'Perfect?' His eyes seemed to twinkle with the word. 'Yes, she is perfect. In looks, in mind, in every way.' He languorously moved over on to his back, stretching out his long legs. This particular movement, I had learned, was one he made only in exceptional circumstances. So he thought this Anson was perfect? Well, he, I had to admit looking away quickly, was the most perfect cat as far as I was concerned.

'And of course she has a very high pedigree and comes from an unusual strain.'

Oh God! How much longer was he going to go on about this pesky female? 'Anson seems a funny name for such a glamorous person.' I snapped cattily.

'Ah well,' William was being serious again. 'Anson is the name of the family who lived at Shugborough, years ago. The name is symbolic of the ancestry.'

What a load of piffle! I stifled a yawn. So this is why I hadn't got to meet his mates. This is why I hadn't been invited along. This explained his frequent absences. William was truly smitten with this Anson. William and Anson – it sounded like a dreary firm of solicitors.

'What about your other friends, the ones over the bridge, in the village? What are they like?' I needed to get away from the tedious she- cat. But my beautiful white knight in shining armour was just not listening. He lay stretched out on his side, paws gently curved in, head resting slightly forward. His big green eyes were gradually closing. Was he dreaming or was it just a complete relaxation?

Thoroughly bored with the way the evening was progressing I turned away smartly and swept into the other room to watch TV. The great lottery mechanism was on the verge of giving away yet more vast amounts of money. I liked that. I liked watching all those little ping pong balls tumbling about. Suddenly a memory flashed at me. My mother, saying what she would do if she won all those millions. And me telling her what I would spend it on if I won. But now, I never would. If I was ever human again....... But I didn't know if I ever would be, and by that time there probably wouldn't be a lottery. And then I turned back to look at William, but he was fast asleep.

# CHAPTER 32

The next morning William watched closely as, after breakfast, (morsels and milk – but not together, you understand) I washed more carefully than usual, in aid of my impending introduction into nearby society. It would not do to have floating bits adhering to whiskers or lumps of fur standing up when they should be laying down. I wanted to look my very best for my meeting with the Adorable Anson.

'But we're not meeting Anson today,' William said catching my eye. (Had I meant to converse or was this super-cat also a mind reader?) 'We are going to see my best friend Tabby. He lives in a cottage just beyond the doctors' surgery.'

'Fine!' I wasn't going to show disappointment or elation at the news. 'So when is Anson day?' I couldn't help adding.

William explained, in the manner of a grown up telling a child, that one did not just 'drop in' on Anson. A time would be pre-arranged.

'You mean she has an appointment system, even for you?' I asked snidely.

'Penny, do not be tiresome.' William could be really haughty when he wanted to. He patiently pointed out that because this precious creature lived in a mansion (and was obviously Puss Queen of the County) cat manners were quite different where she was concerned.

'Who does she live with? Who are her minders?' (I refused to use his term of Master and Mistress.) 'Are there any other cats there and is she a Zoon?' I ran out of eye energy and blinked rapidly, abandoning my in-depth washing. There was no point in exerting myself for someone whose name was, apparently, just Tabby.

'Ah, so many questions Penny Paws,' he said gently. (I quite liked it when he called me this. It seemed like a sort of endearment – but then I could be very wrong.)

Methodically he explained the set-up. Yes of course Anson was a Zoon (probably the Zooniest Zoon in the vicinity, I didn't doubt.) Yes, there were other cats on the estate. Some lived by the farm, some around the shop and café and stables part of the House and yes, a few were Zoons. These were all fed by the various staff who helped to run the estate. But Anson (bless her little cotton socks) actually lived *in* the House.

'Who with?' I challenged, realising at once that I should have at least afforded the great priestess a 'with whom?' But 'who with?' always comes more naturally to me.

'Well,' William was off again, glad of an opportunity too air his specialised erudition. 'Although the place is open to the visitors for much of the year, there are private apartments – rooms which the general public can never enter.'

'Why? Who lives there?' In spite of myself I was curious.

William gave himself a good shake. 'That part belongs to Lord Lichfield's family – he was a cousin of the Queen. A highly esteemed photographer.'

Silence. Mainly because I didn't know quite what to say. Eventually I managed, 'And you are telling me that Lady Anson is a Lord's cat?' Things were getting worse. Competition like this I did not need.

William sniffed. 'Lord Lichfield was a very private person. What he did in his apartments when he was in residence is nothing to do with anyone else, us included. Cat Anson lives somewhere in The House but I don't pry into the ins and outs of the arrangement. What she wants me to know, she tells me but I do not ask questions that may be embarrassing. Although I respect her confidences I also respect her privacy.'

So, I thought, it's a fair guess that even if you knew exactly what goes on, you wouldn't tell me. So, I stretched in my most pronounced fashion to illustrate that I wasn't really very interested after all. 'So, what's Tabby like?' I quizzed, although I couldn't have cared less about that either.

Crossing the bridge later with William was not as scary as I expected it might be. The day was still and the river seemed quieter. We passed no cyclists or pedestrians and in my pleasure that I was jogging alongside William, I almost forgot to be nervous or frightened. Making our way up the narrow road, after the river bridge, we passed over the canal bridge and the restaurant house where I had had my first meal with William. I strained my neck to try to see if the charred remains of the Swan the Third were still tethered to the bank somewhere above the locks. Several boats were moored there and, as I hurried after William, I could not make out whether my last floating home was amongst them.

'Come on!' he admonished, I think to dissuade any thought I may have had about deviating from our decreed route.

'Yes, yes!' I snapped back, secretly thankful not to feel obliged to pay my last respects to the old boat.

Beyond the restaurant there was a third bridge which, this time, we walked under. The high stonework was slightly green with moss and weed near to the top. I looked up enquiringly.

'Railway,' William said briefly. 'Main line. Quite busy. We can hear the trains in the distance from the cottage. And, just along there,' he pointed his nose back to where the canal curved away towards a wood on one side and open fields on the other. 'Just there, is where the trains are supposed to pass, every hour. They never do, of course, one or both are usually late, or cancelled. But I have known it to happen. When we hunt in the woods or fish by the river we see them.'

I digested this useless information as we passed the doors of a row of pretty cottages squatting at the sides of the narrow road, which was made even more narrow by vehicles parked tightly on either side.

'Turn right here!' We duly turned right, past the doctors' surgery car park and started up the hill. Cars whizzed past but William kept well into the hedging at the side.

'Hello!'

Tabby was sitting on his front doorstep and had watched us coming up the road. He was a young cat, probably just a little older than me. And very presentable (well, certainly for someone with a name like Tabby). Introductions were made and the usual small talk conversation started. 'I've heard all about you, Penny,' was his opening shot. (How original!)

'And I – you,' I replied easily, lying through my teeth.

Tabby, I decided after a few minutes, was a likeable rogue. But he seemed genuinely fond of William, whom I gathered he regarded as a sort of role model. After chatting for a while - they spent most of the time talking of people and events which I knew nothing about - William and I made our way back to the restaurant house for our morning snacks.

'Tabby is a great young guy. Rather lecherous though, but he will not bother you as he knows you are my family.' William seemed to feel he should reassure me.

This was nice. I liked the way he put this, though, again, I might have been way off course. But I did think William was warming towards me.

On the way back home we ran into two Zoon cats from the farm who were out hunting on the river bank. They both acknowledged me genially and showed great interest when William explained that I was the one who had escaped the furnace of the stolen burning boat.

'Oh!' they said in unison, eyeing every inch of me.

'And she saved our rabbit, Benjamin, from a savage dog attack.' William added for good measure.

'Oh!' they both said again. Then they both chattered on, saying pleasing things, like how brave I must have been and how courageous I was. I hung my head modestly and smiled up at William feeling very happy. As we left I wondered if they were twins as they seemed to say everything together.

'Yes of course they are,' William replied. 'Nice types,' he added. 'Either they or Tabby are the first ones I would turn to if I needed help. And that goes for you too Penny. You could call on any of them, any time.' I didn't really see why I should ever need to ask anyone else for help but was grateful to be meeting William's friends at last.

'Thanks!' I acknowledged briefly. 'What about Anson – wouldn't you turn to her?' The question thought was out before I could stop it. Knowing it sounded churlish I amended, 'Or maybe not. Tabby looks a good fighter and so do the twins.'

William shook his head almost wearily. 'Oh Penny!' he said, 'I think it is about time you met Anson, then it would stop all these rather silly remarks.'

I huffed up my fur in an attempt to demonstrate my non-silliness, but then I said sweetly, 'Yes. It is about time we met – now that I am 'your family'.

For a moment it looked as if he might make some thoughtful, deep, William-type reply but after a brief pause to look, rather patronizingly I felt, at my ridiculous vertical coat, he ambled on.

That night, snuggling up to William, I had a good think. Trying to remember my human past was becoming almost impossible. Snatches came and went. Then I concentrated on the old minder couple and my cat mother, Penelope. Then – and oh, then! on Tina. For several minutes I wallowed in Tina. So many unanswered questions floated in and out of my pussy head. Why had she gone to America with – whatever his name was? Why had she left me (dumped me) at the farm with that horrible family? Then, Minnie and Sooty. Why hadn't I had the pluck to infiltrate their homely set-up and risk being told I was not wanted? And Robbie and Ben? How could they possibly cope without me? How could they carry on with their vulnerable business and honour bookings if the canals had frozen over? Then I remembered Swan the Third and old Jim. So many question marks. And now, William and me and the Honourable Anson. (Or was it William and Anson – and the dishonourable me?)

Throughout my feline life, my feelings had been strictly cat to human (except for Minnie. I really did like her.) But now, suddenly, I admitted there must be more to life than curling up against William's magnificent curved spine. Although I was fighting it, there was definitely a certain feeling creeping in. Not a sexy, lusty feeling but a warm affectionate 'wanting William to notice me' feeling. Laying there, cuddling close to his rhythmically breathing body, I wondered, tentatively, if I might just be just a tiny bit in love? Cat love, that is.

Long ago, Tabatha had told me that most cats do not love. They put up with, instruct, control and occasionally reward their human owners with small friendly gestures. Affection given is based purely on the standard and regularity of feeding, comfort of bedding, and amount of fondling offered. Love doesn't actually enter into it. I personally think this is rubbish as I'm sure many owners love their cats as much, if not more, than their human partners. And I know, from experience, that cats do love their people. Also, Tabatha said, love from one cat to another is even more unusual. More often than not it is a quick fling, accompanied by loud squealing and hissing. Something no self respecting Zoon, who could remember his human roots, would contemplate. But then later, when you become complete cat, maybe your habits change automatically – something which you may have no control over. Ugh! The thought terrified me. I could not (would not) imagine my William behaving with anything less than consideration. I had assumed that his gentlemanly, but distant, behaviour towards me was purely good manners. But perhaps it was because he was betrothed, promised, engaged (or whatever cats do) to this aristocat, Anson. Perhaps this is why he continually treated me like a sister. Or perhaps he just did not recognise that we might, one day, be more than just friends. Turning my back to his, I vowed to change all this. From tomorrow there was no way he was going to ignore me. I would see to that.

But ignored I was. Well not actually ignored, but not noticed enough in the personal sense of the word – it felt almost like being ignored.

When I awoke at dawn he had already gobbled up a precise half share of our cat biscuits. The milk dish was exactly half full, and William had gone. I breakfasted alone and washed and got trodden on by Di and scolded by Megan.

"Go out for a walk," she said crossly. "And get out from under my feet!"

"Get out of my way – I'm late for work!" Di grumbled. "Why don't you go out with William? I expect he's gone already for his morning visit up at the House."

So they knew all about it! They were party to the William and Anson thing. I was just to be the little stray bystander. Feeling desperately sorry for myself that morning I ambled about the cold crisp garden until the house was empty, then I crept back through the flap into the warm kitchen. Benjamin watched me intently, fluffing up his bunny coat and waggling his nose (How did he manage to twitch it up and down and from side to side without a second's break in the movements?)

'Daft rabbit!' I told him huffily, so he predictably turned his puff tail to the wire so that all I could see was his bottom. Charming! 'Daft rabbit!' I spat again but he simply juddered his tail through the mesh in order to convey his feelings.

The house was still and quiet and warm. I finished off the milk and plumped up our bed so it would be fresh for our next relaxation. Then William appeared, slinking, smiling, purring.

'Have a good walk?' I asked casually, feigning combat with an imaginary fly.

'Yes,' he said, grinning so widely that his eyebrow whiskers wobbled a little. 'Excellent! I have been up to the Mansion House.'

As if I couldn't have guessed. He looked absolutely gorgeous and, I had to admit, happy and contented. My chances were nil.

'This afternoon,' he announced, 'After lunch,' (we never had lunch but William felt the term pinpointed a middle time of the day.) 'You and I will go to the House. I will introduce you to Anson.'

Ah! I noticed straightaway that he didn't say, 'I will introduce Anson to you.' But then I'm not royalty, I thought, or important, or betrothed.

'Great!' I said, shaking my head as if I were ever so slightly cheesed off.

And when he went into the other room for a nap on the couch I set about giving myself an unusually thorough bath. Every hair of my coat was washed and combed down with my tongue. I popped outside to eat some of the special long grass that would clean my teeth and freshen my breath, then I attended to finger and toe nails. I made sure the under part of

279

my tail was pristine and that there was nothing unsavoury caught between the tops of my back legs. My tummy fur was all puffed and fluffy and I even scraped out the top parts of my ears. Satisfied but exhausted I flopped down in our basket to rest, taking care not to disarrange my coiffeur too much. My tongue was aching from non-stop action and the back of my throat felt as if several tiny hairs were lodged there. In future, I resolved, I would wash a little more conscientiously, a little more often so that when an occasion loomed, all this last minute hassle would be avoided.

I was just about to inspect the insides of my eyelids when William leaned over. 'Come on!' he said, 'There's no time for going to sleep. You've had a nice long rest, let us get going.'

He might have had a rest but I felt shattered, not the best frame of mind in which to be presented to her Ladyship.

'Have you washed or are you going to?' he demanded, giving himself a good shake – his coat was always immaculate, even after he had been walking in rain. (I was glad mine wasn't white. There was no way I would ever manage to keep it clean. Maybe there was something one could spray on, to stop the wet and dirt getting into the hairs. Something like – well, whatever it was we used to spray on our shoes to make them waterproof. Why, suddenly, I asked myself, had I remembered this utterly pointless fact from my human days?)

'Well?' he asked again looking at me intently as I uncurled myself carefully. 'Though I must say you look fine to me.'

Stupid man! I thought, then, turning towards him I said, 'I washed earlier. Let's not make a drama out of it. It's only visiting a neighbour after all.' As I stretched slowly to show off what good shape I was in - although I would have felt better if I had been able to have a small sleep - I yawned loudly. Surely he must have got the message at last, that I was completely bored by this whole Anson subject. 'Let's go then,' I said.

And, pushing through the flap, we trotted off, up the pathway towards the Mansion House.

# CHAPTER 33

The audience at the Mansion House was scheduled to take place in the courtyard, as it was a fine day. We were to wait by the (closed) shop door and Her Ladyship would come out to meet us.

'Where do you normally meet her?' I questioned as we went out into the garden.

'Oh, various places,' William said vaguely, swishing his long white tail.

I'll bet! I thought bitterly. Probably she entertains him in the banqueting room with chicken livers or, on a warm day, for pilchard sarnies on the back veranda. I must have scowled because William flicked his ear against mine, which, as all cats know, is a fairly intimate gesture.

'I am very proud of you, Penny. I know Anson will like you,' he said softly. Great! I thought, but what about me liking Anson?

We walked up the pathway from the cottage, past the shrubs and graceful trees, on towards the Mansion House. Because the daylight was bright and the afternoon sunny, the Christmas tree lights had not yet been turned on, though I presumed that these would be lit before dusk. The festive trees looked quite grandiose, standing each side of the huge doors, flanked by the gracious stone columns. We avoided the driveway immediately in front of the long stone steps leading to the main entrance, and kept to the verges of greenery opposite. As neither of us blended well with the short grass William felt it prudent to move slowly alongside the fence where there was more undergrowth. This meant getting our legs and feet very wet. When we emerged from our cover, opposite the entrance to private apartments and the administrative office building, it took some minutes of titivating before we were in a fit enough state to pass through the impressive stone archway which led into the courtyard. William had pointed out that the first archway we reached – the one with the huge clock set into the brickwork above it –

was permanently closed. The tall metal gates were only unlocked and opened for special or estate vehicles to pass through. This led to a small open area between some of the buildings. The arch we were interested in had no gates so we were able to enter freely. This larger paved courtyard was deserted and we strolled over to the first shop building. There was also a National Trust shop at the far end, with lavatories and access to the café nearer to the entrance. The centre of this almost square area was taken up by a long low stone wall which encircled much of the middle of the place.

'What is that for?' I couldn't help asking.

'That is a midden,' William supplied knowledgeably. 'Really it is an old fashioned rubbish dump. In times past, they used to pile all their rubbish here, empty out the debris from the stables. You will notice that there is a small gap over there? That is where a man could get in and the larger opening is where a horse would back up its cart so that the contents could be tipped straight on to the pile.'

'How nasty,' I said, adding generously, 'But very interesting.'

'You should see all this during the summer, especially the school holidays,' William said. 'Sometimes you can hardly move in the shops.'

'Mmm,' I said, trying to imagine this quiet tranquil place turned into a bustling tourist trap. The old stone outhouses had been renovated and around the enclosed yard, windows and wooden doors overlooked us, some of which were open to let air into the rooms, I supposed. 'So, where is your Anson?'

There was no-one, no life, in sight except for a few rather elegant birds. (They were quite ordinary birds truthfully, not peacocks or anything exotic – the sort one might have expected to be patrolling the grounds – but the setting and atmosphere seemed to lend an air of graciousness to everything, so they looked elegant. I shook myself, briefly and hoped that I too looked elegant. What a deliciously descriptive word that is, I decided. Descriptive words and phrases appealed to me. Maybe this was why, in my human life, I had often thought I should like to write. How could I remember this so well?)

William tutted. 'Anson will come when she is ready,' he remarked and sat down to wait. I wondered how many times he had waited for her previously. There was so much I should have asked before this meeting with his lady-friend but it was too late now. I lowered myself beside him, as decorously as possible so as not to ruffle my fur too much.

'You look very good,' William told me, reading my thoughts.

I snorted and turned away to give the impression of it not mattering in the slightest, but inside I was pleased at what he had said. I tried to remember my human reactions when someone complimented me but, sadly, nothing could be recalled. It was pleasant sitting in the watery sunshine but I soon became fed up with just waiting. 'Where is she? Why is she so long? How does she know we are here? I mean, we could sit here all day,'

William shuffled himself around to face me. 'When I come to see Anson,' he explained, 'I arrive, she looks out to see if I am here, then she comes out.' I wriggled about impatiently as there was nothing to say to this. The arrangement seemed logical but she certainly appeared to have William at her beck and call.

'Ah!' he said, getting up and straightening his back, 'There she is!'

I stood obediently and followed his gaze. From an open wooden door a little way around the block, the small frame of a cat appeared. Very slowly she moved towards where we stood. I half expected William to leap forward to meet our hostess but he remained quietly and still until she reached us. From William's sketchy descriptions and remarks of 'high pedigree' and 'unusual strain' I had been prepared for the meeting with Anson to be a mind blowing experience. A Burmese, Persian, Abyssinian or something very oriental was definitely on the cards. Tall, statuesque and definitely haughty was the least I had expected.

Standing my ground I was ready to hold my own. I dropped my chin a little to scrutinize my front paws; better not let the others see I was in the least bit apprehensive. At my side William gave a happy little sort of grunt so I looked up impatiently.

Well, well! I tried not to show my complete surprise at being confronted by a small, low backed, almost crouching creature with the appearance of being a rather commonplace, if slightly mangy, tortoiseshell. As she more or less scrambled up to us William bowed his head slightly and I wondered, ridiculously, if I should attempt a curtsey. Turning my eyes to heaven I asked, 'What is all the fuss about?' Then I looked down at her again. Yes, down, as I seemed to tower above her.

William drew himself up. 'Anson,' his straight gaze said clearly, 'May I present, Penny?' (Of all the drivel! I thought inwardly, looking away quickly.)

The other cat shook her head slightly and pulled her legs closer together, making her back rise and straighten fractionally. I looked at her closely for the first time and realised that she was a very, very old cat. Her eyes were a clouded grey and when she looked at us to speak, the timbre was hesitant; if this had been a human voice it would have been rasping and breathless.

'Don't be so formal, you old fuddy duddy!' she chuckled, 'Hello Penny! William has said so many nice things about you. Why has he kept you away from me for so long?'

'Penny, this is my great friend, Anson,' William said gravely.

I smiled at her and twitched my whiskers just a little. This usually means either friendship or, which was more accurate in my case, relief. 'Hello!' I said, completely baffled. I had been prepared to meet a glamorous celeb-type, young feline person with whom my William was totally besotted. Instead, the old, worn, completely average looking cat who was struggling to keep steady and upright was ancient enough to be William's grandmother and, probably, my great-grandmother.

'Should you rest?' William's eyes asked her as, ever solicitous, he hovered between us.

'Rest?' she retorted, quite loudly and with some inference that she might have felt insulted. 'Whatever for? No, my lad. You, I and your delightful Penny will go around into the garden. No too far, mind, as it will soon start to get cold again. There's that sunny spot just outside the café. The paving will be dry and warm and we can sit there and chat.' She took a few deep breaths and started to work her way slowly towards the archway. William shortened his pace to stroll alongside her and I followed behind, still dazed. No one spoke as we made the short journey and I suspected Anson might easily become out of breath. She obviously had difficulty in turning her head to look sideways at William and it would have been even worse for her to attempt to engage me, four paw paces to her rear, in conversation.

'This is one of our favourite places when there's some sun,' she said flopping heavily down on to the paving slabs. These, were, as she had predicted, surprising warm and comfortable and amply sheltered from the wind. William indicated that I should sit by her side which I did, leaving a comfortable space between us to enable room for stretching, scratching and shaking should this be necessary. William settled himself carefully between and in front of us, minding not to keep the sunshine from either of us.

'He knows I like the warmth on my face,' she said, closing her eyes with the pleasure of it for a few seconds.

'I love the sun, too,' I said. Accurate, but it seemed a little inadequate. I just didn't know what else to say.

'Well, I prefer it on my back,' William said firmly, washing some dirt from his front paw. '

'And how do you like Shugborough, my Dear?' Anson asked me kindly.

'Very well,' I said slowly. This elderly cat was certainly no competition. There was really no cause to fear or antagonize her. 'But this is the first time I have been up to the Mansion House. Before, in the few days I have been staying at the cottage, I've only seen it from a distance. So this is my first real visit.'

'You will certainly come again and again I hope,' she replied warmly. Then her head dropped down and her eyelids faltered.

I nodded my head, waiting for William to add something or to direct the flow of talk. But he didn't and we just sat for a while enjoying the welcome warmth. Anson opened her eyes and for a moment they seemed to sparkle in the sunlight.

'Penny, my Dear,' she said with some vigour, 'I do insist that you come to see me again soon.'

I stammered, 'Yes, of course, I would like that.' I wouldn't mind at all, I decided. It would be a change from dallying around the cottage all day.

'I should like that too,' she said thoughtfully. 'As you can see I am a very old lady and I do not have many months or even weeks left..'

'What nonsense! With respect,' William interrupted, 'That is absolute nonsense! You will outlast most of us!'

Anson laughed lightly. 'That may possibly be,' she agreed wriggling her nose at him, 'You might all fall into the river and I would be the sole occupant of the estate. But that really is unlikely.' I shuddered to be reminded of the river and its rushing waters in this context but realised she was poking fun at William's indignation. (I was dying to ask how old she was but knew this would be bad form.) 'Anyway, as I was saying,' she continued, looking at me. 'As I am old, I have acquired some wisdom. Much of it has already passed to William but, as you are now going to become his family, I must make sure you know as much as possible.' She stopped for breath and to take in more sunshine. I felt a little embarrassed so I said, 'What sort of wisdom? Do you mean things about the estate – the Mansion House?'

Anson tapped her forepaw on a paving slab in amusement. 'Gracious no! I mean all about humans and Zoons. Things that have happened to me, to William and to you, and things that will happen in the future.' I was somewhat surprised at her words and looked to William for some lead but he had stretched out and remained laying motionless with his eyes firmly closed.

'Well, ' I faltered, 'It sounds intriguing but how does what has happened in the past affect what is going to happen?'

'Ah!' she responded at once. 'You might be surprised! You may well ask.' I waited but she just sat and stared.

'Are there many, er, Zoons here, on the estate?' I asked, really to fill what I feared might be an awkward gap.

Anson shook her head. 'Very few,' she replied, putting her head on one side as if she were mentally counting. 'Just William and me and the twins from the Park Farm. Two of the cats that the office people feed are, but we do not have a lot to do with them.' She appeared to be concentrating so I kept quiet, but I couldn't help wondering why the office cats were kept at a distance. She nodded. 'Perfectly acceptable creatures but well, not really part of us.' She made a slight gesture with her right forepaw. 'There were two more of us, actually they were our relatives,' she continued, stopping to blink her eyes which had misted over. 'They were superb!' She lowered her head as if the thought upset her.

I looked across at William hopefully but he had turned over, facing away from us.

'Were? What happened?' I didn't want to ask but knew I had to.

'Killed!' she said vehemently, 'Stone dead! Some crazy truck driver ran over them.'

'How terrible!' my eyes said and my whole insides jolted.

'Crazy man!' she reiterated looking me straight in the eye. 'One of these stupid money-making weekend things they hold here. Some sort of festival where they erect those hideous enormous tents and sell fizzy drinks and food things with smelly onions in them. The van just backed over them whilst they were asleep.' She was silent for a while and I didn't know what to say. 'I am sorry.' I signalled and she nodded in acknowledgement.

Then William uncurled himself and stretched out a rear foot. Balancing on his front legs he pulled himself up into a sitting position.

'You do have a strange way of getting up,' Anson scolded, sniffing, but I could tell she was glad of a diversion.

287

'Ah, well,' he grunted, 'You're not the only one who is getting older each day. We all are.'

'Very profound,' she sniffed again, this time in his direction. 'But let us not get maudlin in front of our very welcome guest. Now, I feel I am getting tired. You will both have to excuse me in a little while. Penny, will you come up tomorrow to see me? After you have had your morning meal? If you look across from your cottage you will see a large light coloured lorry with writing on the sides parked at the front of the House. If you come up any time after it drives away, I will be ready.'

I nodded, noting that this was not so much an invitation or request as an instruction. 'Thank you. I will look forward to it. That is, if it's all right with you?' I enquired of William who was doing some stretching and shaking; something behind his neck was certainly bothering him but as we all know, it's not good manners to scratch in company.

'Of course it is all right with him!' she exploded. 'Nothing to do with him, anyway,' she pointed out, 'It is just a ladies' meeting.' I smiled to myself. For decades now we have said - 'girls' time out' or 'girlie meet' -but I supposed she would never have heard of this.

'Fine with me. I'll have some peace for a change.' He glanced provocatively in my direction and I smiled back. It had given me considerable pleasure when Anson referred to me becoming part of William's 'family'. Suddenly I felt happy, happier than I had for some time. Not only was I accepted by the Morgan family and this very elderly Mansion cat whom William held in such high regard, but William himself seemed to be drawing me in. Also, the relief of there not being a rival for his attentions seemed overwhelming. Then it dawned on me, frighteningly, that I was now acting like a cat; I was starting to think and feel like one. Somehow it was quite relaxing, not the stressful push and tug sensation that it had been a few days earlier. Part of me revelled in the realisation that I was at last getting the hang of it all, although my waning human side wondered where it would end. It was like being in no man's land – a wilderness of uncertainty; a cliff that one did not know whether to jump from or not. Then I recognised I no longer shook and trembled when remembering cliffs and jumping. Why didn't this seem to affect me now? For a few moments, there in the sunshine, I forced my mind back to the accident that had killed me. But the sharpness had disappeared and I could not think of any of the details. Quite soon there would be nothing to remember. The memory would be erased. No recollection of it would remain.

Anson was watching me carefully. 'That is settled then, my Dear. I will see you tomorrow morning and we will have a good chin-wag.'

I grinned, thinking I had not heard this expression in a long time. Talking with Anson may prove to be like getting some sense out of my old grandmother, many years before. But I suspected my rendezvous the following morning may prove to be a little different, even quite interesting.

# CHAPTER 34

'What shall we talk about? Why does she want to talk to me? Did you know she was going to make me go to see her?' I cross-examined William as we turned in front of the now lit Christmas trees on our way home.

'Anson is not making you go to see her. It was just a friendly suggestion. You ask too many questions,' he grunted, quickening his pace.

'If,' I said ominously, 'I had asked more questions before, there would have been no misunderstanding and I wouldn't have got so worked up about everything.'

'I presume you mean getting in a tizzy about Anson? That is up to you entirely. What you chose to believe, making two and two equal goodness knows how much, is your prerogative. I told you she was beautiful and she is. And wise and kind. What muddle you made in your mind of it all I have no idea.'

I was tempted to hit his smug bottom, bobbing about beneath his upwardly pointing tail as he fair galloped along in front of me. 'You made me think she was young, more than just a friend. You led me on.' I accused lamely, wishing I had kept my eyes shut and not entered into this exchange.

William made his snorting sound with which I was becoming familiar; it meant my remarks did not warrant a reply. But he did turn around to say, 'Anson is certainly more than just a friend. And lead you on? Never, Penny Paws!' He was poking fun at me yet again but I was too weary to make a snappy rejoinder. Again, angry though I was with him, the familiar 'Penny Paws' made my tail twitch with pleasure. As we crossed from the gravel to the tarmac path more questions formed in my head. More than a friend? Not for the first time I wondered...So I blurted out, 'Is Anson your mother or some other relation?'

William stopped so abruptly that I almost ran into his rear. (There would definitely have been a collision if I had been able to keep up with his fearsome speed more effectively.) 'Good Heavens! No!' He seemed utterly astounded at the suggestion.

'Well, what then?' I demanded, panting in a most un-cat like manner.

He sat down on the deserted laneway and shook his head theatrically from side to side. I slumped thankfully in a heap near him, rather wishing I had chosen a more appropriate moment to instigate what promised to be one of his explanation-type discussions. It was getting very cold and dark and the warm kitchen was the place to be, not sitting getting frozen hindquarters. Here it comes, I thought.

'Anson has been my guide,' he started, sighing. 'When I was a tiny kitten she rescued me from the road that runs through the village, where I'd been left at the side. The only thing I can remember clearly is that it was very cold and raining. She ripped open the sopping cardboard box and carried me in her teeth along the lane and over the bridges. Presumably she would have taken me to the Mansion House.'

'She didn't?' In spite of the cold creeping into my buttocks I was becoming interested. There seemed to be a story in everything.

'No,' he affirmed. 'We made it at far as the locked gates by the cottage but the bars were too close together for us to get through joined as we were. The same with the fence railings – the bigger gap there was only made for me much later. She just couldn't manage to go any further. She was exhausted by this time - Anson was never a strong cat – and her mouth must have ached so much. I do recall how she lowered me to the ground, so gently. And then she collapsed herself into the grass. I didn't realise the vulnerability of my situation and I crawled out into the lane by the cottage gate.'

'Yes?'

William didn't really need encouragement but I do think he was having some difficulty in calling up the details.

'I don't remember very clearly as I was only tiny,' he admitted, 'But Megan saw me and with Anson laying there close by, tired out, she probably partly guessed what must have happened, although she could never have known where Anson found me or the distance she had carried me.'

'And so you were adopted?'

'Yes, I suppose I was.' He seemed unwilling to go on. I waited for a few seconds until he said briskly, 'Well, that's more or less it. One of the two cats that were run over, that was mentioned earlier, was Anson's heir – some close relation but certainly not her own as she never had offspring. He was to have taken over her role at the House when she became too old. We all understood this and I think the humans who mattered did too, although things and people change. Anyway when he, and his sister, were killed, she turned to me.'

'William?' I pleaded. (If we had this out now we could dispense with it for ever – and it would give me time to get my breath. Forgetting the cold momentarily I was ready to hang on his every word.) 'William – what do you mean 'her heir' and taking over 'her role'. What role? I just don't understand.'

He looked at me silently for a moment. 'I cannot tell you, Penny. All I can say is that when Anson feels she is past it, she will leave the House and finish her days with the other cats in the stables and outbuildings.'

'You mean, go away to die? That sounds horrible. But why should she have to go from wherever she is in the House, living with her fine family, to stay outside with animals she doesn't know and who aren't even all Zoons?' Now that I had met Anson the idea was appalling.

'She will not *have* to go. She will *choose* to go. When cats are near their end it is best they are with their peers unless, of course, the individual is a personal pet and has been in a loving home.'

'Yes, but, if you are to take her place as an 'heir' - whatever you mean by that - does this mean you will have to move to the House? Why should you? And what would Megan and Di say about it? They won't understand.'

He sighed deeply and shivered slightly as the wind whipped at his coat. 'I think they may understand,' he said slowly, 'And I have always spent time up there with Anson. In a way, I suppose, I have been learning the ropes.'

I tried to digest this but it all seemed like mumbo jumbo to me.

'It is all to do with tradition,' he went on, 'It is not necessarily what we want to do, it is what we must do.'

This didn't make things any clearer. Then a thought struck me.

'Me?' I squawked, 'What about me? I am just settling in with you all. What will I do – will I come with you or will they let me stay with them at the cottage?'

'You will not be able to come with me,' he said, 'It is a single post, if I can put it that way, although I should love to take you. Of course you will be able to stay at the cottage and I shall see you whenever I can.'

I swallowed heavily. 'That won't be the same,' I stammered but I reminded myself, be careful Penny, don't say anything you might regret later. 'I thought we were getting closer,' I dared, hesitantly.

'We are! My goodness we are!' he said heartily, leaning over and giving my ear a quick lick. Immediately my furry chest started to pound rapidly and I pretended a small sneeze so that he wouldn't notice. 'Anyway,' he shook his whole body as if to clear his mind of unwanted thoughts. 'Anson, in spite of what she says, is as fit as a fiddle. A little slow and a little stiff maybe, but nothing that need cause concern to any of us. Tomorrow you will see. You will see how strong and positive she is. Just be patient with her movements and walk leisurely and you will have an enjoyable hour or so.'

I cheered a little at this and also stood up to shake. Bits of leaves and dust flew from my back, up into the wind. William shepherded me in front of him, shielding me from the icy blast. 'We will go at your speed,' he said grinning. 'Though don't go as slowly as a snail like you usually do.'

We walked together closely and companionably. I really hadn't found out much more about the mysteries of the Mansion but perhaps Anson would enlighten me more the next day. I invited William to escort me up to the House but he declined firmly, saying he had to see Tabby and then go on to the school where the children were putting on a Christmas concert. 'A sort of nativity play, I think. They always do something before they break up for the holidays.'

I nodded but didn't ask how he would get himself accepted into the hall as part of the audience. I supposed people were so used to seeing him outside at the school gate that someone would invite him into the warm and feed him the treats he was no doubt anticipating.

'Anyway,' he reminded me, 'Yours is to be a 'ladies' meeting'.

So I set off by myself. No sunshine that day. Still windy with a hint of rain or even snow. I had waited patiently for the big van to disappear from the front of the Mansion House, as Anson had instructed, but it stayed almost all morning. It was about midday when I reached the House. As before, I waited outside the courtyard shop and Anson appeared quite quickly from the same wooden door. 'Too cold out here. No sitting outside today,' she greeted me. Beckoning me to follow, she led the way round the yard and in through another, wider door. 'The stables,' she informed me.

These were definitely stables but not the cold, musty, smelly type. These were old buildings, attractively renovated and decorated. They had been restored, for display to visitors, to how they must have looked many years ago. But considerably cleaner, I imagined. In the first room, the manger was filled with dry hay, and chains for securing horses hung from huge iron rings in the wall. It all looked so realistic that I half expected to hear neighing or whinnying and the sound of clattering hooves outside. Wooden and metal implements decorated the sides of the area and the cobbled floor was uncharacteristically spotlessly clean and shiny.

'They have the heating on when people come,' Anson explained and, sure enough, the huge old fashioned radiators were clearly visible, though subtly camouflaged wherever possible with sacking, saddles and various things standing prominently in front of them. The stables had obviously been used by visitors for many years after they had been occupied by horses. 'Today, though, it's cold out here. The inner rooms are warmer, but you and I will sit in luxury in one of the carriages.'

We made slow progress through more rooms, until Anson stopped when we entered a long area that was filled with old fashioned carts and coaches. 'Some of these are very famous. And valuable,' she added. 'Let me see. Today, I think, we will choose this one. Inside are comfortable velvet seats and cushions.'

She paused as if she were considering an alternative but I could at once see why she was recommending this rather drab looking coach. The high step and even higher partly closed window would have precluded any attempt by her to gain access, even I would have had some difficulty. But the roof of the vehicle was being recovered or repaired and there was a large convenient hole to one side. Against the stone wall of the building a small metal stepladder was propped, the top comfortably leaning against the carriage roof. Whatever work had been started had been postponed or abandoned for a while, judging by the dust on the ladder and the roofing material.

'We can pop up here and drop down inside. On one seat, cushions are piled almost up to the gap in the roof so it makes an easy landing.'

I turned away as my eyes smiled, thinking that this was obviously one of her favourite haunts; a frequently used hide-away. 'Would you like me to go first?' I asked, half doubting she would be able to manage the steps.

'Good heavens, no!' she blasted. 'I will go ahead to make sure it is safe for you.'

I followed her as she laboriously climbed upwards. "Manners maketh man", my mother used to say, and they certainly made Anson. It only took us a few seconds to drop down on to the dusty cushioning.

'Now we can talk,' she said as she sank back and closed her eyes. (Obviously we couldn't talk whilst she had her eyes closed so I sat and waited.) 'Tell me about yourself,' she instructed, suddenly alert. 'William has given me some information but I should like to hear it from you. Where were you born, and how long ago?'

This was going to be like an interview I thought but hastily said, 'I don't really know where, but my mother, my cat, mother, was called Penelope and my minders were elderly - mature people,' I amended, in case she might take offence at the word elderly.

She nodded, 'Go on,' she said.

Go on? What? So I racked my mind as to the chronological order of things that happened afterwards. Anson did not interrupt. At one point I thought she had fallen asleep but as soon as I paused to draw breath she was sitting ramrod straight and demanding that I continue. To condense one's life seemed to take very little time and I was soon at the, 'and that is how I came to meet you,' point. She nodded and I wondered secretly how much she had heard, understood or was particularly interested in.

'What of your human life? What can you remember?' she fired at me suddenly.

I snuggled back into the cosiness of the old velvet material. Human life? What could I remember? Not too much, not much at all.

'I was young,' I started, she waited. 'At school, college, I mean.,' I went on. 'But almost at leaving age. Parents? Yes my mother and dad. I liked sports, anything athletic. Maybe I was a bit of a show off. I fancied a guy and would do daft things to get him to notice me. Can't remember his name now. Sometimes he and his mates did daft things so I tried to join in. I did something very stupid. On a bridge.' I stopped, sighed. The bridge and the twanging rope materialised just inches in front of me. 'Showing off,' I felt my eyes smarting, saying, 'Being one of the boys. I jumped....'

Silence. And then she said, 'And here you are, my Dear.' I nodded. 'Anything else – can you recall more?' She spoke quietly and unhurriedly.

Searching my memory, I shook my head. 'Only trivial things,' I said, 'Like sayings my mother used or people's names who now mean nothing to me. It's all rather a blur I'm afraid.'

'Normal,' she interjected. 'Quite normal. In fact, that you remember some things still means you are not yet complete cat.' I wondered uneasily whether to be reassured by this or depressed. 'Soon though,' she continued, rearranging her body on the cushions, 'You will forget it all, even the jump. And then you will be cat.'

I nodded and twitched my whiskers. 'Can you remember anything?' I countered. 'About your human life?'

She shook her head heavily. 'Nothing,' she said. She lifted her head and looked directly at me again. 'You do know about Zoons, don't you? William told me you have some knowledge.' Again I nodded. 'As you may know I am very old and nearly at the end of my natural cat days.' (Oh, dear, I thought, not another one of these embarrassing monologues.) I tried to switch on my interested, eager look but couldn't think of the right comment to make. She coughed delicately, reminding me then of Tabatha in one of her more sensitive moments. 'As you may also know it beholds older members of the species to educate the younger ones.'

She held up a paw as I sat up and said, 'Well, it has been explained to me.'

'Yes,' she said quickly, 'I am sure it has. But I am the oldest cat you will probably ever meet and as we gain more wisdom about these things the longer we live, I undoubtedly know more than anyone you have spoken with before. Therefore, I wish to make sure that you are au fait with everything there is to possibly know about these important matters.'

I moved my shoulders a little. Not actually a shrug but some small action to convey I was listening without really interrupting. 'I wish you to listen because William, as I am sure you know, is very dear to me. He must think a great deal of you as he has asked me to talk like this with you. He feels that you should understand as he does.' So he had arranged it all!

'Why didn't he tell me himself, then?' was my reaction, though I said it nicely so that the old lady could not mind.

'Yes. He could have, I suppose,' she agreed, 'But, as I think he has explained, he might be under some obligation with responsibilities at the Mansion House himself some day soon, so he might have felt it better coming from me – who does not know you as well as he does.'

I shook my head. It was all getting too much for me to get to grips with. 'What is all this about him being an heir to the Mansion?' I asked, hoping that Anson would clear away some of the woolliness.

'Is that what the dear boy said – an heir? Well, not quite.' She appeared to be amused and sat silently for some minutes. Again, I felt she might have dropped off to sleep. In fact, it was so conducive there that I wouldn't have minded a nap myself.

'I cannot tell you much,' she started again. 'William will move up here and supervise the animals. He will also become the House cat – as you will have observed he is most presentable and smart – every inch a suitable representative to appear before the public.' She made it sound as if he were going to star at a London theatre, or do a cabaret turn in the car park instead of perhaps occasionally being spotted by gawping tourists on their way between the House and tea room. 'I cannot give you any detail. There is more to it than that, of course, concerning his place with the humans in the House. But there again, things change and future residents here may not feel obliged to follow tradition. Goodness, we might have lions and monkeys here one day in the gardens – they do have them at some stately homes, you know - and you certainly could not have a cat in charge of all that! Many of the old houses are being turned into – what do they call them? Theme parks? Safari centres? Why they cannot stick with cats and, yes, I am afraid so, dogs, with a few others like our unusual breeds of cattle and pigs, I don't know.'

Anson nodded to herself for a while. 'Right!' she straightened her front legs and gave a lady-like yawn. Resettling herself she proceeded. 'Penny, we will now talk about how being a Zoon will affect your future and the life that follows.'

I valiantly attempted to appear fascinated though inwardly I feared there was more nonsense to come that I wouldn't be

298

able to understand. It was all like a bad dream. And it didn't seem to be getting better.

# CHAPTER 35

I shifted my position to get more comfortable as I realised this might be a long sitting-still, saying-nothing session. 'I'm ready,' I told Anson, 'Tell me about being a Zoon.'

To my slight surprise she asked, 'First. You tell me just what you know – what you have gleaned so far.'

'Fine. That's easy. I've met a few, er, Zoons. Tabatha - a cat, then some seagulls, a mouse, other cats, oh, and yes, a dog and, well, lots of others.' I finished airily.

'And did they all tell you something?' Anson enquired, fixing me with a rigid stare.

'Well, I don't actually remember who said what. But, well, the main thing seems to be that if, when you were a human you voiced a wish, a desire to come back next time as something else, then that's what happens. You die, you come back as a pheasant, or a camel or whatever.'

'Or a cat?' she supplied for me.

'Absolutely!'

'So? Yes – go on?' she waited again.

'Yes, well..' I really wasn't enjoying this one bit and I couldn't see the point of any of it. 'Well.. So here I am as a cat. I understand that the next step is that if, whilst I'm being a cat, some mortal says something like, "You are almost human", or anything that's like this, then, hey presto! When you come to the end of your life as a cat, then we're born again as a person in the real world.' This was as much as I could manage. I really did need a sleep, or at least a cat nap.

'Very good!' Anson applauded. 'And quite accurate. So what else do you know?'

I thought for a bit, slightly nonplussed – what more was there? 'Nothing,' I said defensively. 'I don't know anything else. What more is there? You're a human, then you're a cat, then you're a human again. It just goes on and on I suppose. Then one day when the wishes run out you just become a worm or a lump of earth or just disappear off the planet.' This might have sounded rather rude, I supposed, but the feeling of being fed up and extremely drowsy was overpowering me.

'That is a little flippant,' she observed. 'This is quite a serious subject, I think. But,' she sniffed, 'If you do not want to know what else happens next....I will just tell William I think he had made rather a mistake...'

Although I didn't quite know what she meant, this didn't sound too good. I felt indignant that she might tell William anything about me; I certainly had no wish to be the object of critical discussion between them. I took a deep breath (mainly to stay awake) and said. 'Forgive me. I'm just a bit tired. Yes, I should like to know more about it all. I am curious, though, why what I know or do not know concerns William.'

Anson sniffed again, taking her time in more re-settling movements. 'My bones are stiffening up,' she pointed out, moving her back legs this way and that. 'You wait until you get to this stage. Not very pleasant at all,' she spoke matter-of-factly, without hinting for sympathy.

I realised that if this were human life, we would probably be having tea and cakes or small cucumber sandwiches and she would be fluttering around like the perfect gracious hostess. There wasn't much she could do about providing goodies to munch on, but she was endeavouring to be a good host. We were warm and comfortable in quiet, interesting surroundings. Feeling churlish, I smiled at her and twitched my whiskers. 'Please tell me more?'

'Well you know most of it,' she said rather grumpily. 'And if the answer to your question about William is not self evident, then you are not as astute as I thought you were, Penny. You must know how he feels about you. I will wager it won't be too long before you become, how do they say nowadays? Yes – an item.' She beamed at me, realising that I really hadn't known and wasn't just being coy.

'I had, well, hoped that, well, you know,' I shuffled about, feeling pleased and happy at what she said, yet a little stupid. 'I do want to be really accepted, but, well William hasn't given any indication.'

'Ah!' she nodded so vigorously that her pointed ears seemed to click to and fro. 'He was possibly waiting until you became just a little more complete cat. The last thing he would want to do is to offend you by making any move or suggestion you might find unacceptable.'

We sat in silence whilst I thought about this. Yes, I supposed it made sense. My mind whirled uncontrollably. Half of me wanted to become closer with William but the other half still abhorred any thought of us being on more intimate terms.

'But even if this happens,' I paused not really knowing what I was saying. 'Then, well, what do we do next? When - if,' I hastily corrected myself so as not to cause her any upset, 'William has to go to the Mansion House? I'll be just left behind? And that's only if they want to keep me at the cottage.'

She wiggled her ears (probably to make sure they were still operative after all that head nodding). 'Do not fret about that. You will be taken care of once William has fully made up his mind about things. If you and he have decided to be together, you would naturally go where he goes. But if you are, well, still independent, you would have to stay at the cottage. But they are kind people and you would have a good life there. Anyway, it will all be sorted out in good time.' Her words seemed vague and brought me no comfort although they proved to be oh, so true. I doubt, though, that she had any inclination as to what was to happen so soon afterwards.

'Now,' she went on, this time exercising her front legs one at a time. 'Let's get back to our discourse on Zoonery – if there is such a term, which I rather doubt. When a cat is born a Zoon it gradually loses all previous memories. This is why it is important for old cats to let the younger ones know what will happen – to give them some preparation.'

'But,' I chimed in, 'What about humans? They don't get any warning, no one tells them they will come again as a horse or an elephant.'

'Very true,' she said, 'But, humans when they get older usually have a sort of flash back to any previous animal life, if they had one. As we all know, when a human lives to, say, their 70's – occasionally it happens earlier – their memory starts to fade. This is why old people become forgetful and get disorientated. Some become senile and are completely incapable of living normal lives. They start to really believe that their dog talks to them or that their budgie knows who's going to win the 4.30 at Kempton Park.' Anson wrinkled her nose and sniggered to herself. Then she said soberly, 'This usually happens about the same time as some old people become incontinent or severely depressed.'

I squirmed about on my cushion, praying that I wouldn't ever have this curse, either as a cat or a person. This conversation was getting really nasty.

'They revert to type. To use this rather unsavoury lavatorial instance as an example. If these humans were, in their past, say, a wild creature, completely undomesticated, they could stop and relieve themselves wherever they wanted to. In their elderly human state they are simply going back to this. This is not the explanation for all old people,' she added quickly, 'It's not inevitable. Many do not have any problems.'

She paused and I leaned forward, taking a deep breath, 'And?' I glanced away from her. This was all too much to be taking in but I had to be polite and hear her out. This was obviously very important to the old girl.

'It's not just an accident of fate that some older folk live long healthy lives. These are usually the ones who've not been animals before. It's only the others who might go, as we say, do-dally. Living, in their minds, this dual role, there is no way in which they can remain wholly rational. Often, they have days, weeks, maybe months when everything seems normal, then for no apparent reason they go vague and seem peculiar to their families and friends. This is when they are, in their minds, reliving parts of their previous animal lives. Reminding themselves, I suppose, of what might come again.'

This lengthy explanation obviously made the elderly cat weary, for she gradually closed her eyes and started to breathe more deeply. I sat perfectly still. She looked so peaceful that I couldn't disturb her. Also I was worried that she might be utterly exhausted and that, heaven forbid, she might drift away in front of my very eyes. I would leave her for a few minutes then rouse her gently, I thought. But my eyes also seemed too heavy to hold open so I didn't bother to try.

Although thoroughly convinced I had slept for only for a short while, when I felt her paw stroking my head, just between my ears, my feet and body felt colder. Time had passed. It was much later in the day. Trying hard to stifle my yawn I stretched and sat up. 'I must have fallen asleep,' I apologised, trying to sound astounded at the very idea. 'But I really do feel much better now.'

Anson nodded. She had altered her position and was also sitting; I think she had had a wash as her coat looked a bit damp. 'I slept too,' she admitted, looking slightly uncomfortable. 'I do not normally allow myself to drop off like that when I have guests but I usually do have five minutes or so in the early afternoon when I'm on my own.'

'It probably did us both good,' I said smoothly, stretching out again on the warm velvet. 'But I really think I should be going. It does seem to be getting colder.' She seemed to stare at me hard, so I said hurriedly, 'But is there anything else I should know. Something more you would like to tell me?' I rather hoped not.

Anson shrugged her shoulders and lay down again. 'Where did I get to? So, to put it in a nutshell, humans who voice a wish to return as an animal get their wish. If they were animal in a previous life they have a flashes of animal memory which can last for days, weeks or months, when they seem to be able to call up their previous animal life – this is what makes them go strange.'

I sighed, wishing I'd slept for longer. 'It all sounds terribly complicated,' I drawled.

Anson said firmly. 'It is good for you and all young Zoons to know as much as possible. I often think that if an animal is born again as human it should, as it gets older and start remembering, attempt to write all this down so that everyone would know about it. The sad thing is, though, when people get too old and incapacitated they probably wouldn't be able to physically write. The only way might be if they have someone they could confide in who could help them. Maybe you, Penny, may think of a way. For your age, you have led an interesting life. Some cats are born, live in a household and die. That is their life. But, you, my Dear, have something to tell, something that would interest and perhaps amuse. It would be a way of letting mortals know what they might expect. It would be helpful for them to know about Zoons and how we understand even though we cannot talk.'

'It's all so way out. But really interesting,' I tagged on quickly, thinking, deep inside, that it was all a load of rubbish.

'But,' she said, immediately sensing my impatience, 'I have kept you too long. It is getting late. Little light now. You should go, or William, and probably the Morgans, may be getting worried. I really have talked for far too long.'

'No,' I said courteously as I stretched, preparatory to getting up. 'Not at all.' (Thinking to myself that we had apparently slept for much longer than we had talked.)

'Yes!' She lent against the back of the velvet seat and wriggled into a sitting position. 'We must adjourn. We will talk again another day. But at least I've given you the gist of all this. I hope I have not bored you?'

'Not at all,' I repeated. Then a thought struck me. 'Anson, may I ask you one last thing?' She smiled obligingly.

'Most certainly. Providing,' she paused, 'That it is not about the Mansion House.'

'No it isn't. It's just - what happens if humans die young, like I did, and don't live to be really old and have flash back memories?'

Anson pondered for a moment, probably not because she hesitated about the answer but more in order to put it to me so that I would understand more easily.

'Yes, you, Penny had your accident and stopped being human quite suddenly. Because of this, you have retained your human thoughts and feelings much longer. You are really only just starting to forget about your previous life, but those who passed on as old humans, acclimatize more quickly to being animal. Also,' she blinked and lifted her head slightly, 'It's interesting to know that Zoon people have an affinity with

305

whatever animal they were. For example, if they were a hamster, then they would automatically want to own a hamster themselves. That is why cat and dog owners feel close to their pets – because this is what they were themselves. They understand its requests and needs. They truly feel they can communicate.'

'What about someone who was a lion before? They could hardly go out and buy one?'

Anson chuckled. 'They would probably drool over magazine pictures of lions, watch every television programme on them, visit wild animal parks and go on safari for their holidays. They would have a stuffed toy lion somewhere in their home, or they own the wilder type of cat and fantasise they have the real thing. Believe me, I've heard all sorts of stories in my time.'

Although I was quite absorbed, in spite of myself, for one dreadful moment I feared she might launch into some of these tales, so I came in quickly, 'It's all a bit muddling. Difficult to understand.' As an afterthought I added, 'What about the other animal animals?' Did I really want to know? Now is the time, I thought firmly, to end all of this. I couldn't take much more.

Anson sighed, moving her front legs again, signalling some discomfort. 'Who knows?' she said. 'I only know about Zoons because of the information handed down from one generation to another. As we cannot communicate with the others, there's no way of knowing.'

'The ear wagglers?' I offered.

She grinned, 'Yes, the ear wagglers as you call them, we all have our own favourite names for them, usually not very complimentary. As we can't speak with them we have no idea about their life patterns.'

'Is there ever such a being as a half-Zoon?' I asked, wondering if, like a foreigner, sometimes a few words or gestures could be understood.

Anson threw back her head and laughed, her eyes glinting in the dim light. 'Oh, Penny, What a question! No, I don't think so. At least, I have never come across or heard of such a being. No. We are either one thing or the other. You really have asked lots and lots of questions. Do you think you understand now? You're a bright girl – I'm sure you are right for William and I know by your manner that he's right for you. You will make a great couple.'

I flicked my whiskers and wiggled my nose and gave my right ear a quick scratch. I was suddenly so absurdly elated that I didn't trust myself to just sit still. I felt that I needed to run, jump and leap about, for some reason. My tiny heart seemed to swell with each gasped breath and just as I was fighting to discipline my inner emotions a great burst of purring boomed out of my head and gave the show away.

Anson stood up slowly, balancing precariously on her crumpled cushion. 'Just be patient,' she advised quietly. 'William will not make a move until the time is right. He will want to be certain of your acquiescence. Now,' she said more briskly, 'Just remember what I have said. Lock it away somewhere in the back of your mind – you may never need it except when you get to be an old animal. Then you will be able to tell it all to someone younger. And forget all I've said about the Mansion House and William. Again, things will take their time. Don't worry. Just take each day as it comes.'

I too stood, and shook each back leg in turn, then I gave my side a speedy wash, particularly the bit I had been laying on. This part of my coat was all flat and lank, and was sticking against my skin.

'You look very tidy,' Anson reassured me, 'Anyway, by the time you get home the wind will have ruffled you nicely. Come, follow me. I'll lead the way out. They always leave the doors open until I have retired for the evening and there's no gate or anything on the entrance to the courtyard.'

Very carefully she picked her way up on to the pile of cushions, slightly dislodging the top one. She was easily able to make the short jump up through the hole and up out on to the roof of the carriage. The material which was being repaired bounced up and down but did not pull at the hole, which remained wide open. I watched as Anson crept forwards until all four paws were safely on the top of the step ladder. For me it was no trouble, although the wobbly top cushion tumbled down as I made my spring upwards. I took great care not to move the roofing too much as I slithered towards the metal steps. We left the coach hall and retraced our route through the other rooms and the outer stables. The sky had darkened when we reached the yard but Anson insisted on escorting me to the entrance by the shop.

'Take care, Penny, it is nearly dark. Go straight down the pathway, not across the field or by the gardens into the woods. One never knows what might lurk there after dusk. Thank you so much for coming to see me and for listening to an old woman so enthusiastically.'

She wiggled her whiskers and bowed her head slightly, which I gathered was the accepted alternative to shaking hands or embracing as humans would have done on parting. I followed her example and said, 'And thank you for having me. I have enjoyed talking with you, Anson, and I've tried to take in all you said.'

She smiled, 'We can always go over it again, any time you wish, but I promise you next time you come it will be lighter. We will talk of interesting things and you can tell me more of your adventures.'

As she bowed slightly again I could see she was worn out. Her legs seemed unsteady and her tail was drooping down, almost touching against the cobblestones. Then something made me burst out, 'Anson! I must tell you. When William talked about you at first, I really thought you were his, well, his girlfriend. I am so relieved!'

She looked me straight in the eye. 'If I were considerably younger,' she said evenly, 'That might well be the case!' She sniggered. 'But yes, I think he was teasing you a little, quite intentionally. Probably to see how you would react.'

'And I did react, and I shouldn't have done.'

'It did no harm at all to let him know you like him. This will give him more confidence to approach you when the time is right. But it will also reinforce his determination to wait until you have fully become cat, so as not to spoil everything. You will both know when. But,' she started to turn away, 'In the meantime just have fun. Enjoy your family life at the cottage, and it will be Christmas very soon. Special food and, I suspect, some treats for you from the Morgan people. Goodbye!'

She turned away immediately and hobbled towards the open door.

'Goodbye!' I shouted after her but she was facing away from me, concentrating on reaching her destination.

I started to trot happily in the direction of the cottage but spots of rain dampened my mood and sheets of sleet prompted me to break into a rapid run. But, I was going to my home, to my warm home with food, bed, good minders and William. When I finally got there I resembled a drowned rat.

# CHAPTER 36

William was waiting for me outside the back door. 'I was just starting to worry,' he said in a most parental tone.

'Yes, sorry. We were talking for longer that we intended. You know, it just seemed to go on.' I shuffled ahead of him through the cat flap and when he arrived beside me in the warm kitchen he said, knowingly, 'I bet you both fell asleep. Well, did you? I know you women!'

I tried to look nonchalant. 'Only a tiny shut eye,' I corrected him.

'Mmm. And I bet you got really comfortable in one of the carriages – that's one of her favourite places, especially in winter time.'

'Oh, so you're a real know-all!' I tossed back. 'Anyway, now I know all about everything.'

'Not everything,' he retaliated at once. So I pushed my tongue out at him and brushed past towards the welcoming fire. I expected William to question me on what Anson had told me but he said nothing. After dinner I even opened the conversation for him but he didn't seem at all interested. 'What you chatted about is none of my business,' he said, turning to watch the television.

The next day Di and Megan put up a small Christmas tree in the corner of the living room. Di fixed up a string of minute lights and Megan clipped on silky bows and miniature baubles. Cards had already been decorating the mantle shelf and window ledges for days – ever since I had arrived in fact – and some rather luxurious looking garlands were draped around the rooms. These were a gift from the Mansion House, William told me. They also provided the tree and a substantial turkey and other foods. I gathered that Di was a highly respected member of staff. William said there was always a good monetary bonus which meant that Megan could have a really special present. Although Di loved his job it seemed it was not at all well paid.

I was so happy to be part of all this, particularly at this time of celebration. As I lay curled up in our bed (the floor, even in front of the fire with its closed doors, was draughty) I frantically tried to recall my human Christmas times. Nothing would come. I gazed at the little tree, unlit until Megan returned from work, and up at the lush garlands, glittering in the dim firelight, but no memories would emerge. What did I have as presents, the last Christmas before I became cat? I looked around the room. Nothing served to remind me. Maybe I never had a Christmas? Did it matter? It was possible that next year I wouldn't understand the festivities at all. Just a lot of lights, and food and Di and Megan at home for a while. This depressed me as I had always really enjoyed the holiday. I would ask William what he could remember, when he came back from wherever he had gone to spread good tidings - his words, not mine.

Although he was quite a bit older than I was, and had been a Zoon for longer, he still appeared to understand it all. His current knowledge had not been clouded by becoming cat. Cheered by this I felt happier. Just as Anson had said. Enjoy every day. But, when was Christmas? I couldn't read the calendar that swung from the knob on the kitchen cupboard. William would know.

As we lay side by side in our comfortable bed William said, in answer to my questions, 'Tomorrow is Christmas Eve. Megan and Di will go to work in the morning and come home at midday. The next day is the Big Day, when we eat the turkey and have things that they put under the tree for us. They will be home for a few days. I'm not sure how many this year. Each year it seems different.'

I nodded, pleased that I knew what to expect, and when. 'What about Anson?' I had to ask. 'Will you, or both of us, go to see her sometime?'

William twitched his whiskers. 'I will go alone tomorrow, Christmas Eve, late afternoon. Only a short visit. Then we will both go the following morning to wish her 'Happy Christmas' – that is if you'd like to?'

'Yes, of course!' I knew then, that I wanted to see Anson again soon. I liked her, in spite of, or perhaps because of, the fact that she was old and very tired and seemed so cat-wise.

Listening to William's steady breathing lulled me to sleep – not that I ever had any trouble in that direction. He didn't usually stir more than once. This was when he made his nightly prowl around the garden, checking that everything was in order after he had attended to his more necessary activities. Sometimes I woke, sometimes I didn't. That night, however, William constantly tossed and turned. His legs were digging into my back and he kept sighing (at the top of his voice) and juddering his teeth, as one does when approaching danger or an especially tasty prey. Several times he shuffled about, standing up, turning around and laying down again in exactly the same position as before, as cats do.

'Oh do go to sleep, you're making me cold,' I complained, but all I got was a muttered, 'Sorry!' Eventually he roused himself completely, climbed out of the basket and disappeared into the garden. He had been so restless that it was with considerable relief that I settled myself more comfortably. After a while I felt him probe his way carefully back into bed. Then he went promptly asleep whilst I stayed awake for hours, trying not to think, trying to dream, trying to relax and not keep telling myself what a wreck I would be if I didn't get my proper sleep. Christmas Eve, and I would be staggering about not fully compos mentis; a dangerous situation for anyone – human, animal or Zoon.

William, of course, was up bright and early. He seemed full of joy and energy whereas I, who had at last managed to drop off just as Di started rumbling about the house, preparing for work, crept about as if I were only half conscious. When Megan and Di had rushed off, William and I finished the remains of our breakfast and milk.

'So, what is the plan for this Christmas Eve – our first together?' I ventured sheepishly.

He straightened up and cleaned his whiskers. Early morning care had obviously been lavished on his coat as it gleamed and shone. His legs and tail looked immaculate and he wore a determined, purposeful look. What a lovely creature!

'Well,' he started firmly – it was evident that he got it all mapped out. 'When you have finished slurping we'll go to call on Tabby. This will be the only time we can see him over the holiday as he's going with his people to visit relatives. But he doesn't go until this evening so I have to wish him all the best.'

I nodded, giving myself a quick flick over with my tongue. Poor Tabby, I sympathised silently, remembering my dismal journeys in cat boxes.

'We'll get there as soon as we can then we can do a spot of hunting – just for an hour or so, then stop off at the restaurant house for a drop of late morning milk – they will be closed in the afternoon and on Christmas Day - then come back here to get warm and have a few minutes rest before Master and Mistress get back. (Why would he not simply call them, Di and Megan? I thought irritably.)

'That sounds like a very full morning to me,' I said, 'What hunting? You've never taken me with you hunting before.' This sounded much more organised than my solo attempts at mice and small things that rush across the garden. 'We're not going down by the river, are we?' I tried to keep the anxiety from my voice. Although I wasn't too bad now about heights and jumping up or down, the possibility of ice cold water enveloping my shivering, shaking body seemed frighteningly real.

William laughed. 'No. We will cross the bridge, collect Tabby and go into the woods. Now that there are no leaves on the trees and bushes, there won't be much cover for our quarry.'

'I haven't really been to the woods, only the near one at the end of the garden. The ones on the other side of the river are bigger aren't they?'

He nodded, turning to scratch his neck. 'Much taller trees,' he said. 'Between the river and the canal there's only a narrow strip of copse but on the other side of the canal past the railway, there is a good piece of woodland. It goes for quite a way and leads up to a meadow. Today it should be very pleasant. The sun will be quite warm by the time we get there and the frost has almost gone already.'

He was right. There was no crispness on the grass as we crossed our lawn and strolled towards the hole in the railings. 'I'll go first,' he told me, 'Just in case there's something unpleasant waiting on the other side.' I smiled at him. Ever the gentleman.

We walked briskly over the bridge, in single file – again William leading in protective mode, meeting only one elderly couple of walkers who obediently stepped into one of the passing places to let us through. How strange, I thought to myself, that crossing the river did not bother me at all. All the same I kept to the centre of the pathway and wished the side walls were just a little higher. I was glad not to be a dog because then I might be able to see over the edge. A big dog would certainly have a good view of the water and would probably be quite afraid of falling over and into it. How did the horses used to manage? I wondered. They would only have to lean against the wall and they could topple. By the time we had reached the other side I'd succeeded in frightening myself silly again.

'You all right, Penny?' William turned.

I gulped and nodded bravely. 'Fine, Fine!'

We walked quickly up the hill towards Tabby's house. His folks were out so we were invited into the kitchen to warm ourselves. Not a very civilised place. No fire or cosy-looking heater; just some old fashioned radiators which seemed to gurgle a lot and not give out much heat. I squeezed right up to one but it was only lukewarm. Frugal folk whose heating went off when they weren't there, I gathered.

Both William and I declined the offer of some rather sour looking milk so Tabby said, 'OK. Let's be off. No point in washing this morning if we're going wooding. Have to do all that before I go off tonight. Not looking forward to it. Not one bit,' he chuntered, as we paraded in line through his mud encrusted door flap. 'Where we're going they've got a house full of kids,' he muttered. 'Not my style at all. Though the area

314

where they live is nice. Lots of kitty totty, if you get my meaning?'

'We do,' William said quickly, 'But how lovely it must be to have children around. Are there other animals? Zoons?'

'They've got a cat, not Zoon. Just had kittens, so I heard. So all the attention will be on them. They'll get the best bits to eat I suppose.' He looked mournful for a second as we crossed the road and walked past the church. 'But their next door people are great. Always letting you in their house, which is quiet – big thick carpets and chairs you can get lost in. And, they have the most gorgeous and very willing…'

'Yes!' William interrupted, 'Now where are we going to start? Come on Tabs, let's have suggestions. You come out here more than I do. This is your home ground. Let's get there and you can show Penny just how quick you are!'

Tabby took the lead and we marched behind him alongside one of the houses and past lawns and vegetable plots. 'Just across the field and we come out high above the train track,' Tabby explained to me. We walked more slowly in a line across the meadow, looking down on the wood, the railway, the canal and the river. Way across the far fields, the Mansion gardens sprawled out into more greenery. Only parts of the buildings were visible, most being obliterated by evergreen shrubs and trees. To the left of the House, down towards the farm, cattle ambled about and the brilliantly blue sky was alive with circling birds, hurrying about their purposes whilst the day crept towards its warmest peak.

'It's beautiful here,' I stopped and stood, staring into the distance. The others were quiet as if respecting my unvoiced wish for a short space. I broke the silence myself. 'So, when do we start this hunt? And what do we do?'

'Let's get down to the wood.' We trailed after Tabby as he strode towards the fence, crawling through just below the hikers' stile. The trees were tall there, and straight. Some were very old and knurled and some had massively wide strong trunks, looking absolutely indestructible.

'Wind's been at them,' Tabby observed turning his head towards broken branches that sprawled about the ground.

'And, look over there!' We glanced over the grass, down towards the canal where an old thickly-barked tree was bending over dangerously, just above the water. Some of its branches had already snapped off and were floating about, creating a sizeable obstacle for any boat needing to pass.

'Are we staying this side of the line or going over by the canal?' William asked Tabby, who shrugged. 'Search me,' he said, 'Makes little difference. Let's start here and if there's nothing doing, we'll cross over.'

'What about trains?' I was a little apprehensive.

William sniffed. 'No need to worry. Main line but not that busy. Anyway you can see in plenty of time. The lines make a humming sound if it's a diesel and the overhead wires crackle if it's an electric train. But.. we'll stay here, this side I think,'

Tabby looked as if he might argue but thought better of it. He shrugged again. 'Nice and warm?' he winked at me, walking rather close, I thought.

'Right!' William must also have thought this. 'First thing to look for is holes, tracks, anything that suggests sport.' I knew all this. Didn't he remember that I had killed a Leader Rat? (Then I recalled just how I had killed a Leader Rat and told myself to shut up, and let these experts do their teaching.)

Whilst they rushed about, alternately getting excited and squeaking, then creeping along on their bellies silently, I found a dry sunny place between two fallen tree branches which was sheltered and reminded me of a bed, or safe nest. Making sure the men were immersed in their boy-scout operations I carefully selected the best way of entry and eased my body into an unobtrusively curled up position, resting my chin on the side so that I could keep an eye on what was going on. Suddenly, something tiny scurried across the crackly leaf path ahead and two sets of forepaws sprang on the unfortunate wretch. After much fuss and rustling about in the undergrowth, the victors emerged, shaking themselves. What a commotion about such a small thing, I smiled to myself. Well, let them play! Both Tabby and, surprisingly, William, seemed to have forgotten all about me and, laying warmly and comfortably, I was glad, but knew my respite would be short lived.

It was only a few minutes before William turned towards where I rested. 'Penny! Where are you? Where's Penny?'

Tabby stopped chasing his tail and looked round. 'Branches,' he nodded with his nose. 'Over there. Crashed out, I shouldn't wonder. Aren't you playing with us?' he yelled.

I scrambled out of my hide and dutifully hurried over to them. 'Of course! I was just sitting watching how it's done. Good spectator point I found.'

William glanced at me with his disbelieving look. 'Well, you can come and do some work,' he said.

Tabby cut him short exuberantly. 'Over there,' he whispered. 'See, a young squirrel at the bottom of that thin tree. There are no branches that reach out to other trees. No way for him to jump off and escape. Go on, Penny, this one's yours! Chase him up and we've got him!'

I looked helplessly up at the tall tree which was almost a sheer climb before anything jutted out higher up.

'Go on!' Tabby hissed, 'Or we'll lose him. Get him going up. I'll come after you to frighten him, so he'll run down the other side of the trunk into William's waiting arms.' I looked from Tabby to William. What a romantic phrase, I thought dreamily, 'Into William's waiting arms'. Then I realised with a start just what was being suggested. I stared at William who immediately came to my rescue.

'Penny's had a fall. She's not too brilliant on heights again yet. You chase – you'll soon have it berserk, then I'll catch what's left when it comes to ground again.'

Tabby flashed me a 'no comment' look and dashed away towards the tree whilst the squirrel stood virtually waiting, with his back to us. Sensing, rather than hearing Tabby's enthusiastic approach, the animal sprang on to the tree, its claws digging in passionately. Quick as a flash it shot upwards with Tabby (who was fast, mark you) losing distance as he streaked behind. The animal ignored the lower stumps sprouting from the trunk and made straight for the top where the branches were longer but thinner. Studying the tree shape I knew that Tabby was right and that there could be no springing from one safe perch to another. What was squirrel going to do when he reached the top? But he did not reach the top. About two thirds of the way up he halted. Knowing that Tabby was losing distance he allowed himself to turn and evaluate the situation. The tree above him was almost bare. After hesitating for only a fraction of a second he streamed outwards from the trunk along a precariously thin branch which, as it was so long, waved violently the instant he clawed into it. Tabby was nearly with him and put a forepaw on the bough causing it to sway in great wide sweeps. 'Clever!' hissed William through his teeth. The squirrel ran on towards the end of the madly moving limb. William tensed and hurried away from the trunk to stand expectantly below where the squirrel would land when the long branch snapped. I stood at the foot of the tree trunk watching William's waiting upturned face a few yards away. But the branch didn't snap, it just bent right over and waved, and as it swished inwards vertically, the squirrel seized his opportunity and sprang from its branch back to the tree trunk, firing himself down the trunk again before any of us could see what was happening. (To be fair, if he had come down my side I would have had him, no question about it.) He scurried down the other side and made straight for the nearest safe tree with branches interwoven with its neighbours. Squirrel was out of sight within seconds. Tabby was making his way down from aloft, always a longer journey than going up, and William had run in to circle our tree before seeing that squirrel was out of reach.

Mission aborted as unsuccessful, I surmised silently. Or - how three cats can easily miss trapping one small squirrel.

CHAPTER 37


After a few more successful, and even more unsuccessful, attempts to exhibit their powers of catch, my two male companions started to lose interest in the proceedings. 'Let's go and do a spot of fishing?' Tabby suggested in between pouncing on stray leaves that took off in the breeze.

I shuddered.

'Come on,' William said shortly, 'You know Penny's fall was into the canal. Not fair to suggest water sports just now.'

Tabby looked at me crossly. 'Can't climb, can't go near water. What are we good at then?'

I found his tone quite belligerent and turned away to give my back a hasty wash. Whatever was decided, there was no way I was going anywhere near the river or the canal. I told myself that I was quite capable of getting to the top of the bank and crossing the bridge to get home by myself. (As long as I kept my eyes straight in front of me.) It was clear that William did not care for his friend's tone either and I prayed there would be no harsh words on my behalf; these two had been close long before I came on the scene. But William, being William, had already thought of a compromise. 'Look,' he said, 'We'll cross over with you and sit just the other side of the train track. We'll watch you slide into the canal,' he teased.

Tabby was mollified. 'OK!' and he was off at speed, charging down into the dip between the trees and then deftly climbing the overgrown bank to the railway. He had crossed to the other side before William and I reached the track edge. Tabby raced along the side of the canal towards the stone pedestrian foot bridge which spanned the waterway. Away on the other side of the canal I could just make out two small cat figures weaving towards the river bank.

'The twins from the farm,' William had seen them too. 'Old Tabs will join them I expect. They fish in the river shallows and it's just as much fun as the canal, which can be quite difficult to get down to.'


319

'Will we see him again?' I felt mean at having broken up the party.

'Surely,' William was quite laid back about it, 'We'll catch up with him later. But, come on, let us cross here.'

I had never been this close to railway lines as a cat and not many times as a human. One usually crossed by bridge, I knew, or once or twice, I suddenly remembered, I had used a level crossing. Negotiating the lines without the infill of wood or concrete looked much more daunting, especially when one is so close to the ground.

'Easy!' William said, springing neatly over the first rail and waiting for me.

'No problem!' I agreed copying his move.

'And again,' he led, 'Come on – this is the safe zone between the two sets of tracks.

There was nothing to it, but all the same I looked up and down the railway, just in case. Over to the side of us Tabby had almost caught up with the twins. We paused for a couple of seconds before negotiating the second pair of rails.

'I'll go first,' William said, 'Just follow me quickly. Nothing to worry about.' He sprang away.

As I hopped over the next rail the cold steel brushed against my stomach and I shuddered. I stumbled, on landing, then glanced both ways again, just in case, then started towards the final rail. But something in the middle of the track was pulling at my back leg. Cursing, I turned. Damn and blast! What was holding on to me? Then to my horror I saw that my foot had become entangled in a small circlet of wire. From the sharp feel of it, barbed wire.

'William!' I shouted but he was facing away, ready to descend the slope down towards the canal. Then, thankfully, he seemed to notice that I wasn't at his side and he turned. Seeing me immobile on the railway, he started to run back towards me. 'Penny, come on!' he instructed, 'This is not the place to hang about,'

'I'm not hanging about!' I screamed at him. 'My leg is stuck!'

'Stuck?'

Was this man stupid or what? 'Wire,' I shouted, 'I'm caught on wire!'

'Pull free!' he was beside me then, crouching down.

I tried pulling my foot, and the blood gushed down on to the jagged stones beneath the shinning metal. The pain became unbearable and I felt dizzy and sick.

'Penny! Ease your foot backwards slowly to unhook it, then pull forwards again.'

I did this blindly but the barb in my leg went deeper.

'I'll try!' he yelled pushing and pulling at the wire with his teeth. Why were we shouting at each other? It was so quiet and peaceful.

He laboured away with his mouth, to try to dislodge the thing without hurting me too much. It was stuck fast. Then his front paws attempted to find the other end and he clawed away at the stones and debris, digging as a dog does. But the wire had worked further and further into me. He tried so hard to pull out the end from the track, but it was firmly wedged under the metal rail.

'I'll try and gnaw it through,' he said desperately but his mouth soon became all bloody, and strips of skin hung down where he had been speared. 'Penny!' his eyes were full, apologising and saying how this was all his fault.

Strangely, though, the agony was so bad that it was almost as if I were floating above the torment. 'I'm all right,' I said calmly, forming the words carefully before my eyes might close.

We sat there for a brief second looking helplessly at each other. 'Oh, Penny!' he said, 'We must get you out of here before…'

But it was already too late.

It started as a faint, distant sound then the noise changed to a definite hum. Everything around us seemed to shake. 'Penny!' he whispered, 'There's a train coming!'

We shared one vital thought. Which line was it on?

'Get down!' he snarled, 'Lie in the hollow between the rails, right down, flat!'

I collapsed down, my barbed wire tether just allowing me room to flatten my shivering body. In the distance the front lights of the oncoming express rounded a bend and started towards us. I lifted my head with as much energy as I could summon and William turned and screamed at me.

'Get down, Penny, my love, get down! If it's on this track, I will try to stop it!'

As I lowered my head on to the cold rough edges of the stones I watched William, my adorable William, run towards the hungry train.

The driver would have to see him. Even in bright sunlight, a white cat would surely stand out amongst the brown of the track. But do express train drivers stop for animals? Could he at that speed, safely apply brakes without risk of derailment? Would he even know he had hit something in his path?

Opening my eyes briefly, I could see without doubt that the humming, wailing monster was definitely on our rails. As my head dropped leadenly, the last thing I recollect was a small blob of white between me and the blinding headlights.

Everything shuddered in a frenzy around me. Firstly it was like thunder in the distance. Then, getting closer and closer, booming and banging, Everything was shaking. The world seemed to be moving and shuddering. The enveloping, deafening roar seemed to go on for ever. On and on. Louder, louder. I knew I was going quite mad. Then, without warning, the noise, the rumbling, the humming were gone. Nothing moved then. There was no sound at all. I lay, still flattened, not daring to breathe much. It was not cold or warm. It was just nothing. Probably minutes passed before I took courage enough to move my ears; they still moved.

Very, very gently I started to raise my head, hysterically certain that the nightmare was still there, on top of me. Pounding into my brain. But it was quiet. I forced my body into a sitting position, although I knew I was lopsided. I tried moving my tail; this worked all right. Then each of my paws. Then my mind registered sharp pain and ache, and I remembered. But, strangely enough, I could move both back legs. Turning around I studied my feet. Attached to one, the extremely bloody one, was a short piece of rusty wire whose end was waving about loose. Realisation that the train's considerable weight must have moved and dislodged it from the rail seemed almost irrelevant then.

I struggled forwards along the dip between the tracks, dragging my leg chain, one end of which was still firmly embedded in my skin. Sense told me I should climb over the rail to the safe area but what little energy I had was needed to crawl forwards. (Anyway, I thought vaguely, another one won't come yet and any going the other way will be on the opposite track.) But then I did climb over the smooth steel to the bank side and collapsed down on a clump of grass. It was so quiet, so silent. I rolled my head back crazily to look up at the sky. Yes, birds were flying, zooming, circling, fluttering, but no sound – no cries.

I staggered along the grass that ran by the railway in the direction the train had come. My sore eyes searched along the ground, between the rails, and at the edges of each track. Forcing my front legs to move faster, the rest of me followed somehow. I felt no discomfort now in my leg and even though the end of my manacle caught on debris as I dragged on, there was no feeling, just numbness.

Then, there, in front of me, lay the white fur, in the grass and weeds. Faster! Go on! Worming my way forward I wondered briefly if this were a mirage which would disappear when I got close. But it remained there, still and lifeless. It was just fur; white (now dirty) with a unique black marking. Just a lump of fur. Along, in front of me a bit, by the other track, my staring eyes caught a blur of something else. Tottering forwards, I stumbled wearily back across the twin rails on to the safe centre between the two tracks. My front feet stopped just short of the gory mess that was splattered over the stones. I turned and hung my head across the nearest rail and vomited.

William's voice came then, clearly and distinctly, reminding me that the express trains to and from London crossed somewhere along this way. I turned blindly to gaze back over at the opposite track where I had lain, pinned to the ground. Where William had run ahead to save me. Then I pulled my body away from the horror near my paws, and instead of my head resting on the cold metal, I pulled my body so that I balanced on my stomach, laying fully along the rail. It was curiously comfortable and didn't feel as cold as it had before. It was almost like laying on a flat, obliging fence in the sunshine.

How long must I wait?

I willed myself to concentrate, on anything. I tried to recall Robbie and Ben and their beautiful boat with the fairyland lights. But the image was brief and then was gone. Gull and Tabatha – they were just fleeting memories. The burning boat, my near-drowning in the canal; or had it been a figment of my imagination? But then my mind settled and I could clearly picture Anson, waiting in her courtyard for William to come for his Christmas Eve visit. Moving slightly, I turned my head so that my other ear leaned against the rail, so that I could not see the sticky heap of squashed and battered innards amongst the tiny tufts of white fur. I sensed no pain, no anxiety, in fact I felt quite serene. But the silence was almost deafening.

Then, my body trembled, just a slight tremor at first. When the humming started I clamped my eyes tightly together to stop them from opening and seeing the oncoming lights. The movement and sound formed a rhythm that vibrated through my body. I smiled to myself as my back started to slide from the rail; no matter, I clung on urgently with my front paws, resting my head between them.

Then my mind cleared.

There, in front of me, was William. Resplendent in his shinning, spotless white coat, his ears slightly forward and his tail almost vertical. I opened my mouth to call to him but he vanished and in his place was a smiling woman with auburn hair holding out her hand to me. She seemed somehow familiar.


I would have expected to feel a thud; hear an enormous bang. Losing one's life in this way should be noisy and dark and lonely and cold. But I felt warm – too warm. It was as if I were swimming, or rather floating, and it did not seem dark – not scary dark. It was almost a familiar feeling, one I had experienced before somewhere. My body was rocking back and forth and the soft peculiar gurgling sounds were comforting. But I was getting uncomfortably hot. I wanted to breathe but I couldn't. Suddenly I felt I was being propelled forwards and my body kept bouncing against something. Then my face felt a rush of air and my head was cool. There was a sensation of crawling slowly towards light. Soft hands touched my body and a young voice said,

'At last, Tina! Here is your little girl!'

There were clanking noises and people murmuring. I was lifted about and gently wrapped in softness, cocooned and warm again.

'Are you up to holding your daughter?' the same cheerful voice came again.

Although my eyes would not open there was no need to see.

'Hello!' was all she said, but that one word burst joy into my new life. Laying in the crook of her soft arm, smelling her smell, being warm against her warmth, being part of her once again – this was happiness. Tina! My Tina! Nothing had gone before, I could think of nothing but Now.

'Michael, isn't she beautiful?' Tina asked softly and a warm masculine voice replied, 'My darlings! My darling family!' His big fingers brushed against my arm and his smell, too, was good.

Tina was speaking again. 'Michael,' she said, wonder in her tone, 'She's going to have red hair, like mine. Look!'

The young nurse laughed. 'Don't bank on it. They all change their hair colour. But I must admit, this little one's is unusual.'

'It reminds me,' Tina said drowsily, 'Of a lovely pusscat I once had.'

'I didn't know you had a cat,' Michael said, 'What happened to her?'

There was a silence and I could hear Tina crying quietly. 'I went off to America and left her.' She sobbed.

'Stop that, silly,' he said tenderly, 'Whatever you did, you had a reason for doing. She will have forgiven you. But..' he said gruffly, and I could tell he was smiling. 'Should we not introduce little Mary to her brother?'

I know I stopped breathing. In all this happiness, now a dreadful thing was about to happen, I just knew it. I worked frantically on my eyes but they remained stubbornly shut. Who was this brother? A child. Hurt whistled through me at the reminder of the cruel children at the farm. Tina stopped crying and sniffed loudly. She struggled to sit more upright and feet shuffled nearby as she was helped.

'Mary!' she said. Yes, this must be me. 'This is your brother. He arrived just a little before you, a few minutes ago.'

This other thing must be laying in her other arm, I deduced, as she didn't lift or move me, just a slight change of position.

'And,' she directed her words away from me. 'And, William, this is your sister!'

With a crash I opened my eyes, staring indignantly across the bedclothes. There, smothered in blanketed softness lay the most ugly thing imaginable! A sort of giant red wrinkled walnut with its mouth hanging open. In the same instant its eyes sprang open to stare back at me. They were round and very, very green. Its head was covered with a fuzzy film of whiteness.

Oh Mercy! Great Mercy! William! I felt as though I had been hit by a thunderbolt.

# CHAPTER 38

My name is Mary and I am getting to be an old woman now. In fact, very old. I have had, long ago, my three-score-years-and-ten that the Bible promised but I cannot remember my age or when I was born. Or where. It really doesn't matter. Things like this are not important. But I do know that I have had a good life

I am sitting in my comfortable chair. There is nothing like the feel of upholstered arms and a firm high back behind you when you sit. And the seat is the right height. Safe and rigid, holding buttocks securely, it's not too low down. Not like these great squashy things that you sink right down into and can never climb out of again. I close my eyes briefly, then spring them open again to look across at the special hideous chair they all clubbed together to buy me last Christmas. Dreadful, dreadful contraption! You get on it and wriggle your bottom and the leg rest shoots up. If you lean back too suddenly the whole thing swings down like a bed. I can't work out how to operate the knobs you must press to get upright again, so I have to lie there, suspended in mid-air, until someone releases me. Although I do not want to appear ungrateful, I don't get on it now when there is no-one else in the house. I do much prefer my little armchair which has served me well for so many years.

And often, there is no-one in the house. My son works hard and is away a lot and my daughter-in-law has a very good job doing something or other. My granddaughter, Katy, is home though, after school. She is my joy. She helps me to live with purpose, despite this warped and worn out old body I'm lumbered with, and my odd ways and funny thoughts. She is the only one who doesn't seem to mind, who almost understands.

Katy and I share a secret. I have confided to her about my leading a double life – that I'm a sort of Walter Mitty or a Billy Liar (though she didn't know who these were.) Because I am sure this is unusual, I asked her to help me to let other people know about it. I have always been a writer – stories, articles, and my letters of complaint are a testimony to my hidden talents. (Admittedly my main works – or attempts at works – have not been fairly recognised. I am, as yet, unpublished.)

Now, since I have been having these, sometimes worrying, thoughts and quite clear memories, this seemed to be my chance to create a tale that would indeed be unique. Nowadays, though, even holding a pencil is difficult so it would take far too long to write it all down - and I don't think I have too long. But when I told Katy, she came to my rescue. We went into the study in the main part of the house (I live in an add-on bit – a sitting room, bedroom and washroom). The study is where the most important item of the home is kept – the computer. For years I have banged my fingers across different computer keyboards, an operation I can now no longer manage, but, after a few 'teach-in' sessions, this latest one is so easy. I just sit in front of it and talk and the machine does the rest. These days, such nuisances as spelling, grammar and format are no problem, I just shout at the screen and it obeys, sorting it all out for me. My ally, Katy, sets the machine up each morning and turns it all on, just in case I feel like doing any of my story. She then patiently edits and generally knocks it into shape when she comes in after school or at weekends. She says she likes doing it, and her mother is happy that it keeps her occupied and away from the boys who live up the street. But I don't do much at a time. Sometimes not at all as I get very tired. Katy keeps up with what I do and she is absolutely discreet and doesn't talk about it, even to her mother. She neither criticises nor laughs at my efforts. We have even discussed what would happen should I not be able to finish it, though I didn't go into the most likely reason. I think she thought I meant about getting seriously ill. She assured me she would tie it up neatly and give it a proper ending. I do think, though, that Katy gets a bit bemused at times. Her favourite saying to me is, "What an imagination, you've got, Grandma!"

We are only a small family. Just us here and my twin brother William who lives with his son somewhere by the sea.

(I can't remember just where, but it's a big place with lots of shops.) I don't see him much these days which is probably just as well because he is a cantankerous old fool. Yes, he really is! He always thinks he knows best and will not allow anyone else (particularly me) to have an opinion about anything. Mind you, he's always been bossy and self righteous. Arrogant is the term that springs to mind. And, oh so pompous! It's a wonder he ever married. A wonder anyone would have him. But his son, Stephen, and his wife, look after him well. How they stand him I cannot imagine. Nothing is ever right for him. However hard they try, he will always complain about them. Frequently he rings us up to report their misdemeanours. Why they don't simply push his wheelchair to the edge of the cliff and let it topple over I just don't know.

Sometimes I look back on when we were younger. We always quarrelled, right from when we were tiny but in a funny way we were very close – almost as if we needed each other to fight against. Our parents, Tina and Michael, tried their hardest to keep the peace but I think they must have been thankful when we both left home.

Leaning back in my treasured chair I allow myself to reminisce. How unkind fate was to take them from us well before their time. But, in those days, road accidents were so frequent.

I look across at my giant clock, a gift from Katy on my birthday, whenever it was. It always seems to be my birthday, or Christmas, or Easter, or Mother's Day or Grandmother's Day or some other Day. Everyone makes a fuss and brings flowers that drop petals all over the carpet, or chocolates with rock hard centres that no amount of dedicated sucking will penetrate. Although I can see my clock - clear, and easy to read – the child is so sensible, the hands seem to wobble about and quiver between the numbers which makes it so difficult to tell what time it is. But the creeping darkness means that Katy will soon be in. I lean back and take a deep breath.

The cushion beneath me feels damp again. It seems to be doing this more and more lately and I squirm to the side to try to find a dry spot. The first time I discovered this irregularity I was overcome with embarrassment and remorse, knowing that somehow I must be the culprit. But recently it has become very obvious that it has nothing to do with me. There are vicious, unfriendly forces around, working against me for some reason. I suppose this latest small saturation will instigate yet another mumbled discourse on the benefits of that 'very nice' residential club (they don't call them homes now). My son would say how magnificent the place must be, judging by the fees they charge. My daughter-in-law would reassure me that it was Really Nice, because they let people take in their personal special belongings. I wonder if they might let me take in my beautiful chair. Not that sadistic piece of leather and chrome that tips you upside down; this snuggly, hospitable, very friendly one. When they talk of enrolling me as a 'guest' in this place Katy always looks sad.

It is getting dark now but I'm too lazy to go over to the light switch, even if I could recall where it was. Strange, I muse, how people of my age, whatever it is, have ruled countries, been captains of industry, held responsible roles in the community, and so on. Yet I have trouble in locating the light switch.

I press the back of my head into my chair and relax. Maybe I should take a short nap before they all come in. But I seem only to have just woken up. Never mind, I always needed a lot of rest.

My eyes close whilst I am trying to make up my mind. Yes, I will have a sleep.

I have a very, very deep sleep.

Printed in the United Kingdom by
Lightning Source UK Ltd., Milton Keynes
140096UK00001B/135/P